THE END OF THE TRUCKING WORLD

THE END OF THE TRUCKING WORLD

— BATTLE TRUCKER BOOK TWO —

TOM GOLDSTEIN

Podium

To my family,
who took unreasonable and crucial delight in a story about monsters and a truck driver who swears a lot. Thank you.

This is a work of fiction. Names, characters, places, and incidents are either products of the author's imagination or used fictitiously. Any resemblance to actual events, locales, or persons, living, dead, or undead, is entirely coincidental.

Cover design by Tom Edwards

ISBN: 978-1-0394-4847-6

Published in 2024 by Podium Publishing
www.podiumaudio.com

THE END OF THE TRUCKING WORLD

CHAPTER 1

BREAK'S OVER

As dawn broke, Jill MacLeod gripped a mug of steaming coffee in her hands and inhaled, her eyes fluttering closed in satisfaction. The first rays of sunlight flashed over the Midwestern plains, through the armored windscreen of Bertha, Jill's big-rig truck, and onto Jill, sitting in the driver's seat. To the south, the smoke of a burning city clogged the sky, but to the east it was clear. Jill smiled and took in the wafting scent of coffee. She ignored, for just a moment, all of the stress and horror that had crashed down on her—on everyone—at midnight just a few nights before. When the world as everyone knew it had ended; when technology had failed; when homicidal monsters had come to Earth, thirsting for blood.

The scent of coffee faded, crowded out in Jill's senses by a scene from the night before playing on her closed eyelids: the brothers Babu and Ras Bati, caught on the road like her, fighting for their lives in the dead of night, taking refuge on top of their crashed U-Haul moving truck. Jill's heart sped up as she remembered the brothers desperately holding the monsters off; how Ras's sword had flashed in reflected headlights, how Babu's conjured fire had lit the night.

The two had only survived because with the monsters had come magic, imbuing people with the means to fight back. The magic didn't depend on mystery or esoteric secrets. Rather, all of the powers a person could take were laid out for them in boxes of text, a system of options and statistics suspiciously similar to those found in a video game. Jill had at first dismissed the text-filled blue boxes that had sprung into her vision as hallucinations, but before long, she'd accepted that, no, they were real and that she could gain magical abilities of her own. Every monster she killed gave her experience; enough experience increased her level; every level increased her physical and mental abilities and gave her a class point to spend on a specific ability.

Jill hadn't given herself the ability to cast spells or to infuse magical powers into her guns, or anything else like that. She'd become a Battle Trucker, with nearly all of her powers dedicated to enhancing Bertha. Through luck, circumstance, bullheadedness, and a lot of help from new friends, Jill had gained levels quickly. Her old faithful beat-up big rig had been transformed into a magic-enhanced Soulbound vehicle, which, while truck-sized on the outside, now held an entire burgeoning town on the inside of its dimensionally stretched trailer. Not to mention the half dozen machine-gun turrets on its top and sides, or the horn on the front that blasted out sound waves powerful enough to explode an elephant.

"Good, you're finally up," a voice said from behind Jill. The speaker, Sangita Bati, mother of Babu and Ras, stood between the two seats of the cab. The dark-haired, dark-skinned, middle-aged Midwesterner held a clipboard in one hand; the other was occupied spinning a pen at inhuman speed. From the bags under Sangita's eyes, Jill doubted that the other woman had gotten a minute of sleep. She started to say something else, but Jill spoke first.

"Sangita," Jill said to the woman, "it's officially ass o'clock in the morning, and I haven't gotten any of this cup in me yet. There are less than a dozen people awake in the whole truck—trust me, I can tell—so don't give me that 'finally' duckshit."

"Sorry," Sangita said, not sounding apologetic in the slightest, "but those military folks in the airport are awake and demanding that you meet with them and talk supplies."

"Of course they are," Jill grumbled. "You did tell them that I put you in charge of keeping everyone fed, right?"

Sangita let out a huff of annoyance. "Apparently, I'm not good enough to talk with."

"Bunch of asshats," Jill said. She sighed and gestured at the seat next to her for Sangita to sit. "Gimme five minutes to wake up and I'll go yell at them."

Jill's truck was parked at a gate on the tarmac of Billings Logan International Airport. Bertha had no airlines to compete with for the spot, as there were no flights during the apocalypse. The airport had instead been transformed into a haven for thousands of refugees. Jill didn't know exactly how many, but she and Bertha had delivered a staggering forty-six hundred of them the night before in a deadly rescue mission. The System had rewarded her for saving those people, giving her a mountain of class points.

Rather than spend them, she had collapsed, asleep, at the first opportunity, getting to sleep shortly after midnight after being up for forty-six straight hours. She'd woken blearily just before dawn and forced herself out of bed, fighting a lack of sleep that clung to her like a sodden blanket. That wouldn't normally have been an issue for Jill, as any self-respecting long-haul trucker could go a while on low sleep, and the magic coursing through her should have made it even easier. But constant terror and adrenaline had taken their toll—not to mention being shot and operated on to remove the bullet while still awake. Twice.

Phantom pain flashed through Jill's shoulder and upper chest, where threads of metal had wormed their way through her flesh, extending out from a cursed bullet to torture her. Jill swallowed and shook her head, reaching up without thinking to rub the site of the former injury.

"Is the wound still bothering you?" Sangita asked, a hint of concern in her voice. "I can wake Karen up."

With a flicker of thought, Jill willed a summary of her statistics to appear, and a blue box popped into the center of her vision.

Jill MacLeod
Class: Battle Trucker
Level: 82
HP: 1710/1710 **MP:** 2550/2550 **XP:** 3,355,427/3,403,000
Body: 171 **Mind:** 168 **Spirit:** 255
Conditions: Well Rested
Class Powers: Hold Together (1), Battle Hardened (1), A Deal's a Deal (1), Synergy (1)
36 points available to assign
(+) Bonus to Class Power effectiveness
(+) Bonus to Class Powers that boost Soulbound Vehicle
Dedication slots available: 3
Cross-class dedications available: Malediction Bard

Her hit points were full, and she had no adverse conditions.

"No," Jill said. "It's just in my head." Magic and a night's sleep had cured what would have taken months of recovery. While Jill had invested almost every one of her class points into enhancing Bertha, the stat gains from leveling still represented so much magic coursing through her that she was nothing short of superhuman.

During the hectic fighting of the night before bullets had bounced off of her skin, leaving nothing but welts behind. Not that she was invulnerable: System-enhanced equipment with magic of its own could hurt her easily enough—especially those wielded by someone who had invested their powers into fighting, rather than trucking. Point by point, level by level, offensive and defensive magic were in an arms race with each other, leaving mundane weapons behind.

Jill wasn't just tougher, she was much stronger as well. She dropped her hand back to her mug, gripping it with exaggerated care; thinking about her strength was like thinking about breathing, and she was suddenly acutely aware that she could shatter the mug with the slightest effort. Ceramic shards and scalding liquid couldn't hurt her anymore, but it would be an absolute waste of coffee.

"Just because it's in your head," Sangita said, eyeing Jill's gripped hands, "doesn't make it not real."

Jill snorted. "Tell me a-fucking-bout it."

The past day had been traumatic, to say the least. On top of being physically injured and nearly killed, Jill had been assaulted mentally by both magical powers and just the sheer horror of what she'd been through. First had been the bloody violence of killing monsters. The act of shooting animals was nothing new for a woman who'd grown up hunting with her father and brothers, but there was a horrible difference between killing a deer for food with a single clean shot versus the wholesale exploding slaughter she'd wreaked with Bertha's front grille and machine guns. That had been necessary, though—those monsters had all been hellbent on killing anyone they could get their claws on. And Jill knew that many had succeeded. Thousands of people had died in the towns and cities she had driven through.

But that was yesterday, and today was going to be different. Today her starting point wasn't confusion and terror, it was a giant armored magical truck covered in machine guns, with a whole pile of class points to make it even better.

Jill raised her coffee to salute the dawn and took a long, deep swallow.

"That right there," Jill said with a sigh. "That hits the goddamn spot."

"I'm so happy for you," Sangita said, her voice flat and back to business. "Now get ready to listen. I've got a lot to coach you on if you're going to be getting us what we need."

"My five minutes aren't up yet," Jill said, eyeing the clipboard with distrust. "You know, you were a lot more friendly when you made me coffee at your place."

"That was when you were my guest, not my boss," Sangita said, her disgruntled tone betraying her feelings at their new relationship.

Jill felt the same. She hadn't wanted to be in charge of anyone, but events of the day before had pushed her into the role. It seemed that everywhere she went people needed rescuing; she couldn't in good conscience abandon people to be killed by monsters, and her truck could carry hundreds, thousands of people to safety thanks to its magic. Jill had meant to just drop the newly minted refugees off at the first safe place, but a huge number of them had decided they would rather live inside the truck than out.

The deal had been simple: Jill was going east all the way to the coast; everyone who wanted to come along could, as long as they would help out as best they could and do more or less what Jill said. They could get off any time they wanted, but Jill wasn't going to stop and wasn't going to let anyone else tell her what to do with her truck.

At the end of Interstate 90, Jill's father, brothers, and girlfriend were waiting for her. They had to be waiting for her. If anyone could survive the end of the world, it would be her prepper father, and his bunker of a home would be a natural meeting point for anyone who knew of it. Jill told herself for the hundredth time that everyone was okay and that the worst thing waiting for her was that her father, proven right, would be insufferable.

The door at the rear of the cab swung open and another woman, blonde this time, stuck her head in. "Good morning," she said, yawning. "Is that coffee I smell?" It was Karen, Sangita's sister-in-law. She had showered since the day before, so her hands were clean, but the sleeves of her blouse were still stained brown with blood from her work in the truck's medical bay.

"Hell yes, it is," Jill said, taking another swig. She eyed Karen over the rim of her mug. "You were asleep just a minute ago; I checked. Did you come straight here from waking up?"

"My ears were burning," she said, giving an innocent smile. Karen shut the door behind her and walked over, leaning on the back of the passenger seat. "What are we talking about?"

"How she was nicer to me yesterday," Jill said, gesturing at Sangita.

"Bringing her sons home alive will do that," Karen said. "Just about the only thing that will!"

Sangita fixed Karen with a glare, making the younger woman laugh. Sangita gave out a huff and stared down at her clipboard. "Where are those boys, anyway? It's not like Ras to sleep late, don'tcha know."

Jill raised an eyebrow at Sangita, but the other woman didn't notice. Karen shook her head.

"I'm surprised Babu isn't here," Jill said. "He was so excited about Bertha's mega-upgrade that I thought I would find him sleeping outside of my door, ready with some sort of game-inspired strategy to make us all shit diamonds."

Bertha wasn't just a Soulbound truck anymore. Spurred on by the number of people living inside of it, the truck had undergone an evolution the night before, becoming a settlement and presumably gaining some of the same types of powers that the towns and cities they'd passed on their route already had. One thing, however, was conspicuously absent: the glowing dome of a barrier shield, which helped protect every other settlement from monster invasion.

Sangita sighed. "That would be something he'd be excited about."

Jill opened her mouth to say more, but Karen's now furiously shaking head and a hand drawn across her neck silenced Jill before she said anything. Instead, she closed her eyes and expanded her senses, letting her mind flow into her truck to look for Babu and Ras. Bertha was hers, tied to her by magic in ways that she didn't entirely understand. She could feel what happened to Bertha as if it were happening to her own body, for good and for ill. When her truck was in good shape, running clean and straight down a smooth road, it was as if everything was right in the world. When Bertha was bent and torn, with monsters ripping their way inside, Jill felt excruciating pain.

The same connection gave her a more subtle sense as well, something that, when combined with some of her class powers, gave her an amazing ability to monitor what was happening in Bertha. When she had the chance to concentrate and some mana to spend, she could feel the location of any object, hear any conversation, and even sense if someone truly considered themselves to be working for her.

Maybe one of her later powers would add sight to the mix; that she would take, but she would give smell and taste a miss. There had been far too much monster gore spread on Bertha, inside and out, for Jill to want to monitor those senses.

She took another sip of coffee, holding the ambrosia on her tongue for a long moment to banish the thought of tasting Bertha's deck plates. That distraction gone, she found the brothers soon enough: Babu was asleep in one of the small rooms made by Bertha's Habitation Module, and Ras was slumped down by the cargo doors at the back of the trailer.

"Found 'em," Jill said. "Both are asleep." She stood, threw back the rest of her coffee in one swig, and put her mug onto the dashboard with a clunk. "Sangita," she said as she strode towards the rear of the cab, "how about we walk and talk? You've got things to tell me, and I've got places to be."

"Where are we going?" Sangita asked as she stood.

"Whatever you tell me, it's going to take magic to deal with," Jill said. "So we're going to wake up my chief advisor on super-powered bullshit." She paused her walk and looked over her shoulder to grin at the two women. "Break's over and I've got a truck to upgrade."

CHAPTER 2

RISING CHALLENGES

"Dramatic," Sangita said, moving to stand beside Jill. "Do you have a plan for getting my son out of bed this early? Because heaven knows I've never been able to."

"I'm going to tell them to wake up," Jill said. She pushed mana into one of the powers granted by the Command Module:

> **Captain Speaking:** Jill MacLeod can speak to and receive replies from anyone within "Bertha" or within 14 meters.

"Hey, Babu," she said, projecting her voice into the room where he was sleeping. Anything she said through the power emerged as normal sound at the target destination, but Jill heard what was said there directly in her mind. She realized with discomfort that she could hear two people breathing, and her spatial sense revealed another sleeping body tangled up with Babu's. It was most likely Mia Williams, a rotary-cannon-wielding former school nurse who was riding with them until they reached New York.

Neither of the figures stirred, so Jill projected again, louder. "Hey! Babu, Mia, will one of you wake up?"

"*Mmmflgggr,*" was the only response, though Jill couldn't tell which one had said it. The two were too closely entangled.

"He hasn't gotten up, has he?" Sangita asked, eyeing Jill. From her perspective, Jill was just standing there, staring off into space.

Jill repressed a laugh. "Oh, I'm pretty sure he has," she said back.

She projected the sound of an old digital alarm clock into the room, starting softly and ramping up in volume. Babu moved first, trying to sit up but getting caught on a leg. Mia pushed back and a thud announced Babu falling out of bed, making him cry out. There was a surge of foreign mana and the pop of displaced air; Mia had summoned Blossom, her cannon, out from its usual home in Bertha's front-most turret.

"What was that?" Mia yelled. "Are we under attack?"

"Easy, Mia. Easy," Jill projected. "Sorry for the wakeup, but it's work o'clock."

"What—" Babu yawned. "What time even is it?"

"Dawn," Jill said. "I need your take on magic. Sorry for waking you up, Mia, but Babu's in high demand."

"Are we finally going to talk settlement powers?" Babu asked, perking up. "Did you figure out how to get them?"

"Does a bear shit on the pope in the woods?" Jill projected. "I feel like stretching my legs, so I'm coming to you. And your mom's coming too. Just so you know."

"Oh," Mia and Babu said at the same time.

Jill cut her communication power; whatever drama was about to happen was none of her business. "Are you coming along?" she asked Karen, who had slid into the driver's seat.

"I'll keep watch," Karen replied, yawning. "Okay, maybe I'll just take a nap. This seat is comfy, and it took forever for me to get Kevin to sleep."

"Don't drool on the leather," Jill said, turning to leave. She had a power that could clean up nearly anything that dirtied Bertha, but it was the principle of the thing.

Karen gave a salute and closed her eyes.

"Okay," Sangita said as she caught up to Jill. "The first thing you need to know is that Commander Davis—well, one of his subordinates at least—wanted you to do more rescue missions into the city. And go on supply runs. And stay on patrol around the airport."

Jill grimaced. "All of that is a hard no," she said. "We're leaving."

"That's what I told them," Sangita said. "They said that I didn't know what I was talking about and asked to speak to the person in charge."

"Bunch of cloaca-snorting Karens," Jill muttered.

"I heard that!" Karen said, eyes still closed. "But sounds accurate."

Jill laughed and stepped through the door to the Cargo Module, a lockable hatch more akin to a ship's bulkhead doors than something that could be found in a home. She waited for Sangita to follow her, then shut it and took in the massive room in front of her. The inside of her truck was far, far larger than the outside.

She was proud that someone looking at Bertha from outside would still recognize it as a big-rig truck, though one that had been turned from a freight carrier into a mobile fortress. Seven turrets lined the trailer's top and sides: six with .50-caliber machine guns and one empty one up front, though it usually held Mia's rotary cannon, Blossom. The gun was Mia's Soulbound weapon, a magic-infused gun that could cut through a reinforced concrete building with ease and tended to make lower-leveled monsters explode.

Most of Bertha's surfaces were covered in solid slabs of hardened heavy armor and painted bright red. The magical paint, made from electric eel monsters, made Bertha go faster like any red paint should. It could also electrocute any enemy that managed to scramble on board. The most vulnerable places were the cab's windows, which were a thick crystalline glass that could still take tremendous punishment, and the connection between cab and trailer, where overlapping bands of armor slid past one another to form a flexible joint.

Another memory flashed into Jill's mind: Bertha whipping around a corner, dodging a horde of monsters in a maneuver that would roll any normal truck, with cab and trailer bent at a ninety-degree angle. Tiny feathered raptors leaped onto the trailer, clawing and biting to get inside, only to die from the paint's sting. Even during that crazy maneuver, the path from Jill to the trailer had been straight and clear. Bertha's inside was a separate dimensional space from the outside world, one that obeyed its own rules.

Inside that space resided Bertha's modules, stuck together by magic and steel: the cab, renamed to Command; the inflated trailer, likewise now Cargo; her tiny sleeping area, expanded into many rooms as Habitation; Bertha's firepower, the turrets; and, born out of need, the Medbay. The armor was its own module, forming the boundary between inside and out. That left the Propulsion Module, which was spread out. Some of it was in the wheels, but it was also inside the front of the cab, where the diesel engine used to be. That had been replaced by one that ran on pure mana.

"What did you say back to the military people?" Jill asked Sangita. She walked around the edge of the Cargo Module at a brisk clip, heading towards Habitation. A few people waved to her, and she waved back awkwardly; she didn't recognize them.

It was here, in the Cargo Module, that most of Bertha's residents slept, despite there being another module dedicated to just that purpose. The Habitation Module was only five rooms and a stub of a hallway, while the inside of the trailer was the size and shape of a parking garage, a cube fifty meters on a side and four stories tall. The bottom level was half empty, with a large clear area by the cargo doors across from Jill, and a clear walking space around the periphery along which the doors to the other modules were spread. The middle of the level was filled with airline-style seating. That had been the first way to pack people in somewhat safely that had popped into Jill's head when the refugees arrived. She was hoping that the new settlement powers would let her make something better.

A single ramp gave access to the upper levels, which were all filled with more seating, broken up into clusters to give at least some sense of family and privacy. Jill hadn't gone up to visit the upper floors in person, but she could feel the physical presence of a huge number of sleeping people, along with a few awake.

"I read them a bill for services rendered by Highlander Shipping," Sangita said, "to be paid in food, medical supplies, or material upgrades for Bertha." She smiled, a thin, dangerous, self-satisfied expression. "I mentioned their radars in particular."

"That's how to fucking negotiate," Jill said with a grin. She leaned over and punched Sangita on the shoulder, being careful to use only the tiniest fraction of her strength. "I bet they didn't take it well?"

Sangita rubbed her shoulder but was still smiling. "There was profanity involved."

"Was it any good?"

"After meeting you? No."

The corner of Jill's mouth quirked up. She had an interest in swearing that was bordering on professional; the System had even recognized it, giving her a pair of spells based on cursing and the option to cross-class into Malediction Bard. She added asking how that all worked to her mental list of questions for Babu.

Jill stepped through the hatch into the Habitation Module's hallway.

Babu leaned against the wall outside Mia's room. He wore a gray suit, immaculately pressed, with black onyx cufflinks; his shiny hair stirred as if in a slight wind, and his eyes, so dark brown as to be almost black, flashed as he looked up at them.

Sangita stopped upon seeing her son. "Babu!" she said. "You look so put together!" She hesitated for a moment. "I owe you an apology. I told Jill you wouldn't be awake, but I was wrong."

Babu gave a half smile. "Morning, Mom."

Jill stomped over to him and crossed her arms. "Turn down the magical looks a little bit, will you?" she said quietly. "I'm tired of mind-control bullshit."

He swallowed and leaned in close to her. "I can't!" he whispered in her ear.

"Why not?" She gave him a look up and down; something about his clothes didn't feel right to her mana senses. "Is that suit an illusion?" she asked back, also whispering so that Sangita wouldn't hear.

"We couldn't find my pants and the spell is all or nothing!"

"I knew it," Jill said and chuckled. She walked past him to her own room and opened the door. There was only one chair, tucked under a tiny desk, but Jill could fix that easily enough. Reaching mentally into Bertha she made the metal deck plating of the floor rise up in two stools. A flick of her will turned on the coffee machine, and she waved them in.

"You two ready to help me choose some powers?" Jill asked them once they'd sat down. Sangita nodded. Babu glanced at his mother and swallowed, then nodded his own assent.

"Okay," Jill clapped her hands together. "Sangita, tell me what we need to keep everyone alive, please. Babu, let me know if I miss any solutions in my powers."

Sangita cleared her throat. "First off: water. We filled some containers from the tap in the unoccupied rooms, but it ran out."

"Really?" Babu asked. "After how much?"

Sangita hesitated. "The people filling didn't count, but it didn't last long." She turned to Jill. "Does the room description say?"

"Let me check," Jill said. She pulled up the status box for the Habitation Module and sent it to both of them.

Habitation:
"Bertha" has a Habitation Module with basic amenities for 5. Life support capacity for 12.
Includes: Single Bed, Washroom, Workspace
Add-ons (2/2): Inferior Coffee Machine, Dire Bobcat Fur Bedding

Completed Upgrades:
Restful Sleep: All allies who rest in the Habitation Module receive increased physical and psychological healing rates.

Available Upgrades:
Unseen Servant: Weak manifestations of force will see to the maintenance of the Habitation Module and the residents' possessions. Unlocks **Roaming Servants**.
Bunkroom (1/5): Increases the capacity, life support, and volume of the Habitation Module by 2.4x, and by 1 add-on slot.

"Hey, System," Jill thought, directing a sliver of mana through her mind towards where the boxes came from. "How much water does 'life support' make?"

System Inquiry Detected
Soulbound Modular Vehicle "Bertha's" Habitation Module life support produces 20 liters of new water per person, per day at the cost of 1 Mana per liter. Waste water is recycled into fresh water at a cost of 1 Mana per 100 liters.

She sent that box along as well, speaking at the same time. "Two hundred and forty liters total."

Sangita grimaced. "That's not enough."

"With four more points in Bunkroom, and that one power from the Cargo Nexus to boost it more, life support should go up to"—Babu paused a moment—"594 people and 11,880 liters. That's got to be enough, right?"

"Maybe," Sangita said. "What power from cargo?"

"It gives another class boost to connected modules," Jill said. "Get ready for a longer box; the booster is at the bottom."

Cargo Nexus:
"Bertha" has a cargo bay of total volume 30,408.7 cubic meters, a spatial compression factor of 335.5, and internal dimensions of 50 meters by 50 meters by 12.16 meters. Effective Boost: +1.2
Includes: Doors
Add-ons (1/5): Hearth of the Wolf

Completed Upgrades:
Cargokinesis: Objects inside of and within 14 meters of the cargo bay doors can be slowly moved.
Climate Control: Control the temperature and humidity of the cargo bay. Unlocks **Freezer Control.**
Freezer Control: Non-living goods spoil at 1/22 the normal rate when inside the cargo bay.
Volume (5/5): Per Point Invested: Increase the volume of the Cargo Module by 3.2x and create 1 add-on slot.
Cargo Nexus: The Cargo Module becomes the central hub for Soulbound Modular Vehicle "Bertha." The Cargo Module receives a Class Boost (+.2) for every exclusively attached eligible module. Current exclusive modules: Medbay, Habitation, Advanced Turrets (Small Arms), Command. Ineligible modules: Armor, Propulsion.
Teamster Enhancement: All authorized sapients inside of the Cargo Module and within 22 meters of "Bertha" have their movement speed and spatial reasoning enhanced by 32%. Unlocks **Teamster Tetris.**

Available Upgrades:
Teamster Tetris: All authorized sapients inside of the Cargo Module can teleport non-living objects to other locations inside of the Cargo Module, using "Bertha's" Mana reserves. Unlocks **Teamster Sidestep.** Mana Cost: 1 per kilogram-meter.
Reinforced Module Mounting (0/5): Choose one exclusively attached module. That module's Class Boost increases by +.2. A module may only be boosted once with this power.

Jill squinted at the box. The information was as she remembered, but the text looked different.

"Hey, System," she thought, directing a sliver of mana through her mind towards where the boxes came from. "Did you change how shit looks?"

> System Inquiry Detected
> The adaptive display has been upgraded based on data gathered from local sapients. User confusion is indicative of an unfavorable deviation from mean levels of understanding.

"Fuck you!" Jill said aloud.

"Excuse me?" Sangita said with a glare.

"Not you," Jill said. "The System. The sassy bitch just called me dumb."

"Of course it did. I'm going to ignore the insanity that is your relationship with the System," Sangita said, "and focus on the matter at hand. Twelve thousand liters is a start, but barely enough."

"Doesn't a person only need a few liters a day? If they are just drinking, at least. How many people are coming?" Jill asked, dread rising inside of her.

"2,977," Sangita said quietly.

"Fuck a duck!" Jill rocked back in her chair. "That many?"

"That many so far," Sangita said. "Once word spreads in the airport about your truck and how tough it is, I think we'll get even more."

Jill groaned.

"I think the water is still workable," Babu said. "Jill, you can make a big tank, right? It's just metal, so Customization can do that. Someone must be able to rig up a pump, and then we can fill up at rivers."

"Yes!" Sangita said, snapping the fingers of her free hand. "Then recycle all of the water through Habitation to clean it. The production should be enough to tide us over between fill-ups, and recycling what people excrete will help too."

"Drinking each other's piss. Great," Jill said, mourning the days when she had Bertha all to herself.

"Magically cleaned piss!" Babu said.

"That . . ." Jill paused. "That does make it a bit better, actually. Thank fuck for magic. All right, that's water sorted, at least in theory," Jill said. "Four points into Habitation, then, plus one in Cargo. What's up next?"

"Food," Sangita said. "You had just under ten tons of canned goods left from that shipment you never made, but that's only going to last a few days, even with rationing."

"Can we scrounge?" Jill asked. "I've done deliveries to supermarkets and warehouses all along I-90. We can check and see if they have any, uh, extra. They should have a lot more than a few tons."

Sangita made a note on her clipboard. "You mean steal," she said with a frown. "We do need the food."

"It's only stealing if someone still alive owns it," Jill said with a shake of her head. "Hitting a few stores and depots must buy us a week, right?"

"We can't plan on that, not for sure," Sangita said. "They could be burned, or looted, or people could resist."

"All right, scrounging food is plan B," Jill said. "Maybe a few days is all we need, anyway. Bertha can go hella wicked fast now."

"We have stops to make," Babu said. "Those two military bases where no one magicked any messages back, remember? And, well, if there are other people along the way to rescue, are you really going to leave them behind? All that adds up."

"Dripping fuckburgers," Jill sighed. "You're right. We'll have to grow our own. Someone must have taken a farmer class."

Sangita and Babu shared a look.

"We have a hundred and nine people with some sort of food-producing class," Sangita said, "but you can't grow food on metal. Well, maybe magic can, but it can't be efficient."

"And even if they could, there isn't the space. The Nexus is at maximum size, and we need that space for people to sleep in," Babu said. "We could try buying all of the currently available powers to see if something in the next set would work, but that's a lot of points for an uncertain payoff."

"I could do that," Jill said. A slow grin spread across her face. "But I think Bertha's settlement powers will be a better fit." She leaned over and opened the door to the bathroom. "Take a look at this."

CHAPTER 3

BOXES FOR CREATING MORE BOXES

Jill reached her mind towards Bertha and willed the crystal settlement core to show itself. The night before, it had erupted from the bathroom floor right before she was going to use the toilet. But now, nothing happened. Her mental commands were being refused.

"Jill," Babu said, "that's your bathroom. Did you, uh, make a custom seat or something?"

"I'm trying to get the stupid settlement core to show," Jill said. "It was going to be dramatic!" She scowled and stopped mentally pushing. "Hey, System," she shouted aloud, "why isn't the core popping up?"

System Inquiry Detected Your Inner Sanctum is not secure! Current security settings restrict Core access outside of authorized personnel.

"Inner Sanctum?" Sangita asked. She had gotten the message from the System as well. "Your Inner Sanctum is the . . ." She trailed off, gesturing at the bathroom.

Babu burst out laughing.

"It's not my fault. It's the System," Jill said. "It was messing with me. Like I said before, it's a sassy bitch sometimes."

"To me, it just acts like a computer program," Sangita said. "And a useful one at that."

"It says it's adaptive to its user," Babu said and wiped a tear from his eye. "Now we have proof of that!"

It was Sangita's turn to laugh, though she cut it off after just a few chuckles.

"You two suck," Jill said, spiking each one in turn with a glare. "System!" she barked to the sky. "Make Babu and Sangita authorized to see the core, will you?"

> System Inquiry Detected
> Current security settings restrict changes to settings unless the Inner Sanctum is sealed.

"Oh, for fuck's sake," Jill said and stomped into the bathroom, slamming the door shut behind her. A glowing golden crystal burst from the floor, but Jill had been expecting it, and she leaped aside onto the toilet rim.

"The System really does seem to make things harder for her," Sangita said, her voice muffled by the metal door.

"It seems to tease her," Babu replied. "But I don't think it has ever done something bad in a crisis."

"She must have sworn at it too much. This is why I taught you manners."

"You taught me manners," Babu said, voice laden with skepticism, "in case a magic-power granting program-thing came to Earth and could be offended?"

Jill tuned them out and focused on the crystal.

> Welcome, Settlement Administrator Jill MacLeod
> Your Settlement is ready to configure!
>
> **Settlement Name:** System Go Fuck Yourself I'm Going to Bed
> **Type:** Dimensional Bubble **Core Level**: 1
> **XP:** 1,000,000/3,000,000 **Available Points:** 1
> **MP:** 10,000 **Core Mana Generation:** 16.7 MP per second
> **Shield HP:** 10,000 **Shield Maintenance:** 1 MP per second
> **Residents:** 5299 **Resident Mana Taxed (1%):** 14.1 MP per second
> **Total Mana Generation:** 30.8 MP per second
> **Total Mana Expended:** 1 MP per second

Available Administrative Actions:
Invest XP: Send future or pending XP to "System Go Fuck Yourself I'm Going to Bed."
Set Taxes: Mana and XP tax rates can be raised up to 10%.
Manage Security: Settlement Shield and Inner Sanctum may be configured.
Select Focus: Biological, Technomana, Mystical

Available Power Categories:
Common
Dimensional
Infrastructure
Social

Further options may be unlocked by fulfilling requirements.

"I did not name it that, smartass," Jill thought. "Change the name to . . ." She paused. "Shit, I don't know. How about Berthaville?"

Settlement name changed! Settlement name is now "Shit I Don't Know How About Berthaville."

Jill sighed and projected disappointment towards the System. "I've got something for your adaptive interface to ponder, shit-for-brains," she thought. "Jokes are much funnier the first time."

Usually, responses from the System came instantaneously, but this time there was a pause of several seconds.

Adaptive Interface input processed. Changing Settlement name to "Berthaville."

"Nice," Jill thought. "Now, show me the security options."

> Settlement Security
> **Inner Sanctum:** Core will only reveal itself to authorized personnel. The Sanctum must be sealed to enact changes.
> **Settlement Shield:** Active, Permeable
> Sub-Administrators: None

Jill tapped her fingers on her thigh for a few seconds and thought about who she trusted.

"Set Babu, Ras, and Mia as sub-administrators," she projected to the System. "Let them change whatever they want. And don't require the door being closed—that's just dumb, unless I make the bathroom some sort of armored high-security super-crapper. For Sangita"—she paused for a moment, then nodded to herself—"let her see the settlement boxes, but don't let her change things. Hide the core from everyone else."

> Security settings updated.

Jill balanced and extended one foot over the core crystal. She hooked it onto the door handle, flicked it down, and pushed the door open.

Babu and Sangita turned their heads and took in Jill, standing on one leg on the seat of her toilet, balanced over a spiky golden crystal. They shared a look.

"This is normal," Babu said. Sangita sighed. Then both of their eyes started flickering back and forth as they read the settlement notifications.

"You named it Berthaville?" Sangita asked.

"Yes," Jill said. She jumped over the core and out of the bathroom, ducking her head in midair to avoid the lintel. "That right there is what I named it. No other name. You have a problem with that?"

Babu waved at his mother and shook his head back and forth.

"That's what I thought," Jill said. "Bertha's a kickass name, so Berthaville is too."

"You know it!" Babu said, far too cheerfully.

Jill narrowed her eyes. "Back to business," she said. "First up is picking a focus." She willed the settlement screen to show those options.

Select 1 area of focus for "Berthaville." The choice cannot be revoked.
Biological Focus: +10% to growth and healing rates inside of "Berthaville" for all living things. Unlocks powers related to life and biological engineering.
Technomana Focus: +10% to the crafting rate and effective Level of all Mana-powered devices produced inside of "Berthaville." Unlocks powers related to devices and Technomana applications.
Mystical Focus: -10% to the cost of all spells cast inside of "Berthaville." Unlocks powers related to the direct application of Mana.

"Why this option first?" Sangita asked. "Not spending the point on a power?"

"Well—" Jill started to explain.

"Ope!" Babu interrupted. "This doesn't cost points, but it's permanent! It's just like the choice you have to make when you fully upgrade one of your modules. What it reveals could totally change how the settlement progresses and what power is best to buy first."

"Bingpot," Jill said. The coffee machine beeped, and she reached over to grab the freshly brewed cup. "So, there's the obvious choice of biological focus to help fix our food problem, but I don't think that's the right call long term."

"Bertha is your main asset," Sangita said. "Will the techno one help things that are made through your Soulbound powers?"

"Oh," Babu said. "That would make the choice easy. Does Bertha count as being inside of Berthaville?"

"How can the truck be inside of the things inside of it?" Jill asked, mentally poking the System at the same time.

System Inquiry Detected
Potential spatial paradox detected. Resolving Mana flows.
"Berthaville" occupies the region enclosed by Soulbound Modular Vehicle "Bertha's" dimensional barrier. Integration of exterior Mana flows supporting the Settlement's region will cause dimensional cascade failure. Bertha will not be included in Settlement focus.
Warning! Dimensional cascade failure is not recommended.

"That's a 'no,' then," Jill said. "What do you two vote for?"

There was a beat of silence as everyone thought. Sangita broke it first. "We need food. Badly. But nearly everything else that people here do falls under technomana."

Babu nodded. "People are already crafting things out of monster parts," he said. "Remember that machine shop at the armory back in Boseman? Everything they were doing there would count. Maybe we can ask for some of the airport's trucks or forklifts as payment, and people could upgrade them into battle buddies for Bertha!"

"Or as a more practical priority," Sangita said, "have them make farming equipment, so the focus's bonus will apply to them in a roundabout way."

"I'm more excited about them crafting guns," Jill said, "or armor." She glanced at her tiny closet, where a badass, spiked-shoulder set of leather armor hung. It needed a good cleaning and repair, as there was a blood-covered hole in the shoulder, but Jill could hopefully get it upgraded at the same time. If the armor had been 10 percent better, it might have stopped the round entirely.

Another flash of memory struck Jill: Bertha side-on to a horde of monsters, guns blazing away, while those inside ran out to rescue others. They were exposed in a way that Jill wasn't and would rely on their arms and armor far more. The edge technomana gave them would save lives.

"Right," Jill said. "Technomana it is." She selected and finalized it; a new set of options for the settlement appeared before her.

Technomana Powers
Workshop: Unlocks the workshop structure for placement in the Settlement. This structure provides a facility, bonuses, and further options for item creation. Unlocks **Foundry** at Settlement Level 20.
Direct Mana Feed: Allows for Settlement Mana to be routed into Technomana devices. Unlocks **Overdrive** at Settlement Level 10.
Device Incentives: Experience gain for the creation and maintenance of Technomana devices increased by 10%. Unlocks **Device Spark** at Settlement Level 50.

"Okay," Jill said, "nothing we can use now for food. But I bet that Workshop is what the armory had."

"I'll call them right after we're done and ask Buckman," Babu said. "If it is, he can tell me exactly what it does before we spend a point on it."

"Nice thinking," Jill said. "Now," she cracked her neck, "time to read the rest." She summoned boxes for the other available powers and silence descended in the cabin as they read.

Common Powers
All Common Powers may be taken multiple times.
Size Increase: Increase the diameter of "Berthaville's" claimed region to 1 km. Note: Settlement Shield upkeep is proportional to shield area. Settlement Shield strength in any given place is inversely proportional to shield area. Unlocks **Boundary Shape Control** at Level 15.
Shield Reinforcement: Increases the Hit Points of the barrier shield by 10,000 HP and decreases the shield's upkeep by 20 MP per second. Unlocks **Shield Notifications**.
Core Mana Reinforcement: Increases the Mana of the Settlement Core by 5000 MP, with a consequent increase in Mana generation of 8.4 MP per second. Unlocks **Secondary Core** at Level 50.

Infrastructure Powers
Warning! "Berthaville's" region is currently fully occupied. Increase available space to place structures.
Basic Housing: Creates 20 Basic Housing buildings and allows for the manual placement of more. Each is equipped with housing for 5 and life support for 10, including air, water, and rations, and is self-maintaining. Mana Cost per building: 1 per second. Each rank taken of this power supplies the upkeep for 20 buildings. Unlocks **High-Density Housing** at Level 30.

Social Powers
Tax Increases: Reinforces "Berthaville's" Mana pathways, allowing for a maximum tax rate of 20% for both Mana and Experience. Unlocks **Distributive Services** at Level 15.
Proclamations: Displays messages to all residents through their System interface. Unlocks **Propaganda** at Level 20.
Community Goal: Unlocks Administrator action **Set Community Goal**. Any resident action taken in furtherance of this goal generates 10% more XP, while actions taken against receive a 10% XP penalty. Unlocks **Emergency Action** at Level 10.

Dimensional Bubble Powers
Air Supply: Refreshes the air inside of "Berthaville," maintaining an Earth-standard nitrogen-oxygen atmosphere at 50% humidity. Mana Cost: 1 per cubic kilometer per second. Unlocks **Terrain Generation** at Level 5.
Artificial Sun: Creates a spherical source of heat and Earth-standard spectrum light. The sun can be set to a static or orbital mode. Mana Cost: 1 per second. Unlocks **Seasonal Control** at Level 15.
Interstitial Airlock: Allows access to the Interstitial Realm without contamination. Creates two portals around an intermediate dimensional chamber between "Berthaville's" bubble of causal reality and the exterior Interstitial Realm. Unlocks **Interstitial Gates** at Level 25.
Warning! Exposure to the Interstitial Realm is not recommended at your Level.
Warning! Combat with Interstitial Beings is not recommended at your Level.

"So," Jill said when she had finished. "I'm thinking we put the first point into size increase so that we can set up some farms or hydroponics or something."

"There's no option in the buildings for those," Sangita said. "We'll have to get people to build them manually."

"You said people had farmer classes," Jill said. "I'll give them space, they do their stuff, we don't starve."

Babu raised his hand. "I think it might take a few more settlement levels before that will work," he said.

Jill scowled. "Yeah? Why is that?"

"Well, there being a power called Air Supply is a bit of a red flag, don'tcha know," he said. "It kind of implies that an extra source of air is needed."

Jill snapped her fingers. "Right! It's a dimensional bubble, whatever that means—" She was interrupted by another notification.

> System Inquiry Detected
> Dimensional Bubble type Settlements are pockets of causal reality residing in the Interstitial Realm. Access to the Material Realm is typically granted via anchors or portals. The Interstitial Realm does not contain matter compatible with that of the Material Realm.
> Warning! Dimensional Bubble Settlements cannot draw Mana from the Material Realm.
> Warning! Combat with Interstitial Beings is not recommended at your Level.

"Thanks, Sys," Jill said. "So, whatever we need, we have to bring in from outside, unless it's made from a power?"

"Interstitial Realm . . ." Babu muttered, staring at the wall. His eyes began flickering back and forth, the sure sign of someone reading more System-provided information.

"When I made Bertha bigger," Jill continued, "it sucked in a ton of air, even though I've got some climate control stuff generating air."

"I remember that," Sangita said. "It was like a hurricane blasting through the trailer."

"I bet a whole kilometer diameter of extra space would be a fuckton worse."

Sangita grimaced. "There would be more deaths," she said, tone flat.

"Hey, System," Jill said. "Put warnings on options that are going to straight-up murder people if I take them, will you?"

> Adaptive settings updated.

"Good," Jill said. "Well, it has to be air first." She selected it and braced herself. Every time she had taken one of Bertha's Soulbound powers she had felt the changes in her truck as if they were happening to her own body, and some of them had been truly disturbing. But this time there was nothing. Jill shut her eyes and focused hard, shutting out as much of the room around her as she could to feel what was happening in the rest of Bertha. Finally, she felt it: her truck wasn't spending Mana on creating and filtering the air anymore.

"So, no food production right away," Sangita said.

Her voice snapped Jill out of her introspection. "Uh," she said, "right."

"So is stealing back to being plan A?" Sangita asked and narrowed her eyes.

Jill sighed. "It's kind of a kick in the cooter, but yes. I'll also put food on the top of the list of things to ask for in payment from the commander." She stood. "Hey, Babu," she said.

He didn't answer, still engrossed in reading System boxes.

"Babu," Sangita said, tone sharp.

"What?" he said, jerking backward and looking around.

"We're done for now, but I've got a job for you after you talk to Buckman," Jill said. "For you too," she said to Sangita. "Figure out how to level the settlement as fast as possible."

"Okay," Babu said. "Sounds fun. What are you going to do?"

"Something that's always a giant pain in my ass," Jill said. "Convince someone to pay for a shipment I've already delivered."

CHAPTER 4

THE BERNESE SANDER

Jill stepped out of the Habitation Module into the Cargo Nexus and took a deep breath. The air smelled just a bit different—a hint of grease and metal tickled her nostrils, replacing a slight outdoorsy musk. The new air was being made from magic just like the old had been from the Hearth of the Wolf add-on, but it had a new character: machine rather than nature. Whatever the smell, Jill was glad that something was dealing with the air. The funk of thousands of unwashed people in a building-sized space wouldn't be pleasant without it.

In the time that she, Babu, and Sangita had been planning, many more people had woken up. Some were sitting in little clusters, sharing whatever food they had managed to take with them when they had run from their homes. Others were moving around. A trio of women stepped around Jill with hesitant smiles, heading into the Habitation Module and the few bathrooms there. The cargo doors at the other end of the bay were open and letting in daylight; through them went a steady stream of people in both directions.

Jill's presence had drawn attention. Nothing too overt—a cautious glance here, a change in conversation volume there—but enough to make Jill uncomfortable. Crowds and her didn't get along.

She reached her mind down into Bertha, into her own body, and pulled at the metal decking underneath herself, raising herself up onto a shallow hill. A careful tweak of mana moved the hill and Jill along with it. Satisfied that her control was good enough, Jill crossed her arms, leaned forward, and pushed more magic into Bertha, balancing her body against the acceleration as the wave of metal propelled her forward.

Jill didn't have a power dedicated to surfing through Bertha. Rather, it was a consequence of one of her earliest, but most important, abilities.

> **Customization:** The cosmetic and structural configuration of "Bertha" can be slowly changed, as long as module limitations are not exceeded. Unlocks **Dimensional Customization**.

The word "slowly" in the power description wasn't very accurate in Jill's opinion. How fast she could change Bertha depended on how hard she mentally pushed the ability and how much mana she dedicated to the task. It was like a new muscle, one she was just learning to use, but it was capable of far more than the description had first led her to believe. Jill wondered what else was the same way.

Distracted by her thoughts, Jill didn't see what was coming until it was right on top of her. Her eyes widened, her heart pounded, and time slowed. Charging towards her was an enormous beast, a blur of muscle, fur, teeth, and slobber. A spike of metal formed in Jill's mind's eye, ready to lance upwards from the deck and impale the creature, but at the last moment, recognition broke through her panic. Jill forced herself to relax, dissipating her attack before it had formed.

The creature, a Bernese mountain dog as big as a horse, fell in next to her—easily keeping up—and barked. The single resonant sound was filled with meaning that Jill understood completely, despite there being no true words spoken.

"Hi! Hi! Other Packmaster, are we running? I love running!"

Fondness filled Jill's heart as she looked at the dog, Sander, as he bounded alongside her. The animal was one of the exceptional few that had resisted the tide of magic-induced monsterization that had swept the area, staying loyal to his owners and protecting them long enough to find safety in Bertha. Once there, he had dedicated himself, with the permission of the young girl whom he respected above all others, to comforting everyone he could. Sander radiated happiness, comfort, and safety in a way that only the best dog could.

Jill slowed her surfing to a stop. Her eyes narrowed as she concentrated on the magic surrounding her, willing it to become visible. Glowing lines and clouds of mana emerged in her vision, each coming with bursts of other sensations—smells, sounds, and emotions—telling her their purpose. As she expected, Sander had a cloud of connections emerging from him, each radiating fuzzy, slobbering happiness.

"You're a good boy," Jill began.

"Yaaaaay!!!!!" Sander barked, hopping in a circle and flailing his tail about.

"But," Jill continued, pinning the dog with a glare. His eyes went wide, and his tail fell. "Don't change my emotions. Even to good ones. Got it?"

"Other Packmaster doesn't want to feel good?" Sander barked, this time confused.

"Not through magical mind-control-power bullshit," Jill said. "Got it?"

"That was a bad word," Sander growled.

"Oh, for f—" Jill cut off her profanity. It figured that the only person willing to call her on her language was a family dog. "Just be a good boy and keep your magic off me, okay?"

Sander whoofed out a humid breath. "Okay, but you still shouldn't say bad words."

The magic puffing off of him swirled away from Jill. The intensity of her feelings towards the dog faded. She snorted to herself; even without magic, she still liked the thing. "Thanks, buddy," she said, reaching up to give him head rubs.

"Sorry!" a high-pitched voice called from behind Jill. "Sorry, Ms. Cloud!" A young girl ran towards them, clutching a stuffed animal version of Sander and panting for breath. Jill guessed that the girl was some age less than ten but wasn't sure. Past experience had proved that Jill was terrible at telling children's ages.

The girl stopped by colliding face-first with Sander, trusting in the dog's general fluffiness to bring her to a stop. She clung to her dog and directed him in a serious voice. "Sander, apologize to Ms. Cloud for bothering her."

"It's fine?" Jill said. She turned her head to look for some other adult she could rope into dealing with the girl. "I was telling him to not mess with me, but—"

"He messed with you?" the child said, a note of panic entering her otherwise serious tone. "Please don't do anything to Sander! He's a really good boy!"

"Yay, I'm good!" Sander barked.

"What?" Jill said. "Why would I do anything to the dog?"

The girl put her hands on her hips. "When people bother you, you beat them up and suck them into the walls!" the girl said with a scowl. "I saw you do it."

"That was one time," Jill said, "and they were trying to do a lot worse than bother me." A fraction of the refugees in Bertha had turned out to be the victims of mind control, programmed to turn violent when triggered. Jill had been a particular target; wherever she went they stopped attacking anyone else, focusing entirely on her. But they had been inside Bertha, and Customization wasn't limited to the metal under Jill's feet. In her pain and rage, she had wielded it like a tidal wave, sweeping away the low-leveled, uncoordinated attackers by the dozens.

"You make people disappear forever!" the girl whispered, awe in her voice.

"It's not forever! I'll get to them," Jill said. "I've just had other bull—uh, stuff to deal with. It's been like six hours. They're fine!"

"Uh-huh," the girl said, clearly not convinced.

A man jogged over, wearing a backpack sprouting glowing tubes. His clothes were smeared with the remnants of dried blood and his eyes were ringed from lack of sleep, but he had an apologetic smile on his face.

"Ms. MacLeod, uh, ma'am," he said to Jill and sketched a salute. "I'm Dan, Sarah's dad. Thanks for saving, well, everyone. I hope she wasn't bothering you?" He put a protective arm over the girl's shoulders and rubbed Sander's head with the other.

"What is with people being so mother f—" She clamped her speech off and glanced down at Sarah, who was watching her with wide eyes. "Friendly about bothering me?"

"I just told you!" Sarah said with a scowl. "You're the scariest and get grumpy easy! Pay attention!"

Dan laughed nervously. He nudged Sarah behind Sander. "Kids, eh? They just say stuff. No offense, right?"

Jill snorted. "Oh, don't get your—uh—self in a twist. I can live with being the scariest bitch on the block."

"Bad word!" Sander barked.

Dan gave Jill a pained expression, flicking his eyes at Sarah.

"Aw sh—" Jill took a breath. "Shoot. Sorry about that. Uh, no harm done, right?"

"I'm sure it's fine. Um, if I could ask you—" Dan started to say but was interrupted by Sarah tugging on his hand.

"Daddy!" Sarah said. "I've decided that when I grow up, I'm going to be the scariest bitch!"

"Bad words are bad!" Sander whined.

"That's a great goal, honey, but let's talk about that later," Dan said. "Ms. MacLeod, I've got to ask. Do you have a registry of people that made it into the truck?" He had a half-hopeful, half-resigned expression on his face.

Jill's humor faded. "I've got someone on that," she said. "You want to ask Sangita, Sangita Bati. She's about yay high"—she held a hand out an inch above her own head—"dark hair, dark skin, and a glare that will melt your brain."

"Okay," Dan said and let out a chuckle, "that's not intimidating at all. Thanks for everything, ma'am." He turned to Sarah. "Time to go, honey," he said and guided both girl and dog away.

"Good luck," Jill mumbled to herself once they were out of earshot. Her mind went to her own loved ones, so far away, before she pushed the thoughts away. Action would get her to them, not worrying.

She shook her head and walked the remaining distance to the cargo doors unbothered. Her ears popped as she crossed the truck's threshold, emerging into the chill air of an early spring Montana morning. She walked down Bertha's cargo ramp and onto the tarmac.

"Jill," called a voice from behind her. Leaning against Bertha's rear-most right wheel was Ras. Jill turned to look at him. His clothes were still rumpled from his recent sleep, and the eyes that met Jill's were dull. But his free hand rested on the pommel of his Soulbound sword, strapped to his waist, ready to draw it at the first sign of danger.

"Hey," Jill said and walked over to him. "What's up?"

"Kevin has a dinosaur," Ras said. He yawned.

Jill blinked, then remembered. The night before, Ras's young cousin Kevin had excitedly proclaimed that he had one as a pet. Jill, too tired to deal with it, had delegated the issue to Ras.

"And is it a toy, or . . ." Jill trailed off.

"It's a three-foot-tall feathered stegosaurus. Last I saw the two were curled up together in bed."

"That sounds goddamn adorable, but it's not going to go crazy and try to eat anyone, right?" Of all the monster types that had attacked Jill and Bertha the night before, dinosaurs were her second-most hated. A swarm of velociraptors had even managed to jump onto Bertha and tear their way through the armor, forcing those inside to fight them gun-to-talon. It hadn't been pretty.

"Nope, nothing to worry about. Kevin took a Beastmaster class and says it's tame," Ras said. He shook his head. "Looking at it was"—he paused—"weird. It looks exactly like all the monsters we've been killing, but it didn't feel like them."

"I guess I'll have to live with that," Jill said. She let her gaze sweep over the tarmac. "There aren't many monster corpses out here, and the guns haven't fired all morning. Where are all the monsters?"

Ras shrugged. "No idea. Maybe things have calmed down for a bit."

"Maybe," Jill said. "I collapsed last night faster than a hard-on in ice water. Were we attacked while I was out cold?"

"There was a cluster of vampire bats in the mid-teen levels around three in the morning, but I stopped them before they got too close to the airport," Ras said.

"You were outside?" Jill asked. "Like, on what, a patrol? Shit, you must be exhausted."

"Yeah, I'm tired, but Bertha's only in one place. The rest of the airport was vulnerable," Ras said. "It was good to be doing something. Not much on my plate now."

Jill tilted her head and acknowledged the point. Ras was one of the highest-level people in Bertha, and, as far as she knew, he had taken powers exclusively dedicated to combat. He'd only had his magic for a few days, the same as the rest of them, but he could more than handle himself; Jill had seen his Soulbound sword do incredible things.

"I bet you didn't get paid for that, though, did you?" she asked.

"Um," Ras said, "no? No one asked or anything, it was just the right thing to do."

"Big damn hero, you are," Jill said and punched him on the shoulder. For him, she didn't hold back, and the lazy strike hit with a sound like a baseball bat on a slab of meat. "You've gotta watch out for doing that too much or people will take advantage of you."

Ras didn't acknowledge the impact. "You're lecturing me about helping too much?" he asked and gestured at the people coming in and out of Bertha.

"Yeah," Jill said and scowled. "Do you know how much less bullshit I'd have to put up with if I'd minded my own business?"

Ras chuckled, but there was no heart in it.

"Anyway, I'm going inside to bargain, and I've got a list of shit I want to get for Bertha," Jill continued, "so I'm going to take credit for all of your do-gooder-ing."

"Want me to come along?" Ras asked, sounding hopeful.

Jill shook her head. "Nah, I'll be fine," she said. Her eyes narrowed at the man's disappointed expression. "But I do have a job for you if you're determined to still volunteer. It's going to be annoying at best, dangerous at worst."

Ras stopped leaning on the wheel and stood straight, a spark coming back to his eyes. "What do you need?"

"Prisoner processing," Jill said. She pulled a face. "Well, maybe prisoners, I don't fucking know. We need to deal with all of those mind-controlled schmucks from last night." She extended her senses to the person-sized pockets of air in Bertha's trans-dimensional metal walls, feeling the bodies there. They were still warm, and Jill could feel that Bertha's magic was swapping out bad air for good, so they were still alive. But none were moving.

"They seem comatose," she reported, "but we need to get them sorted before they starve to death. And I don't want anyone dangerous onboard when we leave."

"I'll get some fighters together for security," Ras said, starting to pace, "and maybe you can make a space with bars to hold them?" He paused for a moment in thought. "Right outside the Medbay so we can get one of the docs to look at them if they can't wake up."

Jill nodded. "Good thinking. Get everyone together. I shouldn't be longer than half an hour."

"Will do!" Ras said. It only took him a few steps and a jump, one arm grabbing onto the door frame to spin him around, for him to disappear into Bertha, intent on his mission.

Jill let her eyes wander over her truck, taking in the striped red paint specked with dirt and the machine-gun-toting turrets stained with gun smoke by the barrels. An idle flex of her will and a few mana points, regenerated in just an instant, left Bertha shining with a fresh coat of wax. She cracked a smile at the sight. She missed how Bertha had been just a few days ago, but her home was only getting better.

She turned towards the airport and started walking, fast.

"Time to twist some arms."

CHAPTER 5

NEGOTIATING FROM WEAKNESS

Jill wasn't done in half an hour. Instead, she found herself sitting on a crappy chair pressed up on the side of a bland hallway somewhere in the staff-only section of the airport, which really wasn't wide enough for chairs. She took a deep breath as yet another hurrying person squeezed past her, then blew it out in a long, controlled sigh.

"The end of the fucking world," she grumbled to herself, "and people are still playing power games."

Her entry into the airport hadn't started too badly. She had simply followed the flow of people heading to and from Bertha and into the terminals, where a refugee camp was taking shape. As an emergency place to stuff people the building was pretty good: wide open spaces, lots of seating, working bathrooms, and the power was even back on. Everything that ran on electricity had died when the System had come, but what magic broke, magic could fix.

Someone must have used a class power to fix the airport emergency generators, and they hadn't stopped there: the airport traffic boards and TVs were glowing again too. The former showed an endless string of canceled flights, making Jill wonder just why anyone would have spent the time to get so many of the boards working at all. The latter alternated between the standard airport announcements that anyone who'd flown had heard thousands of times and a single, low-quality clip of Commander Davis.

"Hello, everyone, I'm Commander Davis," he'd said to the camera. "You may not know me, but I've served in this community for close to three years now. As the senior military officer, I am assuming command of this refugee facility until such time as I receive orders from a superior officer or until a properly authorized state or federal civilian official arrives." He paused, still looking into the camera. "What happened to the city isn't going to happen here. It may seem like we're alone out here in a crisis, but we're not. We have each other. Please remain calm and follow all instructions given by security officers. Report any creature you see and keep your distance. Trust in your neighbors and we'll all get through this. God bless."

The message played every few minutes, but no one was paying attention to it anymore. Instead, they were getting on with living as best they could. One TV had been unplugged from the airport systems and instead hooked up to a somehow working laptop. It was deep into the second Shrek movie and had an audience of dozens upon dozens of kids sitting in front of it. The airport restaurants were cranking out breakfasts to a line of mostly patient adults; they had food, at least for now. There was even a makeshift market set up in the food court: some traded things they had managed to take when they'd fled home, and others were using magic to instantly fix things that were broken.

A burst of green light caught Jill's eye; she saw a man retracting his glowing hands from a cell phone, a teen whooping with joy and clutching the device to his chest, and the same teen's face falling when he realized there was no signal and no Internet.

It didn't take her long to find someone to point her in the direction of Commander Davis. She had just headed towards the first person standing around with a weapon attempting to look like they were paying attention to everything. She was a member of the ragtag group of guards that had held off a wave of monsters the day before. From her TSA uniform she was one of the airport's regular staff, not one of the police or civilian volunteers, but the long gun she carried, covered in glowing lines and sporting a wicked animal-horn bayonet, was definitely not airport security standard issue.

The officer had been suspicious at first but had gotten a lot more helpful once Jill told her who she was—or, rather, what she drove. It turned out that Bertha had saved the officer's life the night before. The two of them had had an excellent conversation about how awesome Bertha was as the officer took Jill into the employee-only secured area of the airport, right up to where she now sat.

But since then, Jill had been stonewalled. Through a keycard-secured door on her left, which Jill was sure she could kick down with little effort, was Davis's citadel, the office of the former airport manager. Members of his staff, actual naval personnel from the facility in Billings rather than TSA or volunteers, went in and out, politely giving her the runaround and insisting that Davis was busy. Jill had been patient at first; she was no stranger to waiting for other people to get their shit together after all. But she wasn't just an independent trucker who needed to get paid anymore, and she'd had enough.

The door opened and out stepped a young man wearing navy fatigues, with dark rings under exhausted eyes.

"Hey," Jill said and stood. She took a step sideways to block his path and glared at him. "Is Davis ready yet? I've got shit to do." She threaded just a touch of mana into her voice, not quite activating the Malediction Bard cross-class spell that she'd earned, but enough to give her last statement an edge and make the man in front of her snap his gaze to her.

"Uh, no, ma'am," he said with a wince. "The commander is still busy. Can I get you a coffee, ma'am?"

It was a better offer than anyone else had given her, and Jill felt her ire fade just a touch. The person in front of her wasn't the one causing the problem.

"No coffee," Jill said with less heat, "but you get back in there and give Davis a message: he wanted to talk with me and wouldn't deal with my deputy, so he better make his ass available. And if he's still busy in two minutes, I'm taking that as permission to do what I need to do."

The man gulped. "I'll pass that along, ma'am. What should I, uh, say you're going to do?"

"Leave it vague," Jill said with a smirk. "It's more menacing that way."

He turned around and went back inside. Jill started counting in her head, but she had only reached forty-one when the door opened again.

"He's ready for you now, ma'am," he said, stepping to the side to hold the door open for her.

"I thought he would be," Jill said.

She strode through the door into a bland waiting room—all fluorescent lights, office plants, and gray-upholstered uncomfortable furniture—that led to a half dozen other offices. An older man stood in the open door of one of them with arms crossed. He was in uniform, a modest salad of ribbons and medals on his breast telling a story that Jill couldn't read.

Narrowed black eyes under short-cut salt-and-pepper hair took in Jill, classifying and cataloging her in just the few steps it took her to cross the room.

Jill stopped in front of him and gave him an obvious up-and-down look. "I'm Jill," she said and thrust out a hand. "You're Davis?" The nameplate on the door said *Director MacPherson*, but if the airport director were still alive, he wasn't here.

Davis hesitated just a moment and then shook her hand, hard. "That's right," he said. "Commander Davis." He turned and crossed behind a desk, gesturing for her to follow him. "Thanks for waiting."

"Sure, sure," Jill said. "I'm used to bullshit."

Davis's gaze snapped to Jill's, and they stood in silent tension for a few moments. "Sit, please," he said and followed his own request. MacPherson had either had a bad back or was fond of games himself because the well-worn chair that Davis lowered himself into was far fancier and better cushioned than the one Jill found herself in.

"So, Ms. MacLeod, what can I do for you?"

"Well, what I want is food, medical supplies, and clothing for five thousand people, enough to last a week. Throw in three extra radars, a couple of your forklifts, and open up the hangars for my people to scrounge up as much tech as they can carry. Oh!" She snapped her fingers. "And a shit-ton of toilet paper."

"You're not asking for much," Davis said with sarcasm. "Do you want the F-18 parked out back too?"

"Yeah, that too. I've got no one to fly it, but why not?" Jill grinned and leaned forward. "Now, I'm not getting all of that, so let's negotiate."

"Why should I give you anything at all?" Davis countered. "You're at my airport."

"You're not giving me anything; you're paying for services rendered. Billed and everything, or so I heard. We bailed your over-clenched butt cheeks out last night from a monster horde."

"We would have been fine," Davis said.

Jill snorted out a laugh. "Yeah, some of you would have probably survived, but a hell of a lot of you would've been monster chow. Instead, I plowed Bertha straight through the monsters and put her guns between you and danger. Hell, my people even jumped out and risked their lives to save yours. I'm betting you'd have gladly paid for that kind of help if I'd demanded shit up front."

"Maybe," Davis said. He gave her a shallow smile. "But you don't seem to be the kind of person to do that. I'm not questioning your morals, Ms. MacLeod, or that you've helped us out. Or that in normal, before-yesterday life I'd be dipping into a funding pot to get you recompense. I'm questioning how giving you materiel today, with these new, ah, unique circumstances, helps me get tens of thousands of people through another day, another month. As it stands, well, you've already given me things that can't be taken back."

Jill sighed and tapped her fingers on the armrest of her chair. "Gamahuching giraffes . . . Negotiating after delivery always sucks. You've got a point there."

Davis narrowed his eyes. "You've got a 'but' coming, don't you?"

"Yup! 'Cause I've got something else you really want." She leaned forward. "I've got a radio that can call up an armory in Bozeman, and they've set up a network of magic that talks to everyone else. No more waiting for orders, and you can call in help from all sorts of other people."

"You've got comms?" Davis asked, his face a mask.

"Yeah," Jill said. "And you could use them for the low, low price of a whole bunch of stuff that by all rights you've already bought."

"Or you could just let me use your radio for free. It doesn't cost you anything."

Jill growled in frustration. "You dragged me in here rather than deal with Sangita, made me wait, and have offered me bupkis even after all I've done. Consider me out of generosity."

"You're still asking for a frankly ridiculous amount."

"So, give me a counteroffer! Give me things that you might not need right this second that are going to help me get thousands of people across the country. That's more than fair considering that once you're in contact with the rest of the military and you tell them how many people you're looking after, they'll resupply you anyway."

"That might be the case, but it could also be the case that they have nothing to give." He shook his head. "I could just order you to give me that radio. I'm in charge here, with a whole lot of armed people listening to me. Desperate people who might do a lot to stay alive if I pushed them to."

Jill stared Davis in the eyes. "You could try," she said, "but I saved their lives last night, so they might not budge when you push, and then where would you be? I don't think they'll like shooting their neighbors. Plus, just between you and me"—she mentally composed an abbreviated status sheet with her level and physical stats, then flicked it to Davis's mind—"normal bullets don't work on me anymore. If I didn't have those morals you're not questioning, I could just rip your limbs off and take what I want anyway, before anyone's the wiser."

His eyes flickered once, reading. Davis's face stayed passive, but Jill's magic-enhanced eyes could tell from the artery on his neck that his pulse had picked up from sudden fear.

The shadow of a vindictive thrill flared inside of Jill, satisfaction at a bully getting his due. *Or maybe*, she thought to herself as Davis sat there, silent, *maybe I'm just enjoying being the exact same piece of shit that he just was*. She took a slow, deep breath through her nose and quashed both feelings.

"How about," Jill said, breaking the silence, "we just forget the threats and get back to an honest back and forth. No more bullshit, no more posturing and power plays, just two leaders trying to keep people who depend on them alive."

He nodded slowly, his pulse slowing. "I think I have, to use your language, screwed the pooch on this one, haven't I?"

"Not really up to my standards of cussing yet," Jill said, "but yeah, just a bit. I'm over it if you are."

He extended a hand over the desk. "The name's Jim. Nice to meet you, Jill."

CHAPTER 6

GIVE AND TAKE

"Let's get to it," Jill said after shaking Jim's hand. "The thing I need most is food. I've got plans to grow more, but they'll take time."

"That's what I can spare the least," Jim replied. He raised a hand to forestall Jill's objection. "I'm not trying to be difficult here, but I'm in the same situation you are. Too many refugees, not enough to go around, only I've got twenty times the number of people you do."

"Well, damn," Jill said. "That means I'm going to be stripping a grocery store or a warehouse on my way out of town."

"That I can help you with," Jim said. He stood and crossed the office, opening the door with a jerk. "Smith!" he barked. "Get me that map of food locations. And two coffees!"

He walked behind his desk and sat back down. "We're going to send off a number of resource-gathering expeditions," he said, "so we've been compiling locations from people in the know. How much are you looking to take?"

"Enough for five thousand people for at least three days. If everything goes well, I should get to Boston in under a day, but"—Jill shrugged—"we need some margin."

"I think one of the smaller locations should be enough for you, then," Jim said. "One of my goals is centralizing the food supply for more efficient resource control. We're leaving messages behind so that anyone else looking for food will know to come here. If I give you copies, can you leave them in easy-to-see locations? Somewhere safe from the elements."

"Sure," Jill said. "That's easy."

"Coffee and maps, sir," said Smith at the door. He was the same man who had let Jill into the office. He entered and put down a pair of steaming white mugs and a stack of papers.

"Thanks, sailor," Jim said.

"Can I get you anything else, sir?"

"Not at present," Jim said. Smith saluted and left the room.

There was a short silence as both of them took a long, grateful gulp of hot liquid.

"You know," Davis said, "without international trade, we're going to run out of this."

"Son of a bitch," Jill agreed. She took another swig. "Guess I'm going to have to drive over some borders, then."

"To South America?"

"Bertha's really damn fast."

"Is that so?" Jim asked, putting his mug down and getting back to business. "Then I have an ask for you." He fished one map out of the stack of paper and rotated it so that it was facing Jill.

"These locations"—he pointed at a symbol—"are where we know grocery stores, food distribution centers, and that sort of thing are."

Jill took one look at the map and committed it to memory. The enhancements to her mind weren't as immediately obvious as the ones to her body, but they were still dead useful.

"The farther the locations, the more dangerous it will be for my people," Jim continued. "You have better speed and firepower than anything I have at my disposal. I accept that I owe you already, but if you can do a run here"—he pointed to one of the farthest marks, which was also annotated as being one of the largest—"then I'll owe you a lot more."

Jill thought for a moment, weighing time versus more supplies. Time won. "I'm not available for hire today," she said with a shake of her head. "I have to get driving. That's not a want, that's a need."

"I was afraid you would say that," Jim said. "In that case, it would help me out if you would leave the close locations to me."

Jill nodded. "I can do that. Wherever I go is going to turn into a total shit show somehow, but I can deal with those." She pointed to two of the most easterly marks. "These right here are near my route. That far enough for you?"

"It is," Jim said.

"Then I suppose that's all for food," Jill said. She took a sip of her drink. "I saw some forklifts parked on the tarmac; I want one or two of them to speed up loading. They would go a long way towards making us square. You must have extras you can spare, right?"

"I do, but we have more baggage carrier trolleys and other airport-specific gear that can carry things," Jim said. "What are your requirements here, exactly?"

"I need something that rolls on and off Bertha and that's going to be able to move pallets," Jill said. "Something, too, with a strong enough frame that we can bolt armor onto it and make an enclosed cab. So, a forklift."

"Then I'll give you a forklift," Jim said. He frowned slightly. "Wouldn't enough armor to be useful slow it down too much? The engines aren't rated for that kind of weight on top of a load of pallets."

"Eh, we'll have to soup up the engine with some sort of magic bullshit replacement anyway," Jill said with a shrug. "Speed can be fixed. I'm not just going to be using these for loading, though. I want to make them multipurpose. If I need to send someone without a combat class out of the truck while we're under attack, an armored box to keep them safe to do whatever-the-fuck without getting their head bitten off is a must."

Jill's own experiences with monsters, from before she had out-leveled everything around, intruded into her thoughts: a mutated deer paralyzing her with its gaze of terror, lunging at her with distended teeth; a monster breaking into Bertha's cab, only stopping because of Babu's creepy marionette ability. Her own class, Battle Trucker, was a hybrid between combat, negotiation, and vehicle abilities, but she'd almost entirely neglected the former, and there were a couple of times that she'd only survived because of luck. If she was going to order people as vulnerable as she'd been to go outside Bertha, she was going to give them all the protection she could.

"And you're going to more dangerous places than this, aren't you?" Jim asked and grimaced. He paused for just a moment, then made up his mind. "I have two that would be perfect for you. Bigger than normal, with a fully enclosed seat already, so it won't be too much work for you."

Jill raised an eyebrow. "And you're willing to give me them?"

"We're trying to keep our people alive, right? You need them more than me. But"—he pointed at her—"this is a big sacrifice on my part, and I reserve the right to say no to other things, even if you are giving me access to your radio."

"Got it," Jill said. She took another drink as she considered what to bring up next.

"One thing confuses me," Jim said before she'd decided. "Why did you ask for radars in that door-to-the-face list you opened with? There aren't any planes flying right now, and I wasn't under the impression that rain or snow would stop you. So, what are they for?"

"My people think they can turn them into monster detectors. Maybe take some looted monster eyeballs and merge them in somehow; I don't really know how it works, only that it does," Jill said. "Bertha's biggest weakness is getting caught by something nasty enough to break her, or swarmed by too many targets to kill, or ambushed by invisible enemies that people on the guns can't even see."

Jim sat up straight, alarm on his face. "Invisible?"

"Yeah," Jill said and scowled. "Those fuckers could fly and dodge bullets too, and they killed a kid right in front of me."

Jim winced. "That sounds awful."

"They attacked us in Billings, so if you're going back in that hellhole, watch the skies. I had someone whose scout powers could see through the stealth. So, check with your people and try to get someone with those powers on any expeditions you send."

"I will," Jim said. "Is there any other intel you can give me about monsters?"

Jill thought back. "They seem to appear in"—she waved a hand, searching for the right word—"themes? Like all the monsters in one area will be of the same type and do mostly the same things. Here there were a lot of bugs. But I've seen snakes, deer, bison, and even dinosaurs, of all fucking things."

"Mostly animals?"

"Yes, but also weirder shit. And the higher level they are, the smarter they seem to get. Don't rely on them always coming at you straight on like those bugs that attacked here. And don't rely on them coming from where you can see them. Like I said earlier, we got hit by invisible pterodactyl fliers in the city. But back in Bozeman, there were other things, which could burrow through the Earth like it was water."

Jim had started taking notes as she spoke, rapid pen strokes that ended with a triple underline. "I think that's going to save some lives, Jill," Jim said.

There was a rap on the door; Smith was back. He strode over to the desk, handing Jim a piece of paper. "Hold on just a second, please," the commander said to Jill as he read. His eyes widened a bit as he read, and halfway through they flickered to Jill for an instant before going back to the text.

"Thank you, Smith," he said when he was done. "Please tell them to withdraw."

"Yes, sir." Smith left.

Jim turned back to Jill. "Pardon the interruption. How does an ASR-9 and a GWX-75 sound for radars? I believe we have a replacement for the first on hand and can reclaim the second."

"I don't know dick about radars," Jill said. "You tell me."

"ASR-9s are ground-based air-search radars, good for weather and aircraft. It should work on top of a truck if you can supply enough power," Jim said.

"Bertha can do it," Jill replied. The radar would almost certainly end up being an add-on to one of the truck's modules, with any electricity requirements supplanted by mana. Bertha's mana regeneration and capacity were huge, only really stressed when the truck was firing all of her guns at once or repairing massive damage.

"The GWX," Jim continued, "is a plane-mounted forward-looking weather radar. You'll need to work out how to make that useful, but it's a lot smaller. Potentially portable."

"Yeah, I can work with that," Jill said. "Generous of you, even." She had watched him for any signs of deception while he was describing the equipment; she really didn't know anything about radars and was relying on him being truthful. She didn't think he'd lied about them, but she did think he wanted something. "What are you asking for them?"

Jim cleared his throat and, as he tapped a piece of paper, said, "When you came to see me, I sent a few people into your truck to look around and—"

"Of course you did," Jill interrupted with a roll of her eyes.

"—and they just reported back. They say you've got a full surgical suite and a whole set of nurses and doctors from the hospital to use it. And that you've been able to make prosthetics for people. Is that true?"

"Yup," Jill said. "Bertha's kick-ass enough to have a Medbay Module, and the new arms are from one of its upgrades." Jill hadn't actually known that she had rescued hospital staff, but it made sense. A lot of people had been in and out of the Medbay, and she hadn't heard any complaints of malpractice.

"So, it's System generated? Can you show me the text?"

"Sure," Jill said. They were being helpful to each other after all. She sent over the description and savored the rest of her coffee as he read.

Medbay
"Bertha" has a Medbay Module with basic medical facilities for 3 examination rooms, 3 surgical suites, and care of 2 long-term patients. Generates medical supplies sufficient to treat common ailments at the cost of Mana.
Add-ons (0/2): None installed

Completed Upgrades:
Stasis: While being treated in Surgical Suites, patients do not suffer HP damage from ongoing conditions.
Mana Prosthetics: Missing body parts may be replaced by prosthetics made of Mana. Draws Mana from "Bertha's" reserves to generate, but ongoing maintenance Mana is supplied by the patient. Unlocks **Mana Enhanced Prosthetics**.
Ward Expansion (1/5): Increases the number of examination rooms and surgical suites by 1 and by 1 add-on slot. Increases the number of long-term patient beds by 2.4x.

Available Upgrades:
Mana Enhanced Prosthetics: Enhanced prosthetics have a Body rating equal to the effective Level of the Medbay Module multiplied by 2.8.
Medbay Effective Level: 84

She waited for his eyes to stop flickering. "Like what you read enough to tell me why you're so interested?"

"I wanted to make sure that it really was as good as what my people said before I asked," he said.

"Just spit it out already."

"You were right about us taking casualties from monsters. The airport has an infirmary, but it's not set up for the kinds of traumatic injuries that we have," he said. "There are seventeen people that are stable for now but might not make it long term and another nine who've had limbs amputated. I realize that I'm asking a lot and that you have a limited number of beds, but—"

"Done," Jill said. "Send them over."

"Really? Just like that?"

"Yeah, I've got class points to spend right now," Jill said. "The progression of beds is exponential, so I only need three more points to fit them all. It was something I was going to have to do anyway, given how dangerous things are. Just make sure those people know that I'm heading east before they get in. That's not negotiable."

Jim nodded. "I think they'll accept a bit of travel if it means living. Thank you."

"Yeah, I'm just so nice," Jill said. "Almost makes you feel bad for being such a dick earlier, doesn't it?"

"Yes, well," Davis said, clearly uncomfortable, "I thought we were forgetting about that?"

"Sure, sewage under the bridge," Jill said. "Now, how about tools? You must have spares in those hangars."

The haggling lasted another five minutes, but in the end, Jill got most of what she wanted. Her people would be allowed to raid one of the maintenance hangars for tools in exchange for looted monster parts, and Jim had agreed to give her extra clothes from the airport's lost and found and unclaimed luggage area. It wasn't much, but every bit helped. The only thing Jim really couldn't spare, other than food, was toilet paper.

To Jill's surprise, Jim had suggested that she take a pair of Jeeps that had been left in long-term parking.

"Their owners aren't going to be back for them anytime soon, after all," he reasoned.

"Won't you need them for your supply runs?" Jill asked. She'd leaned back during their conversation and had her feet on his desk.

"Yes," Jim said, "but I think you'll need them more as scouts or outriders. Your bright red eighteen-wheeler is hardly subtle. I've got plans for getting more vehicles, so I can spare two."

"Well, twist my arm," Jill said. "I'll take them." She spun her empty coffee cup in her hands. "How about the rest of your plans? You must have a quarter of the population of the city crammed in here so far. Are you going to try and have people stick it out here or move?"

Jim sighed. "I'm honestly not sure yet. Attacks are down today out here, but we can see swarms of monsters in the city, crawling over buildings and doing God knows what. Part of me wants to get as far away from that hive as we can."

"Sounds sensible to me," muttered Jill.

"But the rest of me," Jim continued, "sees that city as a resource. Not only because of all of the supplies, but also as a source of monster parts. Plus"—he scowled—"we have no guarantee anywhere else will be safer. What if we go somewhere the Bison doesn't like?" He shook his head. "I can't believe I just said that . . ."

The monster in question deserved its audible capital letter. A lightning-crowned, storm-wreathed bison the size of a mountain; the mobile natural disaster had crushed the defenses of the city below them with ease. The only reason the airport still stood as a refugee center was that it had been ignored.

"Weird new world we're in," Jill said. "If you're thinking of staying here, why haven't you made the airport a settlement yet? There are more than enough people. A bunch of magic powers would come in real handy for you, not to mention a big glowing wall."

Davis scowled. "The System reports that we can't, not this close to Billings. The ruins of the old core cause a"—he raised his fingers in scare quotes—"'disruption in the mana' that stops the formation of a new one. We need to send an expedition into the city, through all the monsters, and do some sort of cleanup."

Jill whistled. "That sounds dangerous as fuck."

"There's nothing I could give you to hire you for that, is there?" Jim asked.

"Nope."

"I didn't think so," Jim said. "We'll figure something out."

There was a knock on the frame of the open door. "Commander?" It was another aide, one not in uniform. "Lee from maintenance is here and says that it's urgent."

"Everything is urgent," Jim sighed under his breath. "I think we have an understanding?" he asked, standing up and extending his hand.

She stood and shook it. "That we do," she said. "If anything else comes up, I'll have Sangita call again. Don't blow her off this time."

"Don't be an asshole or you'll tear my limbs off. Got it," Jim said and cracked a small smile. "I'll be down to use that radio, but if I don't see you again: good luck, Jill."

CHAPTER 7

LIKE GIANT METAL ZITS

This seems a little overkill," Jill said. "I'm telling you, they aren't moving."

She and Ras stood in a newly cleared space in the Cargo Nexus, ten meters down from the Medbay. In front of them was the wall where Jill planned on popping out the prisoners. Behind them was a barricade bristling with defenders, chief among them Mia with her rotary cannon, whose bullets Jill had seen collapse office buildings.

"Mind control is terrifying," Ras said back. "Maybe those people aren't moving because they are comatose; maybe they aren't moving because they are saving up energy to strike."

"Did you ask Babu?" Jill said. "Cause of, well, you know." The aforementioned enchanter had several worryingly named class powers that could overwrite the will of others. He had wanted to be present, but Jill had other jobs for him she needed done.

"Yes, I asked Babu," Ras said. "He thinks they aren't a threat." Ras sighed. "He's probably right, but I don't like this. Even if they can't hurt us, there are a lot of people under level ten in the truck who they can, including kids."

Jill cracked her neck. "Well, if they go for anybody, then"—she made a slurping noise—"back into the walls they go. Killing them is a last resort." She turned around and said, louder, "You all get that? No shooting unless they get past me."

Mia gave her a thumbs up. "We're not psychos," she said, then yawned.

"What's with all of the guns, then?"

"Training!" Standing amongst the defenders was a man Jill had seen organizing the various volunteers who took turns on Bertha's turrets. His gym clothes were rumpled now, but his whistle shined brightly from a cord around his neck. "You never know when the Cloud Killers will be forced to defend our home's insides again!"

"The what?" Jill asked.

"It's our team's name," said the coach. "Identity is important for morale."

"I am actually okay with that," she said. "Kickass name."

"Also, a precaution," Mia said. "Maybe five of them merged together and absorbed their weapons to turn into a gun-limbed murder zombie."

Jill shuddered at a memory. "That was one person with a cop car, and we don't even know how it happened," she said.

"So, you're admitting it could happen again," Mia said. "And if it does, I'm going to shred the thing." She gave Blossom a pat.

"Fine. If it's a corrupted abomination, you can shoot it," Jill said. "Now get ready, 'cause here we go." She half closed her eyes and reached into Bertha with her mind, feeling for the prisoner-laden air pockets. She pulled the closest towards the wall and queued up more behind them, being careful to only move it at a walking pace. She didn't want to injure the people any more than they had been the night before. The wall distended in a smooth curve, like the surface of a gray pond with an opaque bubble rising from its depths. "Ready?" Jill asked.

"Ready," Ras said. He stood sideways, one hand on the pommel of his sword. Behind her Jill heard the shuffle and clicks of the defenders readying themselves and their own weapons.

Jill peeled back the surface of the bubble and out tumbled a sandy-haired man. He didn't so much fall as slump forward, spinning, the edges of his body catching on the receding petals of metal. Ras shot forward, catching him before he hit the ground. Jill tensed, ready to do something if the man's weakness was just an act, but nothing else happened.

"He has a pulse," Ras said, a hand to the man's neck. "But it's slow."

"Let me through," a woman in surgical scrubs said as she pushed past the defenders. The last time Jill had seen her she'd been covered in blood up to her elbows. Now she was clean and, unlike everyone else, seemed to have found replacement clothes, as the scrubs she was wearing were pristine. She fussed over the man, hands glowing yellow at times as she activated this power and that.

If the still figures in the walls were like the man who'd just come out, Jill was going to need even more beds than what she needed for the airport's casualties. She took a deep breath and then pushed four points into Ward Expansion.

Mana surged through Bertha and poured into the Medbay. The truck trembled as the module grew. Jill, linked to Bertha as she was, felt as if a new torso was sprouting from her back, but somehow in a good way. She focused her will on the feeling, both slowing the growth down to a more manageable rate and imposing a sensible layout on the new rooms. What had been one hallway turned into a branching network, all growing from a central artery.

Medbay
"Bertha" has a Medbay Module with basic medical facilities for 8 examination rooms, 8 surgical suites, and care of 80 long-term patients. Generates medical supplies sufficient to treat common ailments at the cost of Mana.
Add-ons (0/2): None installed

Available Upgrades:
Mana Enhanced Prosthetics: Enhanced prosthetics have a Body rating equal to the effective Level of the Medbay Module multiplied by 2.8.
Medbay Effective Level: 88

"You just grew Bertha again, didn't you?" Mia asked when the shaking had stopped.

"A whole shit-ton, yeah," Jill replied. She read the last remaining power and paused. The body rating it would give for new limbs was an excessive 246, a solid 44 percent higher than her own 171, and that would only grow with time. A flash of how strong someone could be, should they sacrifice their limbs for upgrades right now, intruded into Jill's mind. But what about the rest of them? Could the torso and spine of a lower-leveled person even support the massive strain the limbs would cause?

She wasn't going to experiment to find out. If there was some volunteer later, well, she would go over the risks with them then. For now, it would be worth a class point to unlock the Medbay's next grouping of abilities.

Experience had shown that when that happened, the System would present her with an either-or option on how to direct the module's growth, and the effects could be extreme. Now wasn't the time.

"Comatose, but this man's brain is very active," the doctor said, finished with her magic-powered examination. She shook her head and looked at Jill. "Think you can magic up an MRI for me? Or steal a working one, somehow? I only have impressions from a diagnostic ability to go on here, nothing precise, and I'm worried about what I'm feeling."

Jill opened her mouth to snark at her but thought better of it. "I'll see what I can do," she said instead.

"Bill, Todd," the coach said, "help the doctor get people into beds." The two people leaped over the barricade, slinging rifles onto their backs as they did, and under the doctor's instructions lifted the man away.

Jill pulled prisoner after prisoner out of the walls, and time and time again they emerged as limp bodies. The atmosphere went from one of tension to controlled chaos as person after person was lifted away.

"Sugar!" Ras cursed. He had fallen into a routine several dozen people in, but this time his hands squelched onto a sweatshirt soaked with blood. He lowered the person to the floor, then shook his head. "She's dead." The reason why was obvious: a hole in her neck, punched clean through.

"Fuck," Jill agreed, her gut turning. She looked at the victim's face and tried to remember her. Jill drew a blank. The woman must have been one of the people Jill had swept into the walls on instinct, part of a tidal wave of people that had borne down on her. Whether the woman had been alive then or had just been a corpse caught as part of a group, Jill couldn't tell.

"Someone get something to cover her with," Ras said. "Then I'll take her to the others." The mood after that was grimmer, the excitement of a new day overwhelmed by memories of the night before. This was far from the first death to have happened in Bertha. She realized that she didn't actually know what had happened to the bodies. She hadn't sensed any place on Bertha that felt like a morgue.

Jill kept pulling more people out of the walls. She wondered how people had been in a good mood in the first place. She already knew part of the answer: the System modified emotions as part of its magic, steeling people to the new realities of the world and helping them cope. She had a bad feeling about what else it was modifying but pushed that away. There was nothing she could do about it for now.

She reached out with her mind to another bubble and pulled it forward. This time the person inside shifted violently, a sudden spasm of thrashing limbs slapping steel. "Hey!" Jill shouted. "We've got a live one!" There was a bang, and a fist print suddenly appeared in the thin metal cocoon. Behind Jill came a whirring noise as Mia spun Blossom up to speed. The doctor and volunteers helping her scattered away and retreated behind the safety of the barricade.

Jill glanced around. Everyone was in position. Ras gave her a nod; she released the metal all at once.

Out stumbled a woman with bloodshot eyes and a rifle gripped with white knuckles.

"Shitdicks!" Jill shouted and the muscle of her thigh pulsed with remembered pain. She recognized the woman. Not only had she shot Jill the night before, but she had the combat powers to have made that shot punch through Jill's buffalo-hide magical armor, through Jill's own passive defenses, and wound her deeply, knocking off hundreds of her hit points with a single blow.

The woman raised her rifle in one smooth motion and pointed the barrel at Jill. Glowing red mana condensed around her in bolts of broken lightning, drawn in by whatever power she was using, but before she could shoot, Ras struck. His sword flashed from its sheathe in one blinding motion, the edge tearing through the air with a sound like ripping cloth, and impacted the gun's barrel. To Jill's shock, it didn't cut through; the long gun must have been a high-level magic item itself, or possibly even Soulbound too. But the blow was still strong enough to rip the rifle up and out of the woman's hands.

"Wait!" she yelled, and Ras's sword stopped mid-swing a split second before it would have again disarmed her, but this time far more literally. "Wait," she repeated at a lower volume. She raised her hands in a slow, cautious motion, showing that she had nothing in them. "Please, don't hurt me," she said, looking at Ras with trembling eyes. "I don't mean you any harm."

"You just tried to shoot me," Jill said. "Again."

"I thought you were more thralls of the mayor." She turned her pleading expression on Jill. "They were everywhere!"

Jill raised an eyebrow. "Damn right about that," she said. "I think I see one of them right in front of me, even." She narrowed her eyes. "I saw you plain as day last night taking aim at me. You ruined my pants."

"I wasn't thinking straight," the woman said. Her expression crumbled into a combination of confusion and anger. "Everything was fuzzy, a floaty feeling. It was like my body wasn't under my control, like I was someone else watching things happen, even though I could feel what actions I was taking."

Jill and Mia exchanged a look. Jill couldn't get a read on the woman, and from Mia's narrowed eyes, Jill didn't think the heavy gunner had either. But the mind-controlled people from the night before had acted in a very particular way, and what the woman described wasn't it.

"And how about just now?" Ras said. "I could feel the power going into that shot. You meant to kill."

"I was confused from being locked up all alone in the dark for who knows how long!" the woman said, angry once more. "I had no idea what was going on, no idea if I would get out or if I'd been buried alive!"

There was silence in this part of the Cargo Nexus, but to Jill the echoing bangs and shouts from the loading going on in the rear were a timer she couldn't ignore. She had to make up her mind now, then get back to getting everyone else who was in the walls out.

Whatever this woman claimed had happened to her, she was powerful. Not as strong as Jill or one of her core trio of monster slayers, but a cut above everyone else in Bertha; if she was telling the truth, she could be a huge help. If not, she would be a big problem.

Jill had two ways of testing the loyalty of someone near her; both were side effects of her powers and mana sense. One was simple: if someone was a resident of Berthaville, their mana would be tied into the settlement around them. For the woman in front of her, the answer was clearly "no," but Jill hadn't expected it.

Instead, she focused on the second way, from one of the several System mechanics that let her profit off the work of others:

> **Synergy**
> Disrupt the static paradigm with groundbreaking synergy! Designate 12 sapients under your command. They receive 12% of Experience you would gain, divided amongst them after other modifiers. You receive 12% of Experience they would gain, after other modifiers. This ability is non-recursive. Requires Level 10 Battle Trucker, A Deal's a Deal (1).

After taking the power, Jill had discovered that she could use it to sense those that were eligible for her to mooch off of, those that considered themselves under her command. More than that, though, when Jill really focused, she could tell just how willing people were to become so or, on the opposite side of the spectrum, how much they opposed the idea. Whereas Jill could get a sense of the feelings of everyone else around, this woman gave her no clue at all. Under Jill's probing her mana was a brick wall.

"I think you're full of shit," Jill said. "But I can't prove it, and I don't lynch people. Are you going to cause problems if I let you go?"

"Of course not!" the woman said, affronted. Again, Jill couldn't tell if she was lying or not.

"Okay," Jill said, "then get the fuck off my truck."

The woman opened her mouth but after a moment's pause closed it again without saying anything. She shook her head and turned for the exit.

"Are you going to give her her gun back?" Mia asked Jill, leaning over close so no one else could hear. "She might need it."

"And she might shoot me again," Jill muttered back. But she was already exiling the woman to life in the airport for the safety of everyone on board Bertha. That was no reason to stop the woman from keeping her weapon.

"Hey," Jill said. "You're forgetting this." She sent a flick of magic at the deck plate under the rifle, kicking it into the air and towards the departing woman, who caught it with one hand.

She looked at it, then at Jill, and nodded once before continuing on her way.

CHAPTER 8

A NEW BUSINESS MODEL

Ninety minutes later, Jill and Aman were seated in the cab, a well-used pocket road atlas spread open in front of them on the dash.

"It's a simple route," Aman said to her, tracing a capped pen over the map. "We cut north around the city, through the heights, and cross the Yellowstone River here," he tapped the pen down on Highway 312 near Huntley.

"I haven't taken that before," Jill said. "This is one of those small local highway bridges, isn't it? Will it be able to take Bertha's weight?"

Aman hesitated. "How much does she weigh?"

"A lot," Jill replied. "Forty metric tons from the armor upgrades plus whatever the turrets weigh on top of her base weight. As for all the people and their shit in the back?" She let out a little laugh. "That must be three hundred tons, probably more. But the real kicker is all the new structure. It's like a parking garage of metal back there."

"All together that must be a thousand tons or more, even though your current construction is far too light to meet code," Aman said. "I don't think there's a bridge in the country that can take that much weight concentrated in a single place."

"Yeah, my big girl's been ruining the roads too," Jill said as she gave the steering wheel a thump of approval. "And she's been getting sluggish on the turns, even with the wheel and speed upgrades. So all that weight must count for something."

"I'm concerned that this truck will collapse the roads entirely and break the water mains," Aman said. "To be honest with you, I'm surprised it hasn't already happened."

"Well, most of Bertha's tucked away inside of a new dimension. That must do something, right?"

System Inquiry Detected
The exterior manifestation of mass and inertia of the contents of dimensionally contained items is inversely proportional to the dimensional warp factor.
Current external mass of Soulbound Modular Vehicle "Bertha": 127,255.8 kg

"Thanks, Sys," Jill said. The System was still being oddly helpful today. "There's no way in the devil's thorned asshole that some little bridge can take that, is there?"

"No," Aman said. He looked confused for a moment but shook his head. "It is close enough that I have some construction and reinforcement powers that should make the difference, but they take time to use. I estimate an hour for repeated casting and then testing."

"So we either gun it and *Dukes of Hazard* from one bank to the other—"

"Please don't."

"Or we spend time reinforcing the bridge, or we get to see if we're waterproof and claw our way up the far bank. I haven't had a chance to try out climbing with the slug wheels yet, but it should work."

"I'm sorry, but the what?"

"Oh, right, you weren't around for that," Jill said. She sent the old notification for the Propulsion Module add-on to Aman.

Slug Feet (Vehicle Add-On)
Level 22, Rare
On toggle, converts the wheel elements of the Propulsion Module into gastropod feet, allowing "Bertha" to adhere to nearly any surface.
Reduces speed by 95%.
Toggle Mana Cost: 1100

His brow furrowed. "This is patently impossible. Your truck is too heavy. Whatever it is climbing would surely collapse, right?"

"Hell if I know," Jill said. "Maybe it releases magic reinforcing slug goo."

Aman sighed.

"Yeah, it's all magic bullshit," Jill said back, clapping him on the shoulder. "But I don't think a riverbank is the best place for a traction test, so let's plan on reinforcing the bridge even if it takes a bit longer."

The door to the Cargo Nexus clanged open behind them. Babu staggered in, his face pale.

"Hey, Babu," Jill said. "You look like shit."

"Hi, Dad, Jill," he said. "Mana exhaustion will do that, don'tcha know, but I'll be better in a few minutes. I, uh . . ." He glanced at his father, then back to Jill. "I did the thing."

Aman raised an eyebrow. "The thing? Really, son?"

"Um, well, Jill didn't want anyone to know, but—"

"Oh no, we're not doing this," Jill said. "I told you to be discreet, not keep things from your folks." She turned to Aman. "Babu's been planting another mind virus."

"Excuse me, what?" Aman said. "Mind virus? Another?"

"Yeah, those were the words I used, but you got the order wrong."

"Ms. MacLeod," Aman said, tone grave, "Please don't make light of mind control. How many died fighting their neighbors last night? And how many are now comatose in your Medbay?"

"Don't worry, Dad," Babu said, stepping closer. "I was canceling compulsions out, not placing them. Just with a self-replicating effect. When it infects someone who is clean, it doesn't do anything."

"Oh," Aman said. Then he smiled. "Well, that's different! Good job, son!"

Jill decided not to mention that the effect Babu was canceling was one that the enchanter himself had put down. It had made thousands, tens of thousands, of people flee from Billings and rendezvous at the airport, likely saving their lives.

Babu half smiled. "Thanks. One thing, though," Babu said, turning to Jill. "Once the counter-spell spread, well, a lot of people changed their minds about staying put in the airport."

Jill groaned. "They're heading back into the city, likely to get killed, and I'm going to have to spend the next colon-load of hours rescuing them?"

"Nope!" Babu said. "They want to come with us!"

Jill sighed. "Bertha kicks ass, so I really can't blame them," she said. "Is someone telling them the deal? They're not going to bitch at me to turn around and head towards their cousin's sister's farm?"

"Mom's on it," Babu said. He glanced at Aman. "I've never seen her so, well, focused on something."

Aman's face clouded over. "We'll talk about it later," he said, pointedly not looking at Jill.

"Trust me, I don't want to know," Jill said. "Family drama sucks. Change of topic. Where are we going to put all of these new people?"

"I have a design for your cargo area that will be better," Aman said.

"Which took him like a minute, Jill," Babu said. "Have you ever been in a building before?"

Jill flipped him off.

"But," Aman continued, suppressing a smile, "more than anything we just need more volume to work with. Have any magical bullspit left to help?"

"Plenty," Jill said and cracked her knuckles. "Thirty-two class points' worth of reality-bending awesome coming right up."

"Yes!" Babu yelled, pumping his fists in the air. He swayed a bit, the effort a little much in his mana-drained state. "I have so many ideas!"

"Heh, I thought you would," Jill said, "but if more volume is what we need, that's what I'm going to do first. The Habitation Module is due for some growth." She raised an eyebrow at Aman. "You have any particular layout you want me to do with it while it's expanding?"

"Ah, no," said Aman. "I'll need to do a redesign based on whatever powers you pick afterwards, anyway."

"Well, okay then," Jill said. She activated her Captain Speaking power and the sound of Bertha's horn echoed throughout the truck. "Hey, everyone," Jill projected. "Uh, this is Jill. I'm making the Habitation Module bigger. I'm going to try and be gentle, but you better hold onto your butts, just in case." She paused. "That means stay put."

She cut the power, closed her eyes, and began.

First, she took a tight mental hold over Bertha's mana in advance of purchasing anything, pushing her mind through her connection to Bertha until she could feel the truck more than her own body. Once she was sure of her control, she put one point into the Bunkroom power. A low groan sounded through the truck, akin to that of a tall tree swaying in the wind. Jill felt the Habitation corridor stretching, at first just an inch at a time. Jill relaxed the tiniest bit, and the growth sped up. The corridor grew enough for a door to appear; a room budded off from it, metal walls reaching out and stretching Bertha's dimensional membrane further into the void. The groaning grew louder each time a new room ballooned outwards, the metal of Bertha's floor, walls, and ceiling an orchestra of creaking metal.

"Huh," Babu said, head cocked to the side. Jill was concentrating on magic hard enough for her to see the dozen threads of mana stretched from his head, each pulsing the tiniest bit as a message passed along them. "Good job, Jill!" he said after a few seconds of listening. "There's less screaming happening than usual!"

Jill rolled her eyes, but the corner of her mouth quirked. "Don't distract me. This is harder than it looks."

She felt the growth rate slowing, so she put the final point into Bunkroom. The groaning leaped up in pitch, the exponential nature of the power's progression pushing the expansion along even faster. Jill let it accelerate for a moment, then held the rate steady. Her body thrummed along, the vibrations coming up from the seat under her combining with the feeling through her Soulbond in a fusion of mind and body that just felt right. But holding the growth steady was getting more difficult. The part of her that let Jill see mana, that felt her connection to Bertha and to the System, grew weary, like a muscle on the hundredth repetition of a low-weight set.

"Um," Babu's voice echoed into her ears as if from down a hallway, "you're starting to, uh, fuzz a little at the edges there, Jill. Are you okay?"

"I'm as fine as a salad of tits," Jill gasped out. She felt herself losing control and cast her mind through the new construction, making double sure that there was no one who'd been foolhardy enough to run inside while it was growing. Thankfully, it was empty. With a gasp, she let go of her control. The groan turned into a shriek and Bertha's mana plunged as more than fifty rooms were made all at once; she couldn't count exactly how many—they were made so quickly.

She pulled up the new description for the module:

Habitation:
"Bertha" has a Habitation Module with basic amenities for 191. Life support capacity for 382.
Includes: Single Bed, Washroom, Workspace
Add-ons (2/6): Inferior Coffee Machine, Dire Bobcat Fur Bedding

Completed Upgrades:
Restful Sleep: All allies who rest in the Habitation Module receive increased physical and psychological healing rates.
Bunkroom (5/5): Increases the capacity, life support, and volume of the Habitation Module by 2.4x, and by 1 add-on slot.

Available Upgrades:
Unseen Servant: Weak manifestations of force will see to the maintenance of the Habitation Module and the residents' possessions. Unlocks **Roaming Servants**.

"That number seemed a lot bigger yesterday," Jill said. "Hey, System, how many people are in Bertha right now?"

The Settlement of Berthaville hosts 5299 residents.

Jill took in a sharp breath, a surge of panic filling her. When she had decided to let people come along, she had expected some small fraction of the four thousand people she'd rescued to sign up. Instead, they seemed to have spread the word, and more than Jill had ever imagined were depending on her. That was just tough shit, though, and it was happening right now, so it was time for her to deal with it.

She put a hand on Bertha's wheel, fingers falling without thought into the grooves they'd worn over the years. Those marks went deeper than anything physical; when she'd Soulbound with Bertha, every bit of damage the truck had taken had been repaired in moments, down to scuffs in the paint. Every bit except for these. She'd never given up on Bertha, and Bertha had never let her down. This wasn't going to be the thing that stopped her.

So Highlander Shipping was changing its business model. It wasn't the first time she'd had to do so to keep rolling, and it wouldn't be the last. She'd been in charge of keeping cargo safe, down to the most fragile of porcelain dolls. People were a hell of a lot more capable of taking care of themselves than that. She just had to do her job and get them what they needed to get going. She could do that. She already was. It was just time for her to accept it and keep driving forward.

CHAPTER 9

TEENAGERS ALSO LIKE TO EAT

Babu poked her in the shoulder. "Are you planning on ripping that wheel off and killing a fear deer with it?" he asked.

"It's you I'd be braining, smartass," Jill said and released her hands. "Right, that was a whole bunch of growth, but not enough."

"You can get another hundred and eighteen rooms right now," Babu said, "but only if you're willing to lock a boost into Habitation."

"What is this from?" Aman asked.

Jill sent the upgrade in question from the Cargo Nexus to Aman.

Reinforced Module Mounting (0/5): Choose one exclusively attached module. That module's Class Boost increases by +.2. A module may only be boosted once with this power.

"Is there any downside?" Aman asked. "Besides locking the rooms onto the trailer."

"Just that I can't change my mind later," Jill said. "If I ever go back to it being just me and the road, it's a wasted point." She smiled and shook her head. "Those days are over, at least with Bertha." She turned a mock accusing glare on Babu. "So, when it's time for my mid-life crisis, you have to get me a magic sports car."

"What?" Babu asked. He leaned away and placed a hand theatrically on his chest. "What did I do?"

"You're the build advisor, so everything that goes wrong with this magical points business is your fault."

"But you're the one making all the decisions!"

Aman chuckled. "My son, here's an important lesson that I learned in the service: spit rolls downhill."

Babu crossed his arms. "I need to get some underlings to blame," he grumbled, but there was a smile on his face. "Besides," he continued to Jill, "with your age, it's not going to be a mid-life crisis. More like eighty percent, don'tcha know."

"Babu!" Aman said. "Don't speak to your grand-elders that way." He grinned at Jill.

"Oh, fuck off!" Jill said, laughing now as well. "Okay, I'm doing this expansion before I die of old age." She was still worn out from controlling Bertha's last growth, but a minute's rest and a few jokes had her feeling good enough. She bought the Reinforced Module Power; one blast of mana, a clench of iron will, and a drawn-out groan later, and the Habitation Module was at its new size.

> **Habitation:** "Bertha" has a Habitation Module with basic amenities for 309. Life support capacity for 618.

"Done," she said. "We're up to"—she paused a moment—"1,236 liters of water generated a day. So recycling is still the plan."

"I'll still set aside room for a water tank," Aman said.

"The other Habitation upgrade makes these cleaning ghost things," Jill said. "We don't need them now, but the advanced powers might grow the module more. That's what happened with the trailer. Any objections to me taking the last upgrades?"

"Finish him!" Babu said, his voice low and bombastic.

"You calling Bertha a him?" Jill asked, an eyebrow raised.

"Ms. MacLeod, that is from a video game," Aman said. "It is something the young people do."

"We're still on that age thing, huh," Jill muttered, narrowing her eyes at Aman. She shook her head and took the Unseen Servants upgrade. Bertha's mana in the Habitation Module churned like a storm cloud, tiny vortices growing larger as they twisted more power into themselves. Three seconds later the storm passed, but the vortices remained: child-sized clouds of mana. Jill focused her attention on her own room, where one of the servants had formed. Tendrils of mana leaped out from it towards the bathroom and bed, presumably to clean.

"Ope!" Babu chimed, putting a finger to his ear. "More screams."

A new upgrade, just unlocked, appeared in Jill's vision. She sent it to Babu and Aman before reading it herself.

Roaming Servants: Unseen Servants are shared with other modules. Unlocks **Roaming Guardians.**

"That's really worth an entire point?" Jill asked, poking a bit of her mana into that part of her mind that connected to the System.

System Inquiry Detected
Mana crossflow between Modules and expansion of Servitor behavioral parameters requires significant foundational changes. System Mana-usage optimization algorithms have several hundred billion times as much data available to them as user "Jill."
Warning! Second-guessing System Mana-usage optimization algorithms is not recommended at your Level.

"Did the System just tell you to shut up?" Babu asked.

"With some sass too!" Jill said. "Nice one, Sys. Well, here goes."

She took Roaming Servants. A web of mana spread from the Habitation Module, shooting out into Bertha. To Jill, it was like gentle, warm threads spreading from her belly into her arms and legs, pulling on her muscles ever so slightly as they passed by. Once the mana reached everywhere inside Bertha, tiny pulses flashed back and forth along the web. Jill realized that the process looked almost exactly the same as the mana around Babu when he was sending and receiving messages.

Half a minute later the communications finished, and the mana web faded from Jill's senses. The next unlocked power appeared before her.

Roaming Guardians:
Unseen Servants will attempt to protect all non-hostile sapients inside of Bertha. They have a Body rating equal to the Habitation Module's effective Level and can interact with non-corporeal entities.
Module effective Level: 90

"Now that's what I'm talking about!" Jill said. Her humor faded. "That would have really helped last night."

"Hindsight, Ms. MacLeod," Aman said.

"Right," Jill said. "I guess so." She took the power. The servants froze. Mana poured into them, but they didn't grow. Instead, they became denser, brighter, and more dangerous.

A thought burst into Jill's mind: what if there were more hostile people inside of Bertha, waiting to strike? Would these mana constructs be able to tell their intentions now, or would they wait until it was too late? No one was prepared for a fresh bout of violence to erupt inside of Bertha.

> System Inquiry Detected
> Guardians act first to protect residents from attack, regardless of hostility designations. Secondary priority is the pacification and removal of hostile entities. Hostile entity classification relies on overt actions or designation by authorized users.

It wouldn't serve as another loyalty detector like Jill's other powers, but if Bertha was ever breached again, like the truck had been several times, the new power would save lives.

The upgrade finished and the mana constructs began moving again. Jill held herself ready to suck people back into the walls if the guardians moved to attack them. But none of the magical constructs did. A line of them formed at the door between the Habitation and Cargo Modules as they began to exit, spreading to the wider truck to clean.

> Congratulations! Habitation upgrades complete! Determining most beneficial new abilities. Only one of the following customized abilities may be selected:
> **Chez Bertha:** Adds a centralized eating and cooking area. Generates up to 618 meals per day. Meals determined based upon resident preferences. Defaults to authentic pizza. Unlocks further food-related upgrades.
> **Shadow Jesters:** Unseen Servants can become audible, visible, and tangible in order to entertain residents, though they always lack facial features. Jesters provide entertainment based upon individual preferences. Unlocks further entertainment-related upgrades.

"Obvious choice is obvious," Jill said after they had all read the notification, "but does anyone have anything to say about the entertainment stuff before I pick food?"

"Teenagers would be using that," Aman said.

"Gross." Jill picked the Chez Bertha customization without another thought and was rewarded with a new box. The scent of coffee exploded in her nose, followed by a flickering series of tastes from different foods. Each one was individually delicious, but the combination made Jill's stomach rise with nausea.

"What counts as authentic pizza?" Aman asked.

"*Pffft*," Jill blew a raspberry and tried to push down her feelings of sickness. "The only real pizza is—" She cut off as a hiccup of stomach acid burst into her mouth.

As fast as it had begun, the kaleidoscope of flavors stopped, the upgrade complete.

> Advanced Habitation Upgrades:
> **An Apple a Day:** Chez Bertha generates 618 apples per day. Fully eating a Berthapple restores 28% of a person's Hit Points and attempts to counteract a negative effect. Counteraction Level is equal to module effective Level.
> **Chez Bertha Takeout Kitchen:** Food prepared in the Habitation Module receives an automatic stasis field that preserves temperature and freshness. Lasts for 10 days, after which the food begins to decay as normal.
> **Luxury Amenities (0/5):** Upgrade the comfort of the module with one of the following: Arcade, Bar, Basketball Court, Climbing Wall, Gym, Hootenanny Hall, Ice Rink, Movie Theater, Performance Hall, Shooting Range, Spa, Swimming Pool, Custom Option.
> **Rested Mana Pathways:** All who have rested in the Habitation Module gain an 8% bonus to Experience gain for the following 16 hours. Unlocks **Sympathetic Alignment**.

She sent the notification to the others and reached out with her mana to include Sangita—if nothing else, she needed to know about the new food generation from Chez Bertha—but the woman wasn't close enough to Bertha for her to contact.

"Oh!" Babu said with an excited inhale a few seconds later. "You have to take Rested Mana Pathways!"

"Yeah, yeah," Jill said. "I know how you feel about experience boosters. They create an 'exponential feedback loop of growth.' But what is up with these amenities?"

> System Inquiry Detected
> Amenities examples are selected from resident desires. Custom amenities may be created by user specification.

Jill shook her head at the casual example of System mind reading. "Right, I'm taking the boost." She did so. Instead of feeling a change in Bertha, she felt a change in herself; the roaring river of power inside of her calmed just a bit and started to flow more easily.

"What was that?" Babu asked, alarmed.

"Welcome to taking Bertha powers," Jill said. "That was, like, the mildest one today." The feeling faded into the background and the unlocked power appeared.

> **Sympathetic Alignment:** All who have rested in the Habitation Module gain an 8% bonus to Power effectiveness when using them on each other.

"And that's another one that's a no-brainer," Jill said, taking it as she sent the description along.

"These are going to add up," Babu said. "More than a little too. We buff each other with all sorts of things already, and that's only going to get more common. All the healing is from powers now too!" He bit his lip. "There's going to be a lot of competition for living in the Habitation Module once word gets around."

"With only 309 rooms," Jill said, "that's going to be a lot of people left out."

"It will help to quarter six in a room instead of two," Aman said. "They can fit if you replace the bed and desk with triple bunks with your Customization ability. Six to a bathroom is fine."

"That's eighteen hundred spots, give or take," Jill said. "We're up to a third of people. I wish some of the new module powers had just let us pack more in." She expected the System to send her a message back calling her dumb and explaining why that hadn't been so, but no boxes appeared in her vision.

"How do you want to handle who goes where?" Aman asked.

"Lottery," said Jill without hesitation. "With guaranteed spots for people who are actively helping Bertha. Either as a defender or an administrator."

"I'm sure Mom will love sorting that out," Babu muttered.

"Once we get more levels in Berthaville we can make some proper housing," Jill said, ignoring Babu, "but until then they'll just have to stay in the trailer."

"I'll add a level of barracks to the plans," Aman said and made a note. "Nothing I haven't built before. Only we'll be leaning on your magic to create almost everything."

Jill sighed. "I'm going to be customizing shit all fucking day, aren't I?"

"Maybe," said Babu. "I think I might have figured something out. Could you show Dad the Command Module?"

Jill did.

Command:
"Bertha" has a Command Module with 1 control station and 1 observer station.
Includes: Seatbelts (rare technology), Airbags (rare technology), Openable Windows, Mirrors, and Doors
Add-ons (1/1): Military ManaNet Radio

Completed Upgrades:
Captain Speaking: Jill MacLeod can speak to and receive replies from anyone within 14 meters or inside of "Bertha."
Available Upgrades:
Capacity (0/5): Add 1.4 control stations, 2.8 observer stations, and 1 command add-on slot.
Sensor Upgrade (0/5): Effectiveness of any installed perception devices increased by 14%.

"So, I was thinking," Babu said. "What is it that a 'control station' would even do? Just another place to drive from doesn't seem enough. So, what if it lets people use all of the other things Bertha can do?"

"Can it?" Jill asked.

"I dunno," Babu said with a shrug. "The System wouldn't tell me."

Jill poked the System herself.

> System Inquiry Detected
> Each Command Module control station can be bound to one upgrade, power, or add-on of Soulbound Modular Vehicle "Bertha." Any authorized sapient can activate and receive information from the bound item. A holographic display gives a visualization of relevant data.

Jill turned to Aman with a grin. "You know what this means?"

He grinned. "It means, Ms. MacLeod, that I can build these barracks however I want."

"Hell yes, it does!" Jill said. She reached over and tapped him on the shoulder. "But you know you'll do a better job at it than I was going to anyway."

"That is true."

Jill purchased a rank in Capacity. The cab around them ballooned outwards, growing wide enough for three seats instead of two and lengthening to add a row of three more seats behind. In front of the new passenger seat, a chrome-plated panel slid out of the dash, covered in buttons. Hovering above it was a slowly spinning icon of a bright red truck with a question mark above it. Jill closed her eyes and summoned the feeling of activating Customization, then threw that at the newly created control station. The icon above the console morphed and shifted as the control station accepted Customization as its bound power, then settled into a three-dimensional cutaway map of Bertha.

"Yes!" Aman said with excitement, thrusting a fist into the air. "Look at how detailed that is!"

"So that's where you get it from, huh?" Jill asked Babu.

The enchanter just shrugged but gave a little smile at the same time.

Jill tapped her fingers on the wheel for a moment, then decided to create more control stations. She invested another point into Capacity and the cab widened even further, this time growing two more control stations and three more observer seats. She bound one of the control stations to the Captain Speaking power and the icon above it shifted to a comms panel that wouldn't be out of place on the bridge of the Enterprise, complete with a full keyboard and glowing indicators. Taking up the left side of the holographic display was a scrollable list of names, with Aaron A. Aaronson in first place.

The other control station she left unbound, but she knew that as soon as she had a working monster-detecting radar to install as an add-on, she would be designating it.

"I know the first thing I'm changing," Aman said, sliding into the chair behind the Customization console. He placed his hands on the controls, then paused. "How do I use it?"

Jill shrugged. "Try shoving mana at it? That seems to work for most things."

Aman nodded and closed his eyes. Jill saw his warm brown mana pulse and stretch, leaving his body in sudden surges but not reaching the console. "A little more," he said and took a deep breath. He let it out slowly, then pushed his mana hard. It finally connected. "Got it!" he said. The floating cutaway diagram of Bertha zoomed in on the cab and things began to change. First was the shape, from a wide rectangle to a smooth oval; the crystal armor windows remained, one large panel to the front and two smaller ones to the sides, but they were curved now along with the room. The driver's seat moved to the center front, flanked on either side by observers. The Customization and soon-to-be radar stations slid around the outside of the cab, settling near the back. Two of the remaining observer seats joined the stations at the back, while the other three moved to the center of the room.

"This is so cool," Babu said.

"This is from *Star Trek*," Jill said, voice flat.

"Not so, Ms. MacLeod," Aman replied. "I kept the seatbelts."

Jill looked around the cab. It felt wrong.

"Bertha's a truck, not a spaceship, and this isn't a TV show," Jill said. She sighed. "I get that we want the control stations easily seen by someone in the middle, so keep them on the edges. But make the cab rectangular again, including those windows, and move the driver's seat to the left-hand side. Someone still needs to be able to look outside at the mirrors to drive."

"Done," said Aman. The seats shuffled around each other as he followed the instructions; Jill clutched the sides of the seat with both hands to stop the sudden motion from dislodging her.

"You've got plenty to do to get Bertha's insides sorted," Jill said to Aman, "so I guess let me know if you need anything. Babu, can you figure out if I need to save any points? If not, I'm of a mind to dump them into the Propulsion Module and get Bertha up to ludicrous speed."

"I sort of have a plan for you," he said back. "I'll flesh it out. How many points do you have left?"

Jill checked. "Twenty."

"Save ten?" he asked. "That should be enough for the start of something really cool."

"Can do," Jill said. She stood up and stretched her back out of habit. "I need a break for now, though; buying so much stuff is exhausting. We've got a plan for food, we've got a plan for water, and we've got a route. As soon as everyone finishes scrounging and gets inside, we're taking off."

CHAPTER 10

SETTING OUT

It was just after noon when Jill finally turned Bertha's mana engine on to bring her truck back into motion. It was later than Jill had wanted to depart, but earlier than she'd feared when she'd seen how the progress of loading all of their allocated equipment was going. Berthaville's population had steadily ticked up as more and more people had come out of the airport terminal, possessions in hand, to board. All of those new people had to filter their way in through one set of cargo doors, throttled by Sangita's volunteers taking their information down and assigning them a place. Berthaville's nascent bureaucracy, despite being cloaked in friendly mountain hospitality, would not be denied the proper time needed to get everyone organized.

Then there had been the goodbyes: hugs and clapping of shoulders and prayers said between former neighbors, entreaties to go or stay, and three fistfights over God knows what. It all set Jill's teeth grinding, but at the same time, she couldn't blame Bertha's new residents. This was the last they'd see of their neighbors, even family, for a long time, even if the actual neighborhoods they hailed from lay in smoking ruins. She was desperate to get home; they were refugees.

Jim and his aides had come and gone, filling Bertha's newly huge cab with the sound of "sir" laden reports. The conversation had been necessarily brief: the magical comms were only a single channel so far, and as the network of facilities needing to use it grew, so shrank the time allotted to any one party. Jim's report on the situation had taken up most of what they had. The rest was a detailed series of strange instructions, all with the purpose of allowing someone to unlock the needed communication powers so that they could tap into the comms network themselves. Jill's favorite was the one that required someone to balance on one leg on top of a building and shout at someone at least five-eighths of a mile away and still be understood.

But all that was done. The engine rumbled to life, filling the truck with a soft but powerful vibration, the promise of speed. Under that were the conversations of those sharing the cab with Jill. At the back was Karen, who had pounced on the Captain Speaking console immediately, and Aman, who was still plugging away at shifting the Cargo Nexus into some semblance of an intelligent design. His brother-in-law Taran, Karen's husband, sat next to him in an observer's seat, pointing at the hologram of Bertha and making suggestions.

"Hey, folks," Jill projected into and around Bertha, "last call. Get in if you're coming, get out if you aren't." She looked into the side mirror and saw a flurry of movement: tearful hugs from some, a final dash to get inside from others.

The door to the cab slid open, a burst of crowd noise coming with it. Jill twisted her head around to see just as Jacob walked in, a man she had last seen mobilizing a community farmers' market to evacuate out of Billings. Instead of the casual jeans and sweater he had been wearing then, he now wore a set of leather armor that matched Jill's, right down to the shoulder spikes, though it was lacking the pair of holes hers sported.

"Oh, hey!" Jill said, eyebrows raising in surprise. "You're alive. Nice. When the fuck did you get on board?"

"A few hours ago," Jacob replied as he walked over. He hesitated. "Is it okay if I sit down?"

"Yeah, sure, go for it," Jill said, checking her mirrors again. "Just don't get in the way." She couldn't see anyone else getting in. "We all closed up?" she projected to Ras, who was overseeing the rear doors.

"Yes," he said back.

Jill grinned. It was finally time to move. Her foot eased down on the accelerator and with the smallest lurch, the wheels started to roll. The terminal slid away on her right-hand side. A quick loop to the left had her heading across a taxiway. With a rocking bump, Bertha rolled over a curb and onto a grass strip, her upgraded wheels giving her a good enough grip not to care. A turn to the right and they were driving down the airport access road.

Jill took a deep breath and smiled, then blew it out. A knot of tension in her back unwound, the simple pleasure of driving washing away a bit of her tension. Her right foot went down, and a light pressure pushed her back as the truck accelerated. She double-checked the road atlas, spread out off to the side, then settled back in her chair. For a minute, it was as if the last few days hadn't happened; just Jill, Bertha, and the road. But then the low stand of trees to Jill's left petered out, revealing the smoldering ruins of the former city of Billings below.

A pall of smoke hung over the city, casting the streets into partial shadow despite the sunny day. The sites where monsters had spawned and erupted from the ground speckled the city like so many burst pimples. In the north of the city, closer to the airport, a convoy of vehicles wound their way through a maze of the less-broken streets. As Jill watched, they stopped in a mostly intact neighborhood and a handful of people emerged from the surrounding houses. She hoped that they would listen to reason and evacuate but knew that not everyone would.

She raised her eyes to look farther and her teeth clenched. The south of the city was a burnt-out wreck of smoking timbers and cracked asphalt. It seemed still and deserted, but that illusion was shattered when a pack of monsters bounded from behind a collapsed building, set on some alien collective purpose. There would be no survivors there.

"Lord preserve us," Jacob said, his face pale. "Half the city is destroyed!" He leaned closer to Jill to get a better look out of her side window. "What made that fire break?" he continued, pointing at a furrow carved through the city, dividing burnt-south from spared-north.

"Those are tracks," Jill said, and a hint of the awe and fear of the creature that had made them washed over her.

When the Boss Bison had stamped through the city, its hooves had left massive gouges and craters carved into the roads and buildings. The mountain-sized creature was so heavy that every one of its steps had not only crushed buildings and fractured roads but also ruptured the water and sewage lines underneath, causing its footprints to become a series of fetid swamps of contaminated water. They led from the west to just shy of the city center, where the city hall itself was simply gone, eaten alongside the settlement core. The final pair of craters, formed when it had reared up in triumph before stamping its hooves down, had cast out spiderwebs of ravines for several city blocks.

Jill shivered, once again thankful the beast had shown no interest in chasing down and eating people. Every other monster seemed hellbent on that one purpose, including the pack of other bison that ran with the boss, small only by comparison. Jill supposed that for a creature of its size, a city was suitable prey; people were little more than garnish.

"And you—you fought the beast that made them?" Jacob asked, eyes wide and staring at Jill.

"What are you, high?" Jill said, banishing her feelings. "We picked people up and then drove our asses away."

"Still—" Jacob began to say but was interrupted.

A tearing roar sounded, barking on and off in bursts. It was Mia firing Blossom, in her turret atop the cab. It was loud, even through Bertha's thick armor. Not painfully so, but enough that anyone talking would need to shout. It was joined a few seconds later by the staccato bursts of the other turrets. Tracer fire bloomed off to Jill's left, bright even in daylight.

> Nascent Mecha-Spider (x3) defeated.
> Your contribution: 27.2%
> 1387 Experience Gained!

"Are we under attack?" Jacob shouted, his face pressed up against the side window. The firing stopped a second later.

"Nah, they just saw some easy XP," Jill said. A bit of light caught her eye: a glowing blade extended from Jacob's left hand. "Put that away, will you?"

"Sorry," he said, and the light winked out. "Aren't you worried about monsters in here?"

"You bet your tits I am," Jill said, "but trust me, if we're under attack from something strong enough to reach us in here, you'll know it." She pulled up Bertha's Armor Module and sent it to him.

> **Armor:**
> "Bertha" has an armored exterior. 14% increase in Durability as armor; damage to this additional Durability does not damage interior systems. Incoming damage is reduced by 14%. Mass increased by 40,000 kg, modified by external dimensions.
> Includes: Transparent Aluminum Viewports
> Add-ons (1/2): Red Eel Paint

Completed Upgrades:
Bulwark (3/5): Each rank increases armor Durability and damage reduction by 14% and mass by 10,000 kg, modified by external dimensions.
Face Hardening (1/3): Each rank reduces incoming damage by 14 points, after other reductions.

Available Upgrades:
Ablative Armor (0/1): When faced with continuous damage sources, incoming damage is reduced by damage taken in the last 1.4 seconds.

"Eel paint?" he asked.

"I like that one," Jill said and sent that as well.

Red Eel Paint (Armor Module Add-On)
Level 19, Rare
An extract of electric eels, which can be used as paint for one vehicle. Upon activation, the exterior of the vehicle becomes electrified for 1 minute. Any enemy creature that contacts the vehicle in this time takes 80 electricity damage per second before resistances. Soulbound Modular Vehicle "Bertha" will also receive a speed boost of 27%.
Mana Cost: 190
This item cannot be modified further.

"You painted it red, and it went faster?"

Jill grinned. "Neat, huh?"

"Yeah. Having your truck must be nice," he said with a hint of bitterness in his voice.

"Yup," Jill said. "It sure beats walking."

He didn't reply, instead looking out the window with a twisted expression on his face.

Jill sighed. She didn't feel like spending the rest of the ride next to someone stewing. "Let me guess," she said. "You ran into some shit getting out of the city?"

"It was hard," he said. "A lot of fighting and people getting hurt."

"Annnnd let me guess," Jill said. "You blame me for leaving you on your own, and aren't I just so lucky to have been so safe and sound inside an armored truck?"

"What?" Jacob asked, sounding perplexed. He turned to look at her. "I heard that you got swarmed by like a thousand zombies all trying to kill you. Your leathers got wrecked by them, and you only survived because Bertha came alive and swallowed them all before you bled to death."

"Uh," said Jill, a bit confused, "not really. I mean it was bad, but wow that is something else." She shook her head. "But anyway, if you aren't jealous, what was with you sounding like your favorite pet got eaten?" She realized a second later what she'd said. "Oh shit, did your favorite pet get eaten?"

"No, I didn't have one," Jacob said. "But my car, a blue Honda Civic that I left behind." He reached out and touched the dashboard. "Maybe I could have Soulbound her too, but in all the rush of leaving . . ." His voice trailed off.

"That's rough, buddy," Jill said. She meant it.

He shrugged, the spikes on his shoulders rattling a little. "That's so stupid, isn't it? After everything that's happened, I miss my car?"

"Yeah, but I'd be worse if I'd had to leave Bertha behind," Jill said. "Emotions are dumb like that."

The guns above fired again, putting pause to their conversation.

Pummeling Puma, Fear Deer (x7) defeated. Your contribution: 27.2% 1958 Experience Gained!

Jill willed away the notifications as they came in. "So," Jill said once the noise had passed, "you have a reason to come up here other than commiseration?"

"I got elected to sit and watch," he said.

"Elected? Who in the name of Athena's tight ass is holding elections right now?"

"The Princeton Avenue Farmers' Market and Home Owners' Association in exile," he replied.

"You've got to be kidding me."

"Well, when you gave that speech, it really lit a fire under us!" Jacob said, suddenly passionate. "It was almost like we were possessed!"

"You, uh," Jill said, her eyes going back to the road, "you don't say."

"Well, we all went and got our folks, and then when we got to the airport, we held a vote. You'd made such an impression, and your truck has just so many guns, and everyone was talking about how amazing it was inside, so we all decided to come along, and then they elected me to be liaison, and here I am!" He said the whole last run-on sentence in one long rush.

"Great," Jill said. She looked at the atlas and let up on the accelerator, letting Bertha slow; the turn to the north was coming up and she didn't want to jostle everyone in the back too badly. Jill turned the wheel and Bertha rounded the corner. Jacob craned his head to get a last look at Billings as it passed out of view; Jill kept her eyes front.

"Fucking finally," Jill said and let out an appreciative sigh. She gestured at the road ahead of them. "Just look at that beauty."

"What?" Jacob asked. "All I see is ranches."

"Exactly," Jill replied. "A nice open road, if a bit hilly. No monsters in sight, no parked cars to dodge, no buildings falling down around me." She eased her foot down on the accelerator and Bertha surged ahead. Within fifteen seconds they had accelerated up to seventy-five miles per hour; a little faster than Jill might normally go on a two-lane, mildly winding highway, but Bertha had the upgrades to handle it even with her higher mass.

Jill opened the Propulsion Module's status.

Propulsion (Ground):
"Bertha" has an engine that converts Mana to rotary motion, which is then transmitted to wheels. Maximum recommended speed: 390 km/h.
Add-ons (1/1): Slug Feet

Completed Upgrades:
Torque Converter: Unwanted rotation along any axis is nullified and converted into Mana. Requires Jill MacLeod to be at a control station.
Utility Wheels: Wheels function over a wider variety of terrain. Rough terrain lowers maximum speed. Unlocks **Distributed Wheels**.
Need for Speed (2/5): Each rank increases maximum speed by 70 km/h.

Available Upgrades:
Distributed Wheels: Allows the number, location, and size of wheels to be changed as needed. Unlocks **Diffused Traction**.

Jill felt the burning desire to put three more points into Need for Speed that very instant but held off. The extra speed called to her, but she wouldn't be able to really use it, at least not in this kind of terrain. One thing Jill had learned the hard way was that when Bertha did crazy maneuvers on the outside, it still threw people around on the inside, despite it being in its own dimensional pocket. Given that the Torque Converter power had already tied down the laws of physics and spanked them with no safe word, she wouldn't be surprised if a future upgrade somewhere fixed the issue. But the System refused to give hints about what future powers it would give and without that the extra speed would be mostly wasted.

"So," Jill said after a few minutes of blissful, uneventful driving. She didn't really count the occasional burst of gunfire and bit of XP flowing into her as an interruption anymore. "Let's circle back to you getting elected to sit up here and watch what happens. Why?"

"Well"—Jacob swallowed—"we want someone in the room when you make decisions, both to see what's going on firsthand but also to make our case. You're in charge after all, right?"

Jill felt the pit of her stomach drop. "The case for your HOA in exile?"

"Yeah."

"Scissor dicks!" Jill said. "Berthaville's one day old, and it's already got an infestation of lobbyists!"

"It's not that bad; I'm elected," Jacob protested.

She glared at Jacob and tapped her fingers on the wheel as she considered what he'd said. "How many people are in your club?"

"With our families, there are nearly three hundred of us."

"Right," she said, "you seem like a good egg, and I like your fashion sense, but that's not enough people. If I let you stay in here, I'm going to have twenty more people clamoring to get in, and when I don't let them, they'll all be pissed off. That sounds like a giant pain in my ass, so"—she jerked a thumb over her shoulder towards the door—"I'm gonna have to ask you to leave."

Jacob frowned at her. "What about them?" he asked and gestured at the others, who hadn't been paying attention to the conversation up front. Taran was still poking at the display and making suggestions and Aman was still responding to him; Karen met Jill's eye for a flash when she glanced back, but then turned her chair away, leaning into the Captain Speaking console and messing with it. "One family seems to be in control of everything around here and no one knows why! That's going to make people angry too."

The conversation between Aman and Taran stopped. Jill snapped her mouth shut, biting back an angry response. She had reasons for trusting Babu and Ras's family, but the luck of Jill rescuing the brothers by the side of the road had played a large part in how things had ended up. She had gone to them and their family first for her needs because they were the only people around here she knew, even if she had just met them.

"Yeah, they have," Jill said, "and I guess that's not really fair. But they're in charge of shit because they stepped up when I needed things done." She pointed at him. "You've stepped up too, you know, both before and now, coming in here." She grinned at him. "Congrats, you've got a new job."

"Oh no," Jacob said. "Not again." The flash of anger had drained out of him, leaving only dread.

"Oh yes. You want to represent people and make sure I don't fuck you all over? That's what you're going to do. Go and figure out what everyone wants—not just your buddies—and come back to me, and I'll see what I can do."

"That"—he hesitated—"seems good?" He took a deep breath, then let it out. "A lot of work, but not so bad."

"And," Jill said, "I'm blaming you anytime they aren't happy."

Jacob sighed. "Yes, ma'am."

CHAPTER 11

TROUBLED WATERS

Bitch-ass motherfucker," Jill said a half hour later. Jacob had left the cab earlier and they had been driving in relative quiet, so her words were easily heard. She eased up on the gas and Bertha began to coast.

Karen cracked up laughing. She was leaning back in her seat, feet up on the Captain Speaking console.

Aman cleared his throat. "Ms. MacLeod," he said, his voice a little louder than it needed to be, "is there a problem?"

"Yup," said Jill. She pulled Bertha over to the side of the road out of habit as they ground to a stop. "That bridge you were going to reinforce? Come look. Something smashed it into pieces."

The three of them crowded forward to see. A wide river cut through the earth in front of Bertha, swollen with meltwater and running fast. The bridge stood in pieces in the middle; three lengths of intact roadway were evenly spaced across the water, supported by pylons, but completely divorced from each other and the highway on each bank.

"Sugar!" Aman said, his mouth falling open. "How?!"

"Yeah, that's a real what in the H-E-double-hockey-sticks sight for sure," Karen said. Her not-a-swear was clearly mocking Aman's, but there was also a note of true wonder in it.

"It's a pain in the ass," Jill said. "Is it going to be faster to drive to another crossing rather than try to fix that?" she asked Aman.

"No, you don't understand," he answered. "The river isn't this wide! This is impossible!"

"A flood?" Karen asked.

"No, look outside," Taran said, leaning close enough to the passenger window to see down to the ground Bertha was parked on. "This is the normal embankment. The river hasn't spilled over. It's just bigger. Three times bigger."

"And the bridge!" Aman said, an arm extended to point. "Look at the damage!"

Jill squinted even though she didn't need to. The edges of the bridge segments were clean and sharp. "It's like it was cut," she said.

"Cut and then the pieces relocated, pillars and all," Aman said, disbelief still in his voice.

"Why would anyone do that?" Jill asked.

No one answered.

"Okay, well, setting aside that there's a mad bridge-mover somewhere out there, we still need to get across the river," Jill said. She ran a finger along the road atlas still spread out in front of them, following the blue line of the river until a road crossed it. "Here's one," she said. "Bundy Bridge."

Taran shook his head. "I don't think any of the bridges are going to be in one piece," he said. "Not if the river itself grew."

"Well, put tentacles in my toilet," Jill said and cracked her knuckles. "Looks like it's time to make this old lady fly again. Bertha can go wicked fast. Aman, if you can build and reinforce a ramp, and I back way up to get a head start—"

"The truck is waterproof," Aman interrupted. "We can drive across the bottom."

"No fucking way," Jill said in disbelief. She sunk her senses into Bertha and probed along the exterior with a tendril of mana. The idea of intentionally driving her truck into water made her gut clench and her mind scream, "Danger!"

"I've spent the last several hours shifting the insides of your vehicle around," Aman said, "and the only points of entry are the doors in the back of the trailer and the ones here. Everything else is seamless and protected by a barrier, even where the turrets rotate."

"Doesn't the engine need air?" Taran asked.

"I don't think so?" Jill said, unsure. "Hey, Sys!" she called out. "Does the engine need air to run?"

System Inquiry Detected
Mana engines run on Mana. The information package "Basic System Terms for Young Children" is available for direct infusion. Proceed?

"Heh, good one," Jill said and shared the box with the others. She pushed the feeling of a high five towards the System, but it didn't respond.

"Did it just . . ." Karen's voice trailed off. All three of them were looking at Jill as if she'd grown another head.

"Let me guess," Jill said and sighed. She was getting really tired of everyone being so surprised. "The System doesn't ever give you any lip, does it?"

They shook their heads.

"Well, sucks to be you. Anyway," she said, "all we need is mana and"—she leaned closer to the windshield and extended her senses towards the water—"yeah, there's plenty down there."

Aman shook his head to snap himself out of his System-sass-induced funk. "The concern I raised earlier is still a problem, though," he said. "The far bank. It is going to collapse under Bertha's weight even if the truck has a perfect grip from those Slug Feet."

"Then let's spread the load out as much as we can," Jill said. She bought the Distributed Wheels power.

Bertha's mana surged and Jill stifled a scream. Through her connection to Bertha came the feeling of thousands upon thousands of legs: her own legs, sticking from every part of her body—eyeballs and all—flailing as they tried to run, tugging at her flesh to pull her along. She was a millipede twitching after being sprayed with poison. No, a cell covered in frantic cilia.

Like all of the sensations that came along with Bertha's upgrades, it stopped as fast as it had started, leaving Jill leaned forward against the wheel, forehead clammy and grip white-knuckle strong.

"Are you all right?" Karen asked.

Jill gave her whole body a shake to rid herself of the feeling of so many limbs. "Just a shitty upgrade," she said. "I'll get over it. Now, where's the next—"

A box appeared in front of Jill.

> **Diffused Traction:** On activation, a web of Mana spreads from the wheels, temporarily stabilizing any terrain underneath. Costs 1 Mana per cubic meter of reinforced terrain. Reinforcement lasts for 12 seconds.

"Hell yeah!" Jill said, then sent it to the others. "That's exactly what we need. Nice job, Sys. You deliver faster than a hangover on Friday morning."

> System Inquiry Detected
> Module powers are determined in advance. Current module powers were chosen upon incorporation of the Propulsion Module.

"Sure they were, buddy," Jill said. "Sure they were." She braced herself for further horror and took the power.

Thankfully, this upgrade was much more pleasant. As usual, she felt her truck as if it were her own body, but this time it wasn't changing. Instead, out from Bertha's eighteen wheels spread a network of mana; tiny burrowing filaments extended into the ground. The upgrade pushed them first a dozen feet deep, then two, the progress slowing as the tendrils branched and connected with each other, forming a tight net around the soil.

Jill had a sudden sense of déjà vu. Her mind flashed to when she had used Customization to surf through Bertha, her mana extending out of her feet. Bertha's wheels. It was the same, but different. With Customization, her mana moved and transformed. With Diffused Traction, it clung and froze. But the feeling of mana flowing out of her to change the environment—that was the same.

The upgrade ended, snapping her back into just her own body. "Huh," she said.

"Did you just do another one?" Karen asked. "You don't look as bad."

"Yeah, I'm fine," Jill said. "No crazy leg shit this time. It just gave me an idea." The echoes of the upgrade were still in her mind's eye: the feeling of the two powers juxtaposed on top of each other. They were so similar; could she use Diffused Traction herself? She resolved to try while the feeling was still fresh.

"Hold on a moment," she said to the three of them. "I need to try something real quick."

She reached out with her mana into the seat underneath her and tried to mimic the feeling she'd gotten from the Diffused Traction upgrade. The cushion froze, still molded in a comfortable shape, but now hard as rock. But Jill frowned; she hadn't actually succeeded. She cut off her magic and the cushion stayed frozen. Instead of using Diffused Traction from her own body, she had instinctively activated Customization and mimicked the effect, truly transforming the cushion into a hard version of itself. She turned it soft again with a thought, then tried again.

Jill closed her eyes and concentrated on the mana inside of her. She watched it ebb and flow for a few seconds, then pushed it down; her thoughts focused on making a web of reinforcing threads through the cushion. Her mana extended downward, and just as it began to leave her body, something deep inside of Jill—but not from her—reached out with a firm grip. In its infinite fingers, her mana took the shape of Customization.

"Stop that," Jill thought towards it. There was a pause, and then it obeyed, withdrawing back into Jill as if it had never been. For half a heartbeat, Jill sat atop mana under only her own control.

"Shitburger!" she yelled as the mana destabilized and exploded. The cushion shredded itself in a small, rumbling, smoke-filled explosion. The force of it jerked her upwards, but her seatbelt held, and she stopped after only going a few inches. The smell of burnt polyurethane filled the cab.

Jill felt her face redden as the three others stared at her again, wide-eyed.

"Jill," Karen said, "that was neither silent nor deadly."

Taran gave a cough that was half from laughter, half from irritation from the smoke.

"Ha-ha," Jill said and rolled her eyes. With a flex of her mind, she repaired her seat and cycled the air. It had felt to her like it always had: she thought about what she wanted to happen, applied mana, and it happened. "I've got a pro tip for you three: don't experiment with mana under your own ass."

"Does that even need saying?" Taran asked.

"Look, it seemed like a good idea at the time," Jill said. "How about you just forget that happened, okay?"

"Please," said Aman.

"Then let's get going again," she said. "One fuckton of extra wheels with magical grips coming up."

First, she duplicated the wheels, filling the underside of the trailer with wheels on both sides. If Bertha still used a normal transmission, the undercarriage would be an absolute mess of axles and differentials. But it didn't. Instead, each wheel was on a short axle that connected to some sort of mana-motor. Like the legs of the millipede Jill had felt, each could move up and down on its own suspension.

Next, she activated the Slug Feet. A thousand mana circulated once inside of Bertha before coalescing onto the wheels, which transformed from knobby rubber to a slightly slimy, distinctly organic slug flesh. The portion touching the road contracted with a little slurp, sucking the truck firmly onto the ground.

"That is so goddamn weird," Jill muttered.

Finally, she activated Diffused Traction and the web of mana roots dug deeply into the ground. She could feel them wind out, lock into place, and then fade over the course of their twelve-second timer. She pushed the power again to renew them and put Bertha into motion. The truck inched forward, the sucking plops of the Slug Feet sticking and releasing, melding into one continuous fleshy squelch.

"Stop!" Aman shouted just as they reached the edge of the embankment.

"What?" Jill asked and gripped the steering wheel tight. "Do you see something? Is the ground giving way?"

"No," Aman said, "but when we go over the edge, we're going to tilt!"

Jill relaxed. "Fuck me, I thought something was wrong. Don't worry about that; I've got it." She thought for a moment. "But I should warn everyone before we go down, just in case."

She switched to her communication power and spread it through the whole truck. "Hi, everyone," she projected. "It's me again. We're about to go down a steep-ass slope. I'm going to compensate, but you might want to hold onto something." She narrowed the focus of power, threading mana to just the turrets. They would be able to see outside, after all. "Once we're down at the bottom, we're going to cross on the bottom of the river. If you're anything like me, all that water rushing over you is going to give you the screaming heebie-jeebies, but don't worry. Bertha can take it."

Profanity-sprinkled acknowledgments came back to her through the power. Jill snorted a laugh at a high-pitched "Since when is this a submarine?!" and cut off the ability. They'd been warned.

She pushed her foot down just a bit on the accelerator and Bertha's front wheels suctioned their way over the edge. As they did, Jill activated the

Torque Converter in the horizontal axis, stopping them from tilting forward. Bertha kept crawling forward, but as she did, more of her extended out into the air, and fewer wheels attached to the ground. The mana roots of Diffused Traction began to strain, and Jill felt a tremble as the ground underneath them compacted under the load. She pushed more mana into the power, making the roots deeper, but she felt that it wasn't going to be enough. Jill needed more wheels to be in contact with the slope.

So, with an unhappy sigh, Jill shifted Bertha so that they were. With the now-familiar groan of growing, twisting metal, the truck unfolded downwards, like an attic stair coming down from the ceiling. A vertical slip joint in the armor formed between each of Bertha's many pairs of wheels, separating the truck into segments. Each of those slid downwards until its own wheels touched the slope and sucked on; from the outside, Bertha looked like a giant red-wheeled staircase crawling its way down the embankment. Inside the dimensional space, everything was normal.

"Ugh," Jill said. "This feels just wrong. It's like I'm an accordion and not in a good way."

"How could—" Aman started to ask, then snapped his mouth shut. "Forget I asked. I do not want to know."

The embankment, reinforced with magic, held. They reached the river's edge and kept going. The water first rose up the grille, then washed over the hood to splash against the armored glass windshield. With a swirl of panic and water, the cab slipped under the river.

"Okay," Jill said a moment later, when she was sure there was no water leaking in, "this is actually kind of cool." Caustic curves of light played across the inside of the cab from the sunlight above, tinted blue-green. The light faded as they descended, but it didn't take long for Bertha's front segment to reach the flat river bottom, so it never grew truly dark. The web from Diffused Traction dug into fine, slippery mud rather than compacted dirt, but under the effects of Bertha's powers, it was as good as concrete. As they inched forward, segment after segment reached the bottom and lined up back on the same level. Jill let out a sigh of relief when Bertha was back in its usual truck shape.

"Well, that is just not right," Karen said and pointed.

"Did that used to be a trout?" Taran asked. "That is terrifying."

Jill squinted and saw a fish. "What's wrong with—oh," she said as the fish's jaw opened wide, revealing a set of teeth that would make a piranha sigh in shame, leave town, and set themselves up on a farm to raise carrots, never to touch meat again. "That thing better not try to—" she said, then cut herself off again with a sigh.

The fish lunged straight towards her, murder in its dull eyes. Its jaws opened wide enough that its teeth formed a phalanx of forward-pointing spikes, and it lunged forward. It hit the armored windshield with a dull ringing *bonk* and stuck there, the tips of its teeth embedded only a sixteenth of an inch deep. Its whole body thrashed, to no avail.

Toothy Trout Level 6 Status: Enraged

"Why do they always go for me," Jill grumbled to herself. She flicked on the windshield wipers and batted the thing away.

Their underwater drive was quiet for another minute, but as they passed one of the bridge's support pillars, Jill saw another fish. And then another. And then a whole school of them emerged from the murk in a silver flash of reflected sunlight.

"Fishdicks," Jill swore. "This is going to bite."

CHAPTER 12

TURTLING UP

"Boooo," said Karen.

"What?" Jill asked.

"That was a terrible pun," Aman said.

Jill sighed and put her foot down on the accelerator. The hum from Bertha's mana engine grew louder, but between the Slug Feet's 95 percent reduction in speed and the water's natural resistance to large boxy objects, the truck barely moved faster.

One of the gunners opened fire; the rapid thuds of the .50-caliber machine gun sounded muted and lower in pitch than usual. A trail of cavitation bubbles filled the water from Bertha to the school of monster trout and beyond, the lines from each bullet merging together into a narrow cone of churning death. The bullets lost their energy quickly, but between magic and the short range, they still held enough to easily kill the onrushing fish.

Toothy Trout (x19) defeated. Your contribution: 27.2% 3256 Experience Gained!

Then the school reached Bertha. The turrets fired in quick bursts, and the river became a churning mass of bullets and fish all centered on Bertha as she crawled past the first bridge segment. The fish were individually weak, easily killed by just one hit, but between the terrible visibility in the water and their natural evasion, it took a surprising number of shots to actually get that hit. They attacked in waves, darting in to chomp on the armor, thrash their bodies, and then slip away.

Jill squirmed in her seat and stifled a laugh. She could feel the bites through her Soulbond with Bertha, but the fish were so weak that it was nothing more than a furious tickling over her body.

"Wow, they can't do shit," Jill said, then lost her battle and let out a laugh. She decided that even though the fish seemed to be harmless, she didn't want to be distracted, so she reached for her metaphysical connection to Bertha and squeezed, pinching the sensations off. It wasn't a complete block, but it was enough for the tickling to fade into distant pricks.

"Since they are mostly harmless," Taran said, "do you think we could catch some?"

"Why would we want to?" Jill said, her breathing still a bit hitched from the tickling.

"Aquaculture," he replied.

Aman sighed. "You want me to make fish tanks too?"

Karen leaned over to Jill's ear and stage-whispered, "His favorite food is fish."

"It's an efficient way of getting protein!" Taran said.

"Just look at them! They'll eat through the tanks!" Aman said.

The hair on the back of Jill's neck stood up and she suddenly felt as if someone was watching her. She knew that sensation: it was someone else's communication power at work.

"Uh, hi, Jill, Dad," Babu's voice shouted through the power. The sound of Blossom boomed on and off alongside his voice as Mia shifted from one target to another, arriving a tiny fraction of a second faster than the sound coming through the water. "Is everything okay down there?"

"We're fine," Jill said. "What's up?"

"I'm just wondering if you're going to use the eel paint," he said. "You could just zap everything, don'tcha know."

Jill shrugged, then remembered that he couldn't see her. "We might as well let the gunners get some practice and XP," she said. "I don't want to hog everything. Hey, how's that build planning going? I'm down to eighteen points left for you to play with."

"Is this the best time to talk about this?" Babu asked.

A fish latched onto the driver's side mirror and shook back and forth, its teeth scoring lines into the silvered surface. Jill glared at it until it decided that it had clearly won and darted away. A second later a storm of bubbles erupted around it, one of the side-mounted turrets having picked that one fish to obliterate.

Her own senses told her that Bertha was only a bit scratched, but Jill pulled up Bertha's status to see what the System thought.

Soulbound Modular Vehicle "Bertha"	
Armor: 35,202/35,700	Durability: 254,881/255,000
Mana: 198,722/255,000	

"Sure, why not?" Jill said. "I might," she stressed the word, "want to repair Bertha once the fish are all dead, but her self-repairs will fix everything fast enough." She gazed out ahead of her at the murky depths; in the distance, she could see the next set of pillars from the segmented bridge. "Besides, we just need to go straight and not stop. I'm not really busy here."

"Fine, fine," said Babu, and Jill felt like she could hear his eyes rolling. "The build planning's as done as it can be for now. I've actually got some really good options worked out for you. Oh!" he exclaimed, more excited. "The next time we find a group of monsters that are weak like this, and we're not in a super rush or underwater or flying or something else crazy, you should come out and fight with us. We can get you to unlock some special abilities."

"Huh," Jill said, "I bet that's going to be a shit show."

"It will totally be worth it!" Babu said.

"Jill!" Karen interrupted, holding a finger to her ear. "Jill, someone has to talk to you." She leaped from her chair and darted back to her control station in the cab's rear.

"Gotta go," said Jill to Babu, and the feeling on Jill's neck winked out. It was replaced by the odd sensation of her own Captain Speaking power being guided by someone else. She glanced to the back of the cab and saw Karen leaning forward, fingers on the controls, her face tight. Jill's mind flashed back to Karen's panicked screaming the first time the other woman had ridden in Bertha when monsters attacked. A day made all the difference. Well, that and a whole lot of automatic weapons fire.

"—through! I really, really need to tell—" A young woman's voice laced with urgency and a small bit of panic erupted in Jill's mind. She recognized the voice as that of one of the volunteer gunners, a teenager who had a so-far unique scouting power that let her see through murk and invisibility alike.

"This is Jill," Jill said. "What do you see?"

"There's a level forty-four turtle coming for us from upriver. It's only walking instead of swimming, but I think it's going to catch us!"

"Well, needle my nipples, that's strong enough to actually hurt some," Jill said. "Hey, what's your name?"

"Uh, Melissa, ma'am," Melissa said.

"Well, Melissa, I can't see shit," Jill said, "so I'm just going to keep driving straight and get us out of the water ASAP. You lot focus fire on the, uh, turtle, but wait until it's in range so we don't stress Bertha's mana. We might take some damage in this fight, but don't worry: Bertha's got the levels, so we'll be okay."

"Got it," was the relieved reply. "What about the fish?"

Instead of replying, Jill activated the eel paint. Mana coursed from Bertha's reserves into the Armor Module and transformed into sparking flashes of electricity. The trout unlucky enough to be biting Bertha at that moment lit up as the current rushed through them, their eyes glowing with light as they exploded. Those swimming nearby took less damage but still twitched with pain as arcing filaments of unnatural lightning zapped through the water. If they had fled, they would have lived, but whatever it was that transformed animals into monsters overrode any instinct for self-preservation, at least for low-leveled creatures like these. The fish, even angrier, charged as one at Bertha. None survived.

Toothy Trout (x179) defeated.
Your contribution: 63%
72,172 Experience Gained!
You are now Level 83! Level gain deferred per user preferences.

"The fish were never a problem," Jill replied. "Call back if you need something." She mentally hung up.

"Attention, everyone," Karen said the moment Jill had cut herself out of Captain Speaking, her voice soft and calm as she leaned down over her console. She had shifted the communication power so that she could address the whole truck. "A dangerous monster is approaching. Do not panic, but hold onto something. Help anyone who becomes injured to the medical bay."

"Tell them to follow the red line on the ground if they get confused," Aman said. "That leads to medical."

Karen did.

Jill raised her eyebrows at the two of them. "Spank me sideways, that was half professional. Where'd you learn to talk like that, Karen? And lines on the floor, Aman?"

Karen blushed and shrugged. "Movies I guess?"

"I got hired to do the last floor renewal at Saint Aubrey's," Aman said. "Color-coded lines just make sense."

"Well, good work," Jill said. She peered out the window but couldn't see the threat, and the turrets were still silent.

Bertha crawled along, and an arm-length trout bumped into the window in front of Jill. The fish might not have been a threat, but they were still a resource, even after they had given up their mana as experience points. Jill reached out with Cargokinesis; dozens of threads of thought guided her magic out into the water to grab fish after fish. She scowled as she realized she didn't know where to put them, thanks to Aman's rebuilding. It was as if she had stopped paying attention for five minutes and her liver wasn't where she'd left it.

"Hey, Aman," Jill asked. "You made a special room for loot, right?" After monsters were killed, the System could, with a simple prompt, render the remainder of the magic out of them and condense it into something physical, usually either a duplicate of part of the monster's body or as a gem of pure mana. Most of Bertha's add-ons were made from loot as was Jill's wrecked armor.

"Second level, to the right of the stairs," he said.

There was no chance of Jill opening a hole in the Cargo Nexus to pull the fish in, but she didn't have to. Physical things couldn't go through the truck's armor—that was kind of the point—but magic could if Jill let it, and for the brief moment between when looting activated and when it formed an item, it was nothing but magic. Flares of golden light erupted in the water next to Bertha as Jill looted the fish—each a flash followed by a trail of sparks leading into the truck—dozens at a time, in a brilliant monochrome fireworks display.

For a moment, all was quiet in the cab. Then a single shot from a .50 caliber thudded, and a line of bubbles reached out to Jill's left, cutting through the water. Jill looked hard, and she just barely made out an enormous shadow in the water.

Jill tapped her fingers on the wheel and wished there was something more she could do, but watertight as it might be, Bertha wasn't built for underwater combat, and there was little chance for fancy driving while moving at a slug's pace. The speed upgrades called to her, but she didn't think they would be at all effective underwater.

Another thud, another test of the range. Jill pulled up the Turret Module's information to see if one of the available powers, perhaps one of the available ammo types, would help them shoot farther.

Advanced Turrets (Small Arms)
"Bertha" has 7 turrets for Small Arms weaponry.
Includes: Firing Station, Viewing Slits (Armored Glass)
Add-ons (7/7): Soulbound Rotary Cannon "Blossom," 6x M2HB machine guns

Completed Upgrades:
Adaptive Mounts: All turrets become better at supporting mounted weapons. All weapons below the turrets' Level receive boosts to their fire rate, range, damage, and penetration sufficient to make them match an uncommon weapon of the turrets' Level while retaining their defining characteristics.
Dakka (4/4): Each rank adds 1.4 turrets with 1 Small Arms add-on slot each.
Mana Substitution: Unloaded Small Arms may fire, drawing Mana from "Bertha" to generate and propel ammunition. Fired ammunition lasts for 84 seconds.
Superchargers (5/5): Each rank increases the damage and fire rate of add-ons by 14%.
Boosted Reflexes: All gunners' nervous systems are modified to have 28% decreased response time. Unlocks **Linked Senses.**
Linked Senses: All gunners gain an instinctive knowledge of what all other gunners are seeing. All perception class abilities are shared between gunners, with the effects scaled by the Level difference between donor and recipient. Unlocks **Hive Mind.**

Available Upgrades:
Ammo Adaption (1/5): Each rank unlocks an ammo type that may be selected depending on the situation. Any weapon add-on may fire any purchased ammo. Select from the following: Knockback, Explosive, Phasic, Acid, Arcane, Entangling. Purchased ammunition: Mana-thief.
Hive Mind: Forms a non-sapient hive mind from the mental contribution of all gunners, allowing for the optimization of target selection and firing patterns. All Class Powers are shared between gunners, with the effects scaled by the Level difference between donor and recipient. Duplicate effects do not apply.

By the time she had finished skimming the many abilities, the guns were firing in earnest, range no longer a problem. Jill glanced left. The turtle was clearly visible now, tall enough that the spikes on top of its shell poked above the surface of the river, and much wider than that. Each of its ponderous steps first ripped a leg out of the river mud, spraying up a concealing swirl of muck, before it crashed down to pull the creature forward. Jill was just glad that it had somehow lost the ability to swim.

Overweight Alligator Snapping Turtle
Level 44
Status: Ornery, Home Waters

Bertha's mana dipped as the turrets fired hundreds, thousands, of bullets at it. None outrightly missed; the snapping turtle was the size of the proverbial barn door. But most of the rounds ricocheted off of shell, leaving scratches and gouges but not doing much real damage. Wherever a lucky shot found a gap between the monumental scutes, it dug deep, and wisps of blood poured into the water from dozens of small holes. They were hurting it, but not quickly.

Jill considered buying Hive Mind; the gunners would almost certainly have different powers to combine to make themselves deadlier. But upgrades could be disorienting, and Jill had a suspicion that this one would be worse than most. The last thing she wanted was for everyone to stop firing because they were puking or catatonic.

Bertha rocked to the side, a dent appearing in the armor of the trailer, and Jill let out a grunt. She looked again at the monster. It was around fifty feet away, feet planted and no longer walking. In its open mouth was a vortex of magic and water: a ball of destruction growing in size by the second.

The gunners shifted their fire, walking their shots into the turtle's open mouth without Jill needing to say anything. The monster flinched, turning to the side and retracting its head into its shell, and it lost control of the attack it had been gathering. There was an explosion of mud in the water, blocking Jill's sight. Five seconds later the turrets stopped firing. Ten seconds and the mud had cleared enough to see, but the creature was nowhere to be found.

The fight was over. Jill pulled up Bertha's stats to see how bad the one attack the turtle had launched had been.

Soulbound Modular Vehicle "Bertha"
Armor: 31,563/35,700 Durability: 253,583/255,000
Mana: 108,951/255,000

Bertha was fine. The ability had hurt, and if the turtle had been free to keep going, it would have cracked the truck open eventually, but overall, it had been no match. But what worried Jill was just how much mana the gunners had spent. Bertha might be getting a bigger mana pool with every level, but the mana cost of each fired round also grew thanks to Adaptive Mounts. It made the machine guns into truly terrifying weapons but didn't help them fire for longer. She would have to either increase Bertha's mana regeneration independently of a higher level or would have to get the turret gunners to be more selective with their shooting.

Jill pushed mana into her repair power, speeding up Bertha's natural regeneration with a jolt of her own magic.

Hold Together: Repairs 1400 Durability worth of damage and increases Physical and Elemental Resistances by 14% for Soulbound Modular Vehicle "Bertha" for 1 minute.
Mana Cost: 10

The pops and groans of metal shifting ran up and down Bertha's hull, and then one echoing *bong* sounded as the trailer's armor popped back into shape. Jill had 2,550 mana when she was full and little else to spend it on while driving, so the repair power was ridiculously cheap. But at the same time, it only repaired around a half percent of Bertha's hull, and it took ten seconds to do so. As soon as the power finished, Jill activated it again, bringing Bertha back up to full durability.

"Is that it?" Taran asked a few seconds later. He had buckled himself into an observer seat, his hands gripping the chair's sides hard enough to turn his knuckles white. "We killed it?"

"Nope," Jill said. "Just drove it away, so no experience for us."

"All clear," Karen spoke into her control station. "I repeat, all clear."

"Oh," Taran said and unclenched his hands. "Good."

"Well, not really," Jill said. The pillars of the final bridge segment appeared in the murk and beyond it lay a band of solid shadow: the far bank. They would be out of the river soon. "I don't want to sound like a murder hobo, but I wish we'd killed it. A monster that knows when to retreat is way smarter than most of them. More dangerous too."

"I wouldn't want to be the next group who tries to cross the river," Aman said.

"Or even gets within half a block," Jill said. "That thing must have a wicked long neck. I bet you a hundred Billibucks that thing is going to make its way downriver and into the city too."

No one took her up on it. "I'll warn them," Karen said. The chrome-plated magic radio had migrated back to be next to her communications console when Jill hadn't been paying attention. Karen poked it. "How far does this even reach?"

Jill almost answered as if it were still her old CB radio. "Uh," she said instead. "I don't know. Shit, that could be important. I should know that. Babu's used it more than me. Could you find out from him and let me know?"

"Will do," Karen said.

The next few minutes passed without incident, and then they were at the riverbank. With a crack of her knuckles and a muttered complaint to herself, Jill unfolded Bertha back into a wheeled, climbing staircase. They rose in near silence, the rock, mud, and roots passing down past the end of the hood. The light grew brighter and the noise of the choppy river surface louder as they grew close to the top. The muscles in Jill's back loosened just a bit; they were almost to the top, almost back to Bertha roaring down a road or turning circles around a monster horde, rather than the horrible crawling they had been forced into under the water. All things considered, the crossing had gone well, but Jill was still relieved it was over.

Harsh sunlight dazzled Jill's eyes as the cab burst from the water. She squinted and raised a hand to shield her eyes from the light, brighter and bluer than she expected. "What the shit?"

> Warning! You have entered into a region of higher Mana density! Expected effects include increased spatial distortion, generation of energetic phenomena, and monster instantiation.
> You are located in the Big Sky Region.
> Mana flow: Very High
> Status: Wild

"Oh," Jill said. "So things are going to get worse. Great."

CHAPTER 13

OVERGROWN

"No, no, no," Aman said and thumped a clenched fist onto the dash. "This is all wrong!" He sat in the central front observer seat, his pocket atlas in his hands. "That," he said, pointing at the T intersection ahead. "We should have passed that half an hour ago!"

"Yup," Jill said. She turned the wheel a few degrees, nudging Bertha into a gentle turn to avoid a boulder sitting in the middle of the intersection. They blew by at ninety miles an hour and blasted dirt and pebbles into the air in an expanding cloud of choking dust that marked their passage.

"And that!" Aman thrust an accusing finger at a sharp-edged mesa of raised stone off the side of the road. "That has never been here, not in my whole life! And it has entirely the wrong geology for around here!"

"Shit's shit," Jill agreed. She started humming a country song that had popped into her head and wouldn't leave, one of those terrible earworms that would only leave you alone if you let it out to infect others.

After they had entered the area of higher mana, things had gotten weird. The road existed only in broken pieces, a dotted line that seemed to go in the right direction but was stretched. Landmarks that should have been a mile away were instead five, and the intervening distance was filled with terrain that had never been there before.

Unfortunately, the new land didn't come with highway. Jill had shifted Bertha's tires away from the high-surface-area, crawling configuration into something more suitable for off-road driving: the truck had eighteen wheels again, but they were all now massive knobby beasts, twelve feet in diameter, which gave the truck much more clearance. The fact that the truck was now terribly unstable through turns didn't really matter, thanks to the Torque Converter. Jill had to admit, she liked the view from up here and might keep Bertha lifted even if they did get back on a proper road.

"And those!" he pointed off to the mountains, pale and hazy on the horizon, which jutted into the sky like blue daggers.

"I get it," Jill said. "They're too far away."

"And too big!" Aman said. "This is the Rockies, not the Himalayas!"

Jill glanced at him. "You seem pretty upset about this."

He glared back. "And you seem far too blasé!"

"Oh, don't worry," she said. "I'm fucking pissed. The instant we clear out this warehouse and have the food we need, I'm calling a full war council. We're going to figure out how to get out of this mother-sucking, shit-fucking, bigger-than-it-looks magic-bullshit county because I am not going to take a week to get home when I should get there in a day!" She took a deep breath, let it out, and continued in a calmer tone. "But we've got to eat, and this place is the plan, so I'm going to enjoy the drive while I can. Now, what has your panties caught in your teeth?"

Aman sighed and stared out the window. "I spent a class point on using this better," he gave the map a tap with the back of his hand, rattling the paper, "and now the world changes how it's shaped. To use your words, it is complete bullshit."

"And that's what has you upset?" Karen asked from the back. She again had her feet up on her console, but Jill could sense a thread of mana connecting her to it. "Not, you know, having to flee home?"

Aman shrugged. "I'd been dealing with that."

"Nah, I get it," Jill said. She eased up on the accelerator a bit as Bertha left the piece of road she'd been on and entered a field positively bursting with flowers and tall grasses. It was certainly prettier than the brown scrub of pre-bloom early spring that Jill was used to this time of year, but it also concealed rocks and ditches that bounced Bertha about, big wheels or not. "The big things are too big. They roll right off of us. But the little things—they're like mud in your tires."

"I guess," said Karen. "I suppose I've been dealing with things better than I expected."

"That could also just be the System mind-fucking you for your own good," Jill said. "Right, Sys?" she asked.

It didn't respond.

"That's right. Nothing to say about that," Jill said with a snort of derision.

"Well, that's going to give me nightmares," Karen said.

"I bet you it won't," Jill said. "But enough of that. Aman, the map power that you bought, what did it unlock?" She snapped her fingers and pointed them at him without taking her eyes off the road. "Because we could really use some better mapping right now."

"It didn't unlock anything," Aman said. "Nothing yet, anyway."

Bertha rocked suddenly as they hit something. A spray of green ichor exploded upwards from in front of the truck and splattered onto the windshield, despite its height. The armored glass sizzled.

Mega Slug defeated. Your contribution: 90% 1710 Experience Gained!

"Gross," Jill said. "But, hey, free experience. I'll take it." As she spoke, the monster gore evaporated off of Bertha in a trail of sparkling gold as her Customization power responded to her desire for her truck to be clean. The slight frosting of the glass cleared in a few seconds as Bertha's passive regeneration handled the slight damage with ease. "How much XP are you getting for rebuilding Bertha?" She asked Aman.

He paused and his eyes flickered back and forth, a surefire sign that he was rapidly reading System messages. "About twenty-one thousand so far, for completing achievements," he said. "Enough for four levels. I thought the System would see using your power to finish building-related tasks as cheating, but . . ." He shrugged.

"But it seems to like cheating," Jill said, finishing his sentence. She tapped her fingers on the wheel. It wasn't an awful amount of experience, especially considering the level of risk involved. "If your class follows a progression anything like mine, you'll see new powers at level ten. Let's make it happen."

She reached out to Mia with her communication power. "Hey, Mia," she said. She didn't feel Babu in her turret with her like usual. "How are things looking up there?"

"Boring," Mia said back. "But boring is good, right?"

"Right," Jill said. "We need to get Babu's dad some XP ASAP. Could you let him on Blossom for a bit? He only needs . . ." She looked at Aman pointedly. Mia's responses were just in Jill's mind, but Jill was speaking aloud as well as projecting her thoughts with the power.

"About fifteen thousand more," he said.

Jill repeated the number. "So, how about it?"

"Sure, he'll get that much in one swarm if we ever hit one out here," Mia said. "But, uh, you know this is going to be hella awkward, right? He's, like, my maybe-new-boyfriend's dad!"

Jill sighed and switched to purely mental projection. "And what? He'll disapprove of you for having a bigger gun than him?"

"Jill!" Mia shouted with a laugh in her voice.

"I can send him to one of the .50 cals if you want," Jill said. "But then he's going to know you told me not to send him up there."

"Damnit," Mia said. "Fine."

Jill cut off the power and shook her head. She vividly remembered the hang-ups of young dating and did not miss them in the slightest. To Aman, she said, "Pop on up and get shooting. You've got leveling to do."

"Yes, ma'am," he said back. He looked confused at himself for a moment, then shrugged, unbuckled himself from the chair, and left.

Jill glanced over her shoulder at Karen, wondering if the other woman was going to take up the mantle of conversation with just the two of them left in the cab, but she seemed content to let the silence stretch.

Minutes turned to an hour, then two as Bertha hurtled over the hills. Despite the occasional thudding chatter of the guns and despite the drive taking too long, Jill found herself relaxing. She smiled as Bertha rocked over a particularly nasty set of rocks, but only lost a little speed. The open road was one thing, but being able to go off-road at will, to really go anywhere—that was something else.

Part of her was worried about not finding the warehouse at all, about getting lost in whatever the hell was going on, but while the road was sliced into pieces and those pieces stretched along, it was still stubbornly all there. The side road they needed to turn down was visible from miles away, the patches of asphalt cutting through overgrown fields.

Jill sat up straight and cut the corner in a wide arc that kept Bertha's speed up without being too hard on everyone inside. They crested a short hill and, in the distance, Jill saw buildings: a pair of warehouses arranged in an L, abutting a single large, shared parking lot and a trio of one-story trailers, the kind that get set up as temporary office space for construction sites. The warehouses were still standing, a good sign for the food that they intended to loot, but they were covered in vines—more victims of rampant plant growth.

"Five minutes," said Jill. "Can you let everyone know?" she asked Karen.

"Can do."

Jill could get used to having someone talk to people for her.

A minute later the door to the Cargo Nexus opened with a brief blast of excited noise and Babu entered. He waved at Karen, who gave him a smile in return, and sank heavily into the passenger observer seat.

"You up here with me?" Jill asked.

"Ras wants me acting as a glorified walky-talky," Babu said back. Jill started to talk but he plowed right on over her. "And, like, yeah, I know you can't talk to people more than fifty feet from the truck, and coordination of people is going to be like the most important job, but still, I'm getting a bit cooped up, don'tcha know. Meanwhile, he's going to—"

"Christ on a cracker, Babu," Jill said, cutting him off. "I thought you two were getting along now?"

He blinked and looked at her, confused. "Who says we're not?"

Karen sighed loudly at the back of the cab. Jill felt the same.

For the whole drive the turrets had been firing on and off, the gunners shooting at anything that tried to intercept Bertha, but as they approached the warehouses, the shooting stopped. The rumble of the tires changed as Bertha pulled back onto a road. Jill let up on the accelerator and the truck coasted, slowing in anticipation of pulling into the parking lot. Loading and unloading of distribution centers like this one didn't stop just because it was after hours; when the System had come at midnight, people had been busy at work.

"Babu, can you sense anyone out there?"

Babu closed his eyes and a surge of mana burst from the enchanter, checked for just a moment by Bertha's armor before it washed out over the buildings. Jill waited as it faded into the distance, impressed by just how far it went. But her spirits fell with every second that passed in silence. The back of Jill's neck tingled, and her eyes began a regular patrol of all her mirrors.

"No one," Babu said.

"Poor bastards," Jill said. "Well, at least no one's going to object to us scavenging. But I'd bet my left tit that whatever killed them is still around."

Another wave of mana washed out of Babu, a bit different from the last. He frowned. "I can't sense anything," he said, confused and worried.

He reached into his pocket and pulled out a tiny vial full of blue liquid, made a face while uncapping it, and drank its content in one choking gulp.

Jill pulled the wheel over and Bertha rumbled into the parking lot, the truck's height giving Jill a clear view over the area. There were a dozen cars still parked inside barely visible lines. Some of them looked nearly intact; others had windows shattered and body panels pierced by intruding vines. But what really caught her attention were the trucks.

The cabs had been breached: windows smashed, doors torn off their hinges, brown smears of dried blood on old seats. The trailers had been slashed in great rips dozens of feet long, plastic and aluminum sides no match for whatever monsters had attacked. The worst was one truck where the trailer had been peeled open like a banana, petals of siding splayed open and the truck's cargo, a shipment of canned goods, spilled out on the ground in a long smear.

Jill swallowed, and she gripped Bertha's wheel, hard. "Something did this," she said, voice rough, "and I want it dead." She turned the wheel and pressed down on the brake pedal, stopping Bertha at the far end of the parking lot from the buildings, where there was more open space. If something horrible came from one of the warehouses, it would have farther to go, getting shot the whole way, before it could reach Ras's crew. And Jill would have enough runway to get Bertha up to speed before slamming all of her angry mass into it, hydra-horn of death leading the way.

As soon as Bertha stopped, the cargo doors slammed open. Dozens of people, led by Ras, ran out of them and set themselves up in ragged lines. Most had System-enhanced guns that they waved from one imagined target to the next, but others gripped melee weapons in tight hands. Jill's gut clenched harder as she realized that she was responsible for all the people outside, that they were going out into harm's way after pledging themselves to her. Or to Bertha at least.

"Did you, uh, did you know them?" Babu asked. "The truckers."

"There's like three million truckers," Jill said, tearing her eyes from her mirrors. "We don't all know each other." Still, she double-checked the wreckage, hoping she wouldn't recognize any of the cabs as belonging to one of the many people she'd met on the road and actually liked. To her relief, none looked familiar.

"I'm putting Ras through!" Karen's voice bloomed in Jill's mind, followed swiftly by a thread of mana coming from outside Bertha.

"Talk to me, Ras," Jill projected once it had connected.

"Nothing but wreckage out here," Ras said back. "I'm going to take a dozen of the highest-level people I have and work forward."

Jill looped all seven turrets into the communications. "They're moving out," she announced, "so watch your fire!"

A chorus of affirmatives answered her.

Ras became visible in the driver's window, sword held in one hand by his side, its blade flashing in the too-bright sunlight. He glanced up at Jill and Babu and gave them a nod as he passed. Following behind him by a car's length were his dozen, clumped together for safety. Ras moved steadily, tension visible in his shoulders.

Suddenly, there was an explosion of mana and Ras was in the air, teleported upwards by his escape power, pursued by a writhing, barbed vine. He shot downwards—his fall powered by more than gravity—and his sword flashed out. He landed in a crouch, bits of plant spattering to the ground around him.

The ground rumbled and the parking lot came alive. The trees and bushes that Jill had thought were just landscaping pulled out their roots, ready to charge; vines exploded into motion, some pooling together to form bipedal monsters, others thrashing as writhing tentacles, rooted to where they emerged from the ground; grass flew into the air, forming into whirlwinds of tiny green blades.

"Oh!" Babu said, excited. "Of course, plant monsters! They must not have brains! No wonder I can't sense them!"

And then everything really went to hell.

CHAPTER 14

CLOSER TO DANGER

A legion of plant monsters burst into motion, all heading towards Bertha and the comparatively fragile string of scouts deployed on the truck's sides. Vines studded with razor-sharp thorns whipped through the air, seeking flesh, and mouths of spike-tipped leaves opened in silent screams, ready to snap shut on their victims. The plants writhed over each other as the more mobile overtook their slower brethren. Asphalt buckled and cracked in snaking lines as underground roots pushed through the earth towards Bertha and her defenders.

Jill cataloged the oncoming wave of photosynthetic predators with half a mind, but much of her attention was fixed on the east warehouse: rising from its green-carpeted roof was a ten-foot wide smooth, green stalk, topped with an even larger closed bulb.

"Ass-grabbing boss monsters," she muttered under her breath. This wasn't the first time she'd run into a horde of themed monsters, and they were invariably led by one apex example that was more powerful than the rest. This one seemed content to grow rather than attack, at least for now, leaving them with only a few thousand smaller plants to deal with.

The turret gunners unleashed a storm of bullets, aiming high to avoid any chance of hitting the people outside of the truck. Scythes of tracer-laden shots swept out, cutting down anything they crossed. Jill mentally dismissed the forming kill notifications before they could appear in her vision, proof that the guns were taking their toll. But this was an ambush with monsters all around and the seven turrets simply couldn't cover enough area to kill them all fast enough. They were going to get swarmed, and soon.

Jill reached out with Captain Speaking but winced as it hit a hard boundary; not everyone was close enough for it to work. The power only had a fourteen-meter, or forty-six-foot, range, and the far ends of the line had spread too distant. To those she could connect to, she shouted, "Get back in the truck!" She turned her head to Babu. "Repeat that to the people far away."

Babu nodded and closed his eyes for a moment. "Done," he said. He leaned forward, closer to the window, and his eyes flickered as he read notifications.

The team outside fell back towards Bertha, a few breaking and running but most backing up while shooting their weapons; it was a tiny contribution compared to the automatic fire from the truck but a contribution, nonetheless. Ras threw his sword into the air. It flashed once in the sun and then split into thousands of copies, forming a whirling wall of blades between him and the oncoming monsters.

Outpacing the plant beings, which were confined to such inferior modes of transportation as limbs, were the flying grass-cloud monsters. They passed through the blade barrier with only a little damage; the duplicate swords were razor sharp and from them fell a smattering of green confetti, but they were no solid barrier. The grass boiled up into the air, the monsters mixing in a giant mass, ready to crash down and slice into their victims. But standing next to Ras was Dan, legs planted wide and hands gripping a pair of nozzles attached to the glowing tubes from his backpack. The grass surged downwards. He threw his hands upwards and blasted out twin cones of billowing orange-white flame.

Where blades failed, the fire thrived. Whatever magic let them fly did nothing to protect them, but instead fanned the flames harder. The monsters recoiled and tried to escape into the air, but the ignition leaped from stalk to stalk. The monsters split from each other and died as rising fireballs, which briefly lit the parking lot in slow, billowing explosions.

Jill whistled. "Well, he just leveled a few times." She glanced at the mana gauge on the dashboard and winced. The continuous gunfire had cost a third of Bertha's mana stores already. "Ease up on the shooting a bit," Jill projected into the turrets. "This is a marathon, not a sprint, and we only have so much mana." Then she scowled: the defenders outside had stopped their evacuation to cheer on the display of firepower.

"Get your asses back into the truck!" she projected to those outside, who, thankfully, were all in range. She felt the cargo doors open again and the first people start jumping back inside.

"You know," Babu said, "most of these plant things are under level ten. Really not that much of a threat! Maybe we should let people stay outside and fight? Get some practice in?" Babu pointed at Dan. "If the other plants are weak to fire, he could hold a whole flank by himself."

"Or something could burst from underground and eat him," Jill said. "I bet you that those"—she pointed at the encroaching lines of buckled asphalt, each hump five feet wide, which in spots now had visible sections of brown root sticking through—"are from that"—her finger swung to the warehouse and the stalk that rose higher and higher above it—"and aren't going to go down easy."

"It's big, but I'm sure—ope!" he cut himself off as his eyes widened. "No, you're right. We should go. Look at the level on that!"

Jill focused her attention on the growing plant and pushed a query at the System.

> Heliophilic Helianthus
> Level 92
> Status: Waking

"Shit dicks!" Jill swore.

"Always a bigger fish," Babu said under his breath.

Outside, the plants reached Ras's blade barrier and threw themselves against it with a sound like an overpowered riding mower driving over a prize rose bush. What emerged on the far side was nothing more than twig salad. But despite being mindless to Babu's magical senses, the plant monsters weren't completely dumb, and after the first wave failed to breach the blades, they swept to either side, seeking a way around.

The cargo doors closed. "Everyone inside?" Jill projected back to Ras.

"Y-yes," he said. His voice cracked and he swallowed loudly.

Jill hit the accelerator and Bertha surged forward. "You okay?" she asked.

"Better than okay," Ras replied. "I just leveled!" There was a hunger in his voice that Jill recognized. Gaining a level came with a System-provided burst of euphoria as powerful as that from any drug. Jill had told the system to stop doing that to her, though in less polite terms, and made a note to talk to Ras, to everyone, about doing the same.

But there was no time for that now because Bertha was out of clear space to drive. Blocking her path was a cluster of animated, decorative trees, bunched together into a forest of waving, clawed branches. Jill could have dodged them. Instead, she reached up and pulled on Bertha's horn.

It wasn't factory original. It was the prize from one of the hardest fights Jill had ever been in: a running battle with a burrowing monster that had outclassed Bertha in nearly every way, from its massive bulk to its straight-line speed, to the ear-shattering horror of its scream. Jill hadn't even scored the final kill herself but had instead lured it into an ambush so that it could be pounded by a Soulbound artillery piece. Some of that monster's power was now hers.

Blast Wave of the Hydra Worm (Vehicle Add-On)
Level 68, Epic Crafted
On activation, projects a short-ranged cone of highly destructive sound that ignores half of a target's physical resistances and pushes enemies up and away. Continuous activation causes the cone to settle into a 5-meter wedge with enhanced damage and force.
Mana Cost: 500 + 100/second

The air rippled as a blast of sonic energy exploded from on top of the cab, the blood-stirring sound of a big rig's horn amplified thousands of times over. It scoured a path thirty feet long in front of Bertha clean of monsters, throwing into the air not just the tree creatures but also chunks of asphalt and dirt. The tree creatures' bodies flexed and shattered, vibrating into shards of wood under the assault.

Roan Razorleafs (x22) defeated.
Your contribution: 90%
18,018 Experience Gained!

Jill released the horn as Bertha blasted through the cloud of debris, wanting to save mana and confident that she could just run over anything that got in her way. She drove the truck in a long snaking curve away from the warehouses, steering towards every concentration of monsters she could. The swarm kept coming, but they were wholly unable to catch the mobile fortress that was Bertha. Experience flowed into the gunners and into Jill.

> You are now Level 84! Level gain deferred per user preferences.

"Karen," Jill said, "get the gunners to swap out for someone else. Not all at once!" She reached for the mana gauge in front of her with Customization and slid it over the metal walls of the cab until it was in front of Karen. "Keep an eye on this too; tell them to ease up their fire if it gets under a third."

"On it," Karen said. "Sangita wants an update on how things are going with the fight. People are nervous about all the gunfire. What should I tell her?"

Jill took in the writhing field in front of her. To a person with no magic, it was certain death, but for them, it was a crop charging towards its own harvest. "Tell her to organize as many people for looting as she can," Jill said. "It's going to take a little while to kill off these things, and there's that boss to deal with, but—"

"Dodge!" Babu yelled.

Jill pulled the wheel hard over to the right and pressed the accelerator all the way down. The force of the turn flung a rooster tail of soil into the air and pressed her hard to the left. Chaos struck the rest of the truck as people went stumbling and falling.

Into the place where Bertha would have been lanced a beam of searing light, a blinding laser that vaporized plants and turned dirt to cracked glass. Just the reflection of it in the mirror made Jill flinch, and the heat of it on Bertha's armor came through their bond like being too close to a bonfire. The beam swept across the ground towards the truck, setting fires as it went and growing closer by the second.

"Hold on to something!" Jill's voice boomed through the whole truck, and then she pulled the wheel hard over in the opposite direction, reversing their turn. The beam swept over Bertha, bonfire heat turning to blistering pain in an instant, then overshot the truck. The outside of the armor melted in that instant of exposure, leaving a swath of the truck's top shiny-smooth and devoid of paint. Jill breathed out a sigh of relief an instant later as the beam winked out.

She kept the turn going until she could see the warehouses out of the driver's side window. The helianthus had grown to its full height, a towering hundred feet into the air, and opened its bulb to reveal a sunflower thirty feet wide. Its petals were mirrored and shaped into a parabolic dish, able to concentrate and amplify the sun's rays into the fiery mixed beam of light and magic. The center of the flower had no seeds: they were replaced with thousands upon thousands of bloodshot, human-looking eyes, all fixed on Bertha.

"Shoot it!" Jill yelled to the gunners, but they were already changing their aim. They knew the score when it came to big monsters: aim for the eyes, the mouth—anywhere that looked vulnerable. Bullets smashed into the mirrored petals, leaving scratches and pits, but they failed to shatter the reflective leaves. They drew lines of gore across the field of eyes, every round rupturing an eye in a shower of purple aqueous humor. The whole flower blinked; a ripple of lids from the center outwards left newly born eyes in its wake.

The sunflower head ponderously turned until it pointed to where Bertha was about to be. Jill's eyes widened as her instincts screamed at her. The sunflower petals turned from shiny to black, sucking all light into them, and Jill pulled the wheel over again, sending Bertha skidding into another course change that threw her against her seatbelt.

It was almost enough. The laser grazed Bertha on the left side of the trailer, clipping one of the turrets, and Jill's perception of time slowed to a crawl. She felt the dagger of heat in her side, its tip digging through flesh—the armor was about to fail. Jill slammed mana into Customization and slid the turret farther down the trailer, where it collided with one of the others with a horrible crunch. Between the heat of the attack and the violent movement, the two were fused together, inoperable until Jill could spare the attention to fix them. But she'd managed to get it out of the way before the heat had broken through and cooked whoever was inside.

The blinding light stopped, leaving just a too-sunny day, and time resumed.

"We're going to get fried!" she said. "Any bright ideas?"

"Um, um, um," Babu put his hands on his head and stared at the flower. "I've got it! It has to turn between shots, and it's slow! The closer we are, the more it has to turn, and the more time we have to hurt it!"

"'Charge straight at the fucker' it is!"

Bertha thundered over the field, crushing plant monsters under her giant tires, as the warehouses grew larger and larger in Jill's vision. She cried out as the world disappeared behind a wall of brightness; the sunbeam was dead center on the cab. Armor crackled, bubbled, and melted under its power.

"Fucking fuckity fuckstick on a—" Jill clenched her teeth and swore to deal with the pain. Through her Soulbond, it was as if her face was an inch from a hot electric stove and her skin was blistering and burning.

Then the pain shifted to her back and Jill was no longer blinded. The warehouse was dead ahead and the sunflower was struggling to look so close to its roots. The field was still chock full of plant monsters, but they weren't strong enough to slow Bertha down.

"Almost there," Babu said. "Now we can circle around it and cut it down!"

Jill pulled the wheel over and they skirted around the outside of the buildings, staying as close as they could. She swore as they slid into the parking lot again; there were cars dead ahead! With no room to dodge, Jill pulled the horn. Sound exploded out and blew the pitiful vehicles up and away, in pieces.

"We have wounded!" Karen announced. She sounded rattled. "Things are getting hot back there!"

"Tell people not to worry. We've fucking won," Jill said. "This thing just can't fight clo—ow! Taint saints!" The pain rushed past Jill's skin and into her muscle, burning and cutting in equal measure. The armor had failed. But the attack cut off even sooner than the last had; the plan was working. Just not enough. Bertha dragged to one side and Jill steered hard to the right to counter it. Three of the left-side tires were just gone. Jill pushed mana into Hold Together and Distributed Wheels at the same time, regrowing the tires as fast as she could.

Soulbound Modular Vehicle "Bertha"	
Armor: 3109/35,700	Durability: 227,929/255,000
Mana: 89,233/255,000	

Bertha was far from out of the fight. It would hurt like having a blazing hot poker shoved through her flesh over and over, but the truck had a huge pool of durability to absorb more punishment. But if that beam broke through the armor with a direct hit, anyone in the way would get cooked, and most of the squishy humans in the back didn't have the levels to withstand it for even a moment.

Jill whipped Bertha into a sliding, spinning turn, throwing up a wave of torn asphalt and dirt. When the truck faced the warehouse wall she sent a pulse of mana into the tires, turning on Diffused Traction to give the truck better grip. Jill's foot was all the way down on the accelerator, and Bertha shot forward.

"Bet you can't shoot through yourself, you overgrown dildo!"

All 127 tons of armored truck slammed into a cinderblock wall. The wall never stood a chance.

CHAPTER 15

FARTHER FROM HARM?

Gray cinderblock rubble and matted pink insulation covered the windshield, blocking Jill's view as Bertha burst through the wall. Jill was already slamming on the brakes; Bertha had more than enough horsepower to plow her way through the warehouse and out the other side if the accelerator was down. Something loomed in Jill's vision, and there was a crash and a jerk, followed by more impacts on the windshield. Cans and boxes rained down on Bertha as the truck punched through a floor-to-ceiling pallet rack.

Jill flooded mana into Diffused Traction to give the wheels a better grip and was thrown forward against her seatbelt by the sudden deceleration. Bertha slammed through another rack, and they finally came to a stop. She froze, her hands clenching the wheel. Were they actually safe here? Would the monster be able to shoot them with that death beam?

Packaged foodstuffs continued to clatter down in ones and twos from the broken racks onto Bertha's back. The truck was lodged at an angle through the shelving, a twenty-foot gap between its rear and the gaping hole in the warehouse wall.

But no monsters attacked. Jill looked in the side mirror as she activated Hold Together, concentrating on repairing the damage to the armor first. For a few seconds everything was still, but then there was movement in the mirror. The horde of plants outside scrambled into view, but its members didn't seem willing to enter the building. They came right up to the edge, then replanted themselves into the ground, together, to form a wall of gnarled branches and green leaves. The warehouse grew darker as the sudden growth choked off the too-bright sun.

"Ope," Babu said, also looking out his side mirror. "I think we're trapped!"

Jill let out the breath she'd been holding. "Nah," she said, "they're still dumb as shit." Hold Together finished its fourteen hundred points of repairs and she reactivated it. It would take just a few minutes for it to get Bertha back into pristine condition. "They think they've trapped us, but we can just punch out the wall somewhere else. In the meantime, we can repair up."

A box appeared in her vision.

> You have invaded the Lair of the Sunflower Queen!
> Invasion progress: 11%

"Oh," Babu said, "a Lair!"

Jill could hear the capital letter. "What fresh hell is that?"

"It's a settlement for monsters," he said.

> System Inquiry Detected
> Lairs are stationary Mana concentrations, generating and being fed upon by monsters. They are a perversion of the symbiotic relationship between Settlements and sapients. Secure the area around a Lair's central control crystal and defeat all current Guardians to claim the Lair for yourself!

"Settlement for monsters, got it," Jill said. "I wonder if that's why the sunflower is so stro—"

The ground underneath Bertha erupted in grasping roots. Quick as snakes, they slithered up the truck's sides and looped over the top. The turrets fired, bullets cutting through wood in just a few rounds, but the monstrous coils writhed over Bertha until they were wrapped close to the turret bases, out of the line of fire. They constricted, pulling the truck down towards the broken concrete floor, magical suspension no match for brute force. Bertha creaked under the stress as the still-melted armor began to buckle.

"Of course it's not going to be easy," Jill said. She activated the eel paint to fry the roots and kept careful attention on Hold Together, making sure to activate it as fast as she could. For a moment there was a balance between her own repairs of Bertha and the crushing force of the roots, but it didn't last. The metal creaks turned to groans and then to shrieks as electricity arced and popped, charring the wood but not stopping it.

"Jill?" Babu asked, his face worried.

"Bertha'll hold for a little bit, but they're breaking in," Jill grunted back. She always hurt when something damaged Bertha, and this time was no exception. Her ribs felt like they were crushed, and it was getting harder to breathe. She eyed the damage the lightning was doing. The roots were smoking, but there was no sign of the paralyzing effect the lightning had on creatures of muscle. They weren't stopping their inexorable squeeze.

She turned to Karen. "Get people ready to—"

> Heavy Machine Gun add-on from "Bertha," Advanced Small Arms Turret 5, removed.
>
> Integrating add-on to "Bertha": Advanced Small Arms Turret 5. Twin Flamethrower detected. Add-on below Adaptive Mount Level; effective Level set to 95. Mana crossfeed enabled. Mana Cost: 475 per second.

The warehouse lit up as fire blasted out from the middle top-mounted turret in twin streams.

"Hell yeaaa—hot!" Jill yelled. "Satan's semen!" Flames raced over the truck's top, searing Bertha and stripping more defensive paint. Jill gritted her teeth. Literal friendly fire was making her repairs fall even further behind the accruing damage.

A flaming, sparking root slapped against the windshield, cracking the armored glass. It reared away and flailed in the air, shaking off ash before Jill's eyes. It then crunched back down into the windshield, and this time the glass caved inwards by an inch, a chaotic spiderweb of cracks radiating out from the impact. The root reared back for another strike.

Jill unbuckled her seatbelt and leaped out of the driver's seat. With a raise of her right hand and a flex of her mana, she willed the metal floor of the cab to rise up. It flowed with barely a sound and covered the failing windshield, blocking their view.

"Aunt Karen," Babu said. He, too, had risen from his seat and stood at the ready, a flicker of fire dancing between his fingers. "You should get out—"

"Too busy!" Karen said back. Streams of mana flowed fast and furious out of her and into her console, then into the rest of the truck. Jill closed her eyes and cast her attention back with those streams, down Bertha's sides, cataloging the damage. The roots would break in other places too, and soon.

"Ras," she both shouted and projected, "I need—"

"Already on it!" he said. Jill heard shouting and children crying in the background. Captain Speaking tugged at Jill's mind, and she let it go back under Karen's control.

There was another bang. More glass crunched, and the reinforcing metal dented in.

"Here we go!" Babu said. His hair blew in an imaginary wind, his eyes flashed, and the flames dancing on his fingers erupted into full infernos up to his elbows.

A terrible shriek sounded as the makeshift barrier at the window tore. Jill cracked her knuckles, bending her fingers backward in a stretch, and the structure of the cab flexed with them, ready to answer her call. When she unlaced her fingers, a forest of jagged metal rose from the floor, walls, and ceiling. If they wanted to break in, fine. She was ready.

The whole windshield burst from its mounting and flew towards them, a mass of twisted metal and cracked glass. Jill jerked her left hand up and caught it in the web of her and Bertha's mana that permeated every inch of the Soulbound vehicle. The debris fell upwards and into the ceiling, sinking into it like a jagged rock into a pool of oil. Two roots slunk into the cab, one on each side, but one lunged straight for Jill. It was burnt and cracked, with whole sections reduced to useless charcoal, but it moved with a deadly strength that could weather storms and shatter rock. Jill twisted her right hand and her makeshift blades chopped at it like so many axes. Chips of charred wood flew through the air.

The intangible wind of mana blowing Babu's hair kicked up in strength, sending his black locks whipping around his head, and jets of flame shot from his hands. They engulfed the two roots on each side and set them freshly alight. They spasmed and abandoned any pretense of subtlety, instead lunging directly towards Babu.

A look of panic crossed the enchanter's face, but before Jill could do anything to help, the root she was attacking broke through her attacks and slammed into her chest. She flew backward and struck an observer chair hard enough to flip over its backrest, her head slamming into the metal deck. The air was driven from her lungs and her vision flashed red. It cleared in a moment, but everything was swimming.

Jill MacLeod
Class: Battle Trucker
Level: 82 (Pending 84)
HP: 1322/1710 **MP:** 1837/2550 **XP:** 3,519,124/3,570,000
Conditions: Well Rested, Moderate Concussion

"Help!" Karen yelled to Jill's left. She had pressed herself into the rear wall of the cab next to her console but was still using it. The root that had just hit Jill snaked towards her. It snapped forward to strike, but a trio of golden specters condensed in front of the woman: Bertha's Roaming Guardians, protecting her against a lethal blow.

"It's not motherfucking nap time," Jill growled at herself, casting one of her two cross-class abilities on herself.

Swampwater Vitality: Your words are so foul that harmful conditions wither before them. Each word in your spell reduces a harmful condition's effect on a target who can hear and understand you by 21.4%, multiplicatively.
Mana Cost: 100 per word

Her mana fell, but her vision snapped into focus. Time froze as she saw the root lunging towards Karen. Jill might not have many class points invested in combat powers, but she was many, many times Karen's level and had all the toughness that came with that. A blow that injured Jill would likely kill the other woman outright.

At Jill's mental command twin limbs of metal shot out from the wall, one on each side of Karen, and grappled the root. The plant flipped back on itself and crushed one of the arms, but Jill just made another to replace it, then a third. Where the strength of her Customization failed, numbers succeeded.

She hauled herself to her feet and glanced over at Babu.

One of his targets was gone, a coil of ash around him all that was left of it, but the other was wrapped around the still-on-fire enchanter. Thorns rippled up and down its surface, tearing at his flesh and spraying blood in all directions, even as the flames ate away at the plant.

Jill's eyes widened in shock, but a voice bloomed in her mind.

"Don't do anything!" It was Babu's, strained but confident. "I've got this!"

Jill hesitated but decided to trust him. She had her own problem to deal with. "Choke on your own shit," she growled at the root and, with a cruel twist of her will, she made thorns of metal appear on her grappling arms, each moving back and forth, tearing at the wood. It took another dozen long seconds for them to cut all the way through. Sap sprayed onto the walls and ceiling as the severed root writhed, then fell still.

> Rabid Mega Rhizome defeated.
> Bonus Experience awarded for: monster kill above your Level (+.8)
> Your contribution: 72%
> 11,923 Experience Gained!

Jill turned her attention to the hole where the windshield had been, ready to slice the roots where they had penetrated the cab, but the charred and broken remains lay dead and still. Her senses swept the truck and revealed great rents torn into Bertha's sides, but no more invading plants.

> 6 Guardians defeated.
> Invasion progress: 41%

"Babu!" Karen yelled, anguish in her voice.

He still stood, but Jill couldn't tell how. Flames licked up and down a body torn to ribbons, bone and guts exposed to the air. His neck had been snapped; jagged shards of vertebra stuck out of stretched and purpling skin.

Babu's body vanished.

"I'm okay!" Babu said. He flickered into visibility standing right next to Karen and scooped his aunt up into a hug. "I'm okay."

"What the hell was that?" Jill asked as she picked her way forward through the ruins of the cab.

"Doppelganger spell," Babu said, his breathing and voice strained by how hard Karen was squeezing him. "A physical illusion. That I set on fire."

"Warn us next time you're going to look dead!" Karen scolded him but didn't let go.

Jill sat back in the driver's seat, debris crunching under her, and closed her eyes. The pain from her bruised chest mixed with that from Bertha's damage made her feel like she'd been worked over by professional boxers for a week before being tossed in an industrial clothes drier. "Well, that sucked," she said and then began the process of repairing Bertha again, activating her repair power every ten seconds. All over the truck, broken metal turned from sharp to smooth, melting and flowing together into solid panels that began to cover up the tears.

She reached back with Captain Speaking to Ras, who she felt standing outside the door to the Medbay, and Sangita, who was near the center of the Cargo Nexus, surrounded by people. "How bad is it back there?" she projected to both of them.

"People are hurt and scared," Sangita said. "What the hell is going on?"

"Monsters," Jill said. "A monster settlement on top of our food. Ras, how about you?"

"Lots of injuries," he said, sounding exhausted. "Coach tried to wrestle a root. You can guess how well that went. Half the Cloud Killers have broken bones from getting hit. But no deaths."

Jill opened her eyes in shock. "What? How?"

"The roots came after me more than anyone else," he said, just a hint of smugness coming through, "and they're slow. Plus, Coach trained everyone up to have a last resort move before he let them fight."

"I really need to get one of those," Jill muttered. Still, she wondered whether the swordsman had been able to see the Guardians, whether it had been them who had saved them from even a single fatality.

She felt another presence join the communication power: Karen was back at her console. In front of Jill, the windshield began to grow back, crystalline armored glass reaching out from the cab's front pillars like ice freezing across a pond.

"Jill," Sangita said, "this has not been a good start to our journey. You're going to have to come back here and talk to people, reassure them that it won't always be like this, and lay out a plan. Otherwise . . ." She paused. "I don't know what, but it won't be good."

"Fuuuuck," Jill drew the word out. "Yeah, I can do that. But I also need this flower dead and this Lair cleared. Ras, you feel up to taking Babu and Mia on a weed-whacking mission?"

"Yes," he said.

"Then get them and get going," Jill said. "Any of the, uh, Cloud Killers that can still fight, I need them to stay here and be ready to keep out any monsters that try to get in. Oh, and what's his name, Dan, the flamethrower dad. He stays on a turret for defense."

"Got it," Ras said. "You'll want to talk to Coach once he comes around."

Jill stood. The cab was sealed again but still covered in ash, wood chips, shattered bits of metal and glass, and the charred remains of the root she had sawed to death. Jill narrowed her eyes and decided she didn't want any of that around anymore. A wave of popping and sparkling golden mana washed over the cab, looting the root corpse and leaving behind a glowing green gem. When it had passed, the room was pristine.

"You got the plan?" she asked Babu. He had just taken another swig from a bottle, which vanished back into his pocket.

"Yup!" he said. "Time to go kill the boss and save the day. What are you going to do?"

"First, I'm spending some points," she said. "We can't move unless we want to get fried, and I'd bet my left tit that we're going to get hit again before this is over. It's time to work on Bertha's defenses. After that . . ." She grimaced. She wished that she could go out to fight instead. "After that, I have to give a speech."

CHAPTER 16

¡HOLA, SOY BERTHA!

Jill leaned forward against the driver's seat and let her head hang down. Babu had left a minute before, but she hadn't started doing what she'd said yet. She needed a minute. Just a minute.

She didn't close her eyes, but the events of the last few minutes played out in her mind with enough clarity that it hardly mattered. In truth, the battle hadn't been as desperate a fight as some she'd had the day before, but with so many more people's lives depending on her, fighting something that strong had been the wrong call. Even though run-of-the-mill monsters had ceased to be a threat to them, Jill knew—she had seen first-hand—that there were still plenty of horrific things that were bigger and meaner than her truck, and the sunflower was one of them. Jill stifled a manic laugh at the idea of calling a monster larger than most buildings the same name as a normal flower.

That gargantuan creature had out-leveled her, and it threw punches that Bertha couldn't take—punches the truck could have taken if Jill hadn't sunk so many points into offense instead of defense. If she hadn't been saving points for emergencies rather than planning for the future. She scowled. She had been saving points, but it wasn't honest to say they were for emergencies. There were just so many different things that needed to be upgraded, not to mention her own completely lacking combat powers, that she'd been paralyzed by indecision. She had eighteen class points to spend, plus another two from the levels she'd put off. All of that was power she had left on the table, putting everyone in danger just because she hadn't been able to make up her mind.

Jill gripped the seat in anger; her fingers tore through leather and foam cushion to bend the metal structure of the chair. "Fuck," Jill swore at herself.

"Jill." Karen's voice made Jill jump. "Clock's ticking, so cowboy up."

A flash of anger rose in Jill, and she snapped her head around to glare at the other woman, but her anger died at the sight of her. Karen looked like she was a wreck, and for good reason. She'd only survived the fight because the roots had more or less ignored her. She'd just seen her nephew die, even if that had turned out to be an illusion. But she was somehow holding it together.

"Right," Jill said and shoved aside the feelings that tormented her. There was no time for sulking.

She unclenched her hands and rested them on the seat, which repaired itself underneath them. A pang of regret welled up inside of her, and she mentally apologized to Bertha for letting her temper, and her hubris, get the better of her. The truck's injuries were fading, nearly gone; the injuries of the people inside would take longer, but not by much. Hit points would come back in ten minutes, bringing with them healing for most injuries. Those serious enough to count as status conditions, such as broken bones, would take longer, but they were nothing that the doctors in the Medbay couldn't fix in just a few minutes. It was the memories that would linger, no matter how dulled by the System they were. Memories of fear and pain, of being injured and causing destruction in turn.

"Right," Jill repeated. She had sunk back into her thoughts. She raised her gaze and looked out the windshield. The pallet rack in front of Bertha was in ruins from the roots, but everything outside was still with no signs of further monsters. For now.

"Can you call Aman and get him up here?" Jill asked. "We need Bertha to be a fortress, and I don't know dick about building defenses that are actually good. I'm going to be out of it for a bit upgrading, so if he gets here before I snap out of it, get him to work."

"That's more like it," Karen said and turned back to her station.

Jill took one step to get around her seat and then slid into it. "Sys," she thought. "Hit me with that experience and level me up."

Euphoria disabled via user preference. Proceed?

"Do it," she thought, before her worry could return.

It didn't start with pain; pain would have been easier. The part of her mind that connected to the System, from where its messages usually flowed with gentle, mechanical precision, erupted with tiny spikes that dove into Jill's consciousness. They pulled behind them threads of mana like so many sewing needles, lines of power that tugged and weaved at her very being. In the breath between blinks, they went from her mind to her body, piercing through muscle and bone with ease. It was an invasion unlike anything she had felt before, and Jill struggled not to panic. Then the threads turned to acid.

Jill staggered forward, though she could barely feel the driver's seat under her hand as it kept her upright. She gasped as the pain stopped as fast as it had started; fire was replaced by ice, which crystalized in the lines left behind. Magic filled in where once there was flesh and bone; flashes of color, smells, and sounds erupted around Jill, phantoms born of whatever was happening to her brain. She squeezed her eyes shut, but that did nothing to stop the false sensations. Time stretched on, though she knew from prior level-ups that it could only have been a few seconds.

And then it all stopped, and she was what remained.

Jill swallowed to clear her throat of bile. "Sys," she said aloud, "that was like having someone shove their unwashed toes down my mouth." Behind her, Karen gagged.

Euphoria is recommended.

"Yeah, yeah," Jill said as she fought to keep herself from shivering. The feelings of leveling up had faded to nothing and she still didn't feel quite right. But it was far better than the alternative.

The squeal of misaligned metal hinges broke Jill out of her thoughts, and Aman walked into the cab. "You wanted to see me?" he asked.

"Yeah," Jill said while fixing the hinges with Customization. "We're stuck in this Lair thing for now, and I think we're going to get attacked again. You have any idea how to make us a tougher target?"

"Yes," he said with a nod. "Plenty. What are the limits on changing Bertha?"

"The outside can't be any smaller than the original truck form," Jill said. "Otherwise, whatever you can think of. Hell, I just made it into a truck-slinky."

He slid into the Customization station. "We don't exactly have clear lines of fire with all these shelves around us," he said, pursing his lips, "and even with this Lair being bigger on the inside like your truck—"

"Huh, no shit," Jill said to herself and leaned forward to get a better view out of the windows. She hadn't noticed in all of the chaos, but the ceiling was higher than it had any right to be. The wrecked pallet rack blocked her view to the front, but looking out the side window, she saw that the row stretched off into the distance.

"—it's still close range for the machine guns," Aman finished. "I'm thinking we turn the outside of the truck into a fort while we're here. Raise the turrets up on towers at each corner so that they can shoot along the walls to scrape monsters off. Lower the bottom all the way to the ground so that nothing can slide underneath and be out of a firing arc."

"Yes to the towers, but we just got attacked by roots," Jill said, "so being on the ground won't stop us from getting attacked from below."

"Right," Aman said. "Monsters do monster things. I need to worry about flying ones too, don't I?"

"And climbing ones dropping from the ceiling. You get on that," she said. Her mind flashed to the class points she had to spend. She pushed down the recriminations that bubbled up; they wouldn't help. "I'm upgrading the bejesus out of the armor."

Jill pulled up the Armor Module status. It would take five points to finish all the armor upgrades: two in Bulwark to thicken the armor and give it a higher-percentage resistance to damage; one in Ablative Armor to help against "continuous" damage sources, whatever those were; and two in Face Hardening to add more flat resistance to damage after everything else. She closed her eyes and took all of them.

Bertha's mana exploded into motion and poured into the armor, transmuting from glowing potential into solid metal. Jill felt her skin thicken and toughen, a straitjacket that made her breathing difficult and bore her down under its weight. Twenty metric tons of plating grew over the top of the already thick armor, plate by plate. Jill's knees buckled in sympathy as Bertha lowered on its suspension.

She growled and willed the straitjacket to release. The upgrades to Bertha were hers to control, not the other way around. She rolled her shoulders at the same time as she cracked the armor forming over the joint between the cab and trailer, turning it into smoothly sliding plates. She pushed mana into the Propulsion Module to reinforce the suspension, and Bertha rose upwards, regaining the foot that the truck had lost. The newly formed armor rippled and shifted as its internal lattice shifted into a harder configuration, the more subtle aspects of the mass upgrades she'd picked taking effect.

She opened her eyes and leaned forward to look at the new armor, but a System message blocked her vision.

> Congratulations! Armor upgrades complete! Determining most beneficial new abilities.
> Only one of the following customized abilities may be selected:
> **Carcinization:** The armor of Soulbound Modular Vehicle "Bertha" crystalizes into an immutable shell. +70% Armor points and +.7% damage reduction per module effective Level. External Customization beyond cosmetic details is disabled unless the shell is discarded, which removes the bonuses until it is restored. A shell in a new configuration grows and hardens over the course of 1 week. Unlocks further defensive options.
> **Armored Explorer:** Soulbound Modular Vehicle "Bertha's" Armor Module becomes optimized for the exploration of hostile worlds. The Armor Module gains Elemental Resistance and Inertial Resistance equal to the module effective Level. Unlocks further adaptability-based options.
> Current Effective Level: 93

From behind Jill, Aman whistled. "Woah, this thing just went crazy!"

Jill turned to look. The hovering holographic diagram of Bertha shimmered and twisted, the shape of the truck flickering between a distinctly crab-like form and one that was sleeker, with less hard right angles than a normal semi and more rounded curves. The latter was subtly different every time the display flicked to it as if it couldn't make up its mind what the upgrade would actually look like.

"New options from the System," Jill said. "Take a look." She sent the boxes to him and Karen. She'd send them to Babu later; he had a job to do. "I swear the System takes sadistic pleasure in this shit."

"You thinking that and treating it like you do might be a self-fulfilling prophecy, don'tcha know," Aman mumbled as his eyes flickered, reading. "It says it's adaptive, after all."

"How is this sadistic?" Karen asked. "They're both useful. Also, Sangita wants you to hurry up."

"Tell Sangita I'm getting there," Jill said. "She can tell people that, uh, I'm making Bertha even stronger to stop this kind of thing happening again. That should calm people down. And it's even true." She tapped her fingers on her leg, the impacts hard enough to make tiny snaps on her jeans. "What's evil about these choices is that I already know which one I'm taking, but the other is stupid good. I'm going to kick my own ass when I need it and don't have it." One corner of her mouth quirked up. "Though, I guess I'm dodging a bullet because making Bertha all crabby would just be wrong."

"Crabby . . . You aren't going for more armor?" Aman asked. His face was blank and there was no judgment in his voice as he gestured outside. "You just said that things out there are going to attack us again."

"Dollars to donuts they will," Jill said, "and I'm sure people will give me shit for not going for maximum defense so, uh, maybe make my life easier and don't spread that story. But being able to shift forms is too important. This magic bullshit is getting even weirder, and who knows when I'll need to slinkify the truck again? Plus . . ." She pitched her voice louder and asked, "Hey, Sys, is that 'Inertial Resistance' what I think it is?"

Inertial Resistance shields the exterior of Soulbound Modular Vehicle "Bertha" from the effects of Inertial Mass and decouples the interior from acceleration. Breaches in the Armor Module will weaken the effect.

"Sweet bouncing mom-tits, that's what I'm talking about," Jill said and sent the information to Aman. "With that, I can finally take the speed upgrades and do some real driving without everyone in the back getting their guts pulped out their assholes like fruit stuffed through a juicer." She paused for a second. "Sys, you must have known I would have to take that if you offered it. Did you think I wouldn't ask, or did you throw super-crab-armor power in there too to make the choice seem hard?"

Module upgrades are determined based on the most beneficial new abilities.

"Sure," Jill said. "Okay, you two, I'm doing more upgrades, so if I zone out or grow a new face, just ignore me until I'm over it."

"Can that really happen?" Karen asked.

"Probably," Jill said with a shrug. She selected Armored Explorer as the advanced option for the Armor Module.

The upgrade started slowly, the mana in Bertha rippling outwards again like before. The cab grew cold around Jill, making her shiver, before abruptly switching to hot. A gentle breeze blew against her face before it was ripped away by a sudden vacuum. Her stomach was gripped in the queasy grasp of weightlessness, and then she staggered as she was pulled down to the floor.

"Hey, Jill, remember not to do this in front of people you haven't warned," Karen said, "or they're going to think you're even crazier."

"Is that possible?" Aman asked.

"Hah," Jill choked out a single sarcastic laugh. All of what she was experiencing was feedback from Bertha as usual. Gravity slid back to normal around her a few seconds later, and the upgrade was finished.

The notice for the module's new advanced powers popped up in her vision.

Advanced Armored Explorer Module Upgrades:
Environmental Suits: Soulbound Modular Vehicle "Bertha" can generate sealed environmental suits with their own back-mounted life support systems. Suits grant the same Inertial and Elemental Resistance as Armored Explorer. Each suit costs 1000 of Bertha's Mana, which cannot be regenerated until the suit is re-integrated. Unlocks **Armored Suits.**
Aligned Adaption: Once per hour a single Elemental Resistance given by Armored Explorer may be doubled and all other Elemental Resistances halved. This effect lasts until a new element is aligned or the ability canceled.
Explorer's Toolkit (0/3): Each rank unlocks one of the following abilities:

Bertha's Brilliance: The exterior of Bertha emits bright light that can only be perceived by residents of Berthaville.
Chameleon's Camouflage: While stationary, the armor changes colors to blend in with its surroundings.
Surface Shifting: The armor's surface moves without intervention to avoid obstacles. Reduces the effect of mobility impairment by 80%.
Nerve Network: Jill MacLeod can perfectly feel temperature and tactile inputs on the armor as if it were her own skin.
Repurposing Repairs: Bertha gains additional passive regeneration of Armor and Durability based on the nearby materials and environment.
Additional Add-on: The Armored Explorer Module gains an additional add-on slot. This option is repeatable.

Jill nodded along as she read through the new advanced powers, recognizing a similar pattern as that of the other modules: there were no direct numerical bonuses to the Armored Explorer Module, one of the options boosted people, and the last was a limited multiple choice.

Aligned Adaption was something she wanted right now; it would have been perfect against the Sunflower Queen's heat beam. She braced herself and took the power. Thankfully, all she felt was a blossoming of potential, like Bertha was ready to make a choice.

"Fourteen points left," Jill said. "Sys, what can you tell me about Armored Suits?"

The Armored Suits ability has not yet been unlocked. A language search reveals that "Armor" refers to a protective layer while "Suit" refers to a set of outer clothing. Further information on words can be found in the informational supplement "Basic Vocabulary for First-Time Speakers." Proceed with download?

"Ha-ha," she muttered. "Witty as always." She only had to remind herself that she was sending Babu, Mia, and Ras out to fight their way through the entire Lair before she decided to take both. She invested a point in Environmental Suits and felt the mana shifting in Bertha as the effect took hold.

The description for Armored Suits appeared before her.

Armored Suits: Environmental Suits may be upgraded to protect the wearer from physical harm in addition to its other resistances. This grants the statistics of an Uncommon Armor of Armored Explorer's effective Level. Each Armored Suit costs 10,000 of Bertha's Mana, which cannot be regenerated until the armored suit is re-integrated.

Jill whistled. Ten thousand mana seemed excessive, especially compared to the costs of her own abilities, and one of Bertha's main limits in a fight was how much mana it could dedicate to making ammunition. Right now, Bertha's maximum reserve of mana stood at 261,000, so making a few suits for people who were going to be outside the truck fighting wouldn't impact the turrets' firepower too much, but she wouldn't be able to protect everyone. Jill took that power as well, and again Bertha's mana shifted about without much fuss.

She threaded her senses through Bertha and found her away team near the rear doors, standing with a half dozen other people. "Hey," Jill projected to them with Captain Speaking, "you heading out soon? Are those folks going with you?"

"Yes and no," Ras replied. "Everyone's staying in until we get back."

"Jill, take a look at this!" Babu said. Through Cargokinesis, Jill felt him raise an arm and that he had something in his hand. "The fruits of our community's crafting labor, ready to wilt some plants!"

"Doesn't she just have that weird mana sense thing, not a camera?" Mia asked.

"Oh," Babu said. "Heh, right."

"I'm sure it's impressive," Jill said. She realized with a start that her own crafted item, the leather armor she still hadn't gotten fixed, was almost certainly obsoleted by the armored suits, and it was doubtful the crafters could make anything even approaching her level yet. On the other hand, what armor they did make wouldn't take up Bertha's mana, so it was still worth investing in.

"Before you go," Jill said, "I've got presents for you." She activated the Armored Suits power, concentrating on the three of them, and pushed the requisite thirty thousand mana out of Bertha's reserves. Screams of surprise erupted in Jill's mind as the deck plates surged up and enveloped them. She laughed and then sent them the power's description. It took another ten seconds for the armor to finish forming and let them move again.

"How's that?" Jill asked. "Wicked awesome or mega wicked awesome?"

"We are the knights who say BE!" Mia said, squeaking her voice on the last word.

Babu burst out laughing. "Oh!" he said. "'Be' for Bertha? Nice." He and Mia fist-bumped with a clang of metal knuckles.

"Jill," Ras said, "these are extremely impressive. We'll have to test just how tough they are, but I think these are going to change our entire approach to defense."

"We can't have that many of them," Jill said, "but I hope so." She explained the mana limitation.

"Expensive! But I have to hand it to you, they look amazing," Babu said. "Like video game armor, only not stupid."

"Yeah?" Jill said.

"I'll show you," Babu said. A tendril of magic connected to her, and an image of the armor bloomed in her mind. It was a cross between full metal-plate armor and biker's gear, with shiny chrome greaves, cuirass, spiked pauldrons, and a jet-black bubble helmet. Connecting them and covering any spots on the suit that would bend was flexible red leather. The image rotated to show that it had what looked like a boxy backpack built in, with green indicator lights arrayed on it: the life support system inherited from the environmental precursor power, presumably. And most importantly . . .

"Fuck yeah! Shoulder spikes. Nice," Jill projected back. "Anything else you need before going?"

Jill felt their heads turn towards each other. Babu patted his armor around the chest and then gave a thumbs-up.

"We're ready," Ras replied.

"Then get going, and good luck."

CHAPTER 17

SPICY BEES

And time for me to get my ass in gear too," Jill muttered. "Tell Sangita I'm on my way," she said to Karen.

"Will do. Who's in charge while you're gone?" she asked.

"Aman," Jill said after considering for a moment. "He's got the experience. Plus, you've got the job of coordinating everyone. Once he's done shifting Bertha around, he'll just be sitting on his thumbs with nothing to do."

Aman sighed. "I feel like there's an officer joke coming."

"Well, not anymore there isn't," Jill groused. She gave a wave at them, opened the cab hatch, and stepped through. The door shut behind her, and she took one more step before freezing in place. Something was wrong with the corridor in front of her.

It was just a hallway six feet wide and twelve feet long—nothing special. She stood at one end with a closed double door on her right and a familiar single door on her left, each within arm's length. In the middle of the hallway, just past the closed doors, were two openings, one on each side, leading to rooms she couldn't see. Opposite her, down the hall, was a third open doorway that led into a larger space, the walls on either side of which were pierced with firing slits. There was a hinged panel on the floor just large enough that when flipped upwards, it would form a waist-high barrier across the entranceway.

Defenses for the cab, Jill figured, to stop any monsters or people that had managed to break in from getting to Bertha's nerve center. That was all fine. Expected, even, from Aman's architectural work.

She took a closer look, trying to figure out what was bothering her. The floor was of gray steel plating, a rubber and cloth strip reminiscent of Bertha's footwell mats running down the middle. Jill reached out a hand and dragged a finger across the white-painted wall. It was glossy and smooth: the durable exterior paint of a vehicle rather than a more typical indoor variety. Everything matched the limited palette of materials that Customization had to work with.

Then it hit her, the reason for her discomfort: this hallway was inside Bertha, but she hadn't made it, or even been consciously aware of its existence.

Jill had felt the changes she had asked Aman to make to Bertha's layout in the same way that she could feel her guts pass a spicy, misbehaving meal through their lengths and curves: something happening in the background that would be an issue later, but for now, didn't require action. But stepping into one of those new places was like looking down to find that the Buffalo wings had redesigned her lower intestines into a chicken coop.

She groaned. Here she was, heading off to reassure everyone she had things under control, but she didn't even know where she was going. She pinched the bridge of her nose. There was too much for her to keep track of these days, but that was no excuse for not knowing her own truck. She eyed the opening across from her and the room beyond. It was busy, filled with people sitting and moving here and there, but none of them seemed to have noticed her or her confusion. That was a relief.

Jill braced her hands on either side of the hatch and closed her eyes, letting her senses flow out into Bertha. It was time to see exactly what Aman had done and figure out where the hell to go. Well, not really see, but rather use her connection to Bertha and her other powers to do something almost as good. The overall layout was something she could tell just by concentrating on her Soulbond, and she had a kinesthetic sense from Cargokinesis of everything in the Cargo Nexus. She could hear anything she wanted and even feel roughly how people felt about her with Synergy.

The little hallway she stood in was part of the Cargo Nexus; the door on her left was to Habitation, familiar because it led to her own room. It was sealed off from the rest of that module completely, with even the ventilation taken care of by magic rather than some gap that an intruding thing could crawl through. If someone wanted to get at her or Bertha's settlement core, the only way in or out was this one door next to the cab.

Unless someone could walk through metal, which Jill figured someone out in the world could. She'd taken crazier abilities herself, after all.

The open doorway past her room on the left led to what had to be a meeting room, as the only thing Jill felt in it was a long oval table and chairs. The closed double door to her right led to the back of the Medbay, bypassing the waiting area. A quick tap into Captain Speaking brought Jill the sounds of busy, stressed people: the doctors and nurses hard at work getting those hurt in the last fight healed enough that their own magical regeneration could take care of the more minor wounds.

The final open door, on the right, led to a small briefing room, complete with a dozen chairs in three rows facing a lectern of metal extruded from the floor. The walls were lined with seven hatches that led to the turrets and half a dozen people were either sprawled on the chairs or standing nearby.

"Gunner's room. Got it," Jill muttered. Then her breath caught as a shifting sensation washed over her: something else was changing, but it wasn't inside of the truck. The armor bent and cracked, like the surface of a frozen pond not quite as solid as expected when stepped on. Bertha's corners rounded and its sides bulged as the truck grew bit by bit. Either Aman was taking the transformation extra slow for some reason, or he just couldn't reconfigure Bertha as fast as Jill could.

She gathered her mana to send a message asking what his plan for the truck was but stopped herself. Her distracting him with micromanagement wouldn't help. Jill had her own job to do, but she still hadn't found where she needed to go. She brought her attention back to mapping out the new interior layout of the truck.

The busy open space down the hallway was filled with tables, chairs, and people. It was an enormous cafeteria, including a door to a food preparation area and a storage room filled with what remained of Jill's original delivery. It was a pitiful number of supplies compared to what Berthaville's residents would need, but that was why they were here, wasn't it?

Off to the right of the eating area was a warren of smaller rooms. Jill's eyebrows rose as she traced them out one after another; they must have taken up fully half of the Nexus's enormous volume! The rooms were identical to each other: a barracks-like rectangle lined on either side with double bunks. At the foot of each bed was a small storage chest extruded from the floor, and cloth partitions gave some measure of privacy.

Jill nodded to herself. It wasn't ideal, but until Habitation had enough rooms so that everyone could fit, it would have to do.

On the end of each barracks room was a door that led to a bathroom, each one a tiny stolen stub of the Habitation Module. For every one of those, somewhere in the Habitation Module two of the hotel-like rooms had been squashed together and stripped of one of their own bathrooms. Jill started to trace the paths through the Habitation Module to see how it lined up with the Cargo Nexus but gave it up when her head started to hurt. There were dozens, hundreds, of folded-space connections between the two modules that turned the whole affair into a dizzying tangle. She wished the hypothetical intruder who could walk through walls luck in navigating that.

On the other side of the cafeteria, through another double-wide opening, was a large rectangular room with a stage on one side. The ceiling was just tall enough that people could stand on the stage without hitting their heads—not even close to the height that Jill would expect some kind of combined gym and theater to have. It felt like a strange choice, but it was the Nexus's total volume that was limited, not its floor area, so low ceilings here meant packing in more rooms elsewhere.

Sangita stood on the stage; the spicy, challenging loyalty to Jill radiated through her Synergy powers in a way that was unlike anyone else inside of Bertha. The room was filled with several hundred, maybe even a thousand, worried people, crowded together. Her Synergy power dispassionately informed her that while nearly all of them were loyal enough to her and the concept of Berthaville for the power to work, that loyalty was wavering. Where before there had been optimism, now there was doubt and the growing shoots of fear.

Jill trickled a little mana into Captain Speaking, just enough to hear and, hopefully, not enough to alert the crowd to her listening.

"—care what you have to say. You aren't in charge, are you?" said a woman's voice with an accent so upper crust that Jill could almost taste money. "I demand to be heard!"

"Don't worry, Barb," Sangita said, her voice out of patience. "You're being heard, all right."

"Why you—"

"Fuck me," Jill muttered and cut off the power. She'd found where she needed to go, all right, but maybe she should check out the rest of Bertha first.

Beyond the living and eating area was a short but wide hallway fortified with defensive positions that finally led into the part of the Cargo Nexus reserved for actual cargo. It resembled nothing so much as the warehouse that Bertha was currently crashed into, with a wide-open area in front of the doors to the outside, also fortified, and rows of shelves broken up by areas with tables. Jill couldn't differentiate the various salvaged goods from the airport from one another, as they were all just shapes to her, but the looted monster parts shone with distinct flavors of mana.

A buildup of magic around one of the tables caught Jill's attention. Three people were clustered around a carefully arranged pile of loot, all pouring their magic into it. With a snap and pop of power, the parts merged together and formed something new. Most of the invested mana sunk into the new item, but some of it poured back into the crafters, from which a little more flowed into Bertha and into Jill. Now that she was paying attention to the flow of mana more closely, Jill saw that hidden amongst the chaotic whirls of everyone using their abilities was a steady current going into her truck, building up bit by bit in the settlement's reserves.

"Are, uh, you okay there, little lady?" a voice snapped Jill out of her inspection.

An older man with salt and pepper hair leaned out of the opening to the turret room. He stared at her with a hesitant expression on his face. "Did you get lost? That door leads to the lion's den, and Ms. Sangita was clear that we're only supposed to go in there if we have to."

"Little lady?" Jill asked with disbelief. The hallway around her flexed in a ripple. "The fuck's that supposed to mean?"

His eyes widened. "Ms. MacLeod, uh, ma'am! Well, shoot," he said. "From your voice, I thought you were my age."

"You sound disappointed," she said with narrowed eyes.

"Well, when you get older," he said, giving Jill a wink and pitching his voice louder, "you'll understand that people are more mature about who they—"

"Oh my God, Grandpa!" shrieked the scout, Melissa, from the room behind him. "It was a mistake!"

Jill rolled her eyes and strode forward. The old man was way too pleased about teasing his granddaughter to have actually meant what he was implying. "You're so off base that you're in the next stadium over," she said anyway, just to be certain. "Call me Jill. Who're you?" She extended her hand.

He took her hand and gave it a firm shake. "Hutcheson's the name. Kraig Hutcheson."

"It's good to meet you. You've been on the guns?" she asked and gestured at the hatches.

"Yes, ma'am!" he said. "Shooting these babies again is like riding a bike: you never forget the rhythm of firing in bursts. Only this bike had a rocket engine strapped on! What did you do to make those old hounds hit so hard?"

"They're attached to Bertha, so they kick ass," Jill said. "It's as simple as that." She leaned around him to look into the turret room. Half the chairs were occupied by exhausted people. Two women were closest to the door, including the red-faced Melissa. Three men were clustered at the opposite corner, one of them keeled over, asleep, with a jacket tented over his head.

"Is everyone here?" Jill asked.

"No, ma'am. Most of A team is here," Kraig said, "and we've got B team in the hot seats right now. But Coach and Dave are in the hospital, and Kyle's out getting us some grub, and Ms. William is off doing high-level commando shit. But, of course, you know all about that."

A notification popped up.

Lair of the Sunflower Queen Invasion progress: 52%

"Looks like they're doing well too," he said. "Do you, uh, want to speak with us for some reason?"

Jill dismissed the box with a wave. "I've got some turret upgrades to choose, and you lot are the experts," she said.

Kraig nodded and stepped into the turret room. As Jill followed, another box appeared in her vision.

New Local Quest: Increase the Loyalty of Berthaville's residents.

"Don't twist my nipples, Sys. I'm getting to it," Jill thought to the System. She continued out loud, "Hey, uh, everyone," and gave a short wave. "I'm Jill. You know who I am, but I don't know you. That's a problem, so hit me with some names."

The red-faced young woman answered first. "I'm Melissa. Uh, Hutcheson!" She gave Jill a tentative smile.

"Right, the one who can see everything invisible," Jill said.

"Connie Newman," said the woman next to Melissa. Brown-haired and grim-faced, she gave Jill a nod but didn't say anything else.

The two seated men were Tristan Kim and Kevin Lindwurm. Jill looked at the last man, but he was still asleep. Kevin elbowed him.

"Ugg, five more minutes," the sleeper muttered.

"Zeke, get your ass up. Jill's here," said Kevin and shoved Zeke again.

"My mom's name isn't Jill," Zeke said in confusion.

Jill snorted. "I'm not your mom," she said, "but she does call me sometimes." She used Captain Speaking to play Bertha's horn in his ear, but she made sure that it was at a reasonable, rather than deafening, volume.

Zeke burst out of his chair and flailed at the jacket in a desperate attempt to get it off of him. "Oh my God!" he yelled as he tripped over another chair and sprawled on the ground. "That Jill?! Why didn't you wake me up?!"

"I tried," Kevin said under his breath.

Zeke finally managed to get the jacket off his head. He stared at Jill for a moment before a pulse of inquisitive mana burst from him. His eyes went wide, and his jaw fell. "Holy fuckballs," he said, "look at what level she is!"

"Yeah, I feel that way half the time too," Jill said. "It's nice to finally meet you lot in person and make sure you're not just voices in my head." That got some obligatory chuckles, but everyone stared at Jill expectantly, not saying anything. Jill coughed. "Right. So. That last fight sucked. How're you doing?"

The atmosphere in the room went from low energy to downright depressed. "We're all alive," said Tristan with a sigh, "but Dave got the shit burned out of him, and Coach got his shit kicked in. Again." He didn't sound angry about it, just tired.

Jill nodded. "I heard about Coach," she said. "I—" She hesitated, then kept going. "I tried to move that turret, Dave's, out of the fire, but I wasn't fast enough. I'm sorry."

Kraig shook his head. "None of that now, little—" He cut off at Jill's glare. "Uh, ma'am. We saw you move him, and it saved his life."

There were murmurs of agreement at that. A knot of worry in Jill eased just a bit. "Right," she said. "So. Anything else?"

"It fucking sucked not being able to do much damage to that giant flower," Connie said. "A flower! We just kept shooting, but it wasn't enough."

"Fucking bullshit ridiculously high-level monsters," Tristan said. "How the fuck did they even get that strong so fast?"

"Does it matter?" Jill asked. "They are. What's going to help you kill them? That's what I want to know."

"We need a BFG," Kevin said after a moment. "Some sort of artillery piece."

"If we find one, we can try," Jill said, "but I don't think we could mount it, at least not yet. The turrets are 'small arms.' Anything matching that description that would help you?"

"More flamethrowers," Zeke said immediately. "Not for all the time," he said, speaking fast as Jill's attention landed on him, "but maybe as close-ranged backups? Dan saved our ass with his and there's enough room to just stick one within arm's reach."

"Hell yes," Jill said, "now that's something we can do. I bet my left tit we've got some loot from a fire aardvark that someone can turn into a flamethrower. Hell, it doesn't even have to be good. Just plug it into Bertha and the truck'll do the rest!"

That was met with grins and a few happy expletives. Everyone liked flamethrowers.

"I've got something to run by you," Jill said. "Another upgrade for the turrets that will let you use your abilities on each other. No more Melissa being the only bad bitch who can see right."

Melissa went red again.

"So, what's the downside?" asked Connie, her scowl coming back. "You'd have taken it already if there wasn't some problem."

"The catch," Jill said, "is that some of these powers do a real mindfuck when I take them. If I'm reading this right, it might stay pretty screwy when you go to shoot too."

"Well, let's take a look," Kraig said. "Then we'll make up our minds."

"We should let the others know too," said Tristan. He and Kevin stood and began opening the turret doors. "Hey!" Kevin shouted into his. "Listen up!"

"Is that how you've been talking to each other?" Jill asked. Her gaze flicked between the open doors.

"That or we shout for Karen," Melissa said. "But it's easier most of the time to have the doors open. And still shout."

"I'll get Karen on getting a better system going," Jill said. "Or we'll shove monster fish parts in your ears until you can hear each other. For now, I've got this." Jill activated Captain Speaking and explained the situation to the B team gunners, then sent the box for the power in question to everyone.

> **Hive Mind:** Forms a non-sapient hive mind from the mental contribution of all gunners, allowing for the optimization of target selection and firing patterns. All Class Powers are shared between gunners, with the effects scaled by the Level difference between donor and recipient. Duplicate effects do not apply.

"Does that mean I'm going to be able to hear what Zeke's thinking?" Connie asked. She pulled a face.

"Hey!"

"Sys," Jill said, "hit us with an answer to that, please."

> Each member of the Hive Mind will remain a distinct entity, but a portion of their mental abilities will contribute to a new whole.

"Huh," Jill continued after reading, "that doesn't seem so bad."

"Will it let us talk to each other?" asked Kevin. "Two birds with one stone?"

> Communication is unnecessary as each member is of the whole.

That box was met with silence.

"Ominous as fuck," Jill eventually said.

"If you don't take it, will you be able to advance the turrets more?" Melissa asked.

Jill raised an eyebrow. "You know about how that works?"

"I might have listened to Mr. Babu for a while when he was explaining it to Mia," Melissa said. Her face turned red again.

Jill groaned. "Executive decision: no love dodecahedrons. That goes for all of you, got it?" She didn't wait for a response. "To answer your question"—she scowled—"maybe. Sys?"

> Ability redetermination may be purchased for a Perk Point.

She had a perk point left from when she had first started out. She'd spent only one to Soulbind Bertha; that had been the single most important thing she'd done with the System. Changing a power for the same cost didn't seem like a very good deal.

"I could," Jill said, "but it would be expensive. Very expensive. And weirdness aside, the ability is bullshit levels of strong."

"Then, uh, it sounds like you've made up your mind," said Kraig, "and we all know who's in charge." He cracked his neck to the side. "Anyone got strong objections?"

Jill could feel the anxiety, but no one spoke up. She met Kraig's eyes and nodded.

"Aman," she projected to the front, "are we clear of monsters?"

"For the moment," he said back.

"Then, everyone, hands off the guns and ass off the seats," Jill said. She waited five seconds and then purchased Hive Mind.

The Turret Module surged to the forefront of her thoughts, an enthusiastic and loyal pet that longed to rip apart her enemies and share with her a feast of their broken remains. It soaked up the mana of the upgrade with eager anticipation.

Jill wobbled her seven turrets and tapped her fingers on her leg as she waited for the inevitable upgrade feedback. So far it was mild. Dan's flamethrower was itching more than usual as its own magic, so foreign to hers, tried its best to work alongside that of the surging upgrade, but that was a minor feeling compared to the bullshit that upgrades often threw at her. The M2HB heavy machine guns were as happy and reliable as ever, the dull, darling things.

She wished she could sense outside beyond the short fourteen meters of Cargokinesis and that Blossom, that fiery gun, would come back so that she could test out a coordinated long-range firing pattern. Jill was sure she could account for the difference in muzzle velocities between the two gun types and make a bracketing spread of fire that would anticipate any enemy movement, but nothing beat getting real practice. For the fun of it, she imagined a moving target at a range of twelve hundred meters, with two hundred meters elevation, moving left to right across Bertha's nose at fifteen meters per second—a typical profile for a bird—and tracked it with four of her turrets.

"I knew it; these things are moving on their own!"

A shouted voice broke Jill out of her upgrade trance and she pulled herself back into just her meat body. "Ass-slapping, coffee-pitting pickup princess!" she spat out in revulsion.

"That bad?" Melissa asked with worry.

"Ugh," Jill said. "I was the turrets and me at the same time." She shivered to chase the strange phantom sensations away. "It wouldn't have been so bad except that I didn't even realize anything was different." She blew out a heavy breath.

"Sounds freaky," Kraig said and grinned. "I'm looking forward to—"

"Jill!" Sangita's voice sounded around them, a restive crowd in the background. "Where are you?" She didn't sound happy.

"Coming!" Jill shouted back. She mentally reached into Captain Speaking, sidestepped Karen's control of it, and flicked Sangita's connection off. "I'll check in again later," she said to the room as a whole. "For now, I've got to go put out a dumpster fire." She groaned. "Sweet Jesus, this is going to suck."

"Anything we can help with?" Melissa asked, a hopeful look on her face.

Jill hesitated. She could use the backup. "Yeah, actually," she said. "I need to calm a crowd down and convince them things are going okay. Maybe they'll trust one of you if they don't trust me."

Melissa stood immediately.

"How many people would we need to talk to?" Connie asked.

"A fuckload. That's what's twisting my panties too," Jill said. "If you don't do public speaking, maybe just, I dunno, shoot the anus out of a sea cucumber from across the room. Convince people that you're all badasses who can kill monsters so that they stop freaking out."

"I like bragging," Zeke said. Connie snorted, but she stood. Tristan and Kevin did likewise.

"We're in."

CHAPTER 18

CHEEK BY FOWL

Jill strode through the central cafeteria area with those four gunners in tow; Melissa and her grandfather decided to stay behind so that there would be at least some backup for the B team in case of emergency. The room was packed with people and hummed with a sound akin to the smell of sour post-panic sweat. Whatever divisions there might have been between different groups of people were rendered moot by the sheer number that wanted someplace to sit and eat. Someone had put together a stew with a scent that made Jill's mouth water; where they'd gotten the meat that now sat in well-stewed, generous chunks she didn't want to know.

Walking through the cafeteria made Jill's nerves grow tight. The nervous chatter grew quieter, and heads turned to follow her progress. She gave what she hoped was an encouraging nod and a set of smiles. A group of people rose to follow her, so her gestures had either worked to reassure them or they were going to try to jump her. Either way, when she made it into the gymnasium, she was followed not just by her quartet of gunners, but also by a solid thirty other people.

The gymnasium was even more crowded and the sounds of the crowd there were far angrier. She was the tip of a wedge that pushed its way through the crowd. At first, they drew angry comments, and one snarling man even shoved Connie. She had been firing at monsters and gaining levels on and off the whole day and must have gotten an absolutely massive bonus for her contribution against the roots. He obviously hadn't, because he was so outclassed in strength that pushing her was like pushing a wall.

He staggered backward and tripped, falling into a trio who hadn't been paying attention.

Fear flickered across their faces, and they moved away from Jill in a panic, bumping into a few more on their way. That started a ripple and before Jill knew it there was a clear corridor between her and the stage. She felt a pang of unease, not of embarrassment, as she moved past the quieting crowd. Without really thinking about what she was doing she'd shown up with some of the highest level, and in turn most dangerous, people at her back. She didn't want to be the kind of person that spread fear where she went.

Jill hopped up onto the stage and strode over to where Sangita stood, talking urgently to a small group of people, the same that she'd mustered to register those coming into Bertha at the airport. "Let's get to it!" she said to them, and they scattered with determined strides, clipboards held in front of them like armor.

"So," Jill said as she reached Sangita. "Here I am."

Sangita's gaze swung onto Jill with an expression of half relief, half annoyance. "You got here eventually."

Jill jerked a thumb over her shoulder at the crowd. "They don't seem happy."

"Really, Sherlock?" Sangita asked.

"You!" interrupted a voice Jill recognized from her previous listening in as belonging to Barb. Judging from the tattered wisps of her perm and her torn, bloodstained cashmere sweater, she had had a rough evacuation from her old life when the System hit. Either that or being on the receiving end of Sangita's ire had done more damage than Jill expected. Still, this was no defeated woman. There was a glint in her eyes like the flash of an assassin's blade.

Barb climbed onto the stage by a set of stairs on the side, surrounded by four people who looked even more haggard than Barb. One man had a nervous tremor in his hands; a woman had long streaks of mascara down her cheeks. Barb marched over to Jill, and her entourage trailed along behind her in a ragged line.

"Are you this Jill woman who I've heard has been driving us around?" Barb asked, her diction precise.

"That's me," Jill said. "Who are you?"

This just seemed to make the woman angrier. "Don't pretend you don't know who I am! Everyone in the city knows me!"

"For fuck's sake, lady," Jill snapped, "I'm not from your crappy town. I don't know who you are."

The woman harrumphed with the ease of one long experienced in that haughtiest of arts. "I'm Barbara Marigold." She said the name as if it meant something. Her follower with running mascara put her hand on her hip and tried to pull off dismissively looking away from Jill, but her desperate glances to see if Barbara had noticed somewhat ruined the effect. Barbara waited a few seconds, then clicked her tongue. "Of *the* Marigolds, you ugly wage slave."

Jill stared at Barbara for a long moment and then turned to Sangita. "You let her on my truck?"

Sangita shrugged. "She wanted to come," she said. "I didn't think she'd bring the attitude, but I should have known better. Sanity has never been high on her list of assets."

Jill snorted a laugh.

"Oh, I see how it is!" Barbara put the back of a hand to her forehead. "You taste a bit of power and just have to put down your betters. And from another woman, no less. For shame! What next, you'll put a gag on my mouth and throw me out so that no one can hear my truths?"

"No!" cried one member of the backup squad.

"We'd never let her!" said another.

Jill looked at them in exasperated confusion, wondering how such people could even exist. "No," she said to Barbara, "I'm not trying to make you shut up. You get the same say as everyone else."

"Humph! Then let me tell you exactly what I think of your so-called—"

"Everyone else is down there," Jill interrupted and pointed at the crowd.

A startled squawk came out of Barbara's throat, and her perm bobbled in indignation. "Why, I have never been treated this way before in my life!"

"Lady, go floss a hippo," Jill said. She waved a hand in idle theater and used Customization to move the floor under Barbara and her entourage. They were swept off the stage in steady safety and deposited into the heart of the crowd. A smatter of grudging laughter came from those close enough to have heard the confrontation, and Barbara stomped off and out of the room in anger.

"That was weird as a duck's dick," Jill said to Sangita under her breath. "What was going through her head? And the rest of them?"

"People do weird things under stress," Sangita replied.

"I guess so," Jill said. "Think she's going to be a problem?"

Sangita shook her head and let out a little derisive laugh. "She's a washed-up heiress whose looks and money are gone. All that's left of her precious society is their petty games of spite."

"Fuck me, history much?"

"A little," Sangita said. "She won't be a problem."

Jill grunted in response and gazed out over the crowd.

There were over a thousand people packed closely together by sheer number. Most of the crowd were refugees who'd fled in whatever they'd thrown on top of their sleepwear, carrying only what they could grab. Some had ridden in Bertha, others had walked, but almost all looked lost and not a little bit angry and afraid. Spread here and there were knots of people with weapons, wearing either shockingly torn clothing or brand-new armor. A quick check with the System showed Jill that they were higher level than those around them who'd simply fled. They seemed to be naturally grouping together with others who'd seen action.

There was more to the crowd than small groups, though; with her view from above Jill started to see the patterns in the people. The easiest to see, so easy that Jill nearly rolled her eyes at herself for not noticing them sooner, were other members of Ras and Babu's Sikh community, dozens of them. The prevalence, though not universality, of darker skin and head coverings kind of gave it away. A kid among them waved at her while jumping up and down. It was Kevin, alongside his father and siblings, with a tiny stegosaurus perched atop his head, clinging on for dear life. Jill let out a chuckle and gave a tiny wave back.

Near the front of the stage on the right she picked out Jacob of the HOA, surrounded by others that Jill vaguely recognized from her time at the farmer's market in Billings. It was their clothing that marked them as a group. None of it was fancy, but it was clean and matched in a way that few others did. Back then, she'd told them to evacuate and they'd listened to her, so they'd had far more time to gather their possessions than the refugees who had only fled once the monster attacks had become serious.

And then, as Jill's gaze continued to scan, there was a blip. Her eyes skipped just a bit too far and the lightest touch of ozone caressed her mana senses. She took a startled breath, the hair on the back of her neck standing on end, and focused on where she'd just been looking, but all she saw was a young girl picking her nose and wiping her finger on her mother's blouse.

"Jill?" Sangita asked.

"What?" Jill said, harsher than she'd intended, and jumped.

"Don't bite my head off," Sangita said with a frown. "I just think it's time for you to say something to them." She gestured outwards. "Now that you're here, that is."

"Yeah," Jill said. She gave her head a little shake. "Yeah, okay." She stuck her fingers in her mouth and tried to whistle, but all that came out was air. She sighed, then used Captain Speaking to project an imagined whistling sound.

"Hey, listen up!" she said. "I've heard that people have concerns about the chickening clustercluck that just happened. So, it's town meeting time. We start in two minutes."

She snapped off the power and turned to Sangita. "What am I in for?"

"They're scared," Sangita said, her voice pitched low. "Half of them want to scream at you, but I bet you can bring all but the most diehard around if you can convince them things are okay. You've got people like that Barbara, who are taking advantage to pull their"—she paused for a moment—"their shenanigans, but, overall, they're just people, Jill. They want someone in charge to reassure them and tell them what to do. They want someone who knows what they're doing."

Jill let out a sarcastic single huff through her nose. "Well, that rules me out."

"Tough tomatoes," Sangita said and rolled her eyes. "You've just got to pretend, like every other politician ever."

"Tie me up and leave me waiting, you just called me a politician," Jill said and pulled a face.

"You walked into the room and pulled power moves twice in two minutes," Sangita said. "If you don't want to be called a politician, don't act like one."

"Stop making sense," Jill said.

"Yes, Supreme Leader," Sangita replied. They stood in silence for a moment. "Have you ever run a town meeting before?" she asked.

"Fuck no!" Jill said. "That's what I have you around for. Think it's been two minutes? I think it has." She used Captain Speaking to sound Bertha's horn in the hall, then spun the mana of that power around Sangita.

"Me? I've never done it with this many people before," Sangita said, her voice booming out over the crowd. It simultaneously quieted and confused them.

"That's what he said," Jill whispered.

Sangita flashed Jill a glare that promised retaliation, then schooled her features into something more professional. "This opens the first town hall meeting for Berthaville. For those of you who haven't realized it yet, standing next to me is Jill MacLeod, owner of Bertha, the truck, and de facto leader of the town. She'll explain how this will work." She stared at Jill as if daring her to contradict her.

"Fair play," Jill said out of the corner of her mouth, then she switched Captain Speaking to herself. "Right, like Sangita said, I'm Jill. Anyone who has questions for me, come up to, uh—" Jill flicked a hand upwards and a raised platform bearing a podium grew out of the floor a dozen feet in front of the stage. "Go there and you'll have your say. But"—she increased the volume of the power to speak over the surge of noise in the crowd—"we're on a timer because if we get hit by something serious, I'll have to deal with it. Don't just repeat what someone already said or ask about something I already said, or I'll kick you off."

There was a brief pause as everyone waited to see if Jill had anything else to say, and then the crowd burst into chatter and motion. It only took a minute before a queue a dozen deep stretched behind the podium, and still, a few of those who had been at the edges of the room were shoving their way towards it. Jill sighed and hoped that the line would shrink as people's questions were asked by someone else.

The first person in line was a large, bearded man, six feet tall and shaped like a powerlifter who'd been retired for a half decade but hadn't bothered to stop eating extra-large meals. He was breathing fast, his hands gripped the sides of the podium with white knuckles, and his face was pulled into a teeth-showing grimace as he stared at Jill. It was no wonder that he had been able to secure his spot.

Jill cracked her neck to one side and met his gaze, her blood rising in anticipation. "Quiet down, everyone," she projected. The noise dropped a little, but not by much, so she blared the sound of Bertha's horn. That did the trick. "All right, buddy," she said to the man at the podium, giving him the benefit of the doubt, "you're first up. Just talk normally and I'll mic you." A twist of her will and Captain Speaking shifted to him.

"Right. Right. Okay," he said, his voice like gravel mixed with tar. "A lot of you know me, but for the people who don't, my name's Logan Bradley." He took a deep breath. "When the, uh, System, I guess, hit us, I lost everything." He said the last word in a roar and slapped the podium.

There were shouts to the effect of "Me too" and "We all did, asshole" from the crowd, but Logan didn't seem to notice. He just kept telling his story.

"We were asleep in bed, so we didn't see the boxes. First thing I know of it all is my dog going mad! The poor pup got monsterized and tried to kill us!" The crowd went silent at this, and Logan's deep, gasping breath echoed. "I had to kill him with my bare hands. I've still got the scars from his teeth!"

Gasps of shock and sympathy rang out. Barely audible underneath them was Sander's woof of "Oh no!" Logan hung his head and swallowed.

Jill felt bad for him, but also confused. She'd expected an angry tirade against her but gotten this story instead. With a pang of impatience at herself for not thinking of it sooner, she tapped into Synergy and gazed at Logan through the prism of mana and intent. Green wisps of magic that smelled of dirt and felt like motor oil swirled around him in anxious spirals. More surprising to Jill was that his connection to her and Bertha was a solid tether, barely frayed at the edges.

"Somehow," Logan continued after he'd collected himself, "we thought to go to the airport. So, we all ran there as fast as we could. Most of you did too, I guess, huh? Anyway, you all know how things were there, how afraid we all were, and how monsters kept running at us over the tarmac all day."

He raised his gaze to look at Jill. "Ms. MacLeod, when you came in with your truck, guns blazing, I thought things were finally going our way. But here we are, still getting attacked, stuffed like sardines into a metal can, getting thrown around and burnt, and having those guns pounding in our ears all the time. My kid got hurt worse inside this truck than they did running to the airport!"

There were angry sounds from the crowd now, agreement and shock. "You tell her," cried one, and "I knew our kids weren't safe!" said another.

"That's right!" Logan said. "Sam." He waved behind him. "Sam, c'mere and show them all your nose!"

Jill followed Logan's gesture and saw just a few steps behind him a tall and skinny preteen who appeared to be in perfect health, with eyes locked onto Jill's, widening in panic. Never before had Jill seen someone communicate so clearly the desire to be sucked into the ground through just a look. A pang of fellow feeling welled up inside of her and she considered granting that wish but knew that she couldn't. The crowd wouldn't understand.

Sam was pushed and prodded up to the podium by the helping hands of those concerned citizens around them. "Dad," Sam whispered, but it was picked up by Captain Speaking and magnified anyway. "I'm fine! It healed in like a second!"

"It was broken!" Logan wailed. "There was blood everywhere!"

Puzzled and exasperated sounds followed this pronouncement.

"A broken nose? Really?"

"I almost lost my arm! What is this shit?"

"I did lose my arm, jackass!"

"Dad," Sam whispered even louder, turning bright red in the face, "stop it! You're embarrassing me in front of everyone! It didn't even hurt that much!"

Jill cut off the amplification for a few seconds so the two could have their whispered argument in relative private. It ended with Sam's face collapsing in relief. The preteen dove back into the crowd a second later. Jill followed with her eyes until Sam had reached another huge man, who scooped them into a public hug punctuated by further cries of embarrassment. It just wasn't Sam's day.

Logan stepped back to the podium, and Jill turned her communication power back on. "Right, uh, so, anyway, my kid only got a little hurt. I guess it wasn't that bad, 'cause of how we kind of all heal by magic now."

Jill felt more than saw the collective sigh at that.

"But it could have been a lot worse!" Logan continued without noticing. "And the rest of what I said is true! So, my question for you, ma'am, is what the hell is going on? Are things going to get any better for us in here, and are we still safe?"

There was a spark in those questions, one that ignited his determination, and the gaze he sent to Jill was full of challenge. It caught with the crowd as well and silenced their skepticism of Logan's story. In the end, he'd asked the important questions, the ones that mattered to them the most.

Jill stood for a few seconds and thought of how to phrase her answers. The silence might have gotten awkward for her, but, luckily, Logan was even more self-conscious than she was.

"Right," he said, then coughed lightly. "So. That was my question. Questions. Thank you and, um, I'm Logan Bradley. God bless." He took a step back from the podium but didn't relinquish the raised platform, instead staring at Jill along with everyone else.

"Those are some good questions," Jill said after pulling Captain Speaking back to herself. "First up: your kid getting thrown around. I've fixed that." There was a murmur of disbelief. Jill raised an eyebrow. "We've all got magic, people. Why is that so hard to believe? I just unlocked this thing called 'Inertial Resistance' and it's up to"—there was a pause for a fraction of a second as she looked up her statistics—"ninety-six percent. You might feel a little tug now and then, but the ride's only going to get smoother as that number goes up." She realized she hadn't actually tested that yet, but there was no choice now but to keep plowing ahead.

She took a breath and moved on to the more difficult issues. "About what's going on outside. You all saw the boxes, right? We're stuck inside a warehouse-turned-monster-Lair tighter than a coffee-less shit the morning after steak night."

She immediately regretted her words. Both the implication that Bertha was in trouble, which might be a bit true but really didn't help reassure people, and also the profane analogy that had slipped out of her. The latter had felt good when it had come out, but she could tell that it had upset some people, and for once, that mattered. The former had set off a ripple of panic that threatened to turn into a flood.

"Calm your t—" Jill checked herself. "Calm down, people. We're doing okay. Bertha's all curled up in fortress mode, and those guns you keep hearing?" She nodded at Logan. "Those are magic-enhanced, .50-caliber fu—fudge cannons"—she really wasn't fooling anyone—"that can shred everything short of a boss monster. The one of those that's around can't reach us anymore." Well, it had stopped trying with its roots at least, so it probably couldn't reach them. "That's why we're in this Lair in the first place, to get away from its attacks. We've got people fighting right now to shove some pain right up its—yeah."

That seemed to have helped calm people down at the very least. Jill turned and paced the stage to burn off a few of her own nerves. "What else is going on," she said. "Right. We're still going east, but we're deep into a high-magic territory where everything is spread out, and it's taking forever to drive anywhere. Crazy shoot is still happening, but Bertha's as safe as anything can be now." As long as Jill spent her points, that is. "That answer part of your question?"

Logan nodded, paused, then shook his head. "So, are we safe here or not?"

Jill sighed. "One hundred percent? No. But I don't think anyone can be a hundred percent safe, not right now." She let her gaze sweep over the crowd. "The fact is that we need food. I took a power to give us some." She brought up the notifications for Chez Bertha and flicked them out, letting them ride along the same strings of mana that Captain Speaking spread through the air. "But we need more, and it's going to take a while until we can grow our own. This warehouse has it now, when we need it, so I took the risk to bring us in here."

She took a deep breath and scanned the room. There was still a lot of anger, but people were listening to her.

"I also get that things are cramped for you," she said, plowing ahead with answering more of Logan's questions. "Right now we don't have enough space in the Habitation Module for you all to have private rooms. The more levels I get and things I unlock, the better that's going to get." Hopefully. There wasn't anything she could take right now, but the System kept insisting that it gave her the most beneficial options. It would come through for her.

"It's not just sleeping," Logan said. "We need better than two big rooms to live in. What about, you know, everything else in life? School for our kids. Weights to lift."

"Buddy, look at the size of you. If you get a few more levels to raise your body rating, we won't be able to fit the weights you need in here no matter what we do," Jill said, and a few people laughed. "But you need more than just a spot to eat and sleep, I get it. Here, all of you, take a look at this." A mental flick sent the box for one of her Habitation upgrades to the crowd.

> **Luxury Amenities (0/5):** Upgrade the comfort of the module with one of the following: Arcade, Bar, Basketball Court, Climbing Wall, Gym, Hootenanny Hall, Ice Rink, Movie Theater, Performance Hall, Shooting Range, Spa, Swimming Pool, Custom Option.

She paused to let people read. She could tell when people reached the middle of the list by the looks of confusion and mouthing of "Hootenanny."

"Sys—uh, the System's up to its usual shenanigans with some of those, but see that 'Custom Option' at the end? Bertha can get anything you want." Excited chatter broke out, even some smiles from the younger people in the audience. Jill let them go at it for a little while, then continued. "We'll put it up to a community vote as soon as we can." She turned to Sangita. "Can you organize that?" she asked, unamplified.

"Why not?" Sangita said. "I don't have anything else to do, don'tcha know."

"So, there you have it," Jill said. "Today's been rough, but things are getting better."

"I guess, uh, that's good," Logan said. He seemed unsure about what to say and settled on a mumbled, "Thanks, ma'am." He turned fast and moved back into the crowd.

The next man in line stomped up to the podium and started talking the instant he reached it, his voice echoing angrily through the hall. "Yeah, so, I'm Steve, or whatever, and all that sounded real good, but I don't buy it for a second. This stupid truck did fuck all to protect us from, what, roots? Some weak ass plant shit! So, when you said just now that we're as safe as we can be, were you lying to us or are you just stupid?"

CHAPTER 19

BARON-IN-TRAINING

"You going to answer me, honey?"

A spike of anger pierced Jill's mind and her fingers twitched a millimeter, the gesture she'd used to suck people into Bertha's walls coming to her nearly unbidden. "Honey?" Jill said, her voice a growl. "I'm not your imaginary girlfriend, so keep your nicknames for your body pillow. If you think Bertha can't help you, feel free to get out and walk. And you can fuck right off with that 'weak plant' bullshit. Want to tell me how many levels they had?"

"I don't have to. They were plants!"

Jill recalled the kill notification and did the math in a blink; an above-level factor of +.8 meant it was eight levels higher than her at the time of the kill, so ninety-two. Another instant and the magic calculator that was now her brain double-checked that the experience total matched that too. "They were level ninety-two, you ungrateful sack of bargain basement monster food."

"I don't care about levels. Coming here and getting attacked was stupid."

"Yeah, I can tell you don't care about levels, you glorified autocomplete. You're what, level ten? Less?" she asked rhetorically. Jill didn't usually check what level people were, but she poked an angry spike of golden mana into Steve, demanding that the System return his stats.

Steve Parker, Level 4 Keyboard Warrior

"Four? Seriously? I've got higher-level pieces of corn in my crap! You couldn't tell me their level because you've got no badger-fisting idea. And why is that? Because you didn't do shit to help kill them and didn't get a popup. I did, and so did a whole lot of brave people who were pulling their weight, unlike you."

"Is that the only defense you can manage? Insulting me?" Steve asked and crossed his arms. "Typical."

"No, I insult you because it's fun, you cuntless creep," Jill said. Angry mutters broke out in the crowd, and she belatedly realized that she had been trying not to swear. "Ah, fudge me. Sorry about that, everyone. Steve, get the heck off of that podium and let someone else talk."

"I have a right to have my question answered!"

"No," Jill said, "you have a right to have me not melt whatever it is that's inside your skull. Get off before I make you get off."

Steve opened his mouth to argue again, and Jill's temper flared. The podium under his feet rippled, sending Steve stumbling. Fear flashed across his face, and he leaped off of it, face red. He stalked away and the crowd pulled back from him as if even being too close to him might hurt them. Which, given Jill's state, wasn't too far from the truth. The fear and anger that she'd been trying so hard to reassure out of the crowd was back. It wasn't so much that they were on Steve's side, but they hadn't liked how she'd handled it either.

The next woman in line was one of the HOA group, brown-haired, and wearing a thick green sweater. She climbed up to the podium slowly, hesitation and nerves written on her face. Jill took the few seconds this offered and closed her eyes. She shoved her anger away; it wasn't useful right now. "Okay," she said a second later, "you're on."

"Hi," the woman said and swallowed. "My name's Jill Waters."

"Well, this is going to be confusing," Jill MacLeod muttered to herself. It still echoed out loud enough to hear.

"Uh, sorry?" Waters said. "Anyway, I guess I got pretty lucky compared to some people. I got out early enough that I haven't had to fight anything. Ms. MacLeod, I'm only level three, and I don't really want to ever fight anything. Does that mean I'm not pulling my weight? That I don't count?"

Jill winced. "You count," she said. "Everyone counts." She took a deep breath before continuing. "Sorry for saying that, everyone. That was me being a bit of a bitch. We need people to fight because the world's dangerous, but that's not all we need. We need doctors and nurses to take care of us. We need food—people to grow it, people to prepare it. We need equipment. We need daycare and classes for the kids. We need a hell of a lot more too; anything that a town has we need because that's what we are now. We might even need"—she gave a shiver—"bureaucrats."

There was a little laugh at that.

Waters relaxed a little. "Thank you, Ms. MacLeod," she said and relinquished the podium.

The next person up was a tall redheaded man sporting a scraggly two-day beard, who introduced himself as Sam Griffiths. "I'm not going to be a dick like Steve was," he said after telling a story of fleeing the city very similar to everyone else's, "but I kind of want to know what he asked at the end. Was it a bad idea to come here, even if we needed the food?"

"Yup," Jill said. "I got cocky. In hindsight, it was pretty dumb." This was met with silence and Jill pressed on. "But it was also pretty dumb for me to go back into Billings to get half of you too, wasn't it? I haven't gotten as far as I have by playing it safe, and sometimes that bites me. But sometimes it saves a heck of a lot of people. That's worth it in my mind, even if I have to put up with town meetings."

That sent the crowd muttering. Some, especially those who were in rougher shape, were nodding, while others still weren't convinced. Jill's last bit of honesty had gotten a few people chuckling, but Griffiths wasn't one of them.

"Was this worth it?" he asked. "In the end?"

Jill shrugged. "I don't know yet. We haven't reached the end. It depends on what's out there," she said and gestured broadly at the walls. "But with the System here, there's a saying that's truer than ever: what doesn't kill you makes you stronger. Think about it. I know most of you didn't get anything, but for some of us, this crapshow has given a truckload of experience. That means levels, which means we're all safer than we were."

"All that video game stuff," said Griffiths. "Does it really matter that much?"

Jill almost laughed at him but remembered her own disbelief at the System in those first few minutes before the brutal reality of magic and monsters had really sunk in. Griffiths hadn't been forced to accept that reality yet, even with all the evidence of it in front of him. Jill felt herself relax a bit. All that meant was that all the effort she'd gone through to protect people had, at least for one person, been enough to spare them some of what she'd experienced. Still, this kind of ignorance was dangerous, so if she could break that illusion for just a few people, it would be worth it.

"How about we show you?" Jill said. "Hey, Zeke," she called out to the gunner, "how many levels did you get in the last hour?"

"Uh," he said and blinked as the attention of the crowd landed on him, "seven, I think?"

Jill whistled. "Hot damn, not bad. How's your body rating?"

"Pretty good, I think? I get two per level, so I'm up to thirty-five."

"Great, then juggle these," she said and extruded a trio of spheres of steel from the floor of the stage. Each of them was seven inches across and had to weigh fifty pounds.

Zeke gulped; he wasn't exactly built. "I'll try, I guess." He squatted down and gripped a ball with both hands, set his feet and back, and lifted it up with an exhale. "Huh," he said, then stood with ease. He took one of his hands off the ball and tossed it up and down. He picked up the other two and tried to juggle them, but failed spectacularly, two of them crashing to the floor with a smashing clang and the last bouncing off his shoulder. It didn't do any harm.

"Okay, we've learned that Zeke can't juggle," Jill said. "But you saw how he could just chuck those metal balls around? That's the smallest bit of what levels can get us. If a monster that could tear through a hundred pre-System soldiers got in here, dollars to Dunkin' Zeke here could punch its face in. And no offense to you, Zeke"—she gave him a wry smile—"but you've got a long way to go until you catch up to some of the strongest of us."

Zeke didn't seem to mind; he stared back and forth between his hands and the metal spheres in mild shock.

"So, how do we get levels?" Griffiths asked. "I'm not a fighter. My class is Apprentice Farmer."

"You get XP for doing things," Jill said. "For you, probably by growing food."

"What if people don't know what they should be doing?" he asked. "Or if they don't want to do their class thing anymore?" There were nods from behind him in the crowd.

"Just try stuff," Jill said. "I'm sure something will work." From the expression on Griffiths's face that didn't seem to be a very good answer, so Jill kept talking. "Go see what others are doing and join them, especially if they seem like they need help. If something gives XP and you like it, keep doing it." She paused for a moment, then snapped her fingers. "People who've already figured their shoot out, do me a favor and recruit, will you? That will help." She gave a huff of a laugh. "I guess I'm first. Raise your hand out there if you have some sort of class power that can repair things."

Dozens of hands went up, some reluctantly.

"Keep them up if you think that those powers can repair Bertha. Read the box over again if you need to."

Over the next few seconds a few hands went down, and some wobbled to indicate that they weren't sure, but others stayed solidly in the air.

"Then all of you are officially invited to be part of the 'Bertha's getting fucked, let's help' squad. If you want in, then talk with me after. Now, how about drivers? Anyone handled a big rig before?"

More hands up, some the same.

"Bertha can drive 24/7," Jill said, "but I can't. Again, talk to me. Trust me, driving brings in the levels."

"Are we going to get paid for this?" one of the men with his hand up for truck driving shouted. "Like, sure, I'm all for helping out, and the levels are cool and all, but eventually we've got to use money, right? Or is this one of those communism situations?" The crowd didn't seem to like that.

"Communism had money, you government cheese lover," Sangita muttered under her breath beside Jill, seemingly unable to help herself.

Jill made a "wait a moment" gesture to the crowd and leaned into Sangita. She made sure she wasn't amplified before speaking softly. "You know about this? I'm good with money for me and Bertha, but I don't know dick about what an entire town needs."

"I studied economics," Sangita said. "We need a medium of exchange, even if basic services are provided by the community. It can't be backed by something physical; the System could probably just make whatever it is and devalue it in an instant."

"Wait," Jill said. "I've got something for this." She sent over the box for one of the class powers she hadn't taken yet. It was from the mostly neglected business aspect of her class.

> **Company Scrip:** You can create a System Currency for your business and can convert any other System Currency you have earned to your own without conversion fees. Transactions converting your Currency to others or vice versa give 12% of their value to you.

The tax made her feel dirty. It seemed like everything in the System that had to do with business was designed to screw someone over.

"Of course you do," Sangita said. "Either you take it or someone else will do similarly. It would be better if it were you."

Jill put her resolution against procrastination into practice and took the power. A feeling of warm greed washed over her, and the sight of the crowd made her grin. Each one of those sentients was another little machine making more value for her.

"Ugh," she said and shook herself. "Well, I have it."

"That asshole 'mayor' must have taken something similar to make Billibucks," Sangita said.

"This or something like it," Jill said. "That was such a dumb name."

"I don't know," Sangita said. "Jillibucks has a certain ring to it."

Currency name set to Jillibucks.

"Sys," Jill said. "Really? 'Cause no fucking way."

System Inquiry Detected Dissatisfaction detected. Checking cultural database. Change Currency name to Jillstonks?

"What the fuck is that?"

"Just make it Berthabucks," Sangita said. "It matches your ridiculous settlement name."

Currency name set to Berthabucks.

"Why are you listening to her about this and not me?" Jill asked. She threw up her hands. "Fine, Berthabucks it is." She wasn't going to tell anyone, but she liked the name. It gave credit where credit was due.

System Currency initialized. Current exchange rate: 1 Berthabuck = 1 Experience Point

A box for a new power appeared before her.

> **Company Town:** System Currencies other than your own cannot be accessed within the borders of a Settlement you own, except to convert them to your Currency.
> Requirements: Be the controller of a Settlement and be the creator of a System Currency.

Jill read it with distaste and dismissed it without sharing.

While they had been figuring this out, the crowd had started making more noise. But to Jill's relief, it wasn't the angry sounds of people about to do something really stupid. Instead, she could hear the snippets of people talking about what they had been in the world before and what they could do now. Her attention focused on an old man in the middle of the crowd with a bright smile on his face. He was gleefully telling the person next to him that this time he was going to make it as a radio actor. Considering that they had audio broadcasting but no video, it wasn't even a bad idea.

Jill cleared her throat and played Bertha's horn noise. "Okay, quiet down again," she projected. "We've got an answer for you. Yes, you'll be paid for the work you do for the community. It won't be in dollars because, well, there's no telling if those are worth more than extra-tough toilet paper right now. I've got a System-backed currency. I'm not sure how much wages will be, but we'll work it out. Let's get the next—"

At that moment a muted, chattering tear sounded in the hall, the sound of the machine guns firing vibrating through Bertha's metal structure despite the closed doors, distance, and dimensional barriers between where they stood and the outside world. A half dozen kill notifications clamored for Jill's attention, but she dismissed them without reading. Connie, Zeke, and the other gunners who had followed in Jill's wake tensed for a moment, but relaxed when the firing cut off and didn't resume. The crowd before her didn't, though. They shuffled and exchanged nervous glances, their optimism from before replaced by worry.

In a sudden moment of clarity, Jill felt why. The vast, vast majority of them had no idea what the inside of the turrets even looked like. The crowd didn't know that when the guns stopped firing so soon after starting, that meant whatever had attacked was no threat. For all they knew, something had gotten past the guns and was trying to break in to kill them.

"It's all good people," Jill said in her best relaxed voice. Then she took the kill notifications that she'd dismissed without a thought and sent them to the crowd. "That attack was just a few minor things being dumb enough to feed us their experience. Eleven monsters, the highest only level six. Not enough to even scratch the paint."

"Sys," Jill thought as those before her read and the faster amongst them relaxed, "could you give everyone here an update on the Lair progress?"

System Inquiry Detected Affirmative.

Which was immediately followed by:

Lair of the Sunflower Queen Invasion progress: 68%

"See?" she projected. "The, uh, special forces team is cutting their way through the Lair. We're okay, people. Now, next person, c'mon up."

Jill spent the next forty-five minutes answering more questions. Some were just repeats and she sent those people away. Others wanted to know specifics about Bertha, which she was only too happy to answer. Jacob got up to the podium at one point and asked if he could announce the elections that he and Jill had gone over. She let him, and that spawned its own set of questions about what their governmental structure was going to be. She let Sangita answer most of those; she didn't need to micromanage every little thing. But she kept an ear out, just in case Sangita tried to promise anything crazy, like her not being the final authority over Bertha.

As more minutes ticked by, the atmosphere in the hall lowered even further as energy waned. The children in the audience especially just didn't care about voting procedures and logistics, and before long, families were heading out. Things were getting boring, which was a nice change.

The calm couldn't last.

Lair of the Sunflower Queen
Invasion progress: 81%
Warning! The Lair's Ruler has been engaged by invaders! The Lair has entered a Frenzy! All sapients, prepare for assault.
Remaining monsters: 131

Gasps rang out. "No one panic!" panicked a man as a tremor of movement rippled through the crowd. The buzz saw rattle of the guns sounded again in a longer series of bursts than before; it didn't make things better. "What do we do?!" screamed someone.

Jill clapped her hands together with a deafening crack, silencing them. "The town hall's over because shit's about to go down," she said, "but we've got this. People who can fight, grab your weapons and get in the Cargo Nexus in case of breaches. If you're not a fighter, stay up here or in the Habitation Module and"—she hesitated for a half second as she stopped herself from saying they should just stay out of the way—"and take care of yourself. Get food ready, make sure none of the kids sneak off, be ready to run messages, that kind of thing."

Jill hopped off the stage and strode towards the exit. "Everyone who thought they could repair Bertha, we're about to test that. Follow me."

CHAPTER 20

NO SIDE EFFECTS AT ALL

What the hell did you do to my beautiful truck?" Jill asked Aman as she stared at the floating hologram above his dashboard.

"Don't you always know what's going on with it?" he asked. "I finished forty minutes ago."

Jill sputtered. "Look, I was busy! I don't see you staring at the back of your hand right now!" Instead, he was looking out the windows, alert for any monsters that appeared out of the maze of palette racks.

"And," Aman continued, "you can change it back anytime you want."

"It's the principle of the thing. Right now, it looks like a shitty sex toy!" Jill said. "Or some sort of spiky death Roomba!"

Her truck was no longer truck-shaped but had instead been molded into a hemisphere with its flat side just above the ground. The turrets sat on towers that stuck out above the rounded surface of the armor so that they had clear fields of fire in almost every direction, and the wheels of the Propulsion Module were tucked underneath in neat rows. The cab was on the top of the hemisphere, and the front and side windows were merged into a circular arc that traversed 270 degrees. A smaller, new window next to the rear door even let someone see behind them, just as long as they didn't think too hard about the internal geometry that was crying in the corner to let them do so.

"Ooh, spiky death Roomba, that would make a great band name," said a woman behind Jill. "Besides, is the old boxy look really so great?" She had introduced herself as Katie Fischer, and she was one of the volunteers with a repair power that might work on Bertha. In total, eighteen people had decided to try to help; they'd followed Jill like engineering ducklings to the cab. Now, half of them were crammed into it behind her while the other half spilled out into the hallway, standing on tiptoe to see what was going on. There was space enough for all of them if they squeezed, but they seemed nervous about getting too close to Jill. All except Katie, who had been chatting with the older woman nonstop, asking question after question about what Jill's first few days had been like and how Bertha worked. For her part, Jill wanted to know who Katie had gotten to make her outfit, which was an enchanted piece of armor that looked like a death knight that had gone through a goth phase but still somehow had taste.

"Oh, can it, you," Jill said and crossed her arms in frustration. "Sweet shoulder spikes will only get you so far."

"Another wave incoming," said seven voices at once. Karen had a connection open to the B team in the turrets, though Jill thought it was a bit redundant to have all of them included. The synchronicity from Hive Mind was freaky to listen to. They'd killed all of the first set of monsters from the Frenzy before Jill had reached the cab, with minimal damage to Bertha despite a few closing into melee range. For all that she absolutely hated how her truck looked, Jill had to admit that the polished-smooth surface gave no weak points for monster claws or teeth to find purchase on.

"Weapons free," Aman replied in a formal voice. Jill had taken overall command once she was back in the cab but had told him to keep coordinating the gunners. His orders that they only fire when he told them they were clear slowed their response down a bit, but it was a lot safer than her usual methods of yelling at them to be careful after they'd already unloaded a few hundred rounds.

They fired just as soon as the plant monsters poked their leafy heads out of the already dubious cover of the racks. Before Jill had taken Hive Mind, the bursts from individual gunners had all blended together into a buzz saw scream of death with no particular rhythm to it. Now there was a distinct tempo to the sound. Three guns at a time would fire in a single burst at one target, blanketing it in a hail of rounds so that even supernatural monster reflexes wouldn't allow them to dodge, followed a split second later by the other three doing the same to another creature.

Not that these monsters were strong enough to be dodging at these ranges, anyway.

> Scorned Rosebush (x7) defeated.
> Your contribution: 17%
> 2499 Experience Gained!

Jill did the math: an average level of twenty-one.

"Is that it?" Jill asked. "I said shit was going down over this?"

"Does she always tempt fate like that?" asked Mathew Harper. He was another volunteer: not one that could repair Bertha, but one who could cast spells on the gunners to help them shoot. He and three of his friends had all taken variants of the Bard class.

"Fate's what we make it, guitar-boy," she said.

"I'm thirty-seven!" he cried and clutched his battered acoustic to his chest.

"Just get in the gunner prep room on your left there," Jill said, "and do your thing. That goes for your friends too; get in there and work out which of your spells combine and which don't." Under her breath, Jill muttered, "What do we call people doing that again?"

"Buffers?" Aman suggested.

"That doesn't sound right," Jill said. "Too much like fluffers."

The noise of machine guns continued, joined a moment later by the stereotypical strains of "Freebird" drifting through the open doors. The fire rate from the turrets picked up, the bullets flew just a bit faster, and the monsters exploded into chunks of wood just that little bit sooner, though it was hard to even tell. The kills rolled in, one after another. Then, the guns stopped.

There was a long period of stillness—twenty, thirty seconds. Then movement caught Jill's eye. She leaned forward, nearly pressing her forehead against the windshield to get a better view. A mass of monsters had gathered. "They're charging!" she said. "From, uh, two o'clock."

"We/I see them," the gunners replied, the first word a blending of sound and meaning that was partially English, partially mana.

"Be on the lookout for a boss monster," Jill said.

The three dozen incoming monsters were a mixture of stomping humanoid trees, crawling vines, and flowers dancing on their roots, all hurling themselves together at Bertha in the hope that a few would make it. Jill felt the guns turn to track them, but none fired. "You going to handle that?" she asked, tone sharp.

Just as she finished speaking, Dan's dual flamethrower erupted. The Soulbound weapon had every bit the potential of Mia's chain gun, concentrated into a close-range cone of burning death, and was boosted up to a massive effective level of ninety-six by Bertha's Adaptive Mounts power. It was held back only by Dan's own abilities: with fewer levels and active powers to boost it, he couldn't match the raw numbers and special effects that Mia could pull off.

But that didn't matter against the swarm approaching them. Box after box popped up in Jill's vision, the highest only clocking in at a harmless level twenty-six. She kicked herself at that thought; that kind of monster was harmless to her and only dangerous to Bertha in extreme numbers but would massacre the vast majority of those in the truck's soft insides. She should take them seriously and so should those in the turrets.

"We/I wanted to give your repair crew practice," the gunner hive said, "but I/we kick too much ass, hooah!" The hive laughed in a discordant cackle.

"Okay, *that* is weird," Katie said.

"Cute," Jill said to the hive, "but that's the kind of thing you ask about before doing, got it?"

"Fine. I/we understand, buzzkill," they said.

"Gunners, report the status of hostiles," Aman said in a stern tone.

"All hostiles dead," they replied.

"So," said another volunteer, one who hadn't given her name yet. "Should we just stand out here, or . . . ?"

"Get in here and sit down," Jill said. She extruded a dozen stools around the walls to join the far more comfortable System-made observer chairs. "So far, so easy, but if we get damaged, we test each one of you in turn to see which of you have powers that work. Got it?"

"Got it!"

"Right," Jill continued, "gunners—"

"Our name is Beezilla," they interrupted and moments later burst into snorts of intertwined laughter.

"Shut it!" she snapped. "Stay serious until we're done with this Lair. I'm convinced there's something dangerous out there. That charge was too coordinated."

"Understood," they said.

Jill tapped her fingers on her leg.

Lair of the Sunflower Queen
Invasion progress: 90%

"This is almost done," Jill said. "It's now or never."

"Jill MacLeod/Leader/Buzzkill," the hive addressed her with its headache-inducing blend of meanings, "someone has arrived with some more prototype flamethrowers. May Gustave and Anna install them?"

"Go for it," Jill said.

"Woohoo!" said Anna.

"Indeed," Gustave agreed.

"You can talk individually still?" Jill asked. "What's with the weird hive voice, then?"

"That's I/we," said the hive, "not me." The last two words were still said in unison but lacked the cohesion of the hive.

"I need more fucking coffee for this," Jill grumbled. "I swear—"

"Contact!" Aman said. He was looking in the opposite direction of Jill. "Something big's coming!"

"Time to see how this fortress does," Jill said.

She turned to look just in time to see a pallet rack ripped away, gripped in the tendrils of a massive arm. The monster was a humanoid collection of granite stone boulders, twenty-five feet tall, with glowing green eyes. It took a ponderous step towards them and for just an instant the movement opened gaps between the rocks, letting her see inside. Pulsing, luminescent green vines lay there, but with a surge of sickly light they pulled the rocks back over themselves, blocking the view again.

Juvenile Ivy Stonewielder
Level 68
Status: Guardian, Favored Daughter, Mindless

"Weapons free," Aman said.

"Don't hold back," Jill added as the first bursts thudded out and the tempo changed from a staccato cadence to one long, drawn-out roar. Bertha's mana reserves plummeted as the truck generated a hail of bullets from nothing, the glowing beams of tracer fire and flashing sparks of hot metal hitting rock and lighting up the dim warehouse Lair. Chips of stone exploded off the monster. Three turrets walked their fire in a perfectly coordinated cross sweep towards its eyes, closing in on their target from three directions, but to no avail: it had already lowered its head in a charge, and it took the fire on an extra-large boulder that served as its helmet.

It took only seconds for it to cross the gap, but in those seconds the gunners switched their target to the gaps in its joints. They opened and closed fast enough that, even with all of the bonuses the gunners had, they couldn't reliably hit them. But seldom wasn't never; the Ivy Stonewielder stumbled as one golden round slipped through and a burst of green gore sprayed out of the joint for a split second before it closed again.

"The insides are weak," Jill said. "Anyone have . . ." She trailed off as it reached them and reared back to strike. The ivy raised its arms above its head and twined its hands together, preparing for a blow that would put Kirk to shame. "Hold on to something!" Jill barked.

The blow, with the full force of the monster's contracting body behind it, slammed down onto Bertha right on top of the dome that was the cab. The sound of the impact, a crashing thud accompanied by the screech of bending metal, battered Jill's ears. She winced not at that, but at a spike of pain erupting in her head: the feedback through her Soulbond from damage. Bertha rocked on its concealed suspension and screeched back five feet despite its immense bulk. But Jill needn't have given her warning to brace because none of the people around her so much as stumbled. To them, the attack was more like the rumble from a downstairs neighbor turning on their washing machine than the attack of a gigantic rock monster.

A quick check showed that Bertha had lost 8 percent of its armor. The monster's follow-up punches were much less effective, but the armor still ticked steadily downwards as cracks and dents marred the dome's finish.

"Repairs!" Jill barked. "Katie, you're up!" She realized that while the cab had a mana gauge that could keep track of how much longer the turrets could fire, there was nothing to give the repair crew feedback. She pushed Customization to make another pair of gauges, one for Bertha's armor and one for its durability, but the power balked. It tugged on that part of her connected to the Command Module, urging her to put another rank into Capacity and make an entirely new control station for this. Jill scowled and pushed harder. This wasn't worth a class point.

"I think it's working!" Katie yelled over the sound of the guns. She sounded delighted.

A yellow and a red meter, for armor and hull, respectively, ground their way out of the front dashboard. Katie was right. The armor was steadily climbing, despite the Ivy Stonewielder's continued punches.

"Great, now switch out!" Jill said.

The lighting in the cab flared as flames washed over the monster, then dimmed as it flung its whole bulk over the windows in another of its two-handed blows. The armored glass creaked, and a single crack raced across its surface, but it held firm. Again, the monster reared back, and bits of stone rained down from it as the bullets kept chipping away. The boulders were noticeably worn down now; they had to be near their breaking point. Bertha was doing fine. All but one of the six people who'd tried had been able to repair Bertha, and by using their powers in sequence they could heal Bertha faster than Jill could with her cooldown.

They were winning the fight—easily, even if it was taking a while. The monster might have an unusually strong defense, so it could soak up a lot of bullets, but it just lacked the levels for its offense to be a true threat.

The song echoing in from the gunner's room changed from "Freebird" to "Thunderstruck," acoustic to metal, and the guns stopped firing. Jill opened her mouth to yell at the gunner but thought better of it. They must have some sort of plan. Their earlier antics were one thing, but they wouldn't mess around against this thing.

She was right. A hum sounded and Bertha's mana dipped, enough for one thousand rounds, sucked in an instant into the Turret Module. Crackles of lightning connected the guns together and a single shot exploded outwards. It shattered the boulder it hit and blew a watermelon-sized ragged hole through the monster. The resulting explosion of glowing goo coated half the windows. That by itself wouldn't have stopped the Ivy Stonewielder, though; even as the broken rock fell away, another was sliding into place to fill the gap. But flames followed the charged shot in less than a second, and magic fire swept into the hole.

A horrid shriek filled the air, vibrating everything, as the monster's insides caught fire, a chain reaction that set it flailing in panic. Jets of fire and steam exploded from between the boulders; with each crack, a high-pressure whistle announced that its shift on this Earth was over. The Ivy Stonewielder raised its arms to do one last futile smash, but first one, then the other crumbled in a whooshing, rattling fireball of stone and burning plant. The smoke cleared to reveal an unmoving pile of red-hot rubble, coated in ash.

Juvenile Ivy Stonewielder defeated.
Your contribution: 19%
1292 Experience Gained!
You are now Level 85! Level gain deferred per user preferences.

"Fuck yeah!" Jill shouted. "Now, that's how it's done!"

CHAPTER 21

WE'RE GONNA NEED A MONTAGE

The notice came less than a minute after killing the Ivy Stonewielder.

> Heliophilic Helianthus defeated.
> Bonus Experience awarded for: monster kill above your Level (+.7)
> Your contribution: 24%
> 3753 Experience Gained!
>
> Lair of the Sunflower Queen
> Invasion progress: 100%
> Congratulations System users! You have reclaimed this Settlement from the monsters! Bonus Experience awarded for: timely reclamation (x2); contribution-weighted Level: +3.2; weighted Corruption: -.1
> Your contribution: 13%
> 213,200 Experience Gained!
> You are now Level 87! Level gain deferred per user preferences.

"Fuck yeah again!" Jill yelled as she read, but instead of excited cheering her exclamation was met only by gasps of pleasure. It seemed that everyone in the cab had leveled at least once—given the amount of experience that seemed to be involved, maybe even five or an unthinkable ten times. Thumps and the sound of sliding cloth on metal rang out as those standing either fell over or stumbled into the walls and slid down them.

A minute passed, then another. Jill tapped her fingers on her leg. The leveling was taking a long time, and even she was starting to get a bit weirded out listening to everyone.

"This is like being the caterer at a Friday night orgy," she said and shook her head. "I've got to get everyone deferring their level gain. At least until they're in private, for fuck's sake."

Ten minutes after those who'd leveled had peeled themselves from the floor, bound by mutual tacit agreement to never speak of what had just happened, Jill stood in the Cargo Nexus by the doors, waiting for the away team to return. She wasn't alone. Everyone had seen the notification that the Lair had been defeated and an excited energy buzzed through Bertha. A crowd even bigger than what had attended the town meeting gathered, all to wait for the victorious heroes. There was a bit of a game ongoing among the more adventurous to get the best view of the doors, and while some had taken to climbing the storage shelves, the clear winner was a man standing upside down on the ceiling.

Mia was the first to hop in, and her appearance was greeted by spontaneous cheers. Her Armored Suit was scuffed, singed, and dirty, showing obvious signs of heavy combat. The only reason part of it was still gleaming was because it was raw, unfinished metal: a deep spiraling gouge that ran up the plating of her right leg, the parting gift of a root's buzz saw attack. She froze in place upon seeing the cheering crowd, her helmet tucked under her arm and her sweat-covered face bright red.

Ras and Babu joined her a few seconds later, the former limping and leaning on his younger brother for support, parts of his armor missing entirely. Ras's mouth fell open a fraction, and he also froze, but Babu surged with energy. Of the three of them, he was the least visibly injured, but there was a shadow to his mana that, to Jill, spoke of deep weariness. Babu grinned and thrust his free hand up in triumph. In it, he held a small potted sunflower, barely a foot tall, which he presented as if it were a championship trophy. It very well might have been, for it pulsed with power.

Jill grinned and cheered along with the crowd. Sangita, followed by Aman, shouldered her way through the press and launched herself at her sons, scooping them both up in a hug.

The sound of heavy machine-gun fire cut through the celebration, popping the mood faster than a terrible two-year-old with a balloon.

"What the shit was that?" Jill projected to the cab and turrets. "I thought the monsters were all dead?"

> Warning! Settlement boundary Mana running low. Boundary integrity at 70%. As integrity falls, more exterior monsters will be able to force their way in. To refill the boundary Mana, new residents must reconstitute the Core.

"Now you tell me," Jill muttered. She activated Captain Speaking again, blasting out Bertha's original horn to the whole truck. "Hey, everyone, listen up! We're going to have to clean up the low-level trash that's outside, so get back to your defensive positions. Then we can finally loot this place to the ground. Time for us to collect some more levels!"

To her shock, the people around her didn't panic or look angry or even shoot her dirty looks. Instead, there was another spontaneous cheer, though this one was more contained than the one that had greeted Mia, Ras, and Babu. Most of the crowd began moving back towards the living areas and Jill joined them, moving with the press back through the Nexus and into the cafeteria. It was truly amazing what a little optimism and an easy fight did for morale.

The fighting was anticlimactic. The initial wave of monsters that had been trapped outside the Lair boundary forced their way in as a huge mass, but without the searing beam of sunflower death to back them up, they just weren't tough enough to be a threat. They broke on Fortress Bertha like water on rock. Katie and two others of the repair crew were in the cab with Jill and Karen, but they had little to do; the machine guns and now multiple flamethrowers reaped a harvest of XP with few of the monsters able to do any damage in return. It was all over in ten minutes, the wave turning into a trickle, then dying out completely.

The three heroes arrived in the cab fifteen minutes after the last monster attacked, trailed by a conga line of new fans. Babu turned at the hatch to keep talking with one of them, but Mia reached past him and closed the door slowly but firmly in the fan's face. Karen got up and gave all three of them hugs, though Jill noticed that the threads of mana from Karen to the communications console never ceased their flickers.

"Welcome back," Jill said, a new cup of coffee in her hands, "and good job. I'd offer you coffee, but you'd have to go back out there to get it."

"Nope," Mia said. She slumped into a chair next to Jill and leaned her head back to stare at the ceiling.

"Jill," Ras said, "it's the afternoon. I want to sleep tonight."

"Pfft. Amateur. So," Jill said and turned to Babu, who still held the tiny sunflower's pot cradled in one arm, "how'd the fight go?"

"There were some close scrapes," Mia said, "and like half of the Lair was a giant maze"—she pulled a face—"but we kicked everything's ass in the end."

"Anything in there worth stealing?" Jill asked. "Now that this little mini wave of outside critters is dead, we've got a bunch of folks going out to loot the warehouse, and all of the monsters that we killed too. But I want to get going from here yesterday, so if there's a maze, I might tell them to just leave it."

"Once out of the warehouse and in the Lair itself there's nothing worth taking," Ras said. "There was a lot of stuff strewn around, but it was all . . . weird."

"Like something drawn by a bad AI image generator," Mia said. "Cans of beans with teapot spouts, tools that were merged with the shelves instead of being on top of them, furniture made of compressed dirt, things like that."

"I think that when the Lair expanded space it tried to fill in the gaps with things that were similar to what was in the original building," Babu said, "but it just didn't do a good job."

"You get drunk or something, Sys?" Jill asked.

> System Inquiry Detected
> Lair object instantiation is not a System function.

"It's not?" Babu exclaimed. "What made it all, then?"

> System Inquiry Detected
> Information denied. Classified access request has been logged.

They sat in silence digesting that for a few seconds.

"Welp, that's a thing," Jill said. "Hey," she said, changing the subject, "what's with the flower?" The yellow plant danced and waved, occasionally humming an alien tune with a voice like the chiming of golden bells.

"It's the loot from the Lair!" Babu said. "The core crystal just kind of went *zoop*"—he brought his hands together—"then *bang*"—he moved his hands apart—"it shattered! But this little friendo was left behind."

"I think it's the big sunflower's loot," Ras said. He leaned against the wall and crossed his arms. He'd needed the attention of the doctors to remove a few status conditions but was now right as rain. "It was in its crisped-up leaves, after all, just sitting there."

"But we didn't have to do the usual stuff to get it!" Babu argued back. "No System window, just *poof, bang*, there it was. And really, if the sunflower was the Lair's owner, is there really a difference between the two?"

"Yes."

"Yes? Just, yes? That's all you've got?"

Jill sighed and exchanged a look with Mia, who shook her head. "They worked perfectly together out there," she said in a low tone to Jill.

"Figures," Jill said. "This is their recreation." She put her coffee down on the dash and clapped her hands together with a crack. "Hey! On topic. What's this super loot do besides look pretty?"

"Here," Babu said, and his mana brushed Jill's, bringing with it a notification.

Smiling Sunflower
Level 1, Legendary
Type: Progenitor Guardian
This friendly, happy sunflower absorbs ambient Mana and will act to defend non-Corrupt sapients. As a Progenitor, it is capable of asexual reproduction. All children are sterile unless this original specimen is destroyed, in which case a random child becomes the new Progenitor.

"Huh," she said. "So, what, it's a tame monster?"

"It's an entire species of tame monsters that only eat mana!" Babu said. "Where has the most mana for this to grow on?"

"Where do you think? My 'Inner Sanctum,'" Jill said with air quotes added to the last words. Mia started laughing.

"We could put it somewhere else?" Babu asked.

"No, no," Jill said. "A little decoration will be nice, help things move along. I've never been a shy shitter. I just hope I don't traumatize the little lady." The flower kept waving and chiming, not seeming to have heard or understood the conversation around it.

"You could always keep it in there most of the time and move it when you, um . . ." Ras trailed off and coughed.

"When I'm fighting for rulership of the porcelain throne?"

Ras looked away and the tips of his ears reddened. "Where are Mom and Dad?" he asked. "I thought they'd be in here."

"They're in the cargo bay organizing the scavengers with Coach," Karen said. "Oh! Sangita's going to be going out as part of her crew that writes everything down and Aman's going along to protect her! That's so cute!"

"There are going to be actual guards too, right?" Jill asked.

"Yup! Coach is organizing the CK's into teams," Karen said. "Oop! One of the gunners is complaining about it, and he's getting yelled at about the importance of physical fitness and getting outside. Classic Coach."

"You're listening in right now?" Mia asked.

"I think she's always listening in to everything," Jill said. Mia and Babu exchanged a fast, worried glance, which Jill pretended not to have seen.

"But we can feel when someone does that," Mia said, "right?"

"You can feel when Jill does that," Karen said. "I've got a"—she paused for a split second—"a lighter touch."

"Oh, fudge sauce," Ras said.

"Wait," Babu said, "you're worried? You?"

"Should I not be?"

"You never do anything worth spying on. Trust me, I know, don'tcha know."

"You—"

Jill sighed, tuned them out, and scooped up the flower. "Karen, Mia," she said, "hold down the fort, will you? Coffee did what coffee does, so it's time to take this lucky girl"—she gave the flowerpot a little pat—"to her new home."

Jill shielded her eyes with one hand against the glaring sunlight and scanned the parking lot around them, on the lookout for more monsters.

"As much as my Scottish skin just loves sunburns," she said, "are you going to finally tell me why we're out here?" When she'd gotten back to the cab, sans flower, Babu had been waiting for her. He'd dragged her outside, insistent that it was time to enact "The Plan."

Her gaze snapped to a subtle movement around a hundred feet away: a vine slithering along the ground. While all the monsters the boss sunflower had gathered were dead, small monsters from the surrounding fields had started to show up. Bertha's guns weren't shooting, though; far too many people were out and about collecting things for that to be safe. The fighters amongst the scavengers were more than a match for everything that had shown up so far, and both Ras and Babu were outside to serve as backup in case something big came. Mia had claimed her usual turret up front just in case they needed heavy firepower, but Jill suspected she was just taking a nap.

"You're too squishy for your level," Babu said, "and it's a strategic vulnerability. But," he said, raising a dramatic hand and the golf tour bag slung over his shoulder slipped. He caught it before it hit the ground and hefted it back on. "But," he repeated, "your points are too valuable for us to just start spending them on your cruddy defensive class powers."

"You calling Battle Trucker crummy?" Jill asked.

Babu shook his head. "No, it gives great stats!" he said. "And all the truck and business stuff too. But it's a hybrid class, and my research is showing that those pay for their versatility by having class powers normally associated with less rare classes. Your combat abilities are close to Ras's Swordsman class, despite his being common to your uncommon."

"He's got some good shit," Jill said.

"Thank you," Ras said from nearby. His hands were in his pockets and his face turned up to catch the sun as he walked past on his patrol.

Babu nodded. "Yeah, he does, but it took him a lot of points to get to the best ones. From what Buckman and I have found so far, the combat classes give a big toolkit before they specialize and start giving things with lots of raw numbers."

"So, Ras has nineteen ways to shove his sword up a monster's ass?" Jill asked.

"Eh," Babu said and wobbled a hand, "more like five ways for that, three ways to escape from a bad situation, four ways to do an alternate damage type, three ways to boost his defenses, something to do damage at range, something to control the terrain—"

"Babu," Jill said. "Focus."

He coughed. "Right, you get the idea. That all works great for him, and it stops some random monster being a hard counter. For you, it's utter crap because you don't have the points for breadth, even on top of the lower rarity."

Jill tapped her fingers on her leg. "Real motivating," she said. "So, what's the plan?"

Babu held up a finger. "Specialization! In particular, we're going to make you the most one-note, boring, infuriatingly cheap, and outrageously effective build that millions of Skyrim play hours have ever devised!" He looked at her expectantly.

"Babu," she said, "I don't play video games."

"Oh, right," he said, sounding a bit disappointed. "Stealth archer. Well, shooter. Maybe stabber? It depends on what you unlock. But we're going to get you at least one power each for stealth, sneak attacks, defense, and escape, and as front-loaded and rare as we can, though I'm suspicious that we haven't really cataloged many of the rare ones compared to what the System really has to offer!"

Jill frowned. "That's a lot. Is this going to delay us leaving? I'm only giving us a few hours here for supplies and then it's time to move."

"Well, you've got to kill a bunch of monsters, but"—he shrugged—"there's like fifty of them right over there." He gestured in the direction where Jill had seen just the vine.

Everything Babu said made sense, but he had an underlying, mischievous glee to his demeanor that pinged Jill's suspicions. "This is going to be like that communication power where people had to climb a building and shout, isn't it?" she asked. "Am I going to have to do some completely ridiculous bullshit?"

"No?" Babu said.

Jill sighed. She wouldn't care except that there were over a hundred members of Berthaville out in the parking lot in small groups of gatherers or guards, and they would all be able to see exactly what she was doing. Many more were in the warehouse and could be summoned to watch if she were up to something truly crazy. On the other hand, a little dignity was a small price to pay for getting stronger and better able to keep those same people safe.

She took a deep breath and let it out. "Let's do it."

"Muahahaha!" Babu laughed in his best impression of an evil movie villain. He reached into the caddy bag and pulled out a gleaming arming sword, its hilt encrusted with a pulsing red gem.

Jill pinged it with her mana and it returned its status box.

Aeeeiiii, I Made a Flaming Sword Too!!! Wait, What Do You Mean Select Name—
Level 13, Uncommon
This sword, infused with the power of a Fire Bunny's wrath, is sharper and stronger than any mundane blade. It is the first creation of Alice Spencer.

She threw back her head and laughed. "Glad to see it's not just me you're fucking with, Sys."

Adaptive Algorithms have detected an increase in group user efficiency.

Jill took the sword and gave it a few inexpert swishes. It was much heavier than a sword its size should have been, heavy enough that pre-System Jill would have struggled to lift it, but Jill of today had superhuman strength, and despite that weight, it was superbly balanced. She drove it through the air with whistling ease, its passage leaving a red streak of burning mana behind it.

"Hell yes," Jill said. "This is so much better than what I thought you were going to spank me with! What's the plan with this bad girl?"

"We're going for an ability called Murder Stroke," Babu said. He reached into the bag and pulled out a pair of metal mesh butcher's gloves.

"Sounds badass," Jill said. "So, what, should I just go and slash that sucker up?" She gestured at the vine, which had slithered its way closer during their talk.

"Nope!" Babu said and handed her the gloves. "You've got to bash it to death with the cross guard, don'tcha know."

"Huh," Jill said. She handed the sword back to Babu, put on the gloves, and took it back, this time gripping it by the blade. She gave an experimental swing. It wasn't too bad, but the exquisite balance was ruined. "Well, time to pulp some plant." She turned her gaze to the vine, which despite not having eyes seemed to sense her attention and froze. "That's right, you thorny bondage toy," Jill said with a grin. "Time for a little revenge."

She charged at it with a yell, arms high in the air. The blow she landed cratered the pavement.

Aggravated Azalea defeated.
Your contribution: 95%
1045 Experience Gained!

"That's nine down," Jill said. She stabbed the Sword of System-Fuckery into the ground, put her hands on her lower back, and stretched. Her body wasn't actually stiff or sore, but she felt like it should be. They had moved farther away from the former Lair, out into the fields surrounding the warehouse, and there was now no shortage of monsters to kill. It had only been a few minutes.

"Just one more," Babu said. He made a note in a black faux-leather bound book—the kind of cheap journal sold in stationery stores for too much money—and tapped a pen to his lips. "Ten did it for other people, so"—he shrugged—"you're done with the sword either way!"

"Pity," Jill said. "I like this thing." She pulled the weapon out of the ground and flipped it in a now-practiced move to grip it by the blade. She strode forward, half looking around for another enemy to harvest and half making herself a tasty target for any monster stupid enough to throw itself at her.

"Ope!" Babu said and pointed. "There's one."

Jill followed his finger and saw movement; the tips of the tall grasses parted in a rippling furrow as something made its way through the stalks below, heading for her straight as an arrow. She tightened her grip on the sword, planted her feet, and got ready to swing. Whatever monster was coming, it had to be small for her to just see the grasses moving and not it, so she adjusted her stance to one more suitable for golf than baseball. She mentally counted down the last few seconds. "Fore!" she yelled and swung.

There was a shocked squeak like that of a dog toy being sat on and the crunching splat of a shattering blow to flesh, and a spinning, bloody, yellow-furred ball flew away, high into the distance.

Electric Mouse defeated.
Your contribution: 95%
570 Experience Gained!

"I almost feel bad for that one," Jill muttered.

Armored Warrior cross-class skill unlocked!
Murder Stroke: Charge a bludgeoning attack with Mana. Increases damage by 2 per Mana spent. Extra damage dealt to unaware or helpless opponents.
Mana Cost: Variable
Select skill? Requires 1 Class Point.

"Finally!" Jill said and sent the notification to Babu. "That's wicked awesome," she said. "I can pump this with as much mana as I want? Throw a shaved cat in my face, that's a lot." Because of her balance of stats, Jill had more mana than hit points, so she would easily be able to throw out attacks capable of crushing her. Once or twice, that is, before she ran out of juice.

"Yes and no," Babu said. "There are lots of damage reduction abilities, and dodging ones too. It's that extra damage that we're really after, though. We'll get you sneaky, or I'll paralyze something for a second and *bam!* You'll blast it away."

"Wicked," Jill said. Then she frowned. "Hey, last time I got one of these cross-class thingies I didn't have to invest a point. I just got it."

"Those were those two swearing-based spells of yours, right?" Babu asked. "I have a theory there."

"Shocker," Jill deadpanned.

"Normally," Babu said without acknowledging her interruption, "with class powers, the System is letting you invest a point to unlock a new way to use your magic. That's what's going on here; you haven't actually done a Murder Stroke yet, but if you take it, the System will guide your mana to let you do it on command."

Jill nodded along. She'd noticed the same thing.

"For your Malediction Bard powers, though, the spell it gave you was the System recognizing something you had already done successfully," Babu said. "And it's super annoying that you can do that kind of thing so easily. Making your own spells is like a cheat code for getting around the issue of breadth versus power! Instead of spending points on unlocking things, just unlock them manually by doing them, then invest the points into the System supercharging you. But no, I spend like three hours working on an enchantment and all that happens is I blow off my eyebrows!"

Jill raised one of her own in response and looked pointedly at Babu's perfectly manicured brows.

"I got better," Babu said in a funny voice.

"So, should I take this one?" Jill asked. "It looks wicked brutal, but after today I just want to dump all my points into making Bertha better."

"Not yet," Babu said. "It's possible we might get something better with a little more work." He took the sword back and slid it into the caddy bag. Out of it, he pulled a double-barreled shotgun. Etched onto each barrel was the glowing outline of a cartoon pony.

Jill shouldered it and checked its sight. "Ten more?"

"Blast away."

"Nothing?" Babu asked.

"Nothing," Jill confirmed. "Maybe because I already unlocked a shotgun-related class earlier?"

Babu shrugged. "Maybe," he said. "I still don't really understand why some things unlock for people but the same things don't work for others. It's a bit of a crapshoot."

Jill handed the shotgun back to Babu and grimaced at the state of her clothes. The last monster had managed to surprise her and get close. Worse, it had been chock full of sap and her shot had exploded it over the both of them. She tried to wipe the goo off of her face but just managed to spread it around. "Hey," Jill said. Babu was completely clean. "A little help?"

He waved a hand, there was a surge of dark mana, and the goo dissolved into motes of black light.

"Handy," Jill said. "What's next?"

Babu pulled out a recurve bow, jet black with lightning bolt engravings down the sides.

"Shit!" Jill yelled as her shot, just like the previous twenty, went wide of the mark. Her target leaped at her, its snarling maw leading the way, its eyes filled with hunger and hate. It found its target, its teeth sunk into flesh, and its red cheeks sparked with electricity, which coursed down its jaws and into Jill.

"Ow! Ow! Ow!" she yelled and dropped the bow, her hands snapping towards her face and the offending creature. Her right hand found it first; Jill grabbed it and squeezed. The monster offered all the resistance of a jelly-filled donut to her level eighty-seven strength. Bones crunched and its guts burst from the gaps between her fingers.

Electric Mouse defeated.
Your contribution: 95%
665 Experience Gained!

"Muh nose!" Jill snarled as she shook bits of monster off her hand.

Babu collapsed to the ground with laughter.

Jill's next arrow flew far into the distance; a second later, she felt a tiny prick through her Soulbond as it impacted Bertha's windshield.

"Wow, it is impressive how much you suck with that," Babu said, admiration in his voice.

"Yeah, yeah."

"Like, you have superhuman strength and dexterity, don'tcha know."

"Get it all out."

"And the draw isn't even much more than a normal bow!"

"You done yet?"

Babu looked to the sky and checked the position of the sun. They still had a few hours before Jill's deadline for their leaving came. "Think we'll have time for you to get ten kills?" he asked with extreme concern.

Jill sighed and looked for another target.

"Huh," Jill said.

"What's up?" asked Babu. "See something big to shoot?"

"No," she said. "Well, yes. Look."

A few hundred yards away rolled a four-foot-tall ball of dirt, propelled by a dozen arm-sized branches sticking out from its surface in seemingly random places. It was, by all appearances, chasing a group of scavengers across the parking lot, but the ball was moving so slowly that all they had to do was keep walking.

"That is the lamest monster I've seen yet," Jill said. "Like, seriously, I'm five minutes into the System and there are fire wolves and fear deer, and everything has all of the teeth, and what do they get? A dirt-stick-ball-thing that can barely move."

"At least we don't need to stop and help them," Babu said. "Want to shoot it anyway?"

"Nah, I'd probably hit them instead," Jill said and laughed.

* * *

Twang! went the bow.

"AAAIIIIIEEEEEE!" cried Babu, an arrow sticking out from his butt.

"Oh, ha-ha," Jill said in frustration. "Fuck off, you faker. You've got that body illusion spell thing going, I just know it."

Babu pulled out the arrow with a ripping squelch, giving another scream of pain as he did. He glared at her.

"Oh shit, really?"

"Next. Weapon," Babu growled.

"I feel like you're punishing me," Jill said as she bludgeoned yet another enemy to death with the stick she'd been given. It wasn't a very strong stick, so she had to be careful or she would break it. This was her seventh.

"We're going for a nature-themed scout power," Babu said. He narrowed his eyes at her. "You'll know when I'm punishing you."

Jill got back to work.

"That's a spoon," Jill said.

"A dull spoon," Babu agreed.

"Ugh."

"You're fucking with me," Jill said with a glare.

"Nope!" Babu said and gave her a brilliant grin.

Jill took the pool noodle. It wobbled. Menacingly.

"So," Jill said and took a bite out of a Berthapple. It was delicious. They were still out in the field but taking a short break. "We both agree, bows are out. I've killed a bunch of monsters with long guns and have the class options to prove it, but no super-duper sneak attack option. What's next for ranged weapons?"

Babu tapped his pen in his journal. "Well, we could try thrown weapons. Daggers or shurikens?"

A high-pitched shriek behind her made Jill spin around. A strange cross between a mushroom and a mini ostrich, only with far too many teeth, was emitting the noise as it charged at her. She whipped the Berthapple at the creature on instinct. It tore through the air faster than any baseball had ever been thrown, pre-System at least, and impacted with a sickening crack and an explosion of feathers.

"Or fruit," Babu said. "Fruit works. I think I've got a banana in here somewhere . . ."

Jill wriggled forward on her stomach through the grass, using her magic-enhanced body to its fullest to stay silent. A tiny movement made her freeze and hold her breath. There was a monster somewhere in front of her. Seconds turned to minutes and the air in her lungs began to feel stale. Then she saw it: an ant, two feet tall at the thorax, its carapace semi-transparent and gleaming like a diamond in the sunlight. It wandered to and fro, testing bits of grass and dirt with its mandibles as it slowly got closer to Jill's hiding spot. It was almost time. She tensed, getting ready for the kill.

There was a flash of light accompanied by a single snicker-snack sound, and the ant fell apart, separated neatly in two and very much dead.

"Goddamnit!" Jill yelled and jumped to her feet.

Ras stood twenty feet away, the look of satisfaction on his face turning to confusion. "Is there a problem?" he asked. "There was a monster right in front of you. I thought you were going to get bit."

"Stealth training!" Jill spat out. "Piss-slurping, steak-blending, coffee-spilling stealth training! That was number ten, Ras. Now I have to find another one."

"Oops?"

"Well," Babu said after she'd finished her tenth stealth kill, "that didn't work."

"Fuck me, that took like half an hour," Jill said. She looked around; the sun had shifted noticeably in the sky, and there were fewer teams of people swarming around Bertha bringing things in. "Think we have time to try again?"

"Just once more," he said. He fished around in the tour bag, searching for something in its odd depths. "I wasn't sure if we'd need this, but it's time to bring out the big guns for stealth."

"Yeah?" Jill asked. "What's that?"

Babu pulled out a folded brown square, three feet on a side, and with a few deft movements turned it into a cardboard box. "Get under this and try again."

The worst part was that it worked.

> Set Slitherer cross-class skill unlocked!
> **What Was That Noise:** Project an aura of Mana around you that cloaks you from sight. It may also confuse lower-Level enemies.
> Mana Cost: 10 per second
> Select skill? Requires 1 Class Point.

The only thing stopping Jill from having a wicked sunburn was that she was absolutely covered in sweat, dirt, and monster goo. She had smashed, leaped, twirled, shot, snuck, throttled, and even bounced on one leg, all trying to kill monsters. If the System was a god that required sacrifice in exchange for power, what it demanded above all else was dignity.

"Only one thing left," Babu said.

"Good," Jill said. "I'm sick of this."

He sunk an arm deep into the golf bag and pulled out what he'd saved for last.

"Persephone's flaming tits, this is what I'm talking about!" Jill said as she took the flamethrower. It was a single-nozzle version, unlike Dan's backpack of doom, and was decorated with a snarling dragon's mouth.

Three minutes, ten kills, a whole lot of fire, and Babu's entire mana pool spent on a water spell to control the fallout later, Jill lowered the weapon from her hand, her task completed.

> You are now Level 88! Level gain deferred per user preferences.

"Ehhh heh heh heh!" Jill's maniacal laughter came to an end. "Oh"—she handed back the flamethrower and leaned over, hands on her knees—"I needed that. We've got just a little time left. Want a go?"

Babu grinned and tossed back the contents of a vial into his mouth. "Why not?"

Jill and Babu stood outside of Bertha's cargo doors, enjoying a final bit of fresh air before going back in. The sounds of organized chaos echoed out from the Cargo Nexus as the task of sorting everything into a sensible place continued, but out here things were getting calmer. The last of the scavenger teams was just now coming back, mostly empty-handed, as the warehouse had at this point been well picked over. Between Jill's own exploits and the combat teams doing their last patrols, the local monster population had been culled to the point where they were starting to get hard to find at all.

"I know we only unlocked half of what you wanted," Jill said, "but I needed that."

"What, crawling around and getting gooped?"

"No, you airborne donkey," she said. "Just the chance to"—she paused—"I dunno, do something different, goof off a little, let off steam. Not be in charge. Plus, there was a lot of fire."

"Well, we need to get the rest of the build completed before you join us adventuring," Babu said, "so we're going to have to do this again someplace."

Jill blinked. "You want me out there killing monsters with the three of you?" she asked. "Like, when you're going after big stuff?"

"You out-level us, and given how much XP gets funneled into you, it's almost impossible for that to change. This Lair"—he licked his lips—"it was tough. We got hurt, and it got close with the sunflower. The big one, that is. Something made it mad, like really, really mad, right before the end. It gave us the chance to finish the fight, but Ras got speared." He shook his head. "Having a high-level sneak-attacker with us to lay in a damage spike would make a big difference, even if you are going to just be a one-trick pony."

"I'd never really considered going outside of Bertha to fight," Jill said.

"Well, think about it," he said. "I'll figure out some way to get you a defense and escape power."

"Maybe I'm crazy, but I'm looking forward to it," Jill said.

CHAPTER 22

A BRIGHT SKY

Jill jumped into Bertha, and as soon as her feet touched the floor, a box popped up in her vision.

> Welcome back, Settlement Administrator Jill MacLeod.
> The Settlement of "Berthaville" has grown to Level 3!

"Nice," Jill said. "Berthaville got two levels." She nodded at one of Sangita's administrators, who stood by the door with a clipboard in her hand, checking people off as they came in.

"Really?" Babu, who had followed her in, lit up.

"No, I'm lying to you," Jill said with an eye roll. She turned to the woman by the door. "Hey," she said, "I'm going to get us moving again. Is everyone inside?"

"Not quite, ma'am. There are"—she paused and flipped the pages on her clipboard to check—"six teams still outside. Should I get them in? It might take a few minutes."

"That's fine," Jill said. "Just send a runner to find me once they're back and you're sure we're not going to leave anyone behind."

"Got it!"

"Thanks," Jill said. She took a moment to survey the Cargo Nexus. What had been mostly empty shelves were now packed with all the food the distribution warehouse had that was still intact. A beeping caught her attention: someone had gotten one of the forklifts from the airport operational, and it was busy moving an entire pallet of cans deeper into Bertha. Off to the side, a trio of people were sorting various plant-themed monster loot into piles. Elemental gems made up the biggest portion of the loot, but there were also leaves, branches, and piles of tufted plant fiber. Knots of armed fighters stood around, keeping a watch on the doors to make sure that nothing bad got in and occasionally helping to move heavy things.

The sound of a minor avalanche drew Jill's attention to the side, where a pyramid of cereal boxes had overbalanced on top of a short black-haired man. He emerged, laughing, and immediately threw one at the woman next to him while claiming she had knocked them over on purpose. She responded with a power that made the box whip around her body in a slingshot to bounce off his face.

Jill smiled, shook her head, and started walking through the Nexus. She'd made deliveries to warehouses where the employees had obviously been overworked, underpaid, and were one intrusively timed bathroom break away from ripping their managers a new asshole. This wasn't like that. She was sure that not everyone was happy—there was no way that the anger and fear that had welled up at the town meeting was gone completely—but right now, here, people were moving like a well-oiled, if unpracticed and just a bit silly, machine.

She and Babu made it to the cafeteria and were greeted by a wall of chatter. A buffet of steaming food lay in front of the kitchen area, and a line of people stretched along the wall next to it, waiting their turn. The tables were nearly full of people, and more still were streaming in and out of the living area, trays in hand. The warehouse supplies were already being put to good use, but there was also a good supply of pizza being provided directly from Bertha.

Jill's mouth watered as she walked through the room, giving a few answering nods to people who called out to her as she went. A tiny swell of nerves clenched inside of her, but she decided she'd had enough of that. "Let's grab some grub," she said. Those in the line tried to move out of her way when Jill and Babu got on the end of it, but she scowled at them until they got back in their place ahead of her. It was moving fast, anyway.

She took herself a slice of pizza and a few scoops of a curry that had mainly come from cans. Jill got to a fresh salad and hesitated; it gleamed with magic. "Where did we get this?" she asked, using just a hint of Captain

Speaking to ensure that the man working behind the buffet could hear her over the noise.

"Which?" he asked. "Oh! The salad." He grinned. "Fresh plant monster. Eat your veggies before they eat you!"

She exchanged a glance with Babu. "It looks normal."

The man shrugged. "There was a herd of predatory lettuce. To quote our illustrious leader, 'the bullshit magic is bullshit, and we should all get used to it. Fuck, shit, damn, tits.'"

Jill sighed and took herself some salad. It was a fair impression.

Thankfully, no one bothered them as they ate. Babu tried to keep their conversation going, but Jill was too busy shoveling food into her mouth to really say anything back. Eating with everyone around, instead of being locked in the cab or her room, was nice, but she was still in a rush. Five minutes later she stood and stretched her back, ready to go. But before she could grab her tray to bus it, it floated into the air, up to and along the ceiling towards the kitchens. Now that she was looking up, she saw that there were dozens of trays, plates, and cups all doing the same, her Unseen Servants at work.

It was a short walk back to her room by the cab. The group of buffing bards was having a jam session in the turret prep room, trying their best to play the increasingly obscure requests shouted at them. Jill paused just long enough to shout, "Play 'My Wife Left Me for My Girlfriend'!" and see the resulting confusion before opening her door and stepping through.

Her room was as she had left it, but the bathroom was starting to get crowded. The Smiling Sunflower still sat on the shelf she'd extruded above the tiny sink, but it had grown to be twice its former size. Another three potted flowers had joined it: one inside the sink, another in the toilet bowl, and a final one hiding in the shower, all of them swaying in the invisible currents of magic that swirled around the room.

"She's spawned already!" Babu said, standing on his tiptoes to see over Jill.

"Huh," Jill said. She prodded the mother flower to check its status. "That was fast."

Smiling Sunflower, Level 13

"I guess it really is legendary," she said. She took the new pots and put them on her tiny desk, ignoring the fact that one of them was dripping toilet water. She had magic cleaning after all.

Babu waited for her in the bathroom, bouncing on the balls of his feet. Jill squeezed in next to him and shut the door. The glowing crystal that erupted from the floor was larger than it had been that morning. She ended up in the shower, with Babu standing on the toilet.

"I need a bigger bathroom," Jill grumbled, then put her hand on the crystal.

The Technomagical Dimensional Bubble of "Berthaville"
Core Level: 3 **Available Points:** 2
XP: 7,301,407/10,000,000
MP: 30,000 **Core Mana Generation:** 50 MP per second
Shield HP: 30,000 **Shield Maintenance:** 1 MP per second
Residents: 5298 **Resident Mana Taxed** (1%): 22.4 MP per second
Total Mana Generation: 72.4 MP per second
Total Mana Expended: 1 MP per second
Available Administrative Actions:
Invest XP, Set Taxes, Manage Security

"So!" Babu said. "What's up first? It has to be the space upgrade, right?"

Jill spent a few moments reading through the available options. Not everything required more space, but getting people housed and fed did. "Yup," she said. She pulled up the upgrade to check it one last time.

Size Increase: Increase the diameter of "Berthaville's" claimed region to 1 km. Note: Settlement Shield upkeep is proportional to shield area. Settlement Shield strength in any given place is inversely proportional to shield area. Unlocks **Boundary Shape Control** at Level 15.

She pushed on the option with her mind, but she found herself blocked as another box popped up.

Warning! This upgrade will cause Mana expenditure to exceed generation. Increase resident tax to 4% to compensate?

"Uh," Jill said, hesitating. "What happens if Berthaville runs out of mana?"

System Inquiry Detected
Mana depletion will cause, in order: the deactivation of active effects, de-instantiation of summoned material, failure of the barrier shield, and failure of space expansion. Warning! Barrier shield failure will cause uncontrolled exposure to the Interstitial Realm. May cause a dimensional incursion into causal reality. Extreme Warning! Failure of space expansion is catastrophic.

"Christ on a cracker!" Jill said and sent the notice to Babu. He let out a low whistle. "Yeah, Sys," Jill said, "increase the tax." She sent another pulse of mana into the core to confirm the size increase.

A dull whomp vibrated through Bertha as every surface vibrated. For a few seconds, there was nothing more, but then Jill felt a breeze on parts of Bertha where none had been before. The Habitation and Medbay Modules of Bertha were tucked inside of the truck's dimensional space and didn't touch the outside world at all, but now there was air blowing against their outer surfaces.

Jill checked the settlement's new mana generation and consumption.

Resident Mana Taxed (4%): 89.6 MP per second
Total Mana Generation: 139.6 MP per second
Total Mana Expended: 125.7 MP per second

"Was that it?" Babu asked. "Normally, you get all weird."

"I think I'm not as connected to the settlement as I am to Bertha," Jill said, "but it's done." She pressed a hand to the wall next to her. After all the shifting of the internal geometry, her room had ended up being on the outside of the chaotic tangle of rooms that was the Habitation Module. She trailed her fingers up and sideways, the gesture largely ornamental, and peeled back the wall to make a doorway to the outside. A blast of wind blew her hair back but died down in a few moments.

A void of air and darkness lay before her.

"Woah," Jill whispered. She glanced down and saw that there was a sheer drop into blackness in front of her. Her eyes widened and she took a half step back. Then, light. A splash of gold bloomed in the distance, first as a single point, then as a spreading ring of shimmering fluorescence. It faded as it grew, but by its light and motion Jill could tell that it was tracing the inside surface of an enormous sphere. "What the shit was that?"

"The outer surface maybe?" Babu asked back, wonder in his voice.

"I think our space problem is solved," Jill said. "We just need to, you know, fill it up, right?" One upgrade she already had, Air Supply, would unlock Terrain Generation once the settlement hit level five. She'd take that as soon as she could.

Babu reached into a pocket and pulled out a small, empty bottle. He gave it an underhanded toss past Jill, and it spun out into the void, flickers of light reflecting off its tumbling form. It kept spinning off into the distance in a perfectly straight line.

"Is that . . ." Jill trailed off. "Fuck me right in the knee, there's no gravity! And I didn't see an option for it either!"

Babu shrugged. "The System will provide?" he asked.

Jill shot him a look. "They can grow stuff in space, right?" she asked. "Like, maybe this just means we can pack more in?"

"I," Babu said, then hesitated. "Maybe? I don't know. But we'll need light no matter what! Want to make a sun?"

"Sweet tits, yes," Jill said. "Let's light this truck up!" She spent Berthaville's last point on Artificial Sun.

> **Artificial Sun:** Creates a spherical source of heat and Earth-standard spectrum light. The sun can be set to a static or orbital mode. Mana Cost: 1 per second. Unlocks **Seasonal Control** at Level 15.

Light bloomed a radiant gold, heat washed over her face, and her pupils shrank in painful protest. She raised a hand to shield her eyes and blinked, hard.

"Wow," Babu said. "I was joking about it being a sun. That's . . . beautiful."

Jill lowered her hand. Shining in front of her in the intermediate distance was a brilliant yellow orb, its mottled surface rotating slowly. She felt a quiver of mana, and an arc bloomed on its surface, looping up before fading away. Now that it was lit up, the boundary shield behind the new sun was a pale, opaque blue, making it look exactly like the sky on a cloudless day, though it still occasionally erupted in rings of gold aurora.

"Windows," Jill said. "I'm getting Aman to make windows." She took a deep breath, gripped the edges of the door, and stuck her head out, looking left and right. A chaotic tangle of metal cubes extended in both directions in a haphazard jumble. "Maybe after he cleans all this up. In the meantime, I'm raising the XP tax rate. I know that it will make us a bit weaker out here, but this deserves priority." She put her hand back on the core and cranked the rate up to its maximum of 10 percent. She felt a light pull on her gut, but it soon faded to nothing.

"I think," Babu said, "that I'm going to go for a flight." He looked younger than he had just a few minutes before.

"Out there? In all that emptiness?" Jill said and pulled a face. "Better you than me! Have fun, I guess. We're kind of done with this for now." A twist of her will as she said the words had the core sliding back into the bathroom floor. "So I'm going to go to the cab and get us moving. And I'm going to move this door to the hall so I can shit without someone coming in to criticize my technique."

"Sure," Babu said, distracted and staring out into the blue expanse.

Jill gave him a clap on the shoulder and left him to it.

CHAPTER 23

JUMP

Jill paused outside her door long enough to listen to a surprisingly accurate rendition of "Danger! High Voltage" and say hello to the group of thirty people that had come to listen before she took the few steps from her room into the cab. She entered and found it only moderately less chaotic: there was a dinosaur running around in it, chasing and being chased in turn by Karen's son, Kevin.

"*Rar!*" Kevin yelled and jumped out from his hiding spot behind a chair. His tiny pet stegosaurus made a peeping noise of surprise and spun around, waving the tiny but wickedly sharp spines of its thagomizer in the air. In so doing, it saw Jill. Its eyes went wide and it promptly flopped over onto its side, playing dead.

"That is a-ducking-dorable," Jill said and walked in. Karen and Taran sat nearby, hand in hand, watching their son play.

Jill used Customization to close the door behind her rather than use her hands; she used one of those to ruffle Kevin's hair instead. "How you doing, buddy?" she asked.

"I'm okay," Kevin said. "But you should pet Spiny's belly feathers. They're super soft!"

Jill grinned and leaned down, stroking one finger along the dinosaur's exposed underside. The appropriately named creature crooned.

"Where did you find him?" Jill asked.

Kevin giggled and shook his head.

"We've been asking that in different ways all day," Taran said. "He refuses to tell."

"Well, this one's cute and doesn't want to eat me," Jill said, "so good enough. How are things going up here?"

"Not too bad," Karen said. She was still connected to Captain Speaking, but her outgoing activity had slowed down. "There hasn't been a monster attack in a while, and everyone's happy with the food. I think things might be actually looking up." Taran squeezed her hand.

"Well, don't say it out loud," Jill said. "You'll jinx it." She slid into the driver's seat and relaxed. It felt like the right place to be. "I'm just amazed that everyone's in such a good mood all of a sudden."

"Not all of them are," Karen said. "Let me guess, you just walked straight here from outside?"

"More or less," Jill said. "So?"

"The people who are pissed off at you are staying out of sight. There are plenty of private places in the barracks and Habitation rooms," Karen said. "No one's saying they want you dead or anything, but there are a lot of whispers about how they shouldn't have come."

Jill sighed. "I knew it was too good to be true," she said. She closed her eyes and sunk into Bertha, sending her senses racing through the truck, keyed into her loyalty sense above all. Now that she was looking, she saw them: knots of people tucked away here or there, indifferent and bitter.

"How many, do you think?" she asked, making an estimate herself at the same time.

Karen shrugged. "I've only got hearing to work with, so it's a little hard to tell. More than fifty, less than a hundred?"

"Yeah, that feels right. I'm at somewhere between sixty and seventy. It could be worse," Jill said and blew out a long breath. "Keep an ear on them for me?"

"I already am," Karen said. "Speaking of which, why did you have Amy send a messenger when everyone's inside?" Karen asked. "She could have just shouted for me."

"You heard that too, huh?" Jill asked. "Pretty close tabs you're keeping on me. If a woman didn't know better, I'd say you had a crush." She winked at Taran, who rolled his eyes. Karen didn't seem impressed either.

"But really," Jill said. "You've been here all day. Have you taken any breaks?"

"I freshened up a few times," Karen said. "I'm okay."

"Uh-huh," Jill said. "And how about food?"

Hesitation warred with hunger on Karen's face, but a rumble from her stomach won the battle. Taran leaned in and whispered something in her ear. "Fine," she said, "I'll take a break."

They said their goodbyes to Jill and left, Kevin leading the way at a run with Spiny atop his head.

For the first time in a long while, Jill was alone in the cab. She reached out a hand to the steering wheel and closed her eyes. "Just you and me, eh, girl?" she said and let out a single laugh at how wrong that statement was now. She spent a few minutes just listening to the sounds of the truck. It was mostly quiet, but the faint noises of people talking and of music could just barely be heard through the hatch. She opened her eyes, leaned forward, and thumbed the button to turn the mana engine on. Its low rumble purred out to join the faint chatter.

"That's more like it," Jill said.

She cracked her neck to the side and got back to work. Their next stop was the first of two military bases. There was a growing network of long-ranged magical communication springing up in the wake of the System-induced destruction of technology, but neither of these two bases had answered when called. Jill had bartered checking them out in exchange for six heavy machine guns—a deal that she thought had less to do with the task itself and more to do with the fact that she'd safely gotten the base's commanding officer, Amelia, to her command without dying. Jill shook her head; she couldn't believe that had been only yesterday.

She took a few minutes to study Aman's road atlas map, still pinned up next to his dashboard. The base was marked with a red *X* and, according to the map, it was less than a three-hour drive away, but that wasn't including the extreme space expansion from the high mana density. She measured the distance on the map from the airport to where they were now and compared it to the distance to go, then scowled. At the rate they were going, it would take days to get there unless something changed.

Jill's frown morphed into an excited grin, and she slapped the wheel in excitement. Something had changed, something big. Bertha had Inertial Resistance now, and Jill knew that it was working; the fight with the Ivy Stonewielder had proved it. No longer was Jill's driving constrained by the need to not kill everyone inside with sudden maneuvers or acceleration. She would finally be able to take advantage of the remaining speed upgrades.

She pulled up the Propulsion Module's box.

Propulsion (Ground):
"Bertha" has an engine that converts Mana to rotary motion, which is then transmitted to wheels. Maximum recommended speed: 390 km/h.
Available Upgrades:
Need for Speed (2/5): Each rank increases maximum speed by 70 km/h.

She immediately took all three remaining ranks in Need for Speed. Wind blew in Jill's face, pulling her cheeks back, and the sound of a roaring diesel engine filled her ears. The feel of tight corners and the smell of burning rubber swirled around her. Bertha was ready to blast down the highway; she needed to be pushed to the absolute limit.

"Hell yeah," Jill said as the feeling faded.

Congratulations! Propulsion (Ground) upgrades complete! Determining most beneficial new abilities.
Only one of the following customized abilities may be selected:
War Rig: As long as the Mana engine is running, all Class Points invested in the Propulsion Module count towards the effective Level of all Weaponry Modules attached to Soulbound Modular Vehicle "Bertha." Increases the Class Boost to all Weaponry Modules by +.2. Unlocks further combat-related abilities.
18-Wheeled Ninja: Noise from the Propulsion (Ground) Module is reduced by 93%, the wheels can be extended with suitable force to propel Bertha to a jump height of 1.4 meters, and the Diffused Traction ability is upgraded to work on fully liquid surfaces. Unlocks further ground movement enhancements.

The image of Bertha with a black paint job, perched on the branch of an enormous tree, a forty-foot-long katana strapped across the top of the trailer came unbidden into Jill's mind. She chuckled and shook her head, considering the two options.

She thought that she knew why the System had generated these two choices: they were going to encounter danger, so either Bertha had to fight, run, or avoid being noticed in the first place. For the latter, a noise reduction was nice, but the 7 percent remaining of all of Bertha's many tons blasting along, tearing up the ground, was still going to be loud. The ability would also do nothing about the sheer size and visibility of a truck in any kind of open terrain.

"Sys," Jill said, "to be honest with you, the stealth stuff chomps balls. It's really not up to your usual standard."

> System Inquiry Detected
> Upgrades are constrained in effect by base characteristics.

Jill let out a huff of a laugh. "So," she said, "you did your best to make a shit sandwich tasty?"

There was no response.

The rest of 18-Wheeled Ninja was also a mixed bag. A little jump might be useful once in a blue moon, but anything that was just five feet tall Bertha could probably blast straight through rather than go over. Being able to drive on water, though, was a serious upgrade. The last river they crossed had been a slow, dangerous pain in Jill's tits. But that one piece just wasn't enough to justify it over War Rig.

Now that was one hell of an ability. The stacking of effective level would boost the Adaptive Mounts power by nine levels immediately, but the real star was the class boost. Jill had learned without a doubt that those were worth their weight in gold: for the turrets, it meant an additional 10 percent boost to damage and fire rate from Superchargers and 4 percent better reflexes for the gunners from Boosted Reflexes. The only reason why it wouldn't add another turret was that the current count from the four ranks she had in the Dakka power was rounding 5.6 up, while with an extra boost, it would round 6.4 down. On the other hand, if she selected the turrets for one of the Cargo Nexus's Reinforced Module Mounting's precious limited slots, then Dakka would be giving 7.2. An extra turret meant an extra Bertha-boosted gun killing monsters. Even if they only had six machine guns, the crafters were already making new weapons; they would come up with something suitably crazy to be worth using.

She was going to take War Rig. It played to Bertha's current strengths, while the stealth option was trying to make a pig fly.

The real question was the Reinforced Module Mounting. Was it worth it to lock in the turrets as that choice forever? Jill let out a sigh. Of course it was, and she should have taken it as soon as the option had presented itself. Unless they just went to meditate in some sterile isolated cave—and boy, did that sound like a nightmare—then Bertha was going to have to keep shooting. That was just how the world was now. She took it.

Magic surged from the Cargo Nexus into the turrets, trying to tie the two modules together even more tightly. Jill realized her mistake a moment later as a foreign entity buzzed in confusion and discomfort, resisting the flow of mana; with the gunners in their seats, the Hive Mind was active, and it was tied into the turrets deeply enough to feel the upgrade. She could have overpowered the consciousness and forced the changes but instead tried to project an apology and an image of growing extra muscles. The hive looked at her, rolled its many eyes, and Jill got the impression of grumbling acceptance. The resistance disappeared and the pent-up magic from the cargo bay shot out like water from a stoppered hose, piercing into the turrets before freezing in place.

Jill blinked.

"Hey," she projected to the gunners, "sorry about that. Upgrades are kind of weird, huh?"

"Hahahaha," came the multi-tonal response. "I can fire even faster now! But, uh, yeah, a little warning next time would be nice. That was really uncomfortable."

"Sure, and sorry again," Jill said. "Another one's coming, so you might want to get out of the seats."

"Oh shit!"

Jill cut the connection and felt the hive diminish as its members got off the guns, one by one. She had the briefest impression of a wink and a wave before it vanished entirely.

One upgrade down, at least one to go. She took War Rig and a scream of righteous diesel fury roared in her ears as mana exploded out of the engine and wheels to spiral into the turrets. She would destroy any who threatened her passengers, shooting them from the sky and grinding them to a paste under her feet. Nothing would stop her; nothing could stop her.

Jill snapped out of the upgrade with a gasp. Her hands had clenched hard enough to bend the wheel; she'd taken nineteen points of damage in the process as shards of metal had pierced her skin. She released them and both healed in seconds. A whisper of Customization later, and the blood evaporated into golden light.

The newly unlocked advanced powers appeared before her.

War Rig Available Powers:
Outriders (0/5): Gain the ability to designate vehicles, each up to 2800 kg in mass, as outriders. Outriders gain 10% of Bertha's Armor and Durability as additional defense. Their maximum top speed is set equal to Bertha's if it would have been slower otherwise. Each rank allows for 1.4 additional outriders.
Brutal Wheels: The wheels become weapons of war. Each gains the statistics of an uncommon melee weapon of the module's effective Level. Unlocks **Voracious Wheels.**
Turbocharger of the Damned: Each enemy slain by Bertha or its add-ons increases the Propulsion (Ground) Module's top speed by 1.4 km/h per Level of the enemy. This effect lasts for 1.4 seconds per Level of the enemy.

She breathed in deeply to steady herself and read through them. Being able to boost some other small vehicles along with Bertha might be a game changer, but she didn't know if they had anything suitable. It was something to check on later. The wheels and turbocharger powers were both obvious choices, and with eleven class points left, Jill could afford them. She braced herself and bought both. Fire burned in her veins, and she felt the sudden urge to kick a fear deer to death, but the feelings passed mercifully quickly. Jill came back to herself to find her jaw hurting from clenching her teeth and sweat pouring down her back.

Voracious Wheels: The wheels hunger for blood. Enemies defeated by the wheels have 14% of their Mana absorbed into "Bertha."

Jill pulled her lips back in a too-wide grin. That was perfect. If there was one thing Bertha needed more in a hard fight it was a way to get more mana for the guns, and it was a perfect excuse for Jill to get in close and grind things under her wheels. She blinked and swallowed, ice running down her spine over the sweat. Her last thought hadn't felt like her. But the reasoning wasn't wrong, so she took Voracious Wheels before she lost her nerve. The hunger returned, stronger than ever. She felt Bertha's mana explode outwards, searching for prey, only to return disappointed.

Jill was as tired and sweaty as if she'd run a mile with a bear sitting on her back. And not a little black bear either—no, a full-grown grizzly at the very least, one that was not trying to eat her only because it enjoyed the wind on its face.

The cab door opened, and Babu stuck his head in. "Are you done doing upgrades in there?" he asked. "Only I could feel the waves of mana even when I was flying, don'tcha know." He saw her sweat-covered face and the corners of his mouth crept upwards in a slow, wide grin. "Oh," he said, "were you doing more than upgrades? Having a bit of a magical time?"

"Shove a sea urchin up your dick," Jill said back.

"Jill!" Babu's voice was full of shock. "In front of a child?!" He moved sideways to reveal a deeply unimpressed pre-teen boy.

"Amy told me to tell you that everyone's inside!" he yelled. "And I've been waiting out here for five minutes while you do your gross stuff!"

"Shit, kid, I wasn't—" Jill started to say, but the child, message delivered, had already disappeared at a run.

Babu entered, closed the door, and then bent over laughing.

"Get it all out," Jill muttered and rolled her eyes.

"You really shouldn't be allowed around kids," he said. He walked forward and jumped into the seat next to Jill.

"I'm working on it," Jill grumbled. "And really, what's worse? A little colorful language or you putting that image in their head?"

Babu waved his hand. "He's too young to understand."

"Bet you five bucks he wasn't."

They bickered back and forth for a few more minutes. The intrusive feeling of bloodlust faded away and Jill relaxed. She was still her snarky, dirty self, and no magic power was going to change that.

"Right," she said after the third iteration of making sure Babu knew she wasn't his buddy, "everyone's inside, the monsters are all dead, and we've looted this place to the ground. Anything I'm missing before we take off?"

"Do you know where to go?"

Jill pointed at the map in front of him.

"Oh," he said and looked embarrassed for the first time since entering. "I think we're good, then."

Jill nodded, then projected the sound of the horn through the truck. "Hey, folks," she said to everyone, "we're loaded up and taking off. Uh, enjoy the food?"

She put her foot down on the accelerator and Bertha glided forward, the crunch of broken pavement under the wheels a now familiar and soothing sound. They turned out of the parking lot at speed, back onto the separated segments of highway, and Jill cocked her head to the side. She'd taken that turn fast but hadn't felt a thing.

She double-checked her route on the map and pushed the accelerator all the way to the floor. Bertha lunged forward, the acceleration hard enough that Jill could just barely feel it through the dampening. The scenery whipped by faster and faster; the tire noise got louder and higher in pitch. According to the System, Bertha's maximum speed was now a staggering 600 kilometers, or 373 miles, per hour; they were now at 300 miles per hour and still rising.

"Shit on a shingle!" she yelled a moment later as the truck went airborne from a small rise. She snapped on the Torque Converter to make sure they didn't tumble, but they weren't in the air long enough for it to matter. They hit the ground hard, but she only felt the smallest bump. She put her foot back down on the accelerator.

"This is incredible!" Jill said, the grin on her face so big that it was starting to hurt. "See this, world?" she shouted. "You can try to make yourself bigger, but Bertha's just going to drive faster!" She twitched the wheel and aimed Bertha at a rise on purpose. They took to the air again, and she laughed in pure delight.

CHAPTER 24

IF YOU CAN DODGE A MONSTER

Jill was in the center passenger seat the next morning, a cup of coffee in her hands and her feet propped up on a ledge she'd extruded from the dash. She was supervising a driving volunteer named Bobby Jordan, an older man with heavy hands and a salt-and-pepper beard. He'd been waiting that morning by the cab along with four others, and all had said they wanted to take her up on the offer of being a backup driver. Bobby had, for a few months in between other work, handled a big rig for a company, so Jill was giving him the first shot. Three of the rest were sitting nearby with coffee of their own, watching and smack-talking Bobby's driving in not-so-quiet voices, while the fourth was trying in vain to chat up Karen.

"Now, I know you can't feel shit because of the inertial canceling," Jill said, "and the engine doesn't sound the same as a normal truck either 'cause it's magic instead of diesel. But you can still see all around so just think about it like a driving sim."

Bobby shrugged. "I've never used one of those," he said. "They just trained me for a day, stuck me behind the wheel, and handed me a bottle of trucker pills."

Jill won the fight against sighing out loud, but that only made it resonate more deeply within her.

"Peachy," she said. "Now, Bertha weighs a fuckton more than a normal rig so take this next turn carefully. No sudden moves until you've got a handle on the Torque Converter."

"The what?" he asked.

"Exactly."

The turn came, a broad sweeping expanse of cracked road chunks interspersed with grass. The tires had good enough traction and the road was scarce enough that it wouldn't have been any harder to just ignore the road and drive straight to their destination; it would even cut down on how far they had to go. But ignoring the road meant losing one of their few landmarks, and the risk of getting lost and wasting time was just too high.

Bobby eased the wheel over and the horizon scrolled by. They weren't going full speed—that was a bit too much even for Jill, not to mention these amateurs—but they were still going over a hundred miles an hour, and what was theoretically a gentle turn could absolutely cause problems if it wasn't handled right. Dirt and rock flew up behind them in a massive rooster tail as the huge knobbled tires bit into the ground, giving them the acceleration needed to change directions, but Bertha didn't slip or roll.

"Not bad!" Jill said. "Not bad at all." She spent the next five minutes coaching Bobby in using the magical features of the truck, occasionally quizzing the rest to make sure they were also paying attention.

The guns fired above, a short simultaneous burst from four of them, which blanketed some target in the distance with burning bullets. It only took three bursts before the kill box popped up in Jill's vision.

Splitrib Spiderdog defeated. Your contribution: 8% 384 Experience Gained!

"Root and toot!" said Bobby. "I just got some experience for that! Was that 'cause I was driving?"

"Yup," Jill said. "Taking XP away from the gunners is kind of bullshit if you ask me, but I don't make the rules. And every bit adds up."

Sometime when she was sleeping it had added up to a whole new level, bringing her to eighty-nine; Jill had forced herself through the searing process of growing stronger while in the shower, after having displaced a dozen more potted sunflowers. Maybe the System wasn't totally wrong for covering that up with its narcotic feelings of bliss, but it took the sensation way too far. Part of her wanted to experiment with toning the sensation down, mixing in just enough System euphoria to stop leveling from being quite so traumatic, but an older, more tired part warned of where that could lead.

Berthaville had leveled at dawn, right after there had been another System quest reward for surviving a day. Three thousand experience for around five thousand people, taxed at 10 percent, had been enough to push the settlement over the edge to level four. After a little thought, Jill had taken the Workshop upgrade.

> **Workshop:** Unlocks the workshop structure for placement in the Settlement. This structure provides a facility, bonuses, and further options for item creation. Unlocks **Foundry** at Settlement Level 20.

She'd stuck the new structure—an open room the size of a barn, lined with workbenches and mysterious tools—off the side of the cafeteria. It would have been more convenient to attach it to the cargo area next to where they were storing the monster parts, but right now that bordered the real world and not Bertha's dimensional bubble. The settlement-generated structure stoutly refused to be anywhere but inside the settlement. She'd have Aman take a look at the whole arrangement later and come up with something more efficient.

"Hot diggity dog," Bobby said. "Time to rake in some levels."

Jill narrowed her eyes and tapped her fingers on her coffee mug. "You're fucking with me, aren't you?"

"What?" Bobby asked. He seemed genuinely confused.

"Dagnabbit, that son of a monkey is just saying bullspit!" Karen said.

Jill snorted. "You, I know, are just being a twerp," she said to Karen over her shoulder, then stuck her tongue out.

She rocked forward and leaped to her feet, being careful not to spill a single drop of the precious liquid in her cup, even if the Habitation Module could just generate more for a piddly amount of mana. She clapped Bobby on the shoulder strongly enough to make him rock sideways but not strongly enough to break him. "Keep us following the road," she said. "And shout at Karen if something big is in our way, or if you just feel like scaring her. She deserves it."

"Got it, ma'am," Bobby said.

Karen stuck out her tongue at Jill as the older woman walked by, and there were chuckles from the others in the cab. They were mostly just sitting around relaxing, but if Bertha stumbled into a big fight, they were ready to cast their support spells. Jill smiled, but she felt just a little off. Her truck wasn't quite ready to run without her but there was a growing set of people taking on roles that had previously been hers alone. It made sense; there were just too many things depending on her for her to get them done in a day if she was also driving all the time. Plus, even if she wanted to take all that on, she had to sleep sometime, and every hour Bertha wasn't driving was another hour they weren't heading east. She'd just have to get used to it.

She was so absorbed in her thoughts that when she exited the cab she almost ran headlong into Sangita. "Were you waiting for me outside the door?" Jill asked. "You can just come in, you know."

"We're not in an episode of *The West Wing*," Sangita said and rolled her eyes. "I just happened to be there. Now, President Profanity, I've got reports for you to read."

Jill pulled a face. "Let me guess, if I don't read them, I won't have any idea what's happening?"

"If you don't read them, I'll be forced to depose you in a coup."

"Well, tickle me with an avocado, I'd hate to kill you for trying," she said. "That would make things awkward with the rest of your family."

It took only a minute for Jill to grab a coffee and a donut, then she stepped into the meeting room opposite the turret prep area. Ras, Coach, Taran, and Jacob were waiting for her. The latter had won a preliminary snap election with a decisive enough lead that Jill had given in and let him come. She had a suspicion that the innocent-seeming man had rigged it given the timescale and sheer margin involved, but she couldn't figure out how. She was probably just being paranoid.

For the next hour and a half they went over the logistics of Berthaville: how many people were in Habitation versus the converted Nexus barracks; the amount of food and number of other supplies they'd managed to take from the warehouse; how many people had found some sort of preliminary job to get themselves experience and help the community; the levels and rotation schedule for the Cloud Killers; salvaging or making suitable vehicles for Outriders; and so on. The biggest bright spot was the situation with water: the scheme to have a large tank in the cargo area and pipes into Habitation, where it could be purified, had worked perfectly. Food would be good for a few weeks, but just in case it needed to last longer, they went over the possibility of eating the more palatable monsters they came across. There hadn't been any health complications from eating the monster lettuce salads the day before, and some had even reported gaining XP from it.

"Anything else?" Jill asked. She'd run out of coffee and was starting to feel antsy.

"Jill!" Babu popped his head around the corner. "It's working!"

Sangita let out a tsk. "Babu, where have you been? You were supposed to be here for this meeting."

"I was busy helping with the casting," he said. "Jill, let's get it installed."

"Get what installed?"

"The radar! We've got a working model!"

With that, the meeting ended.

Jill followed Babu out of the room. She was outwardly silent but used Captain Speaking to project a whispered message to his ear. "Hey," she said, "I know you're excited about this, and Bobbit worms know I hate meetings, but Sangita was right. You should have been there."

Babu shot her a look of sad amusement and used his own communication to mentally reply. "I know you mean well, Jill, but trust me. You don't want me and Mom in a room together for that long."

Jill sighed. "Fine," she projected. "Do you have anything official-like you want to tell me?"

"Yes, actually," he mentally said. "I think we need more magic casters in the Cloud Killers. We've got lots of fighters but no support or healing. I'm holding a meeting tonight to try and do recruitment."

"Good idea," Jill replied, but that was all the time they had for covert conversation before they reached the workshop. And really, there wasn't much more for Jill to say about either matter.

Jill whistled as she walked into the workshop. Hanging suspended by cables from the roof was a rectangular ASR-9 radar antenna, its orange paint now covered in glowing lines. There were mana gems studded into it at intervals, and in the very center was mounted a single eye, two feet wide. Half of the two dozen people in the workshop were standing around this prized creation, while the rest were swearing over their own projects, arguing with the System, and sinking mana into parts.

"This is a serious piece of hardware," she said as she walked around the massive radar. Its main dish was a metal grate with empty space between the bars, but when Jill tried to slip a thread of mana between them, the lines on its surface flashed gold and she was repelled.

"Normally, it's mounted on a tower and has a dedicated power building," said a man by the name of Jim Chen. An aeronautics technician who'd taken to magical crafting like a duck to assholery, he'd been the lead crafter turning the antenna into something that could run on mana. He'd leveled six times from finishing the job.

"Hey, Sys," Jill said, "can we mount this as an add-on to the Command Module?" The module had a power for boosting "installed perception devices," so if she couldn't, she would be annoyed.

System Inquiry Detected
"Piercer of Cloud, Shadow, Earth, and Flesh" exceeds individual add-on Mana draw limit for continuous operation. Calculating. Available for installation with 3 add-on slots.

"Cool name," Jill said. Her two ranks in Capacity, taken to get the control stations, had given her the three slots she needed. "We're good to go, so let's get this on!"

Jill called up to the cab and asked Bobby to stop Bertha somewhere they would have a clear view to look out for ambushes. While he was searching for a good place, they moved the radar out of the workshop. It was big enough that they used a forklift for the initial movement, but once in the Cargo Nexus, it was a simple matter of levitating the radar with her Cargokinesis out the back, over the truck, and down on top of the cab. She shifted Mia's turret back and then willed the radar to connect to the Command Module. Her mind's eye expanded to encompass dozens of miles around, and for just a few seconds she could tell the true number of monsters around them, including a swarm of dozens of them, all above level sixty but with one right at level ninety-nine, heading towards them from the air.

"We've got to move," Jill said. She tied one of the Capacity-created consoles to the radar so everyone else could see the incoming threats. The display morphed into a classic radial radar screen labeled in metric, with monsters appearing as red dots labeled by level every time the radar beam swept over them. Every five seconds the beam completed another rotation, and the dots for the flying swarm were another third of a kilometer closer. Jill did the math in her head: they were coming in at around 160 miles per hour.

Jill kicked Bobby out of the driver's seat and hit the gas. Bertha surged into motion, but there was a problem. Just as they passed 110 miles per hour a sharp pain struck Jill between the eyes. The massive radar was anything but aerodynamic, and it was starting to bend on its mount. Jill raised a windscreen in front of it, but Bertha's structure was so packed with mana that it blocked the radar's beam. The add-on was a massive upgrade to their ability to find or avoid monsters, but if they used it while driving fast, they'd have a massive blind spot ahead of them.

"Hey, Jim," Jill said to the lead crafter, who'd followed her into the cab to watch the deployment, "I've got a new project for you: mana transparent armor."

"Fudgsicles."

They easily outpaced the monsters chasing them, even if Bertha did spend a disconcerting amount of time slightly airborne. Just when the flock was on the edge of radar range they veered away, presumably to hunt some other prey, and Jill breathed out a sigh of relief. Bertha might have won against them, but she had learned her lesson about fighting things higher level than her if she didn't have to. A highly mobile level ninety-nine with support sounded like a terrible time. She kept them going at near maximum speed for another three hours, just to be safe.

They settled down to a more sedate pace, and Jill swapped out for another of the reserve drivers, one Kim Crash, who, despite her name, had assured Jill that she'd grown up driving heavy equipment on a farm. After a bit of practice, she took Bertha up to near its top speed and started to giggle uncontrollably to herself. Jill told her to pull it back a bit but couldn't really blame her.

Then, an hour before sunset, they changed course. The radar had been showing them dozens of monsters at any one time, some in small groups and others alone, and they'd been reaping a steady trickle of kills from the ones dumb enough to get in their way. Jill hadn't deemed it worth it to go hunting, not with how much time that would take. But now, five miles to their south, a dense herd of over a hundred monsters appeared out of their forward-facing radar dead zone. They were in the forty-to-fifty-level range, stationary, and had no paragon of power to protect them.

Jill took the wheel again and turned Bertha south. It only took them two minutes to reach a hill and get a good look at the creatures: they were huge rabbits, at least ten feet tall at the shoulder.

Fibonacci Rabbit Level 43 Status: Multiplying

Jill brought Bertha to a stop so they could observe the rabbits a little longer; there was no need to rush in, after all. The monsters seemed to be just standing in a field, sunning themselves, but every few seconds another one would pop into existence with a flash of pink light. The surrounding rabbits would then converge on the new one—a relatively tiny creature, only the size of an adult human—and sniff it. Less than half of the newborns passed the test. They each got a series of licks from long barbed tongues. Those that failed were torn apart, shredded in moments by sharp, nasty teeth in a frenzy of violence. Then the herd would go still, waiting for their next future friend or meal.

"Well, that's a mess," Jill said after watching a particularly hated bunny's entrails go fountaining into the sky. "Does anyone have any reason we shouldn't slaughter them?" she asked everyone else in the cab. No one did.

"Hey, Coach," she projected to him, "get ready to do that experience-sharing rotation you were telling us about. I think we're about to get a shitload of easy kills."

Jill brought Bertha up to sixty miles an hour and circled the herd. Then she told the gunners to fire.

The rabbits bolted as soon as bullets started exploding flesh, scattering in all directions. They were faster than Jill expected but not faster than Bertha. Jill drove them in a looping circle around the fleeing creatures, trying to herd any getting away back into a central kill zone. In the end, she was only moderately successful, killing maybe half the herd before they had scattered so much that it wasn't worth chasing them anymore. When the slaughter was over, they had to double back over miles of terrain to collect the corpses. Jill let Kim drive again and focused on her Cargokinesis, picking each rabbit up when it was fifty feet from Bertha and levitating it into the open rear doors.

It took half an hour, but Jill deemed it a success. Beyond the loot of mana gems, hides, teeth, and one curious pulsing spiral, the influx of experience had raised the average level of the three dozen or so Cloud Killers by two each. Jill got a nice fifty thousand experience herself for her driving and ownership of Bertha—only a half level for her and not enough to push her over the edge to ninety, but well worth it.

Berthaville had taken its tax of just over 120,000 from the kills, a much smaller portion of the nearly five million experience it needed to get to level five and unlock Terrain Generation. Kills helped the settlement for sure, but there were over five thousand people in the truck. Even the relatively small amounts of XP they generated from living their lives added up to more than just fifty monsters.

It was after dark, and Bobby was again taking a turn driving, when the Command Module's other add-on, the old CB radio now converted into a magical, long-distance transmitter, shiny with chrome, lit up.

"Squawker base to Junkmouth, Squawker base to Junkmouth. Do you copy, Junkmouth?" The voice was scratchy.

Jill strode over to the comms console and snatched up the handset. Activating it cost more mana than she had expected, far more than the last time she'd used it.

"Buckman!" she said. "This is Junkmouth. Great to hear from you. How are things back in your neck of the woods? Over."

"Rough, but we're managing. We had a monster wave from your direction that almost overcame our defenses. Anything you can tell us about that? Over."

"Past Billings is an even higher-mana zone," Jill said. "Things are big in here, and there are more of them, over."

"How's your—" The radio turned to static.

"Say that again? You broke up, over," Jill said.

"I say again, how's your status? Any word on those bases? Over."

Jill checked the map. From the few landmarks they'd spied they'd been able to plot the truck's position, and they were slowly but surely making their way across eastern Montana along Interstate 94.

"We'll be at the first one tomorrow morning if we keep our current speed. Have you heard about the stretched space? Over."

He had, both from Babu and from reports of other people throughout the region that he'd managed to contact with his long-ranged communication ability. What Jill was driving through was by far the worst of any he'd heard of, though.

"It was good talking to you, Ms. MacLeod," Buckman said after relaying that, "but my next scheduled contact is in sixty seconds. Say hi to Babu for me, and drive safe, over."

"Thanks, Buckman. Junkmouth out."

Jill left another volunteer, this one named Tyler Woods, to take the night shift of driving, ate dinner in the mess with Mia, and spent a quiet hour in the corner of the gymnasium-cum-meeting-hall alongside a bunch of other tired people, watching the kids there play. They'd come up with one of those rapidly evolving games involving viciously thrown balls and pain. Coach, who apparently never took any time off, had separated the children into leagues by level to make things at least a little more fair, not to mention safer. Jill found herself cheering as she watched Sarah—a tiny girl who had an unusually high level, thanks to the misfortune of monsters and the protection of her dog—throw a dodgeball hard enough to knock a teenager, spinning and screaming, through the air. They were fine, of course, but rather embarrassed at being owned by someone a third of their age.

Jill went back to the cab but didn't take the wheel. Instead, she sat reclined in the passenger seat, watching the moonlit scenery blur past. The gentle rocking of Bertha slamming down onto the ground after every high-speed jump lulled her to sleep. She only woke up when Karen poked her, hard, in the shoulder and told her to get in bed. She went with a smile on her face, performed her nightly bathroom ritual surrounded by dancing flowers, claimed her bed from the indignant cat that had again appeared in her room, and fell asleep as soon as her head hit the pillow.

And just like that, another day passed.

CHAPTER 25

THE BIRD

There was no smoke. It was far too late for that.

"What in the devil's spiky dick happened here?" Jill asked herself and the crowd of people in the cab with her, who Babu and Mia insisted on referring to as the "bridge crew." Jill was there during most of the day even when she wasn't driving, which was something she was doing less the last few days to give the others more practice; she would only take the wheel either to relax or to deal with something truly dangerous. This was looking to be one of those situations, so she shoved Bobby out of the driver's seat and took the wheel.

"We're too late," Aman said. He had been there since the morning, working with the Customization console to make Bertha's architecture in its dimensional space something other than a dizzying tumble of cubes.

"Look at all those monster bodies," Katie said, her voice trailing off. She was on shift for repairs and had been curled up in her chair with a battered book, legs tucked under her. But now her book lay forgotten. She'd rushed to the windows when Jill had announced that their destination was finally in sight.

She wasn't the only one gathered to see. Coach, Ras, and Babu were all there too, ostensibly so that they could judge the security situation. Jill believed it for the first two; for Babu, she suspected he was just curious. Jacob had come too, bringing with him an assistant and a pile of paperwork. The town was only days old, but already the feel of turning a page of reports haunted Jill's dreams.

Finally, there was a new addition, Jake Foreman, who was watching the radar for monsters. He'd been in the navy, and while he hadn't had anything to do with radar for his specialization, he'd had an overly talkative buddy who did. It was enough qualification for Jill. The thing largely worked on its own, anyway; they just needed a pair of eyes on it that wouldn't get too distracted. He'd done his job well earlier in the day, spotting a hunting pack of high-level creatures, even worse than the one that had chased them last. They'd had to take a detour to stay away from them so had arrived at the base in the early afternoon rather than the morning.

Jill had been expecting something similar to the armory in Boseman: barbed wire fences, some garages for equipment, some old admin building, maybe guard towers if it was an especially secure site. But that wasn't what they'd found. Instead, they'd driven down a short access road off the highway and around a stand of magic-bloated trees to find a five-story office building. It looked brand new and the only remarkable thing about it was the lack of windows on the bottom two floors. A boom gate and a small sign that read "Department of Defense, No Entry" were the only advertised security.

Judging by the absolute devastation of the parking lot and the carpet of monster bodies, "No Entry" had been a lie.

The pavement looked like it had taken multiple hits with explosives, with large craters full of dismembered creatures blasted in a seemingly random pattern. The lot had been half full of cars, all of which were riddled with bullet holes on the side facing the office building, and the decorative trees between parking rows were cut down to jagged stumps. A long row of identical black SUVs had fared better against the bullets thanks to being armored, but Jill doubted any of them would be salvageable. It looked like some creature had decided to just run straight through them, tearing them apart and throwing parts in all directions.

And covering everything were bodies and blood. Hundreds of monsters of all sorts were in the parking lot: mutated animals, bugs, plants, and even some humanoid ones that Jill would have sworn were movie orcs. Most numerous of all, though, were dinosaurs. Packs of small raptors, their colorful feathers ripped and crushed, lay splayed around the torn-apart bodies of larger therapods. One specimen that lay over the crushed bodies of three sedans looked to be a full T. rex. The ground was stained with multicolored pools and smears, enough blood that even the sprinkles of rain the night before hadn't been enough to clear it all out.

The building was no better. All but a few windows on the top floor were shattered, with shards of black-tinted glass glittering on the bland strip of dead lawn. A corner of the roof had been ripped away, looking as if some *kaiju* had leaned over and taken a bite out of it. But the biggest damage to the base was a gaping hole, thirty-feet long, down the side closest to Jill; here, the wall was just gone, exposing the dark interiors of the first and second floors to the elements. Broken desks and shattered cubicles hung partially off the edge of the floor, interspersed with brown-and-white forms that sent a tingle of fear down Jill's back.

She focused on them as she drove them closer, squinting out of habit. What she saw made her gasp. They were the corpses of people, every one of them impaled on a spike of upward-bent rebar and left to bake in the brutal sun. They wore white lab coats, though that color was barely visible compared to the sick brown of dried blood.

There was a trail of more human bodies leading to the building's entrance. Judging by the nearby guns and matching body armor, these had been the base's security. The first lay fallen behind slashed cars amid piles of discarded bullet casings; a few more had been taken from behind as they fell back. Finally, right in the ruined entrance was a pile of over a dozen, their automatic weapons still clutched in stiff hands—at least for the ones whose hands were still attached. The bodies were marred with massive claw wounds that had cut through body armor to expose ribs and lungs, that had torn legs, arms, and heads clean off. It was hard to tell exactly how many of them there had been.

"I guess we know why they didn't answer," Babu said. He looked like he might be sick.

"Fuck," Jill agreed. "Is the radar picking anything up in there?"

"I"—Jake paused—"I'm not sure. The whole place is showing up as this sort of sparkling fog on the screen." He poked the display. "Nothing's ever looked like that before. There aren't any dots that look like monsters, though, and no level numbers."

Jill brought Bertha to a halt just outside the broken gate. "I don't think we're going to find survivors," she said, "and I'm getting a feeling like needles getting shoved in my eyeballs just looking at the place." She tapped her fingers on the wheel. "Is this worth it? We can keep right on going."

"Don't we owe it to the military to check it out?" Babu asked. "They gave us the machine guns for that, don'tcha know."

"The job was to find out why the people here hadn't responded," Jill argued, "and get them in contact if we could. They're all dead. Mission accomplished."

"Do we really know that?" Ras asked. "What if there's a safe room or a bunker inside?"

"Even if there isn't, I would not feel right leaving here without knowing what happened," Aman added in a quiet, solemn voice. "We might have fulfilled the requirements of your deal, we might not have, but we owe it to the dead to investigate. At the very least we can give them a burial."

There were murmurs of agreement from others. Then the System chimed in.

> New Quest: Investigate the facility.

"Piss in my cereal," Jill said. She turned in her chair to make eye contact with Jacob. "How about you, Mr. Civilian Representative? Are you going to stand up in the next town meeting and say you agreed with us checking this place out?"

He pulled a face but nodded.

Jill sighed. "Then we're going in." She put Bertha back into motion and pulled into the parking lot. The feeling behind her eyes spread to her body, a queasy tightening of her stomach and an itching of her skin. The armored glass of the windshield began to frost over as if being hit by a sandblaster, and Jill winced.

"Hey!" Katie yelled and pointed at the repair console. "We're taking damage!"

It wasn't much, just a few points of armor lost per second. The Ablative Armor power activated, and a wave of relief washed over Jill as its extra defense overcame the incoming damage. Bertha's natural regeneration kicked in and the glass cleared as the damage was repaired. Then Ablative Armor wore off, and the damage started anew.

"Sys?" Jill asked. "What's hitting us?"

> System Inquiry Detected
> Bertha currently has the condition "Toxic Corruption Aura." Conditions can be found on the main status page.

Jill felt a little dumb at that and brought up the condition.

> **Toxic Corruption Aura:** Currently dealing 68 acid and Mana damage to Bertha per second. Damage proportional to exposed area. Damage reduced by acid resistance.

The cycle of damage and repair continued every ten seconds as Ablative Armor cycled on and off of cooldown.

"I don't think we're going to be sending many people out to look," Jill said. "Bertha's armor suits have its acid resistance, but anyone outside without protection is going to get their ass melted."

Babu and Ras shared a look. "Hey, Aunt Karen," Babu said, "can you loop Mia in?"

They filled her in on the aura and the armor's acid resistance.

"It should help," Ras said, "but we'll be on a timer. The armor isn't invincible."

"Tell me about it," Mia muttered.

"I want to go," Katie said, a determined look on her face. "I can repair the suits."

"What level are you?" Jill asked.

"Twenty-two."

Jill grimaced and shook her head. "Then you're not going out on this one, sorry. You'll be dead in, what, five seconds if you're exposed?"

"The armor will keep me safe, and I'll keep the armor going."

"Unless we get ambushed by something strong," Ras said. "It doesn't even have to kill you. All it would need to do is poke one hole and stun you and there'd be very little the rest of us could do to save you."

"And before you say it can't happen," Mia said, "it did to me and I almost lost a leg."

"Fine," Katie said and crossed her arms. "I guess I don't want to melt."

"Just us three again, then," Babu said. "We'll get some speed buffs up and get out before we take too much damage. We can relay what we see with telepathy."

"You'll GTFO if you see anything too dangerous?" Jill asked. "This isn't like the Lair; we can drive away."

"We'll be careful," Ras reassured her.

"Then that's the plan," Jill said.

The first challenge was getting out of Bertha safely; Jill didn't want to take any chances on the aura seeping in, not when it would kill unprotected low-level people in seconds. She used Customization to rig an airlock but decided that even that was too risky and instead settled for driving away from the building until the condition went away. She kept the airlock as an emergency backup in case the team needed Bertha to ram in and rescue them in a hurry.

"You'll keep us in the loop?" Jill asked Babu before he stepped out. "That telepathy power of yours doesn't use too much mana?"

He nodded behind the helmet. "I'm good to keep a connection open as long as I don't have to cast too much else," he said. "If things get too hot, I'll have to cut it off. I can't exactly be drinking mana potions if I can't raise this visor, don'tcha know."

A tendril of magic reached out from his mind and connected to Jill. All of a sudden she could hear the sound of him, Mia, and Ras breathing. The other two were already outside.

"What's taking so long?" Mia asked.

"Jill's worrying," Ras said.

"Worry my ass, you ungrateful piffle peddler," Jill said. "I can hear you."

"We'll be careful," Ras replied.

Jill walked fast back to the cab, grateful that people were getting out of her way without trying to talk with her. Word of what had happened outside had spread through the truck and the mood was tense.

She had just gotten back into the driver's seat when Ras's voice spoke in her mind. It made her jump.

"We just started taking damage," he said. "It's much less than what Bertha was taking."

"It's the smaller surface area," Babu chimed in.

"But," Ras continued, "I estimate thirty minutes before we have to turn back."

"Make it twenty, then," Jill said. "Just to be safe."

She jumped as Aman touched her on the shoulder. "Could you share with the rest of us?" he asked. He was tense, and Jill couldn't blame him.

"Aw shit tits, I forgot to loop everyone in," she said. She tugged at the incoming strand of mana from Babu and threaded it through Captain Speaking, multiplying it into enough filaments to connect to everyone in the cab.

"We're approaching the wrecked cars and spreading out," Ras said, keeping up his report. "There's a body in one of them. It looks like they tried to hide, but were found. There's no head left. The body is"—he hesitated—"shriveled?"

There was a pause, and then Mia joined in. "There's a cluster of dead monsters near a crater. They all have small wounds on them. Shrapnel from a grenade, maybe?"

"Could be," Ras said. "Are we collecting loot?"

"We might as well see what they drop," Babu said. "Free resources to pick up on the way back."

There was a pause, then an explosion.

The bottom dropped out of Jill's stomach as she saw the rising fireball. "I'm coming in," she said and reached for the wheel.

"Wait!" Mia said back. "I'm fine. A little lost mana on the escape, but I'm okay."

"What happened?" Aman demanded. "Was the monster booby-trapped?"

"I'm not sure," Mia said. "I used the normal dialog box, and then it just exploded."

"Sys?" Jill asked. "You didn't think to tell us the monsters can fucking blow up when we do that?"

System Inquiry Detected
Corrupted areas are highly chaotic. Caution is advised.

"Okay, then," Babu said. "Look but don't poke it is."

"There's no response to the explosion," Ras said. "No movement from the building I can see. Let's move closer."

"Can you get in without getting close to the dead monsters?" Aman asked. He was standing, staring out the window. "You should treat them like potential IEDs."

"We can go in through the hole in the wall," Ras said after a pause. "There are too many near the door. And it's going to take us a bit longer; there are just so many of them."

For a few moments, there was only the sound of steps and breathing over the link. "I'm near the SUVs," Babu said. "They look like they weren't just cut but also melted? There's some sort of black sludge there too."

"Don't touch it!" Ras said, alarm in his voice.

"Obviously," Babu said back.

A sound behind her made Jill jump, but it was just Karen shifting in her seat. The cab was so quiet that that small noise had been like a shout.

"God in heaven," Mia said.

"What is it?" Jill asked.

"Right, sorry. I'm passing by the front and I have a good view of all the bodies. Parts of bodies?" She sighed. "All I can tell is that they went down fighting. And whatever killed them didn't stop to eat."

"Or come back," Jill said. She frowned. "That's unusual, isn't it? It fucking sucks to say, but the last time we saw a place where the monsters had won there weren't bodies like this."

"Yay," Babu deadpanned, "more mysteries."

The sound of a breath sucked in in shock filled Jill's ears. "I'm at the opening," Ras said. He swallowed. "I took a good look at the"—he hesitated—"scientists? I think they were still alive when they were impaled."

"Why?" Jill asked into the silence that statement made.

Ras continued, his voice sick. "Everything they can reach is smeared with blood, and their hands are torn up."

"The tips of the rebar," Babu said. He must have caught up. "They're bent over. Even if these poor bastards managed to slide their way upwards, they wouldn't be able to get out. The bars are too big at the top."

"That had to have been done deliberately," Ras said. "After they were impaled."

"Whatever broke in was one sick monster," Jill said. "Have we ever seen this kind of thing? It seems, well, cruel."

"It could have been some sort of butcherbird," Katie said. "They put up their kills for later."

"Thanks," Jill said. "I hate bird facts now."

"There's more," Ras said. "Look, there. Writing. In blood. The words 'Our fault' repeated over and over."

"Oh for fuck's sake," Jill said and rubbed her forehead. "This is clearly horror movie shit. Do I have to throw popcorn behind me while screaming 'Don't go in there'? Get your asses back here before an immortal clown jumps out of the murder building and stabs you to death!"

"Hey, Jill?" Mia said. "I don't think going in will be more dangerous than staying outside."

"Ope, I don't like that, don'tcha know," Babu said with dread. "Why?"

"Look at the debris," Mia said. "This hole wasn't made by a monster breaking in. It was made by something busting its way out."

CHAPTER 26

FATE OF THE OBEDIENT

"So," Jill said, "anything trying to eat your face? Because that was a 'something's about to kill me' line if I've ever heard one."

"We call those 'flags,'" Babu said.

"Nothing's moving," Ras reported. "Let's move in."

"Woah, hey," Jill said. "Did you not hear me tell you to come back?"

"Were you being serious there?" Ras asked. "It's hard to tell when you joke around so much."

Jill grimaced. He had a point.

"I think," Aman said slowly, "that we need to know what happened here. The disturbing details make that more true, not less."

New Local Quest: Destroy the source of Corruption.

"Really, Sys?" Jill asked. "You know I like you, but that's as manipulative as a warden with a camera greasing up the soap."

There was no answer, though next to her Aman sighed.

"We're on a clock," Ras said. "Do we go in or come back?"

Jill really wanted to say no. Just being near the base made her feel like she had eyeball ants, and if the disaster that befell the base really was the impaled scientists' fault, Jill wanted no part of whatever they'd been up to.

"Go in," she said, "but make it fast." If she wanted to avoid it, she had to know what it was.

"Thank you," Aman said softly to her.

Jill shrugged. "When you're right, you're right."

"We're inside now," Ras said. "It's some sort of cubicle farm, but there's a path carved through it."

"It's pretty nasty in here," Mia said. "Wet with, like, tons of mildew and mold. It looks like it's been abandoned for months, not a few days."

"That's the high-mana zone growth at work," Babu said.

"What's that sound?" Jill asked. There was a rhythmic sticking and sucking noise in the background that set her teeth grinding.

"That's our boots on the floor. Rain got in," Mia said. "That and monster blood." Jill knew it was from more than monsters.

"We're in a hallway," Ras said, continuing his narration. "The door's been torn off, and there are more dead. Another dismembered pile with guns, but it looks like they were firing down the hall."

"Another point in favor of 'escaped monstrosity,'" Mia said. "God, this sucks."

The sticking noise gave way to the click and scuff of armored boots on debris-strewn tile. Jill snuck a look around the cab and saw pale, stressed faces. Jacob looked like he might be sick. Jill felt the same.

"We're at a security checkpoint, I think," Ras said. "There's some sort of plexiglass airlock."

"There was," Babu said. "It's torn to shit now."

"Moving on," Ras said, annoyed. "There are more bodies. Monsters this time. This must be where the route they took breaking in met whatever was breaking out. There are lots of bullet wounds on the monsters but also claw and teeth marks. Were they fighting each other?"

"Oh my God," Mia said. "Look at this!"

"Oh," said Babu in a quiet voice.

"What is it?" Jill demanded.

"I think it used to be human," Ras said. "But it's not anymore. The monsters weren't fighting each other. They were fighting some sort of hybrid."

"Shit, this is like that car-man-cop thing all over again," Jill said.

"Only organic instead of machine," Babu agreed. "This one has dino claws, this one some sort of shark mouth deal, and this one just has more arms. Like, more human arms! Where did they come from? Who did they come from?"

"I feel like I'm never going to watch anime the same again," Mia said.

"Whatever they are," Ras said, "I think they succeeded? I see more dead normal monsters than dead hybrids. Babu, what do you think?"

"Something really twisted happened," Babu said, "but we're not going to learn what here."

"Then let's keep going. I see an open room ahead. Moving into it and—" His voice cut off.

"Oh my God, I'm going to be sick," Mia said. Shortly thereafter came the sounds of retching and chunky splashing.

"Ras? Mia?" Aman asked. "Are you there?"

"Ras is collecting himself," Babu said, his voice emotionless. "Mia will require cleanup when she has finished."

"What did you find?" Jill asked. "And why do you sound that way?"

"I have changed my mental state in order to retain effectiveness," Babu said. "We've found the remains of another several dozen hybrids. The majority are hanging by their entrails, which have been ripped from their bellies and attached to the ceiling. Evidence from the disposition and physical state of the bodies suggests that the minority dead on the floor inflicted this on the majority."

"Zit-sucking tire popper!" Jill swore. "What in the actual fuck?"

"I agree," Babu said. "Hold a moment. Mia is ready for a cleaning spell."

The telepathic connection wavered but stabilized after only a second.

"You're all going to need so much fucking therapy," Jill said under her breath.

"I agree," Babu said again.

"We're pushing on," Ras said. "I'm cutting a path." There was a sound like a ringing wine glass, then a rain of meaty thumps.

Behind Jill, Karen gagged.

"How's our time?" Jill asked.

"They have six minutes until your deadline of twenty," Aman said. "Another ten after that by the original estimate."

"We are taking slightly less damage than expected," Babu said.

"We're through." Ras's voice was rough but steady. "There's an elevator shaft in front of us with the doors ripped off."

"Look at them," Mia said. There was the sound of scraping metal followed by a heavy crash. "These are camouflaged to look exactly like the walls."

"Heading in," Ras said. "Babu, light." There was a pause. "The car's at the bottom. It looks like its ceiling was punched out by whatever came up. We're heading down."

There was a crashing thump, followed by a second and a third.

"Did you just jump down an elevator shaft?" Jill asked.

"Falls are no longer dangerous," Babu said. "The destruction here is limited."

"I don't think any monsters made it this far," Mia added.

"The aura's damage is higher in here," Ras said. He didn't sound worried.

"Do you need to get out?" Aman asked.

"We're so close," Ras said. "I can feel it." His voice was faster now, more urgent. The sounds of metal screeching filled Jill's mind, then more footsteps.

"Oh, wow," Mia said. "That is a lot of monster gems. Like, hundreds of them!"

"I see active technomana equipment here," said Babu. "There's a hopper and automated feeder mechanism slotting mana gems into a device that has glowing tubes leading away from it. I can sense extreme mana flows coming from it."

"We're following the tubes." Ras continued his narration, his voice excited. "They're laid out on a cable run on the ceiling. There's a locked door here; I'm cutting through!" Again the sound of a ringing glass followed by a crash.

"That is a lot of biohazard warnings," Mia said. Then she yelled, "Watch out!" There was a grinding scrape and then the thunderous, ripping tear of Blossom opening fire.

Jill clapped her hands over her ears, but of course that did nothing. Thankfully, Mia stopped firing after just a few seconds.

"Mia has successfully destroyed a dead, caged primate monster," Babu reported.

"I thought it moved!" Mia said.

"There are dozens of cages with tubes going into them," Ras said. "Each has what used to be a monkey? That's not right." He sounded disappointed.

"They appear completely desiccated," Babu said. "No other wounds. I believe the aura killed them."

"Ah!" Mia said. "That one absolutely just moved!"

"I can't feel any mental activity," Babu said. "The monsters are dead. But looking more closely, it seems that as mana is pumped in, they still experience tissue growth, which then immediately dies. That may explain the movement."

"God, this is fucked up," Mia said. "Hey!" she added a moment later. "I found a lab notebook! Let's see what the hell these people were thinking."

There was silence for a minute, broken only by the sound of breathing. Jill took a few deep breaths of her own to calm her nerves, but her heart still beat too strongly in her chest. Finally, she couldn't wait any longer. "What does it say?" she asked.

"The entry dates indicate that experiments have been active for just over a year," Babu said. "They were focused on the effects of several new strands of viruses on primates. There is a note saying that the airborne rabies data shouldn't be shared with higher-ups."

"That's not going to be in my nightmares at all," said Jill. "Anything about magic?"

There was the sound of flipping pages. "Yes," Babu said. "The entry four hours after System integration describes starting a new series of experiments on the former control group of monkeys. It started with mana infusions from the researchers' own powers, but they moved to mana gems as an external source later that day."

"And when did they switch to mutating their own people?" Aman asked.

Another silence. "I can't tell," Babu said. "The writing becomes unhinged before then. I believe the scientists began experimenting on themselves before others."

"Of course they did," Jill said. "I don't know whether that's commitment or insanity."

"Not here," Ras said, then muttered something under his breath.

"What was that?" Jill asked.

"We need to move farther on," Ras said. "This isn't the source, and we're running out of time."

Jill heard fast footsteps.

"Ras!" Mia said. "Don't move so far ahead! I can't cover you!"

"I'm going down the hall," Ras said, breathing hard. "There's another lab, this one with the door torn out." The sound of scraping. "Nothing!"

"Ras?" Aman asked. "Check in. What are you feeling?"

"One more room, one more room . . . There!" Ras yelled. "I've found her!"

"Ras is compromised," Babu said. "Casting counter-measures."

Jill's stomach leaped into her throat. Compromised meant mind control. He seemed fixated on "her" rather than violence, but if Ras turned against the other two, then an entire silo of elephant diarrhea was about to get sucked through a jet turbine.

The thread of telepathy wavered, then snapped.

"Fuck!" Jill said. "We're—"

A box popped up in her vision, and an instant later the telepathy snapped back on.

"The situation is resolved," Babu said.

Corrupted Caitlin Song defeated.
Bonus Experience awarded for: killing a corrupted sapient (x2)
Your contribution: 13%
18,720 Experience Gained!

Local Quest Complete: Destroy the source of corruption.
Contribution bonus: +.13
13,000 Experience Gained!
You are now Level 90! Level gain deferred per user preferences.

"What happened?" Jill demanded.

"She—I," Ras said, voice shaky. He took a moment. "There was someone talking in my head, begging for help. There was some sort of . . . thing. I guess it used to be a person, but there were no bones left, just a mound of flesh and too many eyes strapped to an operating table. The mana tubes led into her. It."

"And then I shot the shit out of that boneless fuck," Mia said. "Problem solved and quest complete."

"This appears to have been an experiment on the forced injection of monster mana into people," Babu said. "The aura around us has started to decrease, so I believe she was using the injected mana to emit it. I wonder what the effects were on the other subject."

"What other subject?" Mia asked. Jill heard Blossom spin up.

"The one that escaped," Babu said. "The lab we passed without a door was for a person too, and it lies at the start of the trail of destruction. We are facing a mutated human pumped full of thousands of monsters' worth of mana, with the additional XP from slaughtering every person here who was alive at the time of their breakout."

"Can we get the fuck out of here, like, right now?" Mia asked.

"We've completed our objectives," Babu said. "I don't want to stay here any longer."

"I—yes," Ras said.

"Hey, guys?" Mia asked. "Look over there."

There was silence.

"The, uh, exam table under Caitlin," Ras said. "It's dissolving?"

"More like evaporating," Babu said. "It appears that it is turning into mana." There was the wet sliding slap of 150 pounds of ruptured meat falling onto hard tile. "Now the floor is evaporating as well."

"Shit, it's coming towards us!" Mia said.

"Run!" Ras shouted. Pounding metal feet sounded through the link as they all did as he said.

"Right, I'm coming for you!" Jill said. "Get outside!" She put a foot down on the accelerator and hauled the wheel over. Jill braced herself as Bertha surged into motion towards the lab. Her skin itched as the weakening aura again ate into Bertha's armor.

"We're in the elevator shaft!" Ras said. There was the sound of shattering concrete. "Climbing!"

"Faster!" Mia yelled.

"The car beneath us just collapsed," Babu added. "Must climb faster."

Jill aimed Bertha straight for the hole in the wall, but the route was choked with dead monsters and wrecked vehicles. She hauled on the horn's chain and a plow-shaped blade of roiling sound exploded forward, tossing the broken cars and shriveled corpses up and away from Bertha. Surges of sickness flashed across her skin, like being in a gusting rainstorm of grasping centipedes, as the monsters detonated above them. Spikes of broken bone and tatters of leathery flesh bounced off the armor with the sound of hail.

"We're at the main floor!" Ras said. There was a terrible crash and a wet skid. "Sugar!"

"I've got him!" Mia said.

Jill slammed on the brakes and turned the wheel; Bertha slid sideways and stopped just outside the building, her nose pointed outward for a fast getaway.

"We're right outside!" Jill said over the telepathic link. "Aman, get ready to cycle the airlock. Karen, get people away from it just in case!"

The destruction spread out of the lab and under Bertha in motes of mana, rising into the air all around them like flies fleeing a corpse. They weren't black or dark—no, that would be an insult to a moonless night. They were just wrong, each a screaming statement of something that just shouldn't be. The view around them started to tilt as Bertha sank into the ground.

"There's no time for that!" Ras said. There was a clang, then two more, and Jill felt three sets of painful pricks as armored hands dug into Bertha's armor. "We're on! Go, go, go!"

"I've got them," Aman said as bands of metal snaked out of the armor locked around the trio.

Jill hit the accelerator. The truck's many tires spun on ground that had turned to quicksand.

Jill pushed Bertha's mana into Diffused Traction. The upgrade spread a web of grasping roots of power out into the ground around them, attempting to bind the terrain into something stable, but Bertha just lurched and the view tilted further. Everything around them was evaporating corruption, and there was nothing solid for the roots to latch onto to provide the foundation for a solid hold. They needed it to be bigger.

Jill opened the floodgates of Bertha's vast magic reserves and pushed. Ten thousand mana, then thirty thousand, then a hundred thousand! It took only a few seconds, but Jill's body shook and twitched as the power poured out; just the feedback from the sheer quantity of magic being pushed into one ability was enough to make her vision white out. At two hundred thousand mana, the roots had spread to just over 150 feet in all directions, when they finally met sweet, uncorrupted sedimentary rock. The whole web snapped into solidity, then strained as the wheels grabbed on. Bertha shot away, just barely clearing the area before the twelve seconds that Diffused Traction lasted was up. For just an instant the power attempted to renew itself, to grab far more power than was there to take, and Jill's heart missed a beat.

She gasped in pain, but the ability failed before it pulled more. Her vision came back to her, and she brought them to a stop.

She looked in a side mirror; where the lab had sat was a sharply cut crater, three hundred feet across, like some colossal titan had taken an ice cream scoop to the ground.

"That was metal," Katie said. Her eyes were wide.

"Jill?" Karen asked. "Are you all right?"

"I'm fine," Jill said, but her voice was raspy. She shook her head hard to clear it. "You okay out there?" she asked over their shared telepathy.

"I would like today to be over, please," Babu said. He sounded on the edge of tears.

"Make sure you're completely clean before coming inside," Jill said. "But fuck me, you three are done for today." She stood. "Bobby, you're back on the wheel. Aman, get them inside and then plot a route out of here."

"Where are we heading?" he asked. His hands danced over his Customization console and the hologram above shifted, showing the makeshift airlock open and swallow the trio.

Jill grimaced. "The next base," she said, "but get ready to change that and swing us due east. I'm going to call up Amelia on the radio and see just what kind of dried-up cloaca juice she's been snorting, sending us to a goddamn bioweapons lab! If I don't like the answer, or if I think the next base is going to be like this, then fuck our agreement. We're not doing that again."

Before she could get on the radio, the door to the cab slammed open. Sangita burst through, her face pale and hands trembling.

"Jill!" Sangita said. "I need you to follow me. Right now. We've got a problem."

CHAPTER 27

MURDER ON THE BERTHA EXPRESS

"You're telling me this was someone from inside the truck?" Jill asked as she stared with nausea and disgust at the body in front of her. "Not someone outside that got wrecked by that corruption aura? You're sure no one, like, snuck a body on board for some sick prank?"

"Yes," Sangita said. "No one's been on or off since we got here. If I understood Karen correctly, anyone who tried would have melted. Plus"—she hesitated, then sighed—"the body was found an hour ago, but I only got told just now."

"Balls," Jill said and rubbed her forehead.

She was in the Medbay Module in a sealed-off operating room, along with Sangita and Sam Mortensen. The latter was a short, black-haired man who had been a medical examiner in Billings. Until now, his specialty hadn't been required, and he'd joined his fellow doctors in Bertha in patching up the living.

It creeped Jill out just a little bit how comfortable he was poking and prodding the body. It was a dried-out husk of a man: skin, brown leather; hair, white cobwebs; and teeth, black, rotten spikes. No water or blood remained. It and any magic that the man had once possessed were gone, replaced with the sick feeling of mad corruption that Jill was becoming far too familiar with.

"As you can see," Sam said, "there is a rather obvious, but modest, entry wound on the left thigh." He pointed with a glove-covered hand at a small entry hole, now a puckered, dried orifice in brown meat. "But if we examine the back of the leg"—he lifted up the leg and revealed a truly ruinous sight—"we can see that the resulting exit wound was far larger." The hamstring muscles and chunks of the femur had been blown away, leaving a ragged, melon-sized cavity. The leg was really only still attached by the leathery remains of skin and quadriceps.

"Now, a week ago I would have told you that he would have bled out in moments from this kind of injury," Sam said, "but with System-aided healing and toughness being a function of level, and really quite unexplored, it's impossible for me to say for sure."

"Shit, he could have been alive like that?" Jill asked. Her stomach rose towards her throat, but she willed it down. "You know, before he got the bejesus sucked out of him."

"He would certainly have been crippled, but perhaps he could have been alive, yes," Sam said. "If I or one of my colleagues had been there in the room, we would have been able to staunch the bleeding with a flick of our hands. Truly remarkable. Why, one of the men working in the kitchen was terminally ill until last week!"

"Huh," Jill said. "I have to admit, that is one good pickle to go along with the general shit sandwich." She turned to Sangita. "Do we know who he is?"

"Not yet," Sangita said. "We have records of everyone who came on board and are doing a census to see who's missing. We're not saying why, but"—she shook her head and looked Jill in the eye—"there's no covering this up in a community this size."

"Why do you think I would want to cover this up?" Jill asked, angry. A vein behind her eye twitched, sending a spike of pain into her head.

Sangita took a step back. "I'm not saying you do," she said. "I'm just saying people are going to know soon."

"Right," Jill said. "So, do we have any clues?"

Sam coughed. "I do have a power for examining bodies," he said. "It was the first thing I took."

"Of course it was," Jill said under her breath.

"It took me almost all my mana," he continued, "but I got his class and level."

He poked Jill with a bit of magic and a box appeared in her vision.

John Doe, Level 4 Keyboard Warrior

"Colonoscopy bags in a blender!" Jill said. "It was this asshole who got whacked?"

"Jill?" Sangita looked spooked. "You can tell who this is?"

"It's Steve what's-his-name, unless there's another level four Keyboard Warrior on board. Wait, I've got the box here somewhere," Jill said. She flicked through her past notifications until she came to the one she'd gotten in the town hall. "Steve Parker!"

> Local Quest Complete: Identify the murder victim.
> Contribution bonus: +.4
> 2000 Experience Gained!

Sam blinked. "I did all that work and only got 0.6 of the contribution?" he asked. "System, this is a blatant sign of professional disrespect."

> System Inquiry Detected
> Quest contributions are assigned based on results. Direct infusion of the definition of "identify" is available. Proceed?

"Heh, nice one, Sys," Jill said. "But I've got to argue with you there. I didn't exactly have proof until you told me, so did I really identify him? Bit of a loophole if you ask me."

There was no response.

"Oh no, no, no," Sangita said and started pacing. "This is even worse. Jill, people were already pissed about how you blew up at this guy! The best-case scenario here is that they will think one of your cultists killed him without you knowing! Worst case, they'll think you ordered it or even did it yourself! This is a disaster!"

"Back up. My what now?" Jill asked.

"Did Karen not tell you? There are two cults dedicated to Bertha. Yesterday there was only one, but they had a doctrinal split. Both think the truck is Jesus, but one thinks you're Mary and the other Judas."

"Why would I betray my own truck?" Jill asked. "Wait, the others think I gave birth to it? How big do they think my cooch is?"

"Jill, don't try to apply logic, none of this makes any sense in the first place. And it's not important!" She pointed at the corpse. "What's important is that the last person to publicly challenge you is dead!"

Jill tapped her fingers on her leg and stared at the body. "No," she said.

"No what?"

"The most important thing isn't that he's the one who's dead," Jill said. "It's that he's dead at all and killed in such a fucked up way. There's a murderer in Bertha."

"That's really dramatic," Sangita said, "but can't you just find them in like a minute with your not-at-all-fascist loyalty-sensing power?"

"It doesn't really work that way," Jill said. "One tells me if they are willing to work for me and how they feel about it; the other tells me how they relate to Berthaville." She ground her teeth. "Even if I shoved my mana straight down their throats, I wouldn't be able to tell if they'd killed someone, only that they hated me even more. Except for the—and I can't believe I'm saying this—cultists, who think I'm some kind of lemming-sucking religious figure; I bet they'd ping as loyal even as they murdered the asshole right off an elephant."

"Sugar," Sangita swore. "I thought that would be the easy part!"

"I suppose we could start questioning the fifty people who actively want to fuck everything up?" Jill asked.

Sangita stared at her, unimpressed. "You just said it could be one of the 'loyal' ones. And rounding up and questioning every dissenter will help our problem of morale how?"

Jill sighed. "I'm kicking them off when we get back to civilization anyway," she said. "There's no reason for them to stay here if they're just going to cause problems."

"That's profiling."

"It's literal magic telling me their feelings before I've even seen them," Jill said. She snapped her fingers. "What we need is, like, investigation powers. Hey, Sam, did you have any detective buddies that came along?"

Sam flinched and looked away.

"There aren't many cops in Bertha," Sangita said quietly. "Not awake ones."

"Rattlesnake rimjob," Jill said with a sigh. "I'd forgotten that they'd all got their brains turned into santorum by that douche nozzle of a mayor. "

"Ms. MacLeod!" Sam snapped. "I don't know what that means, but by the context I can tell it's nothing good. Those are people, and we're going to make them better."

Jill looked sideways at the man. He wouldn't be any threat at all if it came to a fight. "Some friends of yours in there?"

"Jill! Knock it off," Sangita said. "What's the matter with you?"

Jill pulled a face and shook herself. She didn't know where that thought had come from. "Sorry, sorry," she said. "That wasn't right. I'm just a little worked up over—" She waved at the body but wasn't sure the excuse was true. She'd been feeling worse and worse over the last few hours, and her headache was a constant distraction.

"If this needs an investigation, we should ask my son to take the lead," Sangita said. "People will talk to him."

"Yeah," Jill agreed, "Babu'll charm the shit out of people, even if he doesn't lay down his own mind whammy." She glanced at Sam. "Which he won't, because we've all learned our lessons about that. Look, I really am sorry."

Sam nodded. "Apology accepted. We're all stressed lately, and these things happen."

"I was talking about Ras," Sangita said and looked away.

Jill played back the last few seconds of the conversation. "Hoooolv shit, 'my son'?" Jill asked. She took a step away from Sangita and gave her a withering stare. "Really?"

"It was a—"

"I'm going to cut you off there," Jill said. She pointed at the other woman. "I've been trying to stay out of your family drama, but that right there? That's a festering zit ready to pop all over us."

Sangita closed her eyes and when she opened them again there were tears there. "Ever since Babu was—"

"Nope!" Jill interrupted. "Nope, nopedy, nope nope nope. I am not the one who needs to hear it. Talk to your husband, talk to Karen. Hell, it will do the most good if you talk to Babu." She put a hand on Sangita's shoulder and continued in a softer voice. "We'll put out, I dunno, a wanted ad for a magical therapist. There's got to be someone on board who's doing that. Then, I'll lock the three of you in a room until you starve to death or settle things. Maybe after this whole murder thing is settled."

"A wanted ad?" Sangita asked after a few hard breaths. "Really? On what, the back of cartons of Berthaville breakfast cereal? We don't have a newspaper."

"I'm a therapist," Sam said. Sangita and Jill both stared at him.

"What, there weren't enough dead bodies in Billings to make a living?" Jill asked. "I find that hard to believe."

"Hey!" Sangita crossed her arms. "I grew up in Billings! It was a nice city!"

"Sangita, your hometown sucked. I literally got shot there."

"That was after—ah!" Sangita growled at Jill and pointed. "You're infuriating, and we have more important issues. Like the body in front of us!"

"And Babu's going to take point on it. That work for you?"

Sangita hesitated for a second. "Yes," she finally said.

"Good enough," Jill said. She gave Sangita's shoulder one more squeeze and turned to leave, but hesitated. "You're really a shrink?" she asked Sam.

"Yes, but we don't go by that term," he said with a long-suffering expression on his face.

"Can I send a few people to you?" Jill asked.

He smiled. "Of course."

"Great," Jill said. "Just be ready to hear about some really fucked up shit. Total nightmare fuel."

Sam's smile became a bit strained. Jill gave him a light punch on the shoulder. "Forget I said anything. I'm sure you'll, uh, be fine. Yeah." She turned away from him, pulled a face, and walked out of the room. The door swung shut behind her and she took one step, then staggered. A fresh spike of pain radiated through her head; it was bad enough that she pulled up Bertha's status page, just to make sure the truck wasn't under attack. It wasn't. She was just too stressed. "Fuck me, maybe I need therapy too," she said to herself. "Or at least a nap. Yeah. Right after a few more things."

She took the back way out of the Medbay and emerged in the command hallway, where the strains of "Mad World" wafted out of the turret prep room. Jill stomped into the cab, gave a cursory wave to everyone, and sat down in an observer's seat next to Karen, her console, and the radio. Jill closed her eyes for a moment to gather her thoughts before calling Amelia.

Karen cleared her throat. "I don't think Babu will be up to doing anything for a little while," she said.

"Of course you were listening," Jill replied without opening her eyes. "How about you help him? You must have snooped on everyone in the truck so far. Have any suspects?"

Karen frowned. "A few," she said. "I'll make a list."

"Great," Jill said. She closed her eyes for a moment. "That's good. All right, next thing."

She snatched up the handset to the radio and turned it on. It lit up and the dial made a show of scanning frequencies that were definitely not radio, but it didn't connect to anything. Jill scowled, formed the intention of yelling at Buckman in her mind, and shoved it into the chrome box alongside a pile of mana points. The lights on its face flared and it snapped onto a magical frequency.

"That—Junkmouth?" Buckman's voice crackled through the radio a few seconds later, his speech interrupted by a burst of static. "You're not scheduled for communication right now. Is this an emergency? Over."

"You're goddamn right it's an emergency. We got to the first base, and it was a goddamn biological weapons research lab! Where, by the way, everybody is dead because they went batshit crazy insane and started doing experiments on themselves—experiments that are now running around the countryside doing Bertha knows what! What in God's leaky anus were you thinking, sending us there?"

"I—uh—"

"Did I say 'over'?" Jill snapped. "Get me Amelia right now. Over!"

Aman shot her a startled look. Katie and another of the repair team had been chatting to each other in low voices but stopped dead.

"Yes, ma'am," Buckman said, his voice a professional mask. "The captain will be with you shortly."

"Jill," Amelia said just a few seconds later. "What's this I'm hearing about a bio lab? Over."

Despite all her anger, Jill was still impressed by just how good Buckman was at his job.

"Amelia," Jill said. "That first base was a goddamn slaughterhouse. What the hell errand did you send me on?"

"I didn't—" Amelia's voice cut out with a squeal that sent another spike through Jill's head.

"Say again, over," Jill said, trying to keep the pain out of her voice. She pushed more of Bertha's mana into the radio; it glowed brighter and started to flicker.

"I didn't know it was a bio lab," Amelia said. "As far as I knew it was—vehicle park and regional recruitment center. Over."

Jill weighed what she knew about Amelia and knew the other woman was telling the truth. "Spank me! Fine," she said. "I believe you. But that was a really shitty cover story! What, did they think no one would visit a recruitment center?"

"—worked, didn't it?" Amelia said. "I need to know what happened there. Report? Over."

Jill launched into the story in short, terse sentences. She left the most horrifying details out, mainly because she didn't want to think of them right now. "We barely made it out of the crater," she finished. "Now, I didn't plan on stiffing you on this job, but I need to know right now what I'm driving into next! Over."

The radio hummed and crackled for a few seconds.

"Did you get that? Over."

"—Minuteman facility, over," Amelia said.

"What, like re-enactors with muskets?" Jill asked. "Was the army going to march from Montana to Massachusetts and shoot at some Redcoats?"

"I believe Amelia means that it is a Minuteman III launch silo," Aman said. Jill looked at him without comprehension. "For intercontinental ballistic missiles."

Jill's mouth fell open. "Nukes? You're sending me towards lip-clipping nukes? After all that Sys has done to fuck up tech?"

"—gone," Amelia said. "All of them have—"

"Say again, over," Jill said.

"The warheads everywhere else are gone! They disappeared when the System came! But we don't know about this facility because we can't get in touch with them, over."

Jill blinked. "Gone? Sys, did you steal all the nukes?"

System Inquiry Detected
Information denied. Classified access request has been logged.

"Pfft. That's not a no. So, what, we're just going to double-check that it's the same there as everywhere else?" Jill asked. "And really hope some boss hasn't moved in to make a Lair of the Uranium Dragon?" She gritted her teeth against the pain, which was moving down her head and into her neck. "When we agreed, this was a few hours of delay. Now it's going to be—uh, Aman, how long are we talking?"

"At least three days," Aman said. He stood, walked back to her, and leaned in close. "Those silos are old," he said in a low voice that wouldn't carry, "but they're solid bunkers. If anywhere could hold out against this much mana and all the strong monsters, it would be there."

"Ugh," Jill groaned. "You're telling me there are survivors?" she said back in the same quiet tone.

"I'm saying that it's more likely there than anywhere else."

"Well, twist my nipple rings," Jill said at a normal volume. "I guess we're going after all."

"You have—" Karen started to ask.

"No!" Jill shouted.

"Thank—" Amelia said. "We have to make sure of what happened. Next time I see you I'll—bonus, over."

"You better name your damn child after me," Jill said.

Amelia laughed. "I'm naming her Bertha. She's doing all the work."

"Take care of yourself," Jill said. If they had been in person, she wasn't sure if she would have given the other woman a hug or flipped her off. Probably both. "We'll find your people." She flipped off the radio and slid the handset back into its holster.

"Thank you," Aman said.

"For what?" Jill asked and snorted. "For almost breaking my contract?"

"For changing your mind when you learned there might be people that need help."

"I'm not a fucking monster, Aman," Jill snapped. "What the fuck do you think of me?"

He and Karen exchanged a look. "I think you're a good person," he said levelly. "Are you feeling all right?"

"No," Jill said. "I feel like the anthropomorphic personification of the flu is skullfucking my head."

"Have you considered going to the Medbay?"

"I'm fine," Jill said. "I learned from last time and checked my stupid status."

System Inquiry Detected
Some conditions deliberately hide themselves.

"Then why'd you rag on me last time?" Jill demanded. "Ugh, stupid helpful System giving me stupid crucial information without my stupid self asking."

"You're not swearing," Karen said. She crossed her arms. "I'm officially mutinying until you see a doctor."

"You wench!" Jill said. "Then I'm not paying you!"

"You haven't actually paid anybody yet at all," said Kim from the front.

"Bah!" Jill threw her hands in the air. "Fine, I'll go to the Medbay."

She stomped out of the cab. "Mad World" was somehow still going.

"Will you play something better?!" she said.

The music cut off. There were a few seconds of hushed discussion, then the opening bars of "Highway to Hell" blasted out.

"Yeah," Jill said. She gave a small smile despite everything. "Yeah, that's right."

She went back through the back door to the Medbay, down the beige hospital-like corridor, and out into the waiting area. Two men were chatting behind the check-in desk, but there was no one waiting. Magical regeneration handled most of the minor problems people would normally seek care for, after all.

"Oh!" said one of the men behind the counter. "Ms. MacLeod! What can we do for you?"

"Uh, I think I need to see a doctor," Jill said. "My head feels like my ears have taken an unlubed—" She cut herself off. "It hurts a lot."

She was taken back into one of the examination rooms—though, thankfully, not the one that held the corpse.

It was Sam who entered. "You again?" he asked. "Is there another body for me?" He sounded disturbingly hopeful.

"No, you ghoul," Jill said. "I think there's something wrong with me." She explained her pain and uncharacteristic snappiness of the last few hours.

"You did seem agitated. Well, let's take a look," he said. His hands glowed blue and he put them on either side of Jill's head. He frowned, and the glow flashed brighter.

"Ow!" Jill winced and shut her eyes against the light.

The light cut out. "Huh," Sam said. "Well, that's new and creepy. Tell me, Jill, do you have any enemies?"

"Are you kidding?"

"Oh. Right. Well, take a look."

Curse of Screaming Death: You die in horrible agony.
Mana Cost: Variable, plus sacrifice of a living victim. Effects vary based upon the Level difference between target and sacrifice.

Jill whistled. "That is messed up." She cracked her neck. "Pick an animal."

"Uh, camel?"

"I can work with that." She thought for a moment, then pushed two thousand mana into Swampwater Vitality. "Hey, curse!" she yelled. "You're a camel-spit-gargling, bitch-spawned, cock-juggling thunder cunt of a limp spell. Choke on chode and take a hoof right up your ass!" The power exploded into action: streams of caustic mana reached into Jill, seeking the hidden corners of her magical self where the curse lay. Jill heard a faint scream of shock and rage, which faded along with the pain.

"Heh." She grinned. "I only worked in the camel thing a little bit, sorry. But I'm feeling better already."

Sam's ears were red. "Did you just heal yourself by—"

"Yeah, yeah," Jill cut him off. "It's a thing."

He cast his diagnostic power again. "It's gone," he said. He still didn't sound like he believed it. He frowned. "System! What the hell kind of power is that? What exactly are you encouraging here? Healing is for medical professionals!"

Jill snorted a laugh. "If you get any answers out of it, let me know." She gave him the lightest punch on the shoulder. "I sure as fuck haven't been able to."

CHAPTER 28

BURIED TREASURE

Jill?" Aman asked her the next morning. "Are you listening?"

Jill blinked her eyes open. She was in the center passenger seat again, but despite the coffee she'd poured down her throat, she wasn't quite awake yet. Her nightly take of experience had pushed her to level ninety-one, and her morning shower upgrade had been rougher than usual. It felt like whatever the System was doing to level her was facing more resistance, and with that came more pain.

"What?" Jill said. "Yeah. Wait, no. No, I wasn't." She shook her head and took another pull of coffee. She grimaced. It was cold. "My head's just not in the game yet today. You were saying something about the map?"

He pointed again at a series of pencil marks on his road atlas. "I said that I've been casting a location finder spell every hour since last night—"

"When did you get that?" Jill asked with raised eyebrows.

Aman gave her an unimpressed, red-rimmed gaze. "Last night."

"Right," Jill said. She looked down into her cup and sighed in disappointment. It was now cold and empty.

"Anyway," he said. "I've been plotting our progress. We're slowing down."

Jill looked at the speedometer. "No, we aren't," she said. "Unless . . ." She turned to the driver. "Bobby! Are you slowing your fat ass down when I'm not looking? Do I need to dock your pay?"

"Hell no, boss lady!" he said back, exaggerating his accent. "We're making this delivery at three hundred miles an hour no matter ha-wut!"

"You heard the man," Jill said to Aman.

"Yes, yes, you're both very funny," he said and gave the map a hard tap, "but look. For the last five hours, these have been getting closer together. We might be covering ground at the same speed, but we're not making as much progress."

"Flip my burger," Jill swore.

"Was that obscene or not?" Karen muttered in the background.

"Either way, you owe me a Berthabuck," Katie replied.

"My theory is that we're moving into an area of even higher mana density," Aman said. "Higher density means more space warping. More ground for us to cover."

"I wish the radar could show us that and not just monsters," Jill said with a sigh. "Then we could, I dunno, go around the worst bits."

"It kind of does," Jake Foreman said. "I first noticed at the, uh, murder base. It was all sorts of weird there."

Jill snapped her fingers. "Right! With the sparkles and shit."

Aman groaned and leaned forward to put his head in his hands. "You could have just told me this hours and hours ago?"

"I didn't know it was important!" Jake said quickly. "And it can only tell a bit! There's just, like, a fuzz of background noise that's been getting stronger."

"Huh," Jill said. She walked over to the radar console and studied it. "You're right. There's no detail at all."

"Well, it's not designed to show the mana. It's supposed to filter that out and just show the monsters," Jake said. "But maybe I can tweak it!"

"Hell yeah," Jill said. "And if you can't, go down to the workshop and tell them to get on it." She put her hands on her lower back and stretched. "Aman, go get some sleep. I'm getting more coffee."

Jill took a step and stumbled. "Dicktits!" she said and hopped on one foot. "Did I just step on something?"

"Hey!" Katie yelled. "We took damage!" She extended a hand glowing with warm brown mana and pressed it to the wall. A cool mist settled onto Jill's foot as the damage was repaired.

"We did jerk a bit off course," Bobby said. "I thought we'd just hit a rock."

Jill glanced down at the radar screen. It was clear. Unusually so. "Ow!" she hopped on her other foot. "Bobby, did you see anything that time?"

"No, I didn't—there!" Bobby yelled. He swerved the truck, but it didn't help.

"Shit gibbon!" The same foot again this time. Jill hopped to the front window and stared out. "What did you see?" she asked.

"Something under the ground, ma'am," he said. "Just a flash of color, and it launched this spear thing at us!"

Jill opened her mouth to respond just in time to see the same herself. What had been an innocent patch of dirt and stone shimmered, revealing a multicolored, cone-shaped shell a dozen feet long. It spun in place, and out of a dark opening in the shell's tip shot a four-foot-long wickedly barbed radula, straight into one of Bertha's tires. A sticky, muscular proboscis trailed behind it, pulled taut in an optimistic attempt at reeling in its prey.

"I saw that, you needle-dicked bug fucker!" Jill yelled.

Bertha was too massive and moving too fast for the trap to bring the truck to a stop, and an instant after penetration the harpoon ripped free from its limb. The initial stab hadn't done too much damage, but it had penetrated into the armor and stuck. Every rotation of the wheel drove it deeper in. On top of that, the wheel began to smoke as a hundred kinds of venom ate away at it.

Katie cast her repair spell again and the spine popped out. The venom resisted a bit longer but evaporated all the same.

Jill sighed in relief but it was short-lived; they hit another snail just a few seconds later.

"Dang it, Bobby," Jill said. "Slow down and dodge better!"

"I'm trying, boss!" he said and tweaked the wheel to the side while tapping the brakes. Bertha swerved sideways, wheels throwing up a rooster tail of dirt and dust. They shed speed quickly and were soon down to a more manageable hundred miles per hour. "There's nowhere for me to go. This place is just full of them!"

"I guess we know why there aren't any other monsters around," Aman said. "They must have learned to avoid this whole territory. Either that or they've simply eaten everything here. It really is an amazing bit of new habitat, isn't it?"

"I would be more amazed if they would stop stabbing me! Why didn't we see we'd—d'oh!—driven into a minefield? I thought the—shark taint!—radar was supposed to—dick teeth!—see through dirt?"

"Maybe they have good enough stealth powers?" Jake said. "It's a radar, not magic."

"It is literally—clowns!—magic!"

"Oh. Yeah."

"Ideas?" Jill asked the cab at large.

"Just shoot everything?" Katie asked. "Also, I'm down to half mana. Karen, can you call the rest of the crew?"

"On it," Karen said.

"Let's do it," Jill said. She tapped into Captain Speaking and connected to the turrets. "Hey—ow!—Beezilla," she said.

"We go by Antonio now," came the multivoiced response.

"Antonio, do you see anything to fuck up?"

"Just the disturbed dirt of our passing," they said.

"Sugar," Jill muttered. "You know what? Just blast a path ahead of us. They're out there."

The chattering roar of machine guns and spraying whoosh of flamethrowers filled the cab as the gunners did as she asked. Between the turrets' own purchased abilities and War Rig, the Adaptive Mounts power was running at a full twenty-six levels above Jill's own ninety-one. On full auto, each machine gun consumed a whopping 585 mana per second, so they were restricted to fast bursts. But when they did fire, there were so many bullets with so much punch behind them that their impact carved great trenches in the ground, spraying up reverse waterfalls of dirt and, sometimes, bright blue blood.

> Landbound Rainbow Cone Snail defeated.
> Your contribution: 11%
> 583 Experience Gained!

"Yeehaw! That's a kill!" Bobby whooped. "Hah, they're running, see?"

Jill grinned. The underground creatures might be stealthy while still, but when they moved they left a trail of raised earth behind them. "You know what?" she said. "These things have put me in a bad mood. Hey, Sys! We're spending too much mana throwing dirt in the air. Do any of the ammo upgrades let us fire through shit better?"

> System Inquiry Detected
> Phasic Ammo allows projectiles to ignore 80% of the resistive effect of non-living matter. This reduces the damage they deal by 31.25%.

“These fuckers deserve it,” Jill said. She purchased the Phasic Ammo. A surge of magic curled its way around the turrets as the upgrade took effect, and they cocked their metaphorical heads at her, sniffing the new ammo type to see if it would help them kill. A hunting howl resonated through Jill’s mind as they approved.

“We thought you were going to warn us,” the mixed voices of Antonio complained.

“Ah, slap me right in the cooter!” Jill said. “I knew I forgot something. Still, there’s a new toy for you. How about you try it out and get us all some XP?”

The turrets fired again, the tracer fire from the machine guns now a bright electric blue reaching out to the head of each earthen trail. The rounds slipped into the ground with tiny puffs of dirt rather than giant bursts, and the kills came fast.

> Landbound Rainbow Cone Snail (x17) defeated.
> Your contribution: 13%
> 11,558 Experience Gained!

Bobby pulled the wheel over to dodge a suspicious patch of ground, but he was just a bit too hard. Bertha went into a sideways skid and the wheels dug deep into the earth. Three more kills popped up in Jill’s vision, monsters that had trusted in their stealth to keep them safe rather than running. Mana surged into Bertha’s reserves from the Voracious Wheels, refilling what was lost from the firing of the turrets.

“Keep those swerves up, Bobby,” Jill said. “There’s even more of them out here than we thought! Time for some XP farming, folks.”

The snails were ambush predators—and deadly ones, given that they were completely invisible to Bertha’s radar and able to pierce the truck’s armor. But they were fundamentally short-ranged, slow creatures and didn’t seem smart enough to lay the kind of coordinated ambush required to truly threaten something so much stronger than them. They were easy prey.

Jill handled the looting, sending out pulses of her mana in every direction to trigger the automatic conversion of monster to item. Those that were close she levitated; she’d gotten much better at maintaining her concentration and could handle dozens of Cargokinesis items at the same time. Those farther away she pointed out to Bobby, who grinned as he slid Bertha through murderous slides to pick them up. Jill called the other drivers, Kim and Tyler, into the cab and put them into shifts at the wheel, spreading out the XP between them. None of them leveled; Jill had insisted they follow her lead and defer experience gain until later.

The radar proved its worth. While it couldn't see the snails, it could see when there were other monsters in the distance, and they somehow knew where the territory of death was. That was Aman's cue to call out the next turn. He plotted their course, putting them through first a six-sided sector search of the snail's territory, then an out-to-in spiral. They took a good number of hits on the way, so many that Jill almost ran out of swears. It never stopped hurting. But Katie and her team of Mechanics, Punk Greasers, Mad Scientists, Hot Rodders, and other classes kept up a rotation of repairs.

Jill called off the hunt a little over an hour later. The last twenty minutes had yielded almost no additional kills as they swerved their way over ground that they'd already covered. Some lucky creatures had most likely managed to stay hidden, but not many, and it wouldn't be worth the time to be more thorough. Jill had lost count long ago of the number of gems, shells, meat, and other more bizarre pieces of loot that she'd levitated in, so she willed the System to give her a summary of all the notifications she'd ignored while doing her part.

Landbound Rainbow Cone Snail (x732) defeated. Your contribution: 13% 494,832 Experience Gained! You are now Level 96! Level gain deferred per user preferences. The Settlement of "Berthaville" has grown to Level 5!

"Holy fuck!" Jill said. When she had checked on the core crystal that morning it had needed almost two million XP to get to the next level. As a group, they must have just taken in ten times that amount.

She turned around with a grin on her face and was momentarily shocked at the sheer number of people in the cab with her. It was an "all hands on deck" moment with the three shifts that Aman had organized all there at once for their share of XP, and they were out of seats. "How about that, people?" she asked. A quick mental calculation put the average level of the snails at fifty-two. "We just killed over thirty-eight thousand levels' worth of monsters! Over twenty million XP!"

Tired cheers filled the cab. Some had run themselves harder than others; the repair crew in particular were sweaty messes from repeatedly draining and recharging their mana pools over and over.

"Hey, Mal," Jill said, picking on the youngest member of the repair team, a teenage boy whose class of Cake Apprentice somehow gave him a general-purpose repair power. "Pick a number between one and three."

"Uh, three?" he said.

"Then the night shift gets the short straw!" Jill said. "Stay here and get us back on course. The rest of you, go someplace away from me and level. First shift, you get back here ASAP and take over once you aren't moaning your faces off. Everyone good?"

There were a few good-natured grumbles from the night shift, but nothing serious. Jill joined the crowd of people exiting the cab to find a party starting in the turret prep room, complete with blasting swing music. Jill had to admit, the bard band had range.

She was tempted to join in the dancing—she really needed to blow off steam—but only for a moment. She could tell from the personal space around her, unconsciously granted even in this press of people, that she didn't really belong in this crowd. It would only stifle things to have her there.

She went into her room to level, alone.

CHAPTER 29

ASSUMPTIONS

Jill sat cross-legged on her bed, her eyes closed and her hands resting on her thighs. Breathe in, breathe out. She was Jill, no matter what happened.

"Okay, Sys," she said. "Hit me with the last one."

Threads of magic shot from her mind and weaved their way through her being. She'd thought that spacing out the five level-ups, giving herself enough time to center herself but not forget the last experience, would make the process easier. Instead, it had just made it more confusing. Some of the magic went to the same places every time: her bones, muscles, and joints all got attention, as did her eyes and ears. But the rest of the mana threads went to seemingly random locations. Level ninety-three had almost half the magic concentrated into her bladder, of all things.

Jill clenched her teeth as the threads pulled taut. This step kept getting worse every time, no matter what mental preparations she made. She spasmed as pain wracked her and ended up sprawled on her bed, covered in sweat.

You are now Level 96!

"Axle snapper," Jill said, but there was no energy to it. She peeled herself off the bed and stumbled over to the tiny bathroom. A wave of her hand sucked another twenty sunflowers into Bertha. The progenitor plant, now level forty-seven and four feet tall, was budding so much that Jill had made a pocket in the walls, lined with shelves, to store the offspring. They seemed perfectly happy there despite the darkness, the crop waving in unison in the flow of mana.

She turned the shower to its hottest setting, stripped, and stepped into the flow of steaming water. She didn't have to worry about it scalding her anymore, but the warmth seeped into her muscles, and she felt herself relax just a bit. Right up until, with a pop of displaced air and a happy, golden chime, a flowerpot appeared atop her head.

She answered a knock on her door a few minutes later, a mug of coffee in one hand and a sodden flower in the other. She was met by a wall of sound—the pounding music and laughter of a party still in full swing—and Babu.

"Hey, Jill," he said, exhaustion in his voice. He saw the plant, opened his mouth, but just shook his head with a sigh. He looked fabulous, as the enchanter always did, and there were no bags under his eyes or other obvious signs of tiredness. But the spark of his gaze had diminished.

"Hey," Jill said. "Christ, you look like you need caffeine even more than I do. Come on in. I'll make you a cup."

"We've all got the same add-on, don'tcha know," he said but followed her.

"Maybe," she said, "but I'm the one who can stuff enough mana into it to make something strong. You're stuck with the factory settings, you poor bastard."

The extra magic made the coffee machine shake and a blast of steam escape from the side, but Bertha's regeneration would repair the damage soon enough. Babu took a hesitant sip of the dark brew and his eyes went wide. "Woah," he said.

"Good, huh?"

"I'm just amazed you're still alive, putting this inside you," Babu said, but he took another sip.

"That's what she said," Jill said, not waiting for him to swallow. Thankfully, she had magic to clean up the resulting mess.

"How're you doing?" Jill asked after she'd stopped laughing. "Get some good levels from the all-we-can-kill snail buffet?"

He shook his head. "I didn't take a turn shooting," he said. "The rest of the crew needs the XP more than I do."

Jill pulled out the chair by her small desk and sat in it. "I guess they do," she said. "Can you imagine what would happen if someone—level, what, 30?—got hit with that spike thing? Snail food." She leaned forward. "But you didn't answer my first question. Babu, you look like shit."

"I haven't slept because I see corpses every time I close my eyes," he said. "It turns out that my emotional control power also gives perfect memory when it's on. Yay."

"Well, that sucks donkey dick," Jill said. "Did you see that shrink I told you about?"

Babu sighed. "No."

"Well, do it, doofus," Jill said. "He's a bit creepy around a body but seems like a decent dude." She paused and drummed her fingers on her leg. She didn't want to push Babu, but she'd tapped him to look into the murder and needed that done. "Speaking of bodies, did you do any, uh, investigating?"

He nodded. "I talked to the woman who found the body, Steve's sister. I jumped into her head for a little bit and watched her find him, but she was freaking out so much at the time that I couldn't get a good read on everything." He shuddered. "At least I know she wasn't lying when she said he was just dead on the floor of their bunkroom."

Jill frowned. "You, uh, jumped into her head? And felt what she felt when she found her dead brother?"

"She didn't know who it was then," Babu said, "so it was more like her just finding a random body. But yeah."

"No wonder you're all fucked up. You're going to talk to the doc soon," she said. She pointed two fingers at her eyes, then at him. "I've got magic truck powers to check if you do, and I'll sic your aunt on it too, so don't think of skipping out."

Babu looked down at his cup. "Okay, okay, I will." He paused for a moment. "Hey, Jill, did you do an upgrade earlier?" Babu asked. "I was up with Mia and thought I felt it around us." He sounded a bit sad.

"Yup," she said and sent him the System's message about Phasic Ammo. "We needed a little something. I had a few class points." She paused and checked. "Sugar my donut, I'm up to fourteen free already?"

Babu smiled at her but it didn't reach his eyes. "That's great," he said. "You seem to really be coming into your own with spending them."

"Babu," she said and a corner of her mouth tilted up, "are you jealous that I'm doing stuff without you?"

"No! Well, maybe a little. I was the chief build advisor," he said, embarrassed to be admitting it.

"You are fucking adorable," she said. She took a deep swig. "Listen, I'm getting more used to Bertha because I'd be pretty dumb not to at this point. And I've got Sys on standby to give me terrible advice."

> System Inquiry Detected
> The value of System information is directly proportional to the intelligence of the receiver.

"See?" Jill said. "But what I'm trying to say is that I don't know shit about things other than this big girl." She slapped the wall. "Monster abilities? Other classes? My own powers? Weird item bullshit? Nada. Don't worry, bud. I still need you. You don't get to retire yet."

Babu had turned just a little pink by the end of her speech. He looked away but had a small, genuine smile. "Thanks, Jill," he said.

"No problem," she said. "So, what are the other ammo types I should take?"

"Arcane, entangling, and explosive," he said immediately. "In order of importance."

Jill blinked. "That was fast."

"Arcane deals extra damage to creatures with mana sensitivity; they're rare at our level, but any that we come across are going to be extra nasty and might be highly resistant to physical force. Entangling had competition from knockback, for controlling the movement of enemies, but in the end, enemies with incredible dodge are a real threat, and Bertha can just drive away from normal things instead of knocking them back."

"Makes sense to me," Jill said. "And explosive?"

Babu grinned. "Because everyone loves to see things explode, don'tcha know! Some monsters just need bigger holes put in them. Plus, I just cannot wait to see what happens when a flamethrower gets that as an upgrade."

"Why?" Jill asked. "What's going to happen?"

"I have no idea!"

Jill snorted a laugh. "Then those are the ones I take. Let's see what the next upgrade on the turrets is!"

She almost took the three ammo types right away but remembered to warn the gunners first and check in with the cab to make sure that the coast was clear. The gunners hopped off, she took the upgrades, and the turrets salivated at their new abilities. The mental image of a fear dear, stuck to the ground with goo and seared by brilliant golden light popped into Jill's mind. With a flick of her guns, she shot it one more time. The bullet struck right between those deadly green eyes and the entire head exploded, showering her mindscape with teeth.

Jill shook herself and yet again decided that she should also get in line for therapy.

> Congratulations! Advanced Turret (Small Arms) upgrades complete!

"Uh," Jill said, "Sys, that's it? No new powers?"

> You have discovered that modules by default have 2 Tiers! Further module Tiers may unlock if they are compatible with your Class Evolution.

"Well, shit," Jill said. "I kind of thought the upgrades would just keep on going, don'tcha kn—" She snapped her mouth shut before completing the words and narrowed her eyes at Babu. "I didn't say that. I guess once I finish the ones I have, I'll actually have points to spend on myself."

"Or more modules!" Babu said. "Oh! Oh! We can do what you did with the Medbay and come up with our own!" He reached into his pocket and pulled out a vial.

Jill's eyes lit up. "We're totally going to trick Sys into mounting artillery." Then she saw what he was doing and something in her mind clicked. Her hand shot out with blinding speed, the full strength of her 199 body rating behind a slap aimed at his hand; Babu blurred, an expression of shock on his face, and reappeared two feet to the left. The shockwave from Jill's strike blew back his hair.

"Jill!" he said. "What the fuck was that?"

She pointed at his hand. It still gripped the vial. "I just realized something," she said. "Right before you left for, well, you know where, you said you couldn't drink 'mana potions' with the visor down. Is that one of them?"

"Yeah, so?" he asked. "I spend a lot of mana. I've got like five active spells going right now!"

"So you've been drinking them a lot," she said, "and they're, what, putting someone else's mana inside you?"

"That wasn't efficient enough," Babu said. "We automated production with—with—" Babu's voice died and his face went pale. The vial fell to the deck and bounced, blue sparkling liquid oozing out to coat the floor. "We make them with monster cores now," he whispered. "Oh my God." He started shaking.

"We're going to shut down production," Jill said, "and tell everyone why. Fuck, you can make illusions, right? We can show them exactly what nightmare fuel this shit does so no one does it behind our backs. Dare to not turn crazy and kill everyone."

Babu staggered back and sat on the edge of the desk. One of the half dozen sunflowers Jill had put there bent forward and nuzzled him with its petals.

"Hey," Jill said. "Did anyone using them go fucking nuts yet?" she asked.

He shook his head.

"Then the dose hasn't been high enough for things to go really bad. We're okay," she said. "You're okay."

He didn't answer.

Jill sighed. "C'mon," she said. "We're going to go get you checked out and see if the docs can sense any of that corruption stuff in you."

"What if they do?" Babu asked in a croaking voice. "Jill, I haven't felt like me for a while now."

Jill snorted. "Neither have I, dingnut," she said. "How could we with all this piffling twaddle of a horse puckey going on?"

A flicker of a smile flashed over his face.

"And," Jill said, "if there is something actually wrong with you, we'll twist Sys's nipples until it gives us a way to get rid of it. Now, are you coming, or do I have to toss you over my shoulder and take you there myself?"

"As if you could," Babu said, but he stood. He took a long look at the vial and its puddle, and then a bolt of black fire burst from his eyes. Glass melted, liquid boiled, and Jill winced as Bertha took a few points of damage.

"I'm sure that was very cathartic, but could you not ding up the truck?" Jill muttered. She moved to the door, Babu in tow.

"Jill!" Karen's voice boomed out just as Jill's hand touched the doorknob. "Jill, we've got another, uh, 'problem.' The same kind as last time."

Jill closed her eyes. "Fuck!" she yelled. "Okay, okay. I'm on my way to the Medbay anyway. Tell them I'll be there in a few minutes."

"They aren't in the Medbay yet," Karen said. "The, uh, medical examiner person took a look and thought you'd want to see the actual crime scene this time."

Jill turned to Babu. "C'mon," she said. "I'll drop you off."

He pursed his lips, then shook his head. "No, I'll come with you," he said, his voice still shaky. "This is my job right now and I can do it."

"You sure?"

"Let's go," he said. "I'll be okay."

It was a lie, but Jill didn't call him on it. "Then let's move, chief investigator," she said to him. Louder for Karen, she continued, "Tell the doc I'll be right there. I just have to find him first."

Jill closed her eyes and let her senses pour out into Bertha, seeking out Mortensen. Her attention flashed down the hall, into the common areas, then into the warren of temporary bunkhouses. Nothing. She frowned and pushed on, searching through the Habitation Module, looking for that particular feeling of cleanliness that she associated with the medical examiner's mana.

"Hey, uh, Karen?" Jill said, shock in her voice. "Something's not right. You're going to have to give me directions."

CHAPTER 30

HIDDEN THINGS

Jill was getting sick of looking at bodies. She should have been helping her friend or been in the workshop making sure that the corruption that had infested the last base didn't take root in her truck. Instead, she was in the far corner of the Habitation Module in a room twice the size, and with twice the bunks, of her own. At first glance, it was the same as the other doubled-up rooms, even complete with its own window to the bright sunny sky of Berthaville's dimensional bubble, but it was strangely run down. The beds were unmade and their bedding torn, the floor scuffed with dirt, and the walls spattered with globs of blood.

Strangest of all, Jill couldn't feel the bunkroom through her connection to Bertha, nor sense anyone inside. Stepping into it had been like looking down to find that one of her toes had gone numb and unresponsive when she wasn't paying attention.

"Well," Jill said. "He's dead. What did you want me to see, besides the obvious?"

The body was of a pale, pasty man, who was naked and lying in a pool of his own blood. While he wasn't completely desiccated like the last body, he looked like he might have been on the way there. Jill had seen photos of people as emaciated as he was, but only from places that had been suffering months-long famines. Even if he hadn't eaten at all since magic had appeared, he shouldn't have wasted away so much. That most likely wasn't the cause of death, though; that would be the fact that his head was missing.

"You may be thinking that the cause of death was decapitation," Sam said, "but you would be wrong! Technically."

"Someone took his head after he was dead?" Jill asked. That was an interesting twist.

"Well, no, I'm pretty sure they didn't," Sam said, "and the head being gone is the cause of death. But there was no decapitation! That requires the head to have been cut off. I believe that, to put it in scientific terms, his head instead exploded."

Jill stared at him. At that moment it was just her and Mortensen at the murder scene. The unfortunate person who'd discovered the body had screamed bloody literal murder, so talk of the killing had already spread throughout the truck. Babu was interviewing him to get a second set of eyes on what had happened; Sangita and Jacob were holding an emergency town hall to announce the deaths and had decided that Jill's usual brand of profanity wouldn't help; Ras was down the hall, deep in conversation with a trio of Cloud Killers, who were helping him to keep others out.

Jill didn't really need the help—she could just seal off the walls if she needed to—but she appreciated the gesture.

"Yeah, I can see it's missing," she said, "but exploded?"

"Look at this," Sam said and walked to the nearest wall. The smooth metal was marred by a sharp yellow shard that had been driven into it.

"Steal the lube and—"

"However that expression ends, it is grossly inappropriate," Sam interrupted her.

Jill glared at him. "It's how I handle stress, assclown. Is that bone? Driven into metal?"

"There are shards all over"—he pointed to another half dozen locations on the other walls and the ceiling—"but, curiously, no brain matter, only blood and a few traces of skin. It's as if his brain simply ceased to exist at the same time his skull was propelled outwards."

"That is fucking disturbing," Jill said. Now that she was looking more closely she could see even more punctures in the ceiling directly above the body, places where the skull fragments had been driven far enough into metal to be completely buried. "Could the magical cleaners have just dealt with the brains?"

"But not the pool of blood?" Sam asked.

"Right," Jill said. She rubbed her forehead with her gloved hand.

"The body was found this morning, but I believe he died a little under twenty-four hours ago," Sam said. "Both my prior knowledge and, I have to say, a very handy—nigh cheating—power corroborate that."

"Why is it that whenever I'm with you and there's a body, you're in a better mood and not worse?"

Sam sniffed. "It's nice to be useful," he said. "Class and level," he announced.

A box appeared before Jill courtesy of a poke of Sam's magic.

Level 21 Maiden of Death

"That's just great," Jill said. "Not creepy at all. And there's nothing else you can tell me about how he died?"

"Not particularly," Sam said. "I don't see any gross injuries. No stabs or gunshots or blunt force trauma. I'll have to do an autopsy in the Medbay to find clues other than the missing head and property damage."

"And that's another thing," Jill growled. "What in Zeus's curly duck dick is going on with this room? I should have felt a skull-bomb going off, and it should have healed itself of the damage."

She stepped closer to the wall and opened her mana senses. It seemed to be normal Bertha material, the same kind of metal infused with the truck's mana that made up the walls everywhere else. Jill homed in on a piece of bone and pushed a bit of her own magic towards it, using a mixture of Customization and her own control to try and pop it out. But rather than sink into Bertha's structure, a master and friend welcomed home, her mana was repelled as it bounced off of an invisible barrier. A burst of familiar ozone hit Jill's nose.

A surge of anger ripped through her. Bertha was hers, and she wasn't going to stand for whatever bullshit was keeping them apart.

She snapped on Captain Speaking and snaked her attention down the hall. She felt Babu and Ras in close conversation, the witness long gone. "Babu!" she said, interrupting them. "There's some real magical fuckery going on in here. Can you take a look?"

"This," he said a minute later, a hand on the wall and his eyes closed, "this is really impressive. It feels like my invisibility spell applied over the entire room but making mana flow through instead of light. And there's not just hiding, there's also elements of cutting?" His eyes snapped open.

"Oh! I get it! This whole spell is to make it so that first you can't feel what happens in this room with your magic, and then it cuts it away so that none of Bertha's automatic responses happen either."

"So magic did it. Great. Can you, I dunno, track whoever put it up?" Jill asked. "Is that a thing?"

A pulse of dark mana rippled out of Babu and he stood in silence for a few seconds. He shook his head. "I tried an anti-invisibility spell," he said, "but it didn't find anything."

"Then fuck this thing," Jill said. The anger inside of her burst out in a tide of golden mana that spread over the walls, unformed by the System into a neat, packaged spell, but carrying with it her ironclad certainty that nothing was going to come between her and Bertha. Black-and-green glowing shapes rose from the wall to meet it: runes that turned the eye and sickened the viewer.

They held for a few seconds, but only that. With a sudden series of popping snaps and tiny gold and green fireworks, the runes collapsed one after another.

What had been hidden from her, cut away, was hers again. Then the feedback through her Soulbond struck, and Jill wished it wasn't. The room was a rotten tooth: raw, festering, pulsing. Abused by terrible magic and filled with tiny wounds, this part of Bertha had been crying for help only to have its pleas met by silence. But now Jill could hear. She staggered as a feeling of time passing, of events happening, of magic and death hit her like a baseball bat wielded by déjà vu's sadistic athlete cousin.

Soulbound Paragon advanced skill discovered!
Bond Inviolate: Nothing can come between you and your other half. Dispel any effect attempting to hinder your connection to Soulbound Modular Vehicle "Bertha." This spell is 2.8 times more effective than a standard Dispel Magic.
Mana Cost: Variable

Jill put her hand on the wall. "You're okay, girl," she said softly to it. Groaning pops sounded around her as the walls and ceiling healed themselves of damage, pushing the shards of bone out. They fell to the floor in a macabre clicking rain.

"You just did that thing again, didn't you?" Babu asked, a glowing barrier springing up above his head to deflect the falling bits. "Where you do a spell without knowing it first?" He shook his head. "That is completely unfair."

"I did explode my own ass once," she said and sent him the box for Bond Inviolate. "Ask your dad."

There was a joke there somewhere, but another box popped up in front of Jill before she had a chance to figure it out.

> Delayed notifications discovered! Time delay: 23 hours, 19 minutes, 21 seconds.
> Corrupted Billy Harrison defeated.
> Bonus Experience awarded for: killing a corrupted sapient (x2)
> Your contribution: 85%
> 35,700 Experience Gained!
> You are now Level 97! Level gain deferred per user preferences.

"I killed someone?" Jill asked. "Shut your text hole, Sys. No, I didn't!" She shared the notification with Sam and Babu.

"I—" Sam choked, "I got it too. Only five percent, but . . ." His voice trailed off.

"Why you?" Babu asked. "What were you doing a day ago?"

Jill met Sam's eyes. "We were in the Medbay," Jill said. "Sam had just discovered that I was cursed."

"You were what!?" Babu asked.

Jill sent him that too.

"Jill," he said in a tone of pure suffering. "Why didn't you send me this earlier? You didn't think a spell needing a living sacrifice was related to the murder that had just happened?"

She winced. "Oops?" she said. "In my defense, I felt like shit, and besides, I took care of it."

"If I remember correctly, you blasted it with a string of swears and an even more obscene amount of mana," Sam said. He turned his gaze back to the headless corpse. "If you were still connected to him somehow . . ."

"I blew up his head?" Jill asked. "I blew up his fucking head?"

"To be fair, I think he was trying to kill you," Sam said. "You have a very reasonable self-defense argument."

"And he was the first murderer," Babu said. "Again, that whole 'living sacrifice' thing to cast the curse in the first place, which you should have told me about."

"There was someone else involved," Jill said. "Someone who can hide from me, who did this twisted shit to my truck. I felt them before, during the town hall, but wasn't sure what was going on. Now I know, and I'm going to find them." She clenched her teeth. "And then I'm going to hurt them."

"After a trial, of course," Sam added. He looked at Babu to back him up.

Babu nodded. "We should at least use truth magic first."

"That's not really what I—" Sam said, then shook his head. "Never mind. Ms. MacLeod, how do you know that someone else was involved? Why couldn't this Harrison have done the concealing?"

Jill pursed her lips and put her thoughts in order. She was sure, but it took her a few seconds to be able to put into words why.

"I got a feel of the curse when I popped it," she said, "and the same here." She gestured to the room around them. "The mana behind them didn't match, not even close. One was like a thunderstorm, the other like, I dunno, a leech."

"There's also the missing ten percent of credit for this guy," Babu said. "The System thinks someone else helped kill him."

"Hey, Sys," Jill said, "can you share where that ten percent went?"

There was no response.

"Yeah," Jill sighed. "I didn't think it would be that easy. Babu, this isn't over. Keep digging around later?"

He gave her a salute. "Will do, *capitán*." He turned to go.

"Oy!" Jill said. "I said later! Now I need you to go to the Medbay to get checked out. And then Doc here is going to find you a couch to lie on and talk."

Babu pulled a face. "Can't that wait?"

"Nope," Jill said. "Don't think of skipping out, or I'll lock you in a room till you do it anyway."

"I feel like therapy under threat of incarceration loses some of its effectiveness," Sam said.

"Maybe, but it does happen," Jill replied.

With that, they left. Jill moved the body to the Medbay for further examination by the simple expedient of sucking it and all the surrounding floor through Bertha. Then she went back to the cab. On the way, she noticed that the party had stopped. People were still gathered, but it seemed that the discovery of another murder had soured the celebratory mood.

Jill considered making an announcement telling everyone that the first killer had been found and that she'd dealt with him. But that was giving information to the infiltrator, revealing what she'd figured out so far, and that wasn't something Jill was willing to do. Once the whole mess was over she'd tell everyone everything, and that would have to be good enough.

She spent the next several hours in the Customization seat, ignoring any attempt at conversation. The terrain whipped by, but she wasn't paying attention. Instead, she alternated between having her eyes closed and her senses sunk into Bertha, and studying the holographic map for comparison. If there were any more hidden spaces, she was determined to find them.

The first shift of the cab crew, long back from leveling, switched out for the second. Hours passed, and they swapped for the night crew. But still, Jill didn't find anything. She'd been over every inch of the truck multiple times; everything was as it should be, and there was no hint of the ozone mana.

Her growling stomach finally forced her to stop. Either the concealment spell was so good that it was messing up Bertha's own internal map, or the perpetrator was lying low by not casting it at all. In both cases, Jill had nothing more to gain, not tonight.

She ate in the cafeteria. The monsterized lettuce was off the menu, pending some experiments and very pointed questions to the System about whether or not eating it was "recommended," but there was a big stew and only slightly stale bread for her to dunk. There were few other people there, the rest having gone to bed, and they were clustered in small groups, talking in worried tones. Jill left without speaking to them.

She collapsed into bed as soon as she got into her room, but sleep was hard to come by. She kept seeing the faces of those she'd killed when she closed her eyes, along with the boxes from the System confirming them. Her imagination even made one up for Billy Harrison.

After half of a futile hour, she sighed and got out of bed. If she couldn't sleep, she might as well do something useful. Berthaville had hit level five, and that meant it had unlocked Terrain Generation as an option. She might as well head to the core and select it. Plus, she had to poop.

Jill went into her bathroom, sucked enough flowers into the walls so that she could make it to the toilet, and sat down on it with a sigh.

Berthaville's core crystal rose from the floor to the clunking of displaced pots and helianthic chimes of confusion.

"This is just getting silly," Jill said to the progenitor. "Could you, I dunno, make them show up somewhere else?"

For a few seconds, there was no response. Then a flower popped into existence on her bare lap. At least the pot was warm.

"Fine," Jill said. She accessed the core and navigated to Terrain Generation.

> **Terrain Generation:** Allows for the creation of inert terrain features composed of low-rarity materials for 10 Mana per cubic meter. Terrain does not require maintenance while inside of the dimensional bubble, but will rapidly degrade outside of it. Beings that consume generated material must pay 1000 Mana per cubic meter to incorporate it. Unlocks **Pull Stone** at Level 10.

The second to last line concerned Jill because she wanted people to eat the food they grew inside Berthaville, and a steep mana cost could get in the way of that. But then she realized just how large a cubic meter was compared to a person. Even someone level one could afford the cost without problems for any but the most ridiculous of meals.

She invested a point into the option and smiled as there was no horrid feedback to mess with her mind.

Her next concern was just how much ground she'd be able to make. She navigated back to the settlement's main page to look at the mana balance.

> The Dimensional Bubble of "Berthaville"
> **Stored Mana:** 50,000
> **Core Mana Generation:** 83.3 MP per second
> **Resident Mana Taxed** (4%)**:** 109.4 MP per second
> **Total Mana Expended:** 125.7 MP per second
> **Net Mana:** 67 MP per second

The dimensional bubble was a sphere a kilometer across. Filling it entirely would be counterproductive; they needed room to live and grow food, not just a ball of solid rock. Jill decided to start by making a disc and setting the sun in orbit around it to provide a day-night cycle. That way they'd be able to use both sides, assuming they managed to get things growing at all. Giving the still occasionally flashing boundary a clearance of one hundred meters on each side for safety meant that the disc would be eight hundred meters wide, so a one-meter thick layer would take twelve hours and fifty minutes at sixty-seven mana per second—not all that long to wait, in the grand scheme of things, and it would be manageable to make more than one if needed.

She'd finished her business while working out her plan, so she stood, hiked her pants back up, and flushed. She turned to the wall, took a deep breath, and gestured to the side with her hand to open up the same doorway as last time. Fresh air and sunlight poured into her bathroom. She poked her head out to look at the internal structure of Bertha. What had been a tumbled pile of cubes was now a sleek tower of metal and glass thanks to Aman's efforts, with her bedroom near the middle of it.

"What should I start with?" she asked herself. "Dirt?" No, not dirt. It wouldn't hold together. A layer of rock, then, to hold everything in place later.

Making the terrain was easy; all she had to do was focus on what she wanted while poking that tiny part of her spirit that led to the core crystal. The first chunk, gray granite shot through with veins of glittering quartz, bloomed into existence floating in front of her. Jill reached out a hesitant hand and touched it. It was just rock.

She extruded a dozen hooks from the outside of the tower and nucleated a bit of rock around each, then joined them together. The platform spread out before her; sixty-seven cubic meters per second of coverage seemed an incredible growth rate when standing right next to it, but she had two million in total to go.

Jill smiled and felt the tension in her shoulders bleed out just a bit. Making the rock, watching it grow while the sun warmed her and the air whistled around, combined the best aspects of meditation and usefulness. She took a step out onto her creation but didn't account for the lack of gravity. Her foot pushed down and she shot off into the airy void. It was empty no longer, but filled with obscenities.

CHAPTER 31

TWICE IS COINCIDENCE

"Ms. MacLeod?" A voice rang out in Jill's room and snapped her out of her sleep. Jill's stomach clenched in panic for an instant before she placed the voice: it was the night shift comms person, a friend of Karen's by the name of Amy Pearson. The woman had jumped at the chance to stay up all night every night; when Jill had asked why, the younger woman had deflected instead of answering.

"Ugh," Jill groaned. She pulled the incredibly soft comforter over her face.

"Ms. MacLeod, are you awake? Mr. Woods just saw something, uh, concerning and wants to know if he should keep driving. More concerning than usual."

Jill whipped the comforter off, eliciting a massive hiss from the tortoiseshell cat by her feet, and leaped out of bed. "I'll be right there," she said. Her clothes, which she had thrown haphazardly on the floor before tumbling into bed, were freshly laundered and neatly folded on her desk, courtesy of the Unseen Servants.

The corridor was silent except for the echoing slam of her door as she stumbled out, still buttoning up her jeans. A few steps and she swung the hatch to the cab open, stepping through into the dim chamber. There were just four people there: Tyler Woods on the wheel, the afore-remembered Amy on comms, a woman on the radar whom Jill for the life of her couldn't remember ever talking to, and, finally, one Will Young on standby for repairs. The last, a man older than her with a bushy gray beard, had a tiny ball of red light floating above his head, the light from which he was using to read a newspaper.

Jill strode in. "What's happening, people?" she asked. "We're not under attack, right?"

"No, Jill," Tyler said. He looked over his shoulder and sketched a sloppy salute. "That we know how to deal with." He hesitated, then gestured to the window. "Take a look at this. I don't know exactly what's going on, but I don't want to drive through it."

Jill walked to the front and whistled at what she saw. "Serve me spider sushi, I don't blame you."

Bertha sat stopped at the top of a gentle cliff, overlooking an expanse of rough terrain: prairie badlands that stretched as far as the eye could see. Broken hills cut with grass-filled canyons, sparse forests, and the occasional spire of rock presented a challenging drive that a regular truck would struggle with. Bertha could handle it with only a moderate hit to average speed, especially if the driver embraced the insanity of not worrying too much about impact damage. The truck could jump a surprising number of obstacles by flooring it up a steep incline and launching itself off the top.

What had stopped Tyler were the remnants of a catastrophic battle. Deep gouges and craters marred the landscape, forming a series of sheer, unstable cliffs. Bertha could switch to Slug Feet and climb them, but only at the cost of nearly all her speed. The landscape still bore lingering effects from the creatures that had fought there: patches of burning trees and, somehow, rocks lay interspersed with areas turned to shimmering slag. But worse, much worse, was a gray, luminescent fog that lay over the ground; the plants in it, if they hadn't been burned to a crisp, were withered husks.

A sick, mad feeling crept down Jill's neck at the sight of that fog, one that she recognized from her fights against corrupted people.

"Balls," she said, then turned to Will. "Did you see anything on the radar that could explain this? Any big, high-level things?"

He frowned. "I'm not sure," he said. "I thought I saw two dots in this area, but one kept flickering in and out, and the radar couldn't read the level of the other."

"More fuckery. Great," Jill said. She sighed and rubbed her forehead with her hand, willing her brain to hurry up and get thinking. She hadn't even gotten coffee before coming. "We go around," she said to Tyler. "How much time do you think that will cost us?"

"That depends on how far we have to go," he said, "but not too long. Less than an hour. We might have to jump a few more canyons, but that's the fun part, isn't it?"

Jill clapped him on the shoulder. "Fuck yeah, it is," she said. "Just go in the right general direction towards the dog-spanking nuclear missile silos. What a goddamn thing to say at ass in the morning. If you see more of that horrible fog, keep us away. Aman can always check our position when he's awake and get us back on track."

Tyler put Bertha back into motion, turning them south for a few miles before resuming course. The truck bounced down a ravine and up the far side, the rapid changes in orientation feeling like nothing more than a gentle, barely perceptible rocking. Jill yawned, ready to go back to her room, and Bertha crested a hill. There was a pale light on the eastern horizon.

"Is it dawn already?" she asked.

Tyler shook his head. "No, still a few hours left for that," he said. "We've just been getting aurora the last few nights."

"They're called the northern lights, not the eastern lights," Jill muttered. "Well, if they go crazy, let me know." She got up and went to leave the cab, but paused by Will. "I've just got to ask. What are you reading?"

"This here's the *Berthaville Times*," he said. "It's new." He folded the newspaper and tossed it to her. It was made of paper, but not quite the normal coarse, thin material she was used to for newspapers. It must be some imitation made in Bertha.

"'Head-Exploding Murderer on the Loose,'" Jill said as she read the section titles out loud, "'Sexiest Man Contest Called off Due to Unanimous First Round Vote,' and 'Jill Fashion Watch: Does She Own Clothes?'"

She tossed it back.

"Welp, I got the paper I deserve," she said. "Later, everyone. Yell if you're on fire."

She walked the few steps to her room, went in, and headed straight for the coffee machine. She wasn't going to be able to get back to sleep, not while thoughts of ruined terrain and the remnants of corruption around it gnawed at her mind, so she might as well properly start the day. The overtaxed machine gurgled and hissed as she thought.

The obvious source of the corrupt mist was the escaped experiment. They'd seen hundreds, thousands of monsters since leaving the airport but none of them had carried that sick, unmistakable feeling along with them, and none of them had given the bonus experience that came with corruption either. There was a simple explanation for seeing this rare creature now: they were simply catching up to the escaped one they knew existed.

But that presented a problem because the odds of them randomly coming across the experiment again were tiny. It sometimes didn't seem that way because of the sheer speed that Bertha drove at, but the mana-expanded terrain was mind-bogglingly massive. With the slowdowns and detours included, they had crossed something like three thousand miles, measured by groundspeed, just in the past twenty-four hours—the entire width of the pre-System USA.

Unless this was a truly spectacular coincidence, it meant that the meeting wasn't random. It had to have some reason to be traveling in this direction. Possibly the same reason Jill did.

She finished her coffee and set the worries aside. They would wait for her, but it was time for her to start her daily routine.

She'd gained enough XP in the night to level up; she'd triggered the upgrade during her shower, bringing her up to level ninety-eight and thirteen free class points to spend. She'd intended to keep that number lower, but things kept coming up that demanded her attention. She mulled over her choices for a bit but kept thinking of just how useful the radar had proven to be. It let them pick their prey or run away from predators from miles away, and it had seen something of the battle between fire and mist. She'd neglected the sensor power from the Command Module before because she hadn't had anything it would work on. Now she did.

> Available Command Upgrades:
> **Capacity (2/5):** Add 1.4 control stations, 2.8 observer stations, and 1 command add-on slot.
> **Sensor Upgrade (0/5):** Effectiveness of any installed perception devices increased by 14%.

She'd find out exactly what "effectiveness" meant later, but she'd guess that the add-on would see farther and be harder to fool. That the power would help anything else she'd install later was an added bonus. Seeing it on the list of upgrades, Jill decided to also take the remaining three ranks in Capacity. The cab was getting too crowded when the full crew went into a fight, and she wanted to know what the System had in mind for her advanced module choice.

She took Sensor Upgrade first, all five ranks. The mana of the upgrade coursed through Bertha and drew Jill's consciousness with it. For an endless second her sight spread over miles of plains and hills, into the sky, even through the ground, though not very far there. Monsters roamed, each one a candle flame of danger and opportunity.

Then the upgrade finished and she came back to herself with a gasp. She blinked and shook herself to clear her head.

"Hey," she reached out with Captain Speaking and projected her voice into the cab, "I'm about to make the cab grow. Hold on to something!"

She took the remaining three ranks of Capacity. This upgrade was less disturbing; she just felt like she had terrible gas as the cab's interior volume expanded to accommodate the extra seats and consoles.

A box popped up in front of her once it was done.

> Command Module upgrades complete! Determining most beneficial new abilities.
> Only one of the following customized abilities may be selected:
> **Fortress of the Throne:** The Command Module becomes the Inner Sanctum and Berthaville's Core Crystal is moved there. The Fortress of the Throne gains a localized armor layer with the same statistics as the Armor Module, without add-ons. Any Roaming Guardians inside the Fortress become Throne Room Guardians, receive a bonus of 70% to their statistics, and will prioritize protection of the Core Crystal. Unlocks further abilities related to ruling and defending Berthaville.
> **Berthanet Administration:** Creates a communication network and information web centered on Soulbound Modular Vehicle "Bertha." All installed communication devices receive a range boost of 70% in transmitting and receiving. All data detected by any Control Console or add-on are stored indefinitely in a searchable database. Unlocks further abilities related to information gathering and sharing.

The idea of becoming royalty, even if just by some quirk of System power naming, was gross to Jill. She had power over people because that's how things worked out, not because of some innate factor from her heritage. That said, the bonuses that Fortress of the Throne gave addressed two of Bertha's biggest weaknesses: the fact that the cab could be attacked by monsters directly while controlling the truck and that the settlement core was only really guarded by a hallway, a locked door, and some potted plants. The power would move the core into a space monitored 24/7 and at the same time make that the toughest place in the truck. Plus, she was sick of having to stuff people into her bathroom.

While that upgrade solved problems, but didn't change much else, Berthanet Administration added fundamental new abilities to the truck. Their radio was working but had already started to have problems connecting, and they might have a long way farther to go. The rest of the power would be a surveillance dream—or nightmare, depending on your point of view. Anything heard by someone using the Captain Speaking console and anything detected by the radar would be recorded forever. If Jill attached Cargokinesis to a console, the physical location of anything in or around the Cargo Nexus would be too.

Jill bit her lip. That could be the difference between finding whoever was infiltrating Bertha, whoever had ripped a part of her truck away from her, and not.

"Aw fuck me, Sys," she said. "Why couldn't you give me an easy choice? It's too early to be working this shit out." She decided to wait on picking it until she'd asked her usual people and to also hold off on spending her remaining five class points until she could see whatever new set of powers the choice gave.

What she didn't count on was that the upgrades each had fierce supporters. Jacob was excited by the idea that Berthanet Administration might allow for something akin to the Internet to come back. Karen agreed, except for the ability to record everything she heard; Sangita was adamant it not be, for the same reason. Aman and Ras both voted for the fortress but weren't being very loud about it. Babu said that he wasn't sure, which didn't go over particularly well with Sangita. He left the conference room before it could turn into an argument.

He later asked Jill to let him sleep on it before he gave her his opinion. That suited her fine. The choice was hers, but she just hadn't made up her mind, and the young man tended to see things in a very different way than she did.

The day went on, and there were, thankfully, no more surprise bodies. The miles flew by, sometimes a bit literally, underneath Bertha's wheels, and their mark on the map grew closer, bit by bit, to the nuclear launch facility. They'd arrive that afternoon.

Twice more they passed signs of battle. The first bore the same kind of scars as the area that Jill had been woken up for, but it was off to the side of their new route and didn't require a detour.

The second time happened only an hour before their expected arrival at the Minuteman facility, and the cab was more full than usual. It wasn't an "all hands on deck" crew, but it was close. Half the repair team was playing a card game, and all of them were using magic to cheat in one way or another. Babu, Ras, and Coach were having a talk with Jill about who they could safely send outside given the level of monsters around them; Coach was convinced that a full set of Cloud Killers could handle a monster in the level sixty range, even though they were still in the forties themselves.

"Huh," said Jake on the radar. "That's funny."

"Funny as in a level sixty-nine monster," Jill asked, "or funny as in we're about to get a snake straight up our shit pipe?"

"For a second I thought I saw green dots to the north," Jake said, unsure. "But that's what we show up as. People, I mean. And they disappeared a second later."

"There's smoke that way," Bobby said. "I was going to stay away, you know, just in case it's another of those creepy fight places." Jill stood and moved over to the window next to him to get a better look. They'd been following a ridge line northeast, and from that vantage point, she could see a thin spire of smoke rising into the sky.

"How's the monster forecast?" Jill asked. "Are they swarming your mystery dots?"

"There are a few in the area, but nothing dangerous to us," Jake replied. "The local weather is clear out to about a mile." Another benefit of driving on top of the ridge was that they had a better line of sight for taking potshots at monsters to pick up more experience. The smart monsters hid or ran, while the dumb charged and died. "There's a swarm twelve miles west, led by a boss in the eighties. That could be trouble."

"We'll keep an eye on them," Jill said. "I'd rather not fight that if we can avoid it. But for now, get us to that smoke."

Bobby pulled the wheel over and Bertha charged down the side of the ridge. The sight made Jill's stomach rise into her chest as if she was on a rollercoaster, and she grinned. They bottomed on the valley floor with a massive crash, but Katie fixed the small amount of damage in a moment, and Jill barely felt the impact through the Inertial Resistance.

"Woooweee!" Bobby whooped. "I love this job!"

It took another five minutes for them to reach another ridge overlooking the source of the smoke. In the valley below were the flaming remains of three wrecked Jeeps. Or at least Jill guessed there were three; they'd been torn into enough pieces that it was hard to tell. It took only a minute for Bertha to get down the slope, its huge tires and traction powers keeping them easily under control.

Bobby drove them past a few pieces of flaming brush and brought them to a stop next to the largest intact piece of car: a crumbled engine section sheered away at the A-pillar.

"These fires are fresh," Jill said, "and there's some glowing oil stuff leaking from that engine."

"And the grass hasn't swallowed any of it yet either," Babu said. "With the crazy growth rate from the magic . . ." His voice trailed off.

Jill's stomach sank. "This was today, wasn't it?" she asked.

"Just in the last few hours," Ras said.

"Fuck!" Jill clenched a fist and banged it on the window. "If only we'd been a little faster!"

"Sweet baby Jesus!" Bobby yelled. "There are people out there!"

"Where?!" Jill asked.

Halfway up the far valley wall the ground shifted and split, and loose dirt and stones bounced down an almost sheer cliff to reveal a cave. A figure emerged, waving wildly, followed shortly after by another.

"Incoming!" Jake said. "That level eighty monster just turned towards us! It looks like its swarm is following it too!"

"Ras, Babu," Jill said. She did a fast scan with her eyes, making sure nothing was about to leap at them, then swiped her hand sideways. The armored glass in front of her peeled away, leaving her and the rest of the cab exposed to the searing sunlight and harsh wind. "Get those people inside. Now!"

CHAPTER 32

PETS

The brothers leaped out. Babu had flight spells cast on both of them before they touched the ground, and they sped towards the cave.

"Jill, what the hell are you doing with the armor?" Karen asked. "What if something gets in!"

"Then I'll make it eat its own asshole," Jill said. "Time counts."

Ras and Babu landed next to the survivors. They exchanged words for just a few seconds, then Ras thrust his sword into the air and summoned a flashing blade barrier around the cave. Babu scooped up the two people in front of him and flew back towards Bertha, and Ras followed a moment later. It took them two trips, but they hauled seven people into the cab.

The only interruption was from a monstrous wasp that burst from its underground burrow at the top of the hill and shot towards them, but three turrets opened fire on it before it got halfway. The dozens of rounds that struck it exploded the wasp into chunks of insectile meat that fell to the valley floor.

"That's everyone," Ras said as he landed from his second pass.

Jill clenched a fist and the cab sealed itself again. "Bobby, get us moving again—fast," she said. He hit the accelerator and Bertha surged forward. The truck rocked on its suspension as the huge wheels hit the slope of the valley wall. They spun for a moment on loose dirt, but a web of mana washed out from the Diffused Traction power, stabilizing it. In moments they were up the slope and back on top of a ridge, winding their way northeast at highway speeds and still accelerating.

"Two minutes until they reach us!" Jake said.

"We're about to get hit!" Jill called out, looping in the hive of gunners and the turret prep room as well. "You know the drill! Keep us repaired, swap out if you're out of mana or if your best powers are on cooldown." She switched her voice to a more threatening tone. "And if the band plays 'Stairway to Heaven' as their buff song one more time, I swear to God that I'm going to use them as ammunition."

There was a little laughter at that, and Jill nodded. She just might be getting the hang of this leadership thing.

"What—" said one of the ragged-looking group of survivors. "What kind of truck is this?" Through the smears of dirt and blood, their uniforms were recognizable as air force fatigues.

Jill turned to them. "She goes by Bertha," she said, "and she kicks ass. You can call me Jill. We're in for a little fight but don't worry about it. We've gotten through worse." She eyed them up and down. They were all mobile, but two seemed unable to walk without help; the injuries would be persistent status conditions if their own regeneration hadn't handled the injuries while they hid. "We've got doctors to patch you up, and food too, but I need one of you to tell me what happened here, and soon."

A man stepped forward and saluted. From his clothes, Jill recognized him as the figure that had emerged first from the cave. "First Lieutenant Hayes, ma'am," he said. "I'm fit to give a report."

The turrets opened fire as the first fliers entered range, the staggered bursts of buzz saw death loud through all the layers of armor, and the survivors flinched as one, eyes wide and bloodshot, their hands going to weapons.

The mana around Jill stirred; the Roaming Guardians were on the edge of manifesting. Ras spun around from where he'd been talking with his father, one foot sliding forward, and his right hand went for his own sword. Babu flickered and Jill felt rather than saw a figure step sideways out of where he seemed to be.

"Woah!" she said and raised her hands wide. "Calm your tits!"

"Stand down!" Hayes said to his people, though he looked hardly less spooked. "Sorry about that, ma'am. It's been rough."

Jill nodded. "All good." She turned her head. "Aman, handle this fight, would you? Ras, why don't you take everyone but Hayes here to the Medbay to get checked out?"

"Right," he said and led them off, the invisible Babu following behind. Jill took Hayes to the conference room next door.

"You want a coffee?" she asked him as she made a beeline for the machine. The turrets were still firing, and she was vaguely aware of automatically suppressed kill notifications pilling up for her.

He was just sitting down, relief plain on his face, when Kevin ran into the room, his dinosaur, Spiny, on his head.

"Jill! Jill!" the boy said. "Spiny—"

Hayes threw himself from the chair, panic and fear clear on his face, and reached for his sidearm. He raised it to point at Spiny but hesitated.

Jill threw an arm out and Bertha responded with a cocoon of metal surging from the floor to wrap around Kevin. Hayes pointed the gun at her and his expression turned angry, but before he could do anything else, Jill was on him. She threw a straight jab at his face with her right fist; Hayes deflected it, the impact of hand on arm hard enough to send out a shockwave that blew back Jill's hair. But that had been a distraction. Jill's real attack came a split second later: a lunging grab for the gun.

Hayes was better trained than her and had better reach. That much was obvious from how he twisted away and threw a counter-punch of his own. But Jill had been in a few scraps of her own over the years, was higher level, and over the last week had been in a lot of pain. She let the punch hit her square in the face, breaking her nose, but got a hold of the gun and pushed it sideways. It went off with a deafening roar and a searing red bolt flew out and blew a fist-sized crater in the wall.

A pair of Roaming Guardians condensed in front of Kevin's cocoon and wrapped themselves around it.

Jill tried another jab, but Hayes shifted his stance and batted her fist away. Jill was thrown off balance but didn't relinquish her hold on the gun. A moment later she took another brutal blow to the face that broke two of her teeth.

She spat out the shards, willed Bertha's deck plating to flow over Hayes's feet to stop him from dodging, and kicked him square in the nuts. The blow was hard enough that if his feet hadn't been pinned, her superhuman strength would have catapulted him straight into the ceiling.

And then the fight was over, both because Hayes was collapsed in stunned agony and because backup arrived. Ras arrived in a burst of air with a sword to Hayes's neck and an instant later a half dozen of the Cloud Killers, who had been in the turret prep room across the hall, poured in, weapons ready. Babu was presumably there, invisible. The fight had only lasted a few seconds.

"Are you done?" Jill asked. She wrapped a band of metal around his chest and pulled it and the surrounding floor downwards, sucking him an inch into the deck. "Or do you need a time-out? What the fuck are you thinking, pulling a gun on him?"

"There's a monster in there!" Hayes yelled. He struggled against the restraints, but froze as Ras's sword bit into the skin of his neck, drawing a bead of blood. He swallowed, then collapsed back. "You've got to do something. It's going to kill that kid!"

Jill turned and opened her hand. The cocoon around Kevin peeled open like the petals of a flower. He stood there shaking, clutching his tiny stegosaurus to his chest.

"Kevin?" Jill said. "Take Spiny and go find your mom. Okay, kiddo? Cousin Ras can go with you."

"Okay. Are—" He sniffled and stared at Jill. "Are you hurt?" he asked. One of his hands glowed green with healing mana, and he took a hesitant step towards her.

Jill smiled. It probably wasn't the most comforting sight, given the broken teeth and blood. "I'll be fine in a few minutes, champ." She reached out and ruffled his hair. "Now, do me a favor and let the adults talk?"

He nodded and left. Ras gave her a nod, sheathed his sword, and followed, an arm looped over Kevin's shoulders.

She waited a few seconds for Kevin to be out of earshot, then stomped over to Hayes. "The only reason I'm not throwing you outside for a monster to rip your dick off and make you eat it," she growled, "is because you were trying to protect him. Even if all you did was scare the shit out of a child." She released the bands of metal securing Hayes to the floor. "Now get your ass up."

Hayes opened his mouth but Jill spoke first. "The dino's tame," she said. "A pet that didn't go crazy. We've got a couple of them onboard, though it's the only critter that didn't exist before magic. We've got a few dogs and cats that didn't go full murder mode too."

He looked away and pursed his lips. "We weren't that lucky," he said. "Everything turned. Everything."

"Sucks to be you," Jill said. "But when you're on this truck, you don't attack things that haven't attacked you first. Got it?"

"Yes, ma'am," he said.

"Good," she said and horked up a glob of blood. She could already feel her teeth regrowing, new ones pushing out the old. It hurt like hell, but she didn't really care. "Then how about I pretend you didn't shoot my truck, and you pretend I didn't give you the castrato singing class, and we both sit down with a cup of coffee. Good? Then let's get some coffee, and you can tell your story."

She made coffee with her usual abusive overcharging of the machine and tried to ignore the continuing fight outside as the pain from Bertha taking a hard hit got her right in the kidney. Her people knew how to fight at this point, and things weren't dire enough to need her driving or extra repairs. Even the Cloud Killers, still standing around looking suspiciously at Hayes, weren't really needed right now, not unless things really went south and something broke in.

"Right," she said. "Talk."

"The first to go were our cell phones," Hayes said. "We were on the hardline with command, asking if we were under EMP attack, when that cut out too. We locked the base down, thinking we had saboteurs that had dug down to cut the cable, that maybe it was some kind of combined attack to steal the warheads. We sent out our electrical systems specialist and some guards to find and fix the break, but"—he shook his head—"they were caught out in the first monster wave and didn't make it. It was only later we realized that it was all the new ground growing that had snapped the line."

He took a sip of his coffee and looked at it with raised eyebrows. He gave an approving nod and started to speak.

"We'd only just started playing around with classes at that point. Captain Green—that's the acting wing commander; Major Carey never got back from a conference—anyway, Green wanted to keep us organized instead of just taking what we each liked best. That turned out to be a good idea in the end, but it meant we weren't prepared for that first wave. We lost some good people, but held them off in the tunnels."

"Tunnels?" Jill asked.

"Right," Hayes said, "you wouldn't know. We're from Maelstrom AFB, 342nd missile wing. It's a nuclear—"

"Yeah, we know," Jill said. "We were sent out here to find you."

Hayes blinked. "By who? Do you have contact with command?"

"The armory over at Bozeman contracted me to find out what happened to you," she said.

Hayes furrowed his brows. "Them? Aren't they, like, a tiny little base? Please, don't tell me they're the biggest force left!"

Jill shook her head. "Nah, they just got doubly lucky to have a comms wizard around and me rolling through. They've got contact with your brass. Well, someone's brass. I don't really know the details. Now, c'mon and keep the story going. We're going to get to your base in like half an hour."

"Half an hour? But we were driving for—"

"Buddha boning a bagel, what part of kick-ass truck don't you understand? Story, flyboy."

He took another gulp of the coffee. "Well, we beat back the first attack, figured out how the System's whole level thing worked, and tried to get back in touch with command." He shook his head. "But no one still alive had the options for it."

The somber mood was somewhat ruined as the beat dropped on some nameless techno masterpiece from across the hall.

Hayes shook his head. "We holed up for a while, hoping for contact. We expected some of the local farmers to come to us for refuge, but . . ." He shook his head again.

"Fuck," Jill said.

"We were attacked almost nonstop for the first few days. We started to get hopeful that things were getting better, but the monsters were just regrouping. Organizing."

"Aw fuck me," Jill said. "You've got some sort of smart boss monster around?"

"So that's not just here?" he asked. "It's a T. rex, a huge one, must be forty feet tall. It was at the head of the next group to hit us, and everything changed. They were attacking from new angles, using each other as shields, waiting for reinforcements before launching mass assaults—you get the idea."

"What does the boss do?" Jill asked and leaned forward. "Any special attacks or weaknesses? You must have forced it back."

"We've never come close to hurting it. The damn thing is playing with us, that's what it does! It cut holes in our tunnels for the other monsters to get in, then would just stand by and watch. One time we were winning too fast, and it started launching fireballs at us. Another time, when we were almost overrun, it turned on its own monsters, tore them apart with its teeth, and evened the odds. The only time it ever attacked us for real was the first time we tried to leave"—he clenched his fists—"even then it didn't kill us, just chased us back into the base with our asses on fire." He looked Jill in the eyes. "We are toys to that thing. The other monsters want to kill us, but this damn T. rex wants to make us suffer!"

"Well, that's like an unlubed artichoke right up the ass," she said. Hayes looked pissed off at that, so she quickly kept talking. "You said it's too strong and keeps you in, so how'd you end up out here?"

"The attacks stopped two days ago and so did our sightings of it," he said. "We thought it was a trick so stayed put for a day. When it didn't come back, we figured that that was our shot to try and get help, so we punched out of the cordon and went as fast as we could."

"The cordon?"

"Right, I'm all out of order," he said. "After our first try at leaving, the T. rex made the other monsters maintain a ring around the base. It keeps us in and other things out, at least until the T. rex wants them to attack."

"That's a whole new level of smart. Do you have any idea what level the boss is?"

"The last I saw, it was ninety-nine. But it had been that for days, so either it's stuck somehow or that's a lie."

"Huh," Jill said. "Well, that's not too bad."

Hayes looked at her like she was crazy. "How is that not bad?"

"Well, Bertha gets stronger with me," Jill said, "and I'm level ninety-eight."

Annoyed muttering broke out among the Cloud Killers listening to the story. "I thought we were catching up!" was a common sentiment.

"How did I even hurt you?" Hayes said. "I, uh, never apologized for that. Sorry."

Jill waved a hand. "Eh, it didn't even hurt that bad. Look, my teeth are already back. What happened after you broke out?"

"Uh, sure," Hayes said and blew out a breath. "We drove all night but didn't get anywhere. Things are way more spread out than we'd expected. Then this morning we got hit by these weird floating jellyfish from the air and had to dig a shelter underground. Things were pretty hopeless until you showed up."

"I'm surprised they didn't peel you out like canned beans," Jill said.

"I've got a power to reinforce rock and another for hiding underground."

"Handy."

"The base is underground," Hayes said. "If the System hadn't given us things to keep out attacks from below, we'd be dead by now."

"Sys does come through with those 'most beneficial abilities,'" Jill said. "When we get there, how many people are we rescuing? Can you get them on board fast?"

"There are only fifty-one of us left," Hayes said, "so forty-four to pick up at the base. There's no working radio or anything, so I'll have to run in and—"

"Nah, we'll psychically project your voice," Jill interrupted.

"Oh. Okay, that will help. A lot of them are seriously injured, though. I don't know if it will be safe to take them onto a truck, not in this terrain."

Jill smirked. "Why, is the ride too rough?"

Hayes looked around, then down at the placid liquid in his cup. "What? We must have stopped when the fighting started, right?"

"Nah, we don't stop for that kind of thing," Jill said. "Don't worry about your injured friends. Bertha's one fast, smooth lady, and she's here to rescue them. We'll be there soon."

CHAPTER 33

A SHOCKING WELCOME

"There they are," Jake said. "A solid ring of monsters about three miles across. At this density"—he whistled—"that's a solid four, five hundred of them." His announcement stopped the low conversation between the cab crew. All three shifts were ready to fight now, and the noncombatants in Bertha were out of the cargo bay, where monsters could break in.

Jill stood looking over Jake's shoulder at the radar. "I see mostly level fifties and a few sixties," she said. "That's a lot of mana to spend on bullets, even without their leader." She looked around the cab. Everyone was waiting on her to make the decision they knew she would, even if right now they were chatting with each other. "We go in," she said. "Full speed." She clapped Jake on the shoulder. "Holler if you see something level ninety-nine."

"What are we going to do if I do?" he asked. That question quieted the rest of the cab as all the people definitely not listening in waited for her answer.

"If the big bad T. rex goes for us," she said as she looped in the turret prep room and the gunners with Captain Speaking, "we fight. We're not leaving these people to die. Though"—she paused and mulled over Hayes's story in her mind—"I'm hoping that it won't attack until we actually try to leave. The fucker might think it's toying with us when really it's giving us the chance we need. So if you see it and it's just beating its meat watching us, leave it be. Shoot everything else, but not it."

He nodded and reached down to the radar, tweaking a knob on the side. The screen fuzzed but the contrast increased.

Jill strode to the front of the cab. Babu and Hayes were in the observer seats, ready to communicate with the base. There would be no opening the cab up to possible attack this time: Ras and two dozen fighters were by the rear cargo doors, ready to spring out and help the evacuation. Jill was ready to kick Bobby off the driver's seat if things got too hairy, but for now, she would let the other man get more experience.

"Let's see what these monsters do," Jill muttered to herself.

The terrain around Maelstrom Base was flatter than the badlands they'd just exited, with a long shallow uphill climb to the top of a broad hill, beyond which was the facility. The monsters saw Bertha coming from miles away, and around fifty of them left their posts and charged at them. They couldn't make out anything of the base over the hill; there had been no tall buildings even before the monsters had attacked.

"Steady as she goes, Bobby," Jill said. She grinned. "Have some fun with the horn if any get close enough."

"Permission to fire?" came a multi-voiced question from the hive. Mia's stood out to Jill's ears, and she had the sudden urge to ask the younger woman to tell her exactly what it felt like to be part of the gunner collective.

"Let 'er rip!" Jill projected back.

Blossom shot first and Bertha's mana reserves began to dip. Jill shunted one kill box to the side before it materialized, and then four heavy machine guns joined in.

If they'd wanted to, they could easily have turned and maintained range around the poor slow melee monsters, but they had somewhere to be so only managed to kill half before reaching the charging group. Bobby hauled on the horn and a blast of devastating rolling sound exploded in front of Bertha, shooting out before settling into a shimmering plow. Its initial explosion churned a massive cloud of dirt into the air that blocked their view for a critical few seconds, during which they struck the first monsters.

These were strong enough to survive the brief contact with the Blast Wave of the Hydra Worm, but only just. A spinosaurus was thrown tumbling to the side, the flesh on one side of its body torn away as if it had been hit with an industrial sandblaster. A second monster, a long-necked supposed herbivore whose mouth was just stuffed with jagged teeth, was unfortunately too heavy to be thrown clear over Bertha. Instead, it was flipped upside down and Bertha hit it windshield first at three hundred miles per hour.

It died on impact, splattered like an elephant dropped from a cargo plane. A tremor ran through Bertha, and the truck took several hundred points of damage. The windshield erupted in a spiderweb of cracks but held firm, and they kept driving forward, turrets firing behind them to clean up anything chasing them. The repair team sunk their mana into Bertha and, with a crinkling like stressed ice, the windshield knitted back together. They were through the blockade and would be at the base in just thirty more seconds.

"Sideswipe the big ones, Bobby, sideswipe," Jill said. "And slow us down. Hayes, Babu, get ready."

They crested the hill and there it was. The launch center had never had many buildings above ground, but those that had been, and the barbed-wire-topped fences that had provided casual deterrence, were long flattened. A scarred, pillbox-like short tower of shimmering concrete lay in the heart of a field of destruction. It had signs of being slashed, blasted, and peeled open, before being repaired over and over.

"That the entrance?" Jill asked and pointed at it as they bounced closer. "I was expecting, I dunno, a huge door."

"We have one of those, but it's underground," he said. "We built this over the original entrance to give us a way to shoot at the monsters in the open field—a zeroth line of defense."

"I feel them!" Babu said. His eyes glowed black. "Hayes, you're on!"

Bobby slammed on the brakes and they skidded to a stop, a wall of churned dirt flying up around them. He twisted the wheel at the last second and they just missed the pillbox. They came to a stop.

"H-E-double-hockey-sticks!" he ground out. "I overshot!" He put the truck into reverse and backed them up fifty feet, bringing the back of the trailer right next to the pillbox.

"Not bad for going three hundred to zero, though," Jill said and clapped him on the shoulder.

"Green's agreed to evacuate!" Hayes said, hope and triumph in his voice. "They're getting the wounded ready now!"

"Ras!" she projected to that back, "get in there!" She felt the cargo doors fly open and twenty-five people charged out. The rest of the Cloud Killers, which had swelled to a volunteer force fifty strong, were waiting behind prepared defensive positions inside the Cargo Nexus.

"What are those monsters doing?" Jill asked.

"The ones that chased us are, well, dead," Jake said. "The rest are still in their ring." He flicked the display with a finger. "Huh, that's—"

"Do not say 'that's odd,'" Jill said. "It's bad luck. What do you see?"

"There's something out there, right at the edge of our range," Jake said. Jill hurried over and he pointed. "Right there. The radar can't tell what level it is, and I swear sometimes its color flickers between different shades of red."

"Fuck, I bet that's our T. rex being all freaky, bossy-like," Jill said. She pointed at a part of the ring ninety degrees off from their entry point. "Are those monsters fighting each other?" There was a tangle of dots all together in a clump, with a portion of the ring depleted around them. Then three dots broke away from the mass, running away. The rest spread back out.

"They really are keeping other monsters out," Jake said. "That's almost"—he paused—"helpful?"

"It's not," Hayes said with venom. "Just a monster keeping its toy box safe."

"We'll take it," Jill said. "Babu, progress?"

"The CKs have made contact," Babu said, his eyes still glowing. "Their medical area was at the deepest point." He tilted his head to the side, then grimaced. "The Medbay's going to need to make a lot of prosthetics."

A spike of anger surged in Jill, but she pushed it down. She knew that monsters were, well, monsters, but she'd put Berthabucks on the T. rex having issued specific orders to maim instead of kill. She stomped back to the front of the cab and looked out over the former base. There had been a lot of fighting here, a lot of dead monsters. The people still alive were going to be high level—high enough to be a pain in the ass if Hayes's performance in a surprise fistfight was any indication. Hopefully, they'd be grateful enough for the rescue and healing to follow Jill until they made it back to what was left of civilization.

Something tapped against the window to Jill's right, a hard, clicking noise like metal on stone. She turned to look, but there was nothing there.

"Are you sure that—" she started to ask Jake, but he interrupted her.

"Incoming! A whole swarm just entered radar range, moving in at"—he paused a moment—"over two hundred miles an hour! Maybe fifty of them, all level sixty and above, probably flying!"

"Get ready!" Jill projected. "Aman," she continued with just her voice. "Get us into fortress mode, but get the door on the inside and have us be around the pillbox if we can?"

He tilted his head, then nodded. "Yes, ma'am. Two minutes."

Jill pushed down a flash of self-recrimination. She should have thought to do that earlier, to have them transition the instant they'd stopped. She felt her insides shift and squirm as Bertha began its metamorphosis.

"Antonio," Jake called out to the hive. "Range: four kilometers, bearing: sixty-seven degrees, altitude: four hundred meters." The radar, System made, was of course in metric.

"Fire when you can hit them," Jill said.

She paced back and forth as the guns opened fire, the rest of the crew moving out of her way to give her space. Jill hated having nothing to do in a fight like this. She couldn't even pretend to be waiting to jump back on the wheel; they weren't driving. The fliers came within extreme range, and the guns opened up with a bracketing fire; the swarm scattered to dodge, but all that did was make a target fly straight into a waiting stream of explosive ammunition. It was fragile for its level and lost a wing in just a few shots before falling to its death.

Electrodactyl defeated.
Your contribution: 15%
1002 Experience Gained!
You are now Level 99! Level gain deferred per user preference.

The bright yellow pterodactyls turned and wheeled, electricity crackling between them like bright blue heat lightning on a cloudless day. More of the monsters fell to Bertha's barrage, but the power between them built until it at last overflowed. Lightning bolts began to rain down, first one and then more, faster and faster. The bolts blasted holes in the fortress's armor, tracing lines of destruction on their way to the ground, and Jill winced as the pain hit her like gouges in her flesh.

Katie slumped into a seat in exhaustion, her mana completely spent, and the next repairer took over. Jill began casting her own repair spell as soon as it came off cooldown to help. The frequency of the lightning began to fall as more of the fliers tumbled, broken, to the plain below, and their repairs pulled ahead.

Jill let out a slow breath of relief. That had been a high-offense coordinated ranged attack from a high-speed flying set of monsters; she couldn't imagine something without the Elemental Resistance of the

Armored Explorer upgrade, or something that lacked the range to attack back, surviving long. It was also a force that would have annihilated the small convoy they'd just rescued without breaking a sweat. If it had been ordered to attack them.

The electrodactyls performed one final, unified blast that carved 14 percent out of Bertha's armor in a single hit, then turned and fled. Jill glanced over at the radar and watched them leave. They were slower now than they had been approaching, presumably from mana exhaustion, and dot after dot blinked out of existence as more of them were shot down. A sparse third escaped the range of the machine guns.

Jill crossed her arms and chewed on her lip. So far, so good. The window in front of her stretched and curved as the truck finished forming into a tower-studded dome. "How are things going, Babu?" she asked.

"Checking," Babu said and paused as he waited for a reply. "Hayes says that they'll be here in five minutes!"

Jill grimaced but said nothing. She'd been hoping to be in and out faster than this but trusted that they were moving as fast as they could. The tapping sounded next to her again, loud enough to be heard over the last hammering bursts of gunfire.

"What the shit is that noise?" she snapped. "Does anyone see anything outside? Gunners?"

"I/we see nothing," the hive responded. "I/we will swap in a more perception-focused constituent." One of the guns stopped firing. A few seconds later a confused, terrified, panicked eruption of mixed voices came from the turrets. "Don't shoot! Don't shoot! It's right next to us! Get sexy pants to dispel it! Why is it just sitting there?"

A pulse of dark mana blasted out from Babu just as more tapping sounded.

The wave of revealing magic washed past Jill as she looked again at the sound. First to be revealed was a pair of cruel, hooked claws, their metallic tips an inch away from Bertha's window. Jill's blood turned to ice and time slowed as more of the monster was revealed: a dainty pair of arms sticking from a barrel chest covered in feathers, a forest of massive teeth in a huge set of jaws, a head turned so that a single huge, slitted eye could watch Jill.

The tyrannosaurus's eye widened just a fraction as it lost its invisibility, and its mouth opened a bit more as if in a widening smile. The arm reached out again, a mere two feet from Jill's head.

Tap. Tap. Tap.

CHAPTER 34

PLAY TIME

Uncle-pegging fruitmongers!" Jill yelled as she threw herself back from the window, her heart slamming in her chest. The T. rex's grin widened.

She wasn't the only one to panic at the sight of the predator's arm-long fangs so close. Aman fell out of his chair sideways, Babu yelped and vanished, and there was enough screaming to welcome a boy band on stage. Jill didn't blame them. It must have been a hundred feet long from the front of its fanged mouth to the tip of its feathered tail, and it was bent far over in order to see into the cab.

"Look at all those pretty feathers!" Katie said, peeking out from her hiding place behind Jill.

"The monster is not attacking. I/we are holding fire as instructed, buzzkill," the hive said. "However, I/we must report that several constituents have wet themselves. It is very unpleasant."

Jill's head caught up to the pounding of her heart. The massive dinosaur wasn't hostile; it was just tapping the glass and watching, like an oversized six-year-old at an aquarium. Jill scowled, marched straight up to the glass, and flipped the dinosaur off. It was doing exactly what she'd hoped, but it still pissed her off.

"Lick my hairy armpit, you goddamn voyeur," she yelled, using Captain Speaking to project the noise right around the T. rex's head. "Shoo!" She flung her arms up at it. "Shoo!"

It tilted its head to the side, a forty-foot-tall apex-predator bird, whose toy was doing something unexpected.

"That's right! I'm not afraid of you, you strutting twatwaffle," Jill continued. "Go play your games somewhere else!" She raised a fist in front of her and, using metal from above the window, extruded a triple-sized copy of it outside. Then, with a single metal finger still mirroring her own motions, she flicked the dinosaur right in the middle of its feathered forehead.

Its head jerked back and its jaws snapped shut, but its eyes lit up. A crest of neon-yellow feathers atop its head stood straight up.

"TWATWAFFLE," it bellowed, shaking the truck, and it hopped from side to side in excitement. Then, in a movement so fast that it broke the speed of sound, which Jill's eyes were barely able to follow, its head shot forward and bit the metal fist clean off. It spat out the twisted, sizzling hunk of metal and leaped away from the truck. Then it spun around, feathers whipping through the air, and started to shake its tail back and forth.

"Is it dancing?" Jill asked no one. "Seriously?"

The T. rex looked over its shoulder at them and roared again. Then there was a pulse of mana, and a swirling blue-green vortex of magic appeared in front of the monster. It charged through, and nothing came out the other side.

"It can make portals?!" Babu yelled. "No fair!"

"It can fucking speak!" Jill said. "There's a goddamn level ninety-nine murder machine, with an army of dino minions, that's smart enough to talk!"

"At least it doesn't seem to actually want to hurt us," Karen said.

"Speak for yourself," Jill muttered. "That nip stung."

"Oh, this is not good," Jake said. "The whole ring of monsters at the perimeter just started moving at once! They're charging us!" He looked up at Jill and a note of panic entered his voice. "Some of them are over level seventy!"

"Burger on a brioche bun!" Jill swore. "I guess it didn't like me taunting it."

"Or it wants to see what happens," Babu said. "It seems, uh, playful, and Bertha's probably stronger than anything it's ever seen."

"Of course it is," Jill said. "Hayes, we're out of time. Tell your people to get here now."

She looked at the mana gauge and scowled; it was just over 70 percent. "Hold fire," Jill said to the hive. "Let's recharge our batteries for the main event."

This was going to get dicey. They would have to weather the swarming attacks from all those monsters while Bertha squatted, immobile, over the entrance to the base like a reverse-birthing sea turtle. There was no way the number of creatures charging them could actually fit around the truck to slash, slam, or bite their way in, not with how large the dinosaurs were to begin with. At the same time, there was no way that Bertha could kill all of them at range. They were going to get hit.

"I/we can see the big ones," the hive announced. "Those big long-necked dinosaurs."

"Those are brachiosaurs," Karen said, "maybe diplodocus."

Jill looked at her and raised an eyebrow.

She huffed. "Kevin is a dinosaur fanatic. Why are you surprised I know this?"

"Well, I'm glad he can't see us fuck them up," Jill said. "Antonio, shoot as soon as you won't be wasting mana, but be ready to switch to the flamethrowers. What do you think—explosive ammo?"

"Entangling," Antonio's many voices replied after a moment's pause. "They are packed tightly, and we may be able to delay multiple monsters for each one that becomes stuck."

It was a race between the base's survivors and the oncoming dinosaurs. The long-necked herbivores were the most visible, but Jill was less worried about them than the smaller creatures. Ankylosaurs lumbered close to the ground, heavily armored and with club tails waving in the air, while spinosaurs and raptors darted here and there. The former might be able to crack open Bertha's armor if they had enough time; the latter could dart through those cracks and maraud inside.

Jill's heart sped up as the turrets started to fire long-ranged bursts. The tenor of the guns was slightly different, a deeper, almost hollow note accompanying the rip of rapid-fire rounds. Bright green tracers reached out to the oncoming horde in visible arcs. There was nothing non-lethal about the entangling rounds; the bullets punched into dinosaur flesh, though they had trouble penetrating the ankylosaurs' armored plates.

Once each round's kinetic energy was spent, they burst into ropes of green light; those that penetrated exploded out of the wounds to wrap around their prey, and those that didn't stuck to the surface of their target, doing the same. Dinosaurs fell as their legs were bound, and while they could bite through the ropes in just a few seconds, the disruption was working. The oncoming wave went from a solid, fast wall to a slow, chaotic mass.

"The first people are getting on!" Babu reported. "The more injured are behind them. We're almost there!"

"Aman," Jill said. "Start un-fortifying us. Get us ready to go but keep that entrance covered!"

Everything seemed to be going well, but that, apparently, wasn't very fun. The T. rex stepped out of a swirling portal a few hundred feet from Bertha. It looked first at the truck, then at the streaks of tracer fire, and finally at the tripped monsters. Its mouth opened again in a grin and it bobbed its head up and down, crest flaring with each motion.

Then it started summoning portals, one after another, directly in the path of the oncoming monsters. It would hold each one open just long enough for them to charge through.

The other end of the portals were, naturally, right above Bertha. A chorus of cries came from the individuals of the hive as the dinosaurs rained down upon them.

"Ahh, it's on my turret!"

"Shoot it!"

"Fudging fudgepacker!"

"Get those off of us!" Jill ordered. She turned on the Red Eel Paint and electricity crackled over Bertha's surface.

"Are you sure I/we can't kill that T. rex?" the hive asked, back in control of itself. "It's the one doing this!"

"I am so tempted," Jill ground out. A raptor made it past the bullets and flame and landed above them. It gave a shrill cry and attacked, raking its talons over and over to try and scrape its way into Bertha. Electricity arced over its body, blackening feathers, but the monster persevered. The Red Eel Paint was a good add-on, but it was only level nineteen and just not powerful enough for these enemies.

"We're taking damage!" Katie announced, and she started casting repair spells.

"No shit," Jill said. "It feels like that budget chicken is pulling my hair out." She tried to use Customization to make an arm and bat the raptor off, but it kept jumping over her attempts. After a frustrating five seconds, one of the flamethrower turrets finally had a free moment. Brilliant white flames washed over the top of the cab, searing the paint, and dealt a chunk of damage to Bertha's armor, but it did worse to the raptor. Its charred corpse slipped off the smooth dome of metal and fell to the ground.

Despite the surprise saurian downpour, Bertha was holding on as repairs kept ahead of the incoming damage. The bigger impact was that the fortress couldn't shoot at both the monsters right on top of them and the oncoming horde. What had been a pile of confused limbs and necks pulled itself back into shape and ran again. The T. rex tilted its head back and roared, its ploy successful.

"Everyone's on!" Hayes shouted.

"Get us moving!" Jill said. She pushed her own will behind Aman's efforts at the Customization console, and Bertha exploded the rest of the way back to her boxy self. Bobby slammed a foot down on the accelerator and they surged into motion.

The monstrous wall was closer, but now that they were mobile again, Jill wasn't worried.

"Aim for a hole," Jill said, then shot Babu a warning look before he could make the obvious joke.

"There's no way through," Bobby said back, his voice unsteady.

"There's always a way," Jill said. "Let me show you how this is done." She sat down in the center seat, buckled in, and, with a twist of her mind, pulled the driving controls over in front of her.

It didn't take long for her to find her way. The largest of the brachio-diplo-whatsits was a towering beast with legs bigger than any natural tree, and it wasn't particular about where it slammed them down as it ran. The other monsters stayed away for their own safety; either that, or the ones that hadn't stayed away had already been trampled into meat paste.

"Here we go!" Jill said. She pulled the horn and Bertha roared. The sound exploded forward before settling into its plow form. Jill turned the wheel, aimed Bertha straight for that huge monster, and floored it. They would reach it in seconds.

Then Blossom opened fire in a long roar, aimed straight ahead. The rounds smashed through flesh and exploded, carving huge craters in the titanic dinosaur. Mia—or was it the hive?—walked her shots from the torso to the huge neck and held the beam of burning ammunition on it until it had sawed straight through. The monster fell to one side, dead, and the trunk of a neck and head fell to the other.

"Spoilsport!" Jill said. She twitched the wheel and they thundered past the dead monster before the others could react. "See, Bobby?"

"That didn't end up being very hard," he said back, his arms crossed.

"Maybe not, but now we're home fr—fuuuuu!" Jill's voice morphed into a curse of alarm as a massive weight slammed down on top of Bertha, driving the truck down on its suspension. The truck's nose dug a scar through the earth, and they slowed but didn't stop; the wheels were pushing with far too much power for that. Jill pushed mana into War Rig, and bit by bit the truck rose.

"Buzzkill," the hive reported, "I/we would like to report more soiled pants. We have a new, very heavy feathered passenger."

A roar sounded right above Jill. Then an upside down T. rex grin lowered into view in the front window. It was riding Bertha, and it had bent itself over all the way to look in the cab again.

"TWATWAFFLE!" it bellowed, and instead of fear, Jill felt a moment of understanding. It was enjoying the ride. Because of course it was.

"Will you kill that thing already?!" Hayes shouted. His face was red and his eyes bulged with hatred.

Jill ignored him and opened her mouth in a wide toothy grin at the T. rex. "Nice playing with you, big lady," she projected outside the truck, "but I can't go fast with you on the roof." She took one hand off the wheel and waved. "Bye now!" With the other hand, she pulled the wheel hard over.

Dirt sprayed, and Jill had to use the Torque Converter to stop the truck from rolling. The T. rex, despite all the magical bullshit around them, was not entirely immune to physics. It kept going straight and tumbled off the truck. An enormous portal opened in midair and swallowed it before it could hit the ground.

Local Quest Complete: Evacuate Maelstrom Base.
Contribution bonus: +.4
Noncombat savior bonus: +1.1
55,000 Experience Gained!

Cheers broke out as everyone else got a similar notification. Even Hayes seemed mollified.

"Hell yes, everyone!" Jill said. "Great job. How are we doing, Jake? Are we clear?"

"I think"—he knocked on the radar console with his knuckles—"I think we've gotten away! They aren't chasing us! I mean, there's still tons of monsters around in general, but all the dinos around the base are just going away!"

Jill let out a sigh of relief. Her worst fear had been that after finally making off with the survivors, the T. rex would stop playing and really go after them.

"But," Jake said and let the word hang in the air.

"Don't make me come back there," Jill growled.

"But that other dot! You know, the weird one we thought might be the T. rex? It wasn't, by the way. I saw it when the T. rex was jumping around us."

"And the weird one?"

"It's following us."

They kept driving. An hour later, Jill was back in the conference room with Hayes. This time they were joined by Jacob and Captain Green.

Jill had just given Green the twenty-minute summary of what had happened to the rest of the world, at least the small part she'd driven through. "You and your people have a lot of levels," she said, "and the kind of training that most of my people either never had or have forgotten. I could really use your help."

"So, let me get this straight," Green said. "This whole giant building and weird-ass bubble filled with an entire sun is inside of the truck?"

"Yup," Jill said.

"And there are five thousand people here?"

"A few more."

"And you"—he pointed at Jacob—"are their elected leader, but she"—he pointed at Jill—"is the one really in charge?"

"She doesn't really mess with how we've been setting up the administration," Jacob said.

"But she could," Green said. He turned to Jill. "I'm grateful for the rescue, ma'am, and for the medical help, but I can't in good conscience take orders from a dictator."

Jill winced at the word and tapped her fingers on the table. Until they finalized what their system of government would really be, it was an accurate description. "Okay," she said, "I can respect that. You can get off any time you like. But before you make up your mind, why don't you radio back into your brass and see what they say? I bet they'll tell you to fight with us to keep everyone safe, at least until you leave. You won't be joining me permanently."

"You have comms with someone who can give me orders?" Green asked. "And you'll take me and my men where we need to go to complete them?"

"More or less," Jill said. "Yes to the first. Hell, they even paid me to come out here and see what happened to your nukes."

Green's face clouded, but Jill kept talking before he could say anything.

"Let me guess, super classified? Fine, I don't care that they turned into pixie farts. But as to your second question"—she leaned forward—"I'm heading east. Through this bullshit high-mana zone and out the other side, then on to Boston. I'll drop you off wherever, but I won't detour more than a few hours."

"I'll relay that to my superiors and see what they say," Green said.

Jill nodded and stood, ending the meeting.

A day passed. The air force personnel from the base settled into a barracks of their own that Aman made for them—a traumatized community apart, even though, just as Jill anticipated, they had been ordered to help defend Bertha until she could bring them to another base. Karen listened in on the crackling, in-and-out radio call to see what had happened to the nukes, and later told Jill. They'd vanished, just like all the rest.

The day was normal, or at least as normal as any day inside Bertha could be. Jill spent another several hours searching for places inside Bertha that had been hidden from her but found nothing. The monsters grew thicker over the course of the day, the mana density higher. On the map, they made less progress. The strange radar contact came and went, sometimes heading off on its own for a time, out of range, but always returning to stalk the truck. There was no sign of the T. rex.

Jill had just gone into her room to settle in for the night when a flashing notification appeared before her.

> Congratulations, Battle Trucker Jill MacLeod! You have reached Level 100 and can now evolve your Class to a new form. Determining most beneficial Class Evolution.

"Well, that's nicer than a bed full of tits. What have you got for me, Sys?" she asked.

System Inquiry Detected Users may delay the selection of a Class Evolution by staying at Level 100 until they have met the prerequisites for the desired upgrade. Delay Class Evolution?

"Huh," Jill said and tilted her head to the side. "That's not even close to what I asked. Do you have something really good for me, something I haven't qualified for yet?"

Abilities are revealed upon being unlocked. Delay Class Evolution?

"Sys," Jill said, "if I stay at one hundred, then Bertha doesn't get any stronger. Things are getting bat-fucking-insane out there around us. More monsters, higher levels. Hell, we came across a sheep today that was higher level than the hydra back in Bozeman!" It had been a ram, not a sheep, with glowing red eyes and horns that burned with infernal heat, but to Jill, it still counted. "Is waiting going to be worth it for us?"

There was no response for several seconds.

Checking cultural database. Jilldalf, my old friend, this will be an evolution to remember.

"Great," Jill said. "You're turning into a giant nerd. But fine, delay."

CHAPTER 35

ENEMY ACTION

Piercing, shrieking screams, like golden wind chimes in a hurricane, tore Jill from her sleep. The guardian sunflowers in her room screamed at the top of their questionably existent lungs, all of their faces turned in the same direction.

As she came to consciousness a flashing blue box appeared in her vision.

> New Local Quest: Defeat the Corrupted Sapient! Protect the residents of Berthaville from the Corrupted Sapient!

> Berthaville has been Invaded!
> Protect the Settlement Core! Defeat the Invaders!
> Current monsters in Settlement: 0
> Current invaders in Settlement: 11
> Threat estimate: Extreme

Fire and ice coursed through Jill's veins as she leaped from her bed. She threw her magic into Bertha, not so much sinking as running her senses full tilt into her truck. They were still moving at top speed, the wheels sending up a spray of dirt behind them that vanished as it left the range of her Cargokinesis. The hive of gunners hummed at her, wondering what she was doing but unconcerned. The Habitation Module and converted bunkrooms in the Cargo Nexus were filled with mostly sleeping people and no sign of trouble.

But then Jill realized she couldn't feel the cargo doors. They had been blocked from her senses.

"Bertha is mine!" Jill's words echoed through the truck at a deafening volume as she instinctually activated both Captain Speaking and Bond Inviolate at the same time. Golden mana exploded from her and raced through Bertha as searing lines of light on the walls. The concealment in the Cargo Nexus exploded, and Bertha was whole.

Three figures stood by the cargo doors. Two were fuzzy in Jill's senses, as if neither Cargokinesis nor Synergy could get a good hold on them, but were people-sized. The third was an abomination. Eight feet tall at the shoulder, it had to stoop to fit under Bertha's somewhat short ceilings. It took a step forward, and Jill felt dozens of curved, jointed spines on its torso flex and shift, a mass of grasping too-thin limbs that bent in the wrong way. One of the two figures stiffened and turned their head around as if searching. The two people vanished.

A terrible howl erupted from the creature's throat, loud enough to rattle the stored cargo and resonate through the metal interior of the truck. It flickered forward, lightning fast, towards the crafting area and the workshop. Despite the early hour, there were still a few people working there and in the rest of the Cargo Nexus.

Jill snapped back to herself. "Danger!" she yelled through Captain Speaking, projecting it to the entire truck, even as she started running. "Boss monster in the cargo bay! Get out of there!" Her door slammed open just before she reached it and she ran out.

"What's—" Zeke said from just outside the turret prep room. His mouth fell open at the sight of her.

"Follow me!" Jill yelled. She planted her feet and willed the deck under her to shift and surge in a wave of metal to push her along faster than even she could run. She activated Armored Suits and, for the first time, summoned a set for herself. It was still forming around her as she shot from the hallway like a cork from the world's angriest champagne bottle into the cafeteria. Tables melted away from her path, shoving those few people who had been eating at them aside.

"Zeke," she yelled at the young man who, despite sprinting, was far behind, "get these people out of here!"

Then she saw it skittering towards her, nearly at the single door that led from the cargo area to the cafeteria. What had once been a person was now an emaciated giant of bones, stretched skin, and dripping muscles, a normal-sized head set with glowing green eyes, and a crazed grin stuffed with too many teeth. It didn't use its legs to move—no, not when it was in a hurry. Instead, its dozens of rib-limbs stabbed out in all directions, the tips sinking into Bertha like so many stabbing spears, propelling it along with a rippling motion like that of a centipede.

"It's in the cafeteria!" she projected and prepared to attack.

Then a scream sounded in Jill's mind, endless insanity pressing in around her, and her thinking mind stuttered. Her vision started to go white.

"You tire-popping pus-fucker!" Jill screamed and her mana fought back, Swampwater Vitality doing its work. "Get off my truck!" Her mind cleared, and it was almost upon her.

She thrust an armored hand upwards, fingers raised in a claw, and Bertha responded. Spikes of metal pierced the surprised abomination before it could dodge, puncturing flesh and shattering bone. Jill clenched her hand shut and twisted; the spikes did the same, snapping off rib-limbs and making a ruin of the creature's torso. The spikes twisted and wrapped, pinning and squeezing, around as much of the creature as they could cover. The ribs on the floor spasmed and flopped, black blood leaking from ripped flesh.

It opened its mouth as if to scream, but what poured out was a gray, luminescent fog, a boiling mass of wrongness that warped and twisted everything around it. Jill screamed in pain as it seeped into the floor, walls, and ceiling—into her. The metal crumbled into motes of dust that blew away in a non-existent wind, and it was free. It flexed and a half dozen of its rib-limbs shot at her like supersonic spears. She dodged one, but the other five were on target.

They would have hit if not for the sudden appearance of the Roaming Guardians. They rose up in front of Jill, a phalanx of pale-gold, translucent warriors. The front ranks exploded into wisps of mana as the spines tore through them, but through their sacrifice, the attack was stopped. The rest charged towards the abomination, cracking bones with their every blow even as the horrible mist ate away at their very being.

Warning! Berthaville Inner Sanctum has been invaded! All Administrators, defend the Core!

"Fuck!" Jill yelled. "I'm a little busy!" She let her senses snap to her room, and her heart clenched; two people were battling the potted sunflowers, who launched beams of fire at them, and a third was already in her bathroom, hacking at the floor. Another dozen were in a fight that spilled from her door into the turret prep room, a confused tangle of guns and swords surging with the mana of active powers. Jill opened a connection with Captain Speaking to the cab. "They're attacking the core! In my room!" she yelled. She heard the sound of fighting and screaming through the link. They already knew.

Warning! Berthaville Settlement Core under attack! Core Hit Points at 80%. All Administrators, defend the Core!

They weren't going to make it. She reached out with Customization and slammed a pillar of metal out of the wall of her bathroom, knocking that person out of the small space. But before she could follow up, her instincts screamed and she threw herself sideways. A rib had gotten through the guardians, and the flying spike glanced off of her hip, carving a deep gouge in the metal armor.

She was going to get herself killed if she tried to fight in two places at once.

Advanced Module **Fortress of the Throne** available. Upgrade?

"Do it!" Jill yelled. She braced herself for feedback even as she pulled herself off the floor. She almost staggered as the feeling of her heart being scooped from her chest hit her, but the sensation lasted for only an instant before a wave of automated mana swept it aside.

Leo Sharp defeated. Your contribution: 90% 21,000 Experience Gained. Killing other sapients is not recommended.

"The fuck?" she said but had no time to investigate to see who had been killed, or if the upgrade had worked to save the core, because at that moment the last of her guardians exploded into shards of gold. The corrupted human roared, pouring more corrosive mist from its mouth, and its rib-limbs bit into the floor to propel it at shocking speed towards Jill. She tried to restrain it with more metal from the floor, but the mist clung to the creature like a cloak, and everything that touched it rusted away.

Then it was on her. Its many ribs shot towards her head, and she raised her arms to cover her face, but it was a feint. The real attack came from one of its massive, clawed hands. It slashed her, carving a gouge into her armor starting just above her left hip and traveling across her torso. She flew backwards into the cafeteria and through a set of tables. Pain erupted across her chest, and it wasn't a sympathetic feeling from Bertha. No, it was her own flesh, torn open down to her ribs.

Jill expected it to follow, to shove those spines right into her body and tear her in half. But an explosion of blades erupted in the cafeteria, blocking its path. Ras, shirtless except for a phantom breastplate of magic, charged at the abomination. His sword left a luminescent trail behind it as it cut the air, and every time its edge struck a rib-limb, it won. The creature jumped back and started firing its spines at him, forcing him to dodge and block instead of strike.

Jill pushed herself off the ground and tore the ruined chest piece of her armor away. It had done its job in blunting the attack just enough, but it wouldn't be stopping anything else. It was equivalent to a whopping level 111 uncommon armor, but that wasn't enough. It was a pale imitation of Bertha's Armor Module, and she needed the real thing. Her lips pulled back in a bloody grin as she realized that if she needed vehicle-grade armor, she could just take it.

Ras was back in melee and had done some damage, but he'd also taken hits. His armor flickered and his left arm hung useless and broken. He was losing but giving her the time to do what needed to be done.

Jill reached out around herself with Customization and she pushed. Bertha trembled as she ruined Aman's careful architecture, as she scattered the internal layout of the rooms in order to make the cafeteria adjacent to the outside world. Her push turned to a grasping, rending pull, and red-painted armor from the truck's exterior exploded out of the walls and ceiling to wrap around her. The sliding panels between the cab and trailer formed the joints and the armored glass a visor.

"Round two, motherfucker," Jill said and turned on the eel paint. Snapping electricity coursed over her, and she charged.

It wasn't the best plan; as strong as the monster was at range, it was stronger close-up and faster than her too. But her charge took the pressure off of Ras, who leaped back.

"Get that healed and get back here!" Jill ordered, and he flickered away. She barely ducked a swipe of tearing claws, stepped in, and threw a haymaker at the thing's torso. The punch landed and shattered three rib-limbs, but that was all she managed before she was slashed again and thrown back. She activated the Torque Converter in midair to stop her spin and landed on her feet, skidding. The blow burned, and it felt like her skin was split anew, but it was just the usual feedback from Bertha. There was a gouge but no penetration. Jill pulled more armor from the exterior of the truck to repair the damage, cracked her neck, and stalked towards the abomination yet again.

Before she reached it again, a cracking hailstorm of rifle fire struck the horror from the defensive positions by the Habitation area as the first of the Cloud Killers, backed up by the survivors of Maelstrom Base, arrived to fight. The corrupted person snapped out its rib-limbs to smack bullets out of the air, stopping nearly all of them, but it didn't advance.

Jill sensed weakness. The thing wasn't invulnerable, and with every person that joined the fight the pressure on it increased. Her initial surprise attack had hurt it; the guardians, Ras, and her own punches had hurt it more. Half of its rib-limbs were broken wrecks, twitching shards of bones pierced through rotten skin, tugged on by muscles but unable to move. It could melt her, it could cut her to pieces, but it couldn't keep going forever.

With Cargokinesis, Jill felt two familiar invisible figures enter the room, followed by the pulsing sultry magic of spells being cast, and she knew the fight was won.

"That's right, you shit stain," Jill growled. "I can do this all day!" It was a lie, but that was okay. She just had to keep its attention for a few more seconds. She took another step forward; it took one back. Then the sound Jill had been waiting for rang out in the cafeteria: the spooling of a jet engine in miniature. Jill snarled her teeth into something approximating a smile. "Say hello to my friend Blossom."

A grasping net of dark mana folded around the corrupted creature, pinning it in place. The tips of its limbs glowed gray and they stabbed outwards, tearing into the spell, but it had been held long enough.

Mia snapped into view, wearing pajamas and a furious expression. She stood on top of a table and opened fire as the invisibility spell failed, her legs braced and her massive gun held at her hip. The roar of the chain gun was deafeningly loud in the confined space of the cafeteria, and a solid beam of burning ammunition slammed into the abomination, punching into its flesh before exploding, blowing out chunks of gray meat that boiled into nothingness. It launched itself backward away from Mia, running with its rib-limbs curled tightly for protection. They broke and snapped, and it stumbled with a piercing scream. It was done for.

But then a single crack of a rifle cut through all the other deafening sounds, accompanied by a blast of ozone mana. Mia's fire stuttered to a stop, and the woman looked down, confused. She stumbled to a knee, eyes wide with pain and mouth working soundlessly, and in so doing Jill saw that there was a bloody wound on her back. Writhing tendrils of metal whipped out of it like a nest of worms on cocaine.

"Mia!" Babu yelled. A shimmering black bubble snapped around Mia and he popped into visibility by her side.

"Motherfucking assassin!" Jill yelled, tremors of sympathetic agony breaking out over her as she recognized the wound. "Get her to the Medbay! Now! Everyone else, take cover!"

The need to find the shooter burned within her, but she didn't take her eyes off the abomination, which had taken the momentary respite to regain its feet and keep running, nor did she stop harassing it with spikes of metal from all sides. It leaped across the void of destroyed decking back into the warehouse portion of the Cargo Nexus. Jill moved to follow but stumbled in pain. It had breathed out another of its disintegrating fog banks, this time aimed straight down. It was tunneling its way out of Bertha.

She might have been able to stop it. To wrap it in metal, to rip and tear until the weakened monster was dead. But a cornered rat was all the more dangerous, and it had already shown that it could melt Bertha away if it was restrained. Someone had shot an unarmored Mia with a copy of the single nastiest power that Jill had ever been hit with, and they were still around, presumably getting ready to murder someone else. Jill let the abomination escape.

She spun around, eyes searching the ruined room for the assassin who had shot Mia, but had little hope of finding them. There was too much chaos, too much destruction. A horrible pain drove her to her knees, and she felt the gentle rocking of something catastrophic happening to Bertha on the outside.

Local Quest Complete: Protect Berthaville from the Corrupted Invader.
Contribution bonus: +1.9
Noncombat savior bonus: +2.2
Fatality penalty: -.3
213,000 Experience Gained! Experience gain deferred until Class Evolution complete.

"What the shit was that?!" she projected to the cab.

"We just lost the left-side wheels!" Amy on the comms yelled in her ear. "Ripped all to fuck! We're stopped!"

Jill groaned and pulled up Bertha's status sheet.

Soulbound Modular Vehicle "Bertha"
Armor: 18,022/43,260 Durability: 207,834/309,000
Mana: 289,375/309,000

Between her own borrowing of the armor and the horrible corrupted person cutting its way through the hull on the way out, they were horribly damaged. It had also left them a spiteful parting gift: one final blast of its breath weapon over one side of the truck, melting the wheels to slag. She pushed some of her remaining mana into her repair power, but it was a drop in the bucket of what was needed.

"Incoming!" Amy said. "Monsters coming from all sides!"

"I could be asleep right now," Jill muttered to herself.

Ras appeared beside her in a flash of mana, his arm bound tightly to his body. "Where do you need me?" he asked.

"The cargo bay," Jill said. "That's where they can get in." She focused her attention on the ruined hole between her and the cargo section and activated her repair power again. A bridge of metal extended across the gap, and she ran across it. "Hey," she projected into the cab, "we need reinforcements in the cargo bay!"

They passed the workshop. Its doors were slammed shut and unscarred; the abomination had run straight past it. Jill had the fleeting hope that everyone in the Nexus had made it into that shelter, but the first ruined half of a body they found shattered that illusion. Other crying people crouched half-hidden behind shelves, untouched only because it hadn't bothered to stop and kill them.

"It's gone," Jill projected around the Cargo Nexus, "and I know you're scared, but I need you to get out of here—now. Everyone get to the Medbay."

She had a minute to catch her breath and pump mana into her repair power before the first monsters got in range. Outside, the turrets thundered, and the kill notifications started. The abomination's mist was persistent and kept melting the wheels every time Jill fixed them, but it consumed itself to do so. They just needed a little more time.

They didn't get it. Jill gritted her teeth and closed her eyes against the pain as monsters clawed, bludgeoned, crushed, and spat acid at Bertha. The sound was horrible as the shrieking of rent metal mixed with tortured monster screams. The hive had switched to flamethrowers for this close-in work, and they were burning the monsters alive.

The wall of the cargo bay was peeled back by a pair of terrible claws, and a crocodile-headed humanoid monster shoved its way through the shimmering dimensional barrier that separated outside from inside. It roared at Jill. She charged.

She and Ras fought alone at first, then were joined by a rotating squad of Cloud Killers and soldiers. Coach joined in, wrestling monsters to death and blowing his whistle to change squads whenever they were too worn down. The monsters, thankfully, didn't seem to want to destroy Bertha outright, but rather to cut their way in and satisfy their ravenous hunger. Jill stopped trying to repair the rents in the armor through which they entered and in a free second directed the repair crew to do likewise. All their efforts needed to go towards overcoming the corrosive mist and getting Bertha moving again.

Jill and the residents of Berthaville fought together, and they held. Ras cast aside his bandages after a few minutes, the status condition gone and his bone healed enough to fight again. Between constant repairs and manipulating Bertha's structure with Customization to kill monsters, Jill's mana had started to run low, so she took the swordsman's recovery as a chance to rest and recharge for a moment. She joined the squad of Cloud Killers who were likewise catching their breath.

"Babu," she said, reaching with Captain Speaking into the Medbay, "how's Mia?"

"They are cutting the tendrils of the cursed bullet out right now. She will recover," he said, tone flat. He must have activated his emotion-suppressing power again.

"Thank fuck," Jill said. "Babu, this whole clusterfuck was a diversion. They went for the core."

"I saw the notification," he replied. He was also an administrator. "You defeated their attempt?"

"I had to take the fortress power, but yeah," she said. "Listen, at least one of the coffee-hating bastards who did this died when I moved the core, and there might be other clues about what happened. I have to stay here fighting, but I need someone to follow up on them right now. Can you do it?"

There was a pause. "I'll take care of it," he said.

"Thanks, Babu," Jill said. "You're a lifesaver."

She switched with Ras and went back to fighting. The cargo bay was a wreck, the carefully stowed supplies scattered amid monster corpses and blood, the shelving torn down into twisted scraps of metal. But the tide of monsters was receding. There had only been so many monsters within range to pounce on their vulnerability, and they were reaching the end of that number.

Jill had just finished sucking a twelve-legged fire spider into the metal floor and crushing it to death when she saw movement through one of the rents in the walls. It was the ground moving past, slowly at first but then picking up speed. The receding tide of invading monsters became a trickle, as only the fastest were able to grab a hold of the truck and pull themselves in.

Ras flicked his sword to the side and an arc of glowing blood sprayed off. "I think we did it," he said, relief and pride on his face.

"That you did," Jill said. She turned to the rest of the defenders. "We all did!"

There was an exhausted cheer.

"Ras, I've got to get to the cab and figure out what the fuck happened. Can you stay here and hold down the fort against any stragglers?" A giant hummingbird–mosquito hybrid with a cruel, acid-dripping proboscis buzzed into the cargo bay at that moment, only to explode into bloody chunks as the combined rifle fire of fifteen defenders slammed into it at once.

Ras saluted with his sword. "Not a problem."

Jill jogged back to the cab. Between the truck's natural regeneration and the efforts of the repair team, Bertha was pulling itself back together, the signs of fighting fading bit by bit. The jagged, melted pit between the cargo bay and cafeteria remained, but even it was starting to heal around the edges.

The hallway to the command area was guarded by six people: four with glowing rifles and two with swords. Jill nodded at them as she went past, then strode into the cab. The room was crowded with people. Every single member of the repair crew, plus a few more people that Jill didn't recognize, were sprawled on seats and against the floor, suffering from mana exhaustion from keeping the truck together. Tyler was driving, but Bobby was sitting next to him, pointing out terrain features for them to dodge around.

In the center of the cab was the glowing gold settlement core. Invisible ripples in the air circled around it, the un-manifested Throne Room Guardians ready to defend. Jill's central observer seat had been moved behind it and transformed into a magnificent white toilet, complete with golden scrollwork and shining mana gems.

"Throne was a fucking pun?" Jill asked the System. Her mouth twitched upwards in an involuntary smile, and she shook her head. There were a few strained chuckles, but no one seemed to be in the mood for humor.

"Good one, Sys," she said. "Even if your timing was shitty." She waited a few seconds for a response, but none came, so she morphed the toilet back into a normal seat and moved it back to its position at the front windshield.

"All right, people, we seem to be alive and going fast enough to be mostly unfuckable," Jill said once that was done. "So good job. Now, talk to me. What's the situation?"

"We've depleted the monsters around us," said the night radar operator, a woman named Leah. "The mystery dot ran straight away from us after it escaped, and I haven't seen it since."

"Thank heaven for small mercies," Jill muttered.

"Right now I'm just kind of driving as fast as I can," Tyler reported. "We're kind of going in the right direction, I guess?"

Jill's eyes went to Aman's usual seat, but the man wasn't there. "Good enough for now," Jill said. "Just keep us moving, and we'll get back on course when we can."

"We just sealed the last of the holes," Katie said from the floor. There was dried blood on her face. "Nothing's going to get in, at least not without cutting through again."

Jill breathed out a sigh of relief. "Then we made it," she said. She slumped down into an observer seat. "God, that was awful." She took just a moment with her eyes closed, then forced herself to keep going. This hadn't been random. Someone had masterminded this, had let that horrible thing on to Bertha, all in an attempt to keep her busy and go for the settlement core. People had died. She had to find out who did this.

She opened her eyes and realized that Babu wasn't in the cab either. "Did Babu come through here?" Jill asked.

"He came in and looked at the, uh, body and recognized them," Leah said. She looked nervous. "He was acting really weird."

"Like, excited I've solved a mystery weird, or . . . ?"

"He didn't seem like himself," Leah said. "And the way he said he was going to take care of things . . ." She shivered and her voice trailed off.

"Karen, can you—" Jill started to ask but cut herself off. For a moment she'd forgotten that it was Amy at the communications console.

"Where the ass are all the Batis?" Jill asked, annoyed. "There are like forty of them."

"Oh," Amy said. There was grief in her voice. "You haven't heard?"

"Heard what?"

"Sangita's in the Medbay, in stasis," Amy said and swallowed. She slumped. "She ran out of here to defend the core and took a sword through the back."

Jill froze, and the world seemed to fall away. "But she's alive?"

"She's not dead," Amy said.

"Fuck," Jill said. "Do Ras and Babu know?"

"I told Ras after the fighting was over," Amy said. "He's—let me check." She paused for a moment. "He's still in the cargo area." She looked close to tears. "Babu already knew when he came here."

Dread's claws went from icy to white hot, tearing at her heart. Babu had known, and he'd been in the Medbay with Mia. He had seen his mother brought in, horribly injured and near death. Then Jill had ordered him away, to hunt Sangita's almost-killers, and he had made a breakthrough in finding them. He'd left to handle it, alone.

"Oh fuck," Jill whispered.

She closed her eyes and sent her senses racing through Bertha, reaching for the young enchanter. She was only halfway through her search when a burst of horrible, sick mana flooded into her. She felt as if her stomach were being pumped full of motor oil and, despite being as tough as a superhero, sunk to her knees and retched. She looked around desperately to find the source of the attack; her eyes saw nothing other than the rapidly panicking crew around her, but her mana senses saw a swollen, black worm latched straight onto her. She reached out with her mind and ripped it away. The horrible mana boiled its way out of her body, rejected.

But in that moment, when she was destroying it, she had recognized the worm. It was one of her own Synergy selections, one of only a dozen links that let her share and receive experience from people in her crew. The other eleven were intact.

"No," she whispered, still on her knees. The missing Synergy link had led to Babu.

New Local Quest: Defeat the Corrupted Sapient!

CHAPTER 36

ENOUGH

Jill half ran, half surfed through Bertha, following a beacon of sick mana to a far corner of the Habitation Module. The noncombatant residents of Berthaville had emerged from their hiding places to take stock of the damage to their home and to help with repairs. Jill's reckless passage was met with wide-eyed panic.

Her stomach rose in rebellion as she approached her target room, but she pushed through.

The door was open. Babu stood with his eyes closed in the middle of the bunkroom, the sun from Berthaville shining on his face. Around him lay eight withered corpses, some on their beds, others collapsed on the floor. There was no blood, but one man had been carrying a cup of coffee when he had been killed. His desiccated form lay in a puddle of brown liquid, shards of white ceramic scattered about.

"Babu," Jill said, "what the fuck happened?"

Babu's eyes snapped open. "I did it, Jill," he said in a quiet, cold voice. "Me! I got them for what they did." He walked a few steps towards her, casually stepping on a corpse as he did. "She was using them, and they were using her, and all of them had already eaten so much before getting on that they were far gone, far gone. But they messed up—yes, they did—when they *attacked my mother!*" He screamed the last words, and his body spasmed, the skin on his face bulging as a half dozen other, smaller skulls tried to push free.

"She's okay," Jill said. She took a step into the room and flinched as the horrible feeling of corruption washed over her. "The doctors saved her. She's in the Medbay."

"I know," Babu said and hummed a discordant triad that no human vocal cords could. "I know she's there, probably already waiting to tell me how I did this all wrong, but I know I didn't. They're dead and gone and never even had a chance." He nodded at her. "We're alike now, you and I, I, I." He twitched and the motion rippled through his body, making the joints on his arms and legs go momentarily backward as it passed.

"Sure," said Jill. "Why don't you tell me how?" Her heart felt like it was being ripped from her chest. The other people she'd seen this far gone she'd either killed or been glad when they had died. And now the System wanted her to do the deed herself, right now, to supposedly protect them all. But there had to be another way. He had to be there under the madness. If she could coax out what had happened, find some way to undo what had been done . . .

"I did nothing clever at all, no careful plans of crafted synergetic abilities. I just out-leveled my enemies." He bent over as if in terrible agony, his spine bulging upwards in a row of spikes. Then it passed, he snapped back upright, and he kept talking like it had never happened. "Just like you do so often with your cheating. I didn't sink all my points into a truck, no. I made myself the best battlefield support and control that could be, but that doesn't mean anything to you now, does it, does it?"

Jill opened her mouth to answer but he started speaking again right away.

"They never saw me," he said.

"Who never saw you?"

"You'll never guess! It was all an act, Jill, all an act," Babu smiled that cold smile again. "It fooled me like it fooled you, right up until it didn't, and now she's just skin and bones." He pointed to one of the bodies on a bed. She was unrecognizable by her features, so distorted were they by the desiccation, but a cashmere sweater, pearls, and a wig were enough.

"Was that, uh, what's her name? Marigold?" Jill asked in disbelief. "That crazy Karen?"

"All an act!" Babu said, his cold mask cracking again in triumph. "She was the ringleader: power-hungry, mad, and a mana vampire too! She was feeding, feeding, feeding on all of her hangers-on while keeping them under her control. She cast the curse but routed it through one of her cattle."

"Harrison?"

Babu shrugged, his shoulder blades pushing out and back like the wings of a bat before being sucked back in. "His name is not important. They are dead for their crimes now. Dead because of the power I earned." His eyes lit up. "Invisibility is better without the System. There's no restriction on it at all."

"Without the System?" Jill asked. "You got that working, huh?"

"No, no, no!" Babu screamed, his emotional control spell again shattered for an instant. He was cold again an instant later. "But my guides did. The System doesn't like that, though, and now it won't talk to me. But that's another way we're alike! I'm going to be just like you, using mana as it was meant to be!" His face rippled again.

Jill took a step closer and gestured at the bodies. "So they never had a chance to fight back?"

"No, they did not," he said. "One spell, free, free, free of System restrictions, and I had them paralyzed. Then another, and I was in their heads. and"—he twitched—"they were messed up, Jill, truly twisted. Evil leeches that only wanted to hurt us all, to take over and make us suffer for their hunger." He nodded. "They deserved it! She deserved it! So I ate them."

Jill swallowed. "How did you eat them, Babu?" she asked. "I don't see teeth marks."

"I didn't use my mouth," he said. His jaw split open sideways, two mandibles overflowing with rotten teeth. He cocked his head to the side, and they slithered back into place. "That would be insane. I devoured my puppets, Jill, as I was always meant to."

Ice spread up Jill's back. She remembered that phrase. She flicked back through her notifications to the first day, to a box that Babu had sent her.

> Enchanter evolution, Dark Dominator advanced spell learned!
> **Devourer of Puppets**: Your domination goes beyond the mind and body and extends to the soul. Execute and reap the soul of a creature that you have total control over. The more creatures you slay with this ability the more powerful it becomes, but beware of whispers in the dark. Mana cost scales with Level and remaining Hit Points of the target.
> Mana Cost: Variable
> You do not meet the prerequisites to evolve Enchanter into Dark Dominator.

"You said you weren't going to use that!" Jill said. "Christ, Babu, it's the only power I've ever seen that comes with a warning!"

"It would have been illogical to not use something I spent a point on. I always knew that it would be needed eventually," he said. He twitched and his eyes split into insectile compound structures before coming back together. "But the System was wrong, so very, very wrong. The voices are nothing to be afraid of, no, not at all!" His control spell again failed in his excitement. "The whispers talked math at me, Jill, sweet, sweet math. They laid bare what the future damage progression was, about how the damage per mana increased for everything I killed with it! I needed an attack power. I'd been falling behind, behind, behind! And there it was, the best ratio that would only get better. It said that if I fed it enough, it would grant me pure damage spells that are even better, and it was telling the truth!"

He grinned at her, and for just an instant Jill saw Babu as he had been. Then she realized that the grin had too many teeth.

"Babu," Jill said and took a step closer to him. "You're my chief advisor, right?"

He nodded and the mask of indifference snapped back on. "I am."

"Well, I need a different perspective on this. Then how about we, uh, reframe this. Let's say that a video game character got that power, that voices were whispering to them," she said. "What would you say about that?"

His control spell shattered once and for all and his body rippled. "I know about more than just games!" His voice grew louder. "I studied, I got good grades, I did well!" He was screaming by the end of it, and his mana responded. It thrashed around in all directions, aimless power that howled and snapped, scarring the metal and tearing the air.

The bodies turned their heads to point at Jill, eyeless sockets of sunken leather gazing at her with hunger.

"Fuck yeah, you did, especially with me," Jill said. "You've been here for me ever since I got you off that U-Haul. Remember that? Remember learning about magic?"

He nodded, and his magic settled a little. Jill took another step closer. "It was amazing," he whispered. "So many doors opening. A new life. And I thought I'd done so good, so good at last!" Tears of blood leaked from his eyes, and he smiled at Jill. "I was using fire back then. But think how much easier it would have been with this!" He held out a hand and a ball of inky blackness appeared in it, a hungry, lecherous magic that would only ever take. The whites bled out of Babu's eyes as he stared into it.

"Yeah, that sure would have fucked everything up," Jill said. "How about you put it away when you're inside, though, huh?"

"It wouldn't have been enough!" he screamed and threw the ball. The heads of the bodies turned as they followed its speeding progress. It hit the wall of the room and exploded outwards in a sticky mass. Jill twitched as she felt it eating into Bertha, robbing it of magic.

"You and Ras, Ras, Ras! You were the smart ones, not me, not poor Babu with his numbers and dreams! Soulbound this, Soulbound that. Why is it so strong, why, why?"

Jill held up her hands and stepped over a body on her way to him. "Hey, you could—"

"I tried!" he bellowed.

The body snapped out a desiccated arm and grabbed her ankle. Jill pulled her leg free and stomped down on its head. Brittle bone stood no chance, and the skull crumbled in an explosion of dust, bones, and crackling skin.

"I tried," Babu whispered, and his shoulders began to shake. "It wanted nine perk points. Nine! How could it ask for so many? Why didn't it let me be like you two?"

"Because Sys can be a real bitch sometimes," Jill said with grief.

He let out a mad little chuckle, blinked, and recoiled from the bodies as if seeing them for the first time. "I didn't want to have to do all this," Babu whispered. "I only ever wanted to help. Oh my God, what's happening to me?" His eyes met hers. "Please, Jill, help me."

Jill made up her mind. She thrust her mana at the quest notification, wrapped it in bands of iron will, and tore it to pieces. Then she pushed her mana farther. There was a place that the System came from when it interacted with her, a fortress that she instinctively knew not to try and breach. She visualized Bertha slamming into those fortress gates and pushing with all its might.

Her magic disintegrated into nothing, annihilated entirely for its temerity. But around her time ground to a halt as she felt something from the System respond. Something that was waiting.

"Give me a new fucking quest, Sys," she thought at it. "One that saves him."

New Special Quest: Purge the Sapient of Corruption.

Hope bloomed in her chest. "Yes! Yes, thank you, Sys! Now, how do I do that?"

System Inquiry Detected Abilities are revealed upon being unlocked.

"Bullshit!" Jill raged at it in her mind while showing nothing on her face. "You bend the rules for me all the time, you discount nineties chatbot! Do it for him! I'll pay whatever it takes."

There was a second of delay.

Invest 1 Class Point? Class Points remaining: 10 Invest 1 Perk Point? Perk Points remaining: 1

"Do it," Jill said. She felt something inside of her crumble away.

Unrevealed ability requires complete cooperation from subject.

Time slammed back into Jill. Babu was shaking and crying in front of her, his skin rippling as changes under the surface heralded the arrival of a new form.

"Hey, Babu," Jill said. "Guess what? I just swore at the System until it changed its mind. We can make this better. Do you trust me?"

A glimmer of hope warred with madness in his eyes. "Yes! Yes, I . . . I . . ." He cocked his head to the side. "They say you're lying," he whispered.

Jill reached out and wrapped him in a hug. "They can open wide and breathe in a jet-propelled shart for all I care. Do you trust me, Babu?"

"Yes," he whispered. His arms reached around her in a desperate embrace as blood rolled down his face.

The System reached through Jill and touched Babu. He stiffened and tried to pull away from Jill. She released him to arm's length but didn't let go entirely.

"Jill, are you sure? It wants everything, everything I am! Every class, every experience point, every stat! It's going to make me nothing!"

Jill rolled her eyes. "You doofus," she said. "That's not what you are. You're my smart, funny friend, who stops me from making dumb choices. Not some collection of bullshit magic." She cracked a smile. "You're the heart of our team, Babu," Jill said. "It doesn't matter what you can do for me. You, Babu, are enough."

For an endless few seconds, Jill saw the war in his eyes and under his skin as the corruption tore at his sanity and claimed his body for itself. Then something in him settled—a moment of calm. His gaze met Jill's, and he smiled the right number of teeth.

"Thanks, Jill," he said. "Sys"—he turned his head up—"do it. Please."

His mana imploded. The corpses turned to dust around them, and Babu's body was suddenly lit from within by searing black light. He screamed, the ragged piercing agony of a soul being rent apart, but it was in his own voice. His shoulders shrank under Jill's hands, the System-granted muscle mass from his many body points was sucked away, and the lumps under his skin faded to nothing.

His screaming stopped, and his body went limp; he would have collapsed to the floor if not for Jill holding him up. "Babu!" she yelled. "Hey, buddy, you there?" For a terrible second, she thought that he had died, his life forces sucked away with the magic, but then he took a gasping, rattling breath. His eyes snapped open and they were human once again.

"Fuck yeah!" Jill cheered. "I knew you could kick it! How are you feeling?"

He looked confused for a moment, then opened his mouth and vomited all over her. Gallons of black and green slime, far more than could actually fit inside a human frame, blasted from his mouth like it was a bidet from hell. Jill turned her head sideways and clamped her eyes shut; she released her hands, but he'd gripped her tight to keep himself up.

The blast ended. Jill pulled one of her hands out of his grasp, being extra careful not to use too much force on him, and wiped enough of the slime off of her so that she could open her eyes.

"You're lucky I like you," she said. "That got up my fucking nose!"

He gave a helpless laugh, then spasmed as if he was going to throw up again. Jill turned him so he wasn't facing her anymore.

"Yeah, get it all out," she said and rubbed his back.

He heaved twice more, and then his stomach ballooned outwards. A basketball-sized lump rose up, distorting his ribs and throat as it went, magic making possible what should have torn his body apart. His jaw distended unnaturally wide. There was one more burst of slime, and then a mana jewel, ten inches across and pulsing with a dark, alluring light, erupted from his mouth. It landed with a wet thud in his hands. He blinked at it, looked at Jill one last time, and passed out.

Jill caught him with one hand and the gem with the other. She spent a moment to reflect. Here she was, covered head to toe in foul sludge, surrounded by destruction, and her only company was an unconscious friend who'd just given birth to a rock out of his mouth.

"This is what happens when I don't have coffee," she muttered. She slung Babu over her shoulder and strode out of the room.

CHAPTER 37

THE END OF THE WORLD

She left the unconscious Babu in the Medbay with the rest of his family. They demanded to know what had happened to him; she made up some lame excuse and left. She would leave it up to Babu whether or not anyone but her would ever know what had almost happened.

She finally went back to her room and had her morning coffee. The stress of the morning, of all the fighting and of the people who'd died, hit her all at once, and she staggered over to her bed. She didn't cry—she had too much to do for that—but the tears would come later.

> Rare Class Evolution unlocked!
> **In Bertha Clad**: You have become one with your vessel, making its strength yours against a terrifying foe. Your new Class Powers will enhance your ability to channel Soulbound Modular Vehicle "Bertha's" upgrades and structure in combat.

"Huh," Jill said. "Is that what you were waiting for me to unlock?" Jill asked the System. It didn't reply. "I guess I've been working up to it bit by bit."

She sighed. Objectively, she'd gotten a massive boost to her combat potential by making Bertha itself into her armor. With that level of protection, she had the toughness and raw statistics to fight others of her level. But she still didn't have anything else, and it showed in how, even in the heart of her own domain, she'd still lost.

Before the upgrade, the abomination had nearly killed her with one blow; after it, it had still been kicking her ass. Ras had done better, and he was at least thirty levels below her. She'd held her own later in the cargo bay, holding off the horde of less dangerous creatures, but even down an arm, the swordsman had been killing more monsters than her.

She laughed and shook her head, thinking back to the training session she and Babu had done. His plan of making her a stealth fighter made sense except for the fact that she was Jill MacLeod, and she was the furthest thing from stealthy a person could get. She charged in headfirst and kicked things in the balls.

But she'd always done that because she had to, not because she sought it out. Unconsciously or not, she had always known that combat wasn't her strength, wasn't where her passion lay. She'd invested in Bertha because she'd always invested in her truck, and she always would.

She'd fight when she had to, she'd work on honing her self-made ability to armor herself in Bertha, and she'd even take a few more powers going forward to keep herself from being too vulnerable. But she wasn't going to take a class evolution that focused so much on fighting. It just wasn't her.

"Not bad, Sys, but not for me," Jill said. "Delay again." She stood, threw back the rest of her coffee, and marched out of the room.

For four days they drove east, towards the glow on the horizon that was now visible even in the day. As they progressed less and less on the map each day, as the amount of original terrain amid all the stretching shrank to almost nothing, the geography grew more confused and nonsensical. They thundered over plains and hills, cliffs and rivers, and stranger territory yet. Bertha roared over the top of a hill to find itself in a sparse frozen tundra, then hours later among multicolored lakes with waterfalls going up instead of down. They skirted around an active volcano, wary of the towering figures of lava and rock that they saw in the far distance. The crazy biomes sometimes limited their speed, but Aman estimated that they'd put ten thousand miles under the wheels, give or take a few thousand—enough to go halfway around a pre-magic Earth.

Aman's location power put them barely over the border into North Dakota.

On the second day, Jim from the workshop came to the cab with another device. He had been unable to turn the primary radar into one that could detect both monsters and mana density at the same time, at least not well. So he had just taken the smaller weather radar and dedicated it to mana density detection. It took only a single add-on slot, and Jill bound it to a console next to the primary radar.

What had been vague fuzz turned into a detailed plot of mana density and how much extra volume was being created by magic. In testing, they'd found the effect was nonlinear. Space stayed the normal size up to a critical threshold of mana, then began ballooning faster and faster. They were in such a high-mana area now that even minor pools of extra magic might mean miles more to drive. Their course turned from as straight as they could manage to a winding curve that dodged around patches of more expanded space.

On the other radar screen, the monsters grew both more powerful and more numerous, but at the same time, they stayed more out of the truck's way. What had been a continual trickle of easy kills, broken up by hordes, became lone aggressive bosses, all of them at least level eighty. There were still herds of monsters around, but the one time Jill had diverted to chase and try to harvest them, she had discovered that the monsters were even faster than Bertha.

The T. rex visited them again on the second and third day. Glowing portals in the sky had vomited out a swarm of electrodactyls to shoot at Bertha while it teleported around them, watching and roaring. It danced, crest flaring, as Bertha swerved and drifted out of the way of lightning bolts, and the turrets scored kill after kill.

On the third day, it came alone and just ran with them. It couldn't match Bertha's speed over long distances, not even close, but it would teleport ahead of them, activate some sort of temporary speed power, and run alongside for a few minutes before abruptly falling back.

Jill supposed that she could order the gunners to shoot at it and try to drive it off; after all, they were no longer trying to manipulate it to get Maelstrom Base's people out. But she didn't.

The T. rex was truly monstrous: forty feet tall and a hundred from nose to tail, with massive teeth, a breath of fire, and a slew of magical abilities that put many people's to shame. It had tormented a base full of people with constant attacks for its own amusement, causing horrible injuries. But it was also clearly capable of real thought, and there was every indication that it just wanted to play, even if that play sometimes involved fights to the death.

For now the truce held, and at the end of the fourth day, when it had failed to appear, Jill found that she missed its ridiculous feathered head just a bit.

They hadn't seen the abomination, the corrupted experiment, again. Its strange dot on the radar screen followed them no more, and good riddance. In the end, it had killed seven people in its charge through the cargo bay before Berthaville had stopped it. Another dozen would have died without intervention from the Roaming Guardians.

Jill stayed at level one hundred, and her choice to delay weighed on her. Bertha's strength, and their ability to survive in this crazy ultra-high-mana region, was tied to her level, and until she made a choice, that strength would stagnate.

Berthaville, even grieving for the dead, had not. The five thousand people in the truck kept living their lives, earning XP through all the things that a community of people did to thrive. The System was more generous with its quests than ever before: experience for surviving each day, experience for making good meals, experience for making each other laugh, even. It seemed that every day people were making thousands of XP for the simplest things, and the progress from that overshadowed the XP from killing what aggressive monsters still attacked.

When Jill concentrated she could see the mana blasting in from outside, a torrent of raging power, before it was calmed and coaxed into them all. Were all the quests just byproducts of all that excess magic? Jill had asked the System about it but gotten nothing back but sass.

The settlement hit level six, then seven as the residents' average level climbed. Jill took Basic Housing first.

Basic Housing: Creates 20 Basic Housing buildings and allows for the manual placement of more. Each is equipped with housing for 5; life support for 10, including air, water, and rations; and is self-maintaining. Mana Cost per building: 1 per second. Each rank of this power taken supplies the upkeep for 20 buildings. Unlocks **High-Density Housing** at Level 30.

She had Aman begin making housing blocks out on the earthen disc inside of the dimensional bubble, but they held off on asking people to move there. Reclaiming the volume in order to have the Cargo Nexus deal with more, well, cargo, would be a boon, but the lack of gravity in the bubble was just too strange.

For the other settlement power, Babu—who was still level zero and recovering in the Medbay but demanding to at least be able to help plan builds—had advised Jill to do something to increase its growth rate. She had three choices: Tax Increase, Device Incentives, or Community Goal. The first would double Berthaville's XP gain from 10 percent to 20 percent, but Jill liked how the other ones instead made everyone get more XP for themselves. She ended up taking Community Goal.

> **Community Goal:** Unlocks Administrator action **Set Community Goal**. Any resident action taken in furtherance of this goal generates 10% more XP, while actions taken against receive a 10% XP penalty. Unlocks **Emergency Action** at Level 10.

"Hey, Sys," she said, sitting in the cab with the core crystal raised in front of her, "set the goal to 'Don't be an asshole!'" That had gotten a chuckle from the rest of the cab, but to her shock, the System had done so without issue. "Attention, residents of Berthaville," Jill had projected through Bertha. "The power of friendship now grants ten percent bonus experience. That is all." It was a joke, but it also wasn't.

Food wasn't an issue yet, but Bertha couldn't make enough for everyone, and their stores were going down. Taran, alongside almost a hundred others with food-related classes, had gone floating out into Berthaville each morning to work on making the earthen disc bloom. At first, they had piped in water from the storage tanks in the Cargo Nexus and run the Habitation Module in overdrive to make more. Then Jill realized that water counted as a low-rarity material for the purpose of Terrain Generation and just made more whenever they needed it. The first plants had taken root, and their shoots had broken the surface of the dirt, but it would be a while yet before they were ready for harvest, even with magic powers.

Jill was back behind the wheel on the fifth day, weaving Bertha around the massive trunks of impossibly wide trees in a many-miles-long forest, when they crossed into a new region.

> You have entered the North America Rift Region, Western Branch.
> Mana flow: Singularities
> Status: Wild
> Extreme Caution is advised.

"I guess that's progress?" Jill said to herself. She kept driving. The trees made it difficult to go anywhere close to their full speed, but with creative use of drifting and the occasional sideswiping collision she still kept them going at over a hundred miles per hour.

"Singularities," Aman said. "That means infinite, right? Jill, if space stretches with higher mana concentrations, and the mana is going to infinity . . ." His voice trailed off.

"This fucking trip," Jill said, "is like trying to pass a kidney stone, only for it to really be a badger. Hey!" she shouted at Jake. "What's the density radar telling us? Anything weird?"

"More patches we should avoid," he said, "but nothing yet."

"Keep your eyes peeled," Jill said, "I don't want us to blunder into something by accident, not with 'Extreme Caution' advised."

That, at least, wasn't going to be a problem. A half hour later the light to the east had gone from an ominous glow to a blazing warning. With most of the sunlight from overhead blocked by the canopy, it was as if they were driving towards the morning sun. Rays of blue, green, and white cut around the trees in a shifting pattern, like bright walls in the darkness. It made for beautiful, if harder, driving.

They emerged from the forest an hour later at the top of an endless valley. In the center, impossibly far away and yet within sight, was a solid wall of magic stretching from the sky to the earth, as painful to look at as the sun. Where it met the ground, a conveyor belt of new terrain sprang into existence: cliffs and plains, gushing waterfalls, mesas and mountains, but no plants, no life. Those came into being farther out, where the fires of creation had cooled to being only extreme, rather than intolerable.

> You have gazed upon a Rift.
> Warning! Limiting exposure to Rifts is recommended at every Level.

Jill slowed Bertha to a stop on the top of the ridge.

"How . . ." She swallowed. "How do we get through that?"

"I don't know if we can," Aman said.

"Jake?" Jill asked. "Tell me you see something!"

"The density map's gone crazy," he said. "You've got to see this for yourself. But I think there might be a way through! A fast way, even!"

Jill leaped from her chair to see what he meant.

The mana density radar display had warped so its flat surface was now a three-dimensional contour map of peaks and troughs, as if the geometry of the world around them simply couldn't be represented on a flat surface, even with colors representing different densities.

"We're here, right?" Jake put a finger in the middle of the plot, where Bertha was. "See how the density is all changing?" He started tracing a curve to the east. The display was rippled in valleys and peaks in that direction, growing narrower and sharper as they got closer to the Rift wall itself.

"The high points are, well, crazy," he said, growing excited, "but the troughs! They go way, way down! All we have to do is follow one, and . . ." His finger reached the singularity wall. The display cut out there after shooting upward, the sheer impossibility of it too much for the detector. Jake messed with the display, zooming in as much as he could while keeping it centered on his finger. At the maximum magnification, a ribbon of calm blue was suspended in midair, leading through the wall between two infinite peaks.

"That's our road," Jill said with a grin and clapped Jake on the shoulder. "Way to fucking go!" Excited chatter broke out and a few people whooped with joy.

"How wide is that?" Aman asked.

"Um," Jake rotated the map until the ribbon was next to a scale. "Oh. A meter. Maybe less in places."

Jill sucked in a breath. From the outside perspective, Bertha couldn't become smaller than her original volume, but it could be skinnier.

"Okay, we can still do that," she said. "We make the truck into a giant long snake, right? Long and thin, with joints everywhere to let it bend along the path."

"What about the turrets?" Aman asked. "Or the cab? They can't change their volume very much."

Jill chewed on her lip. "We can do it," she repeated. "We're going to stop here for an hour. Jake, I want you to look for any other ways through and see if any are wider. Aman, you're with me to see just how skinny we can make this big girl be."

For Jill, it was an hour of metaphysical body issues and indigestion, but in the end, she still thought they could do it. They twisted and stretched the truck in every direction before finally settling on something very similar to Jill's initial idea: a long train of narrow, connected cars, with wheels set high and wide to improve stability. The turrets and cab could be shrunk down somewhat to match, but to Jill's frustration they found that Aman was right, and they could only warp those spaces so much. If they wanted to be small on the outside, they had to be small on the inside. The turrets would go unmanned, and the cab more resembled an elongated cockpit with two seats in a row than the triple-wide configuration it had sported before. They suppressed all the other seats and consoles to save space.

Jacob found Jill a few minutes before the hour pause was up. "I'm worried," he said.

"Yeah?" Jill asked. "We've got a path to follow, we're small enough. We can do this."

"Jill," he swallowed down his fear. "What if we can't? What if we get in there and the magic is just too much? There are five thousand people on board, and look at that thing we're trying to drive through. I can feel the magic coming from it from here!"

Jill had been feeling it for days but didn't say that. "I have to try," she said instead. "I have to! Otherwise, what, we go back? I just abandon trying to get to my family?"

"If we go back, we'll try again. Maybe spread the word through the military network, see if anyone far to the south or north sees an end to this—this Rift?" He smiled at her. "We'll get there. I want to see this mythical east coast of yours."

Jill snorted a laugh and sighed. "Fine. You're right, this isn't the only option. I'll turn back if things get too bad."

"Thank you," he said. He gave her a little salute and left her to it.

Jill took a deep breath and slid into the driver's seat at the very front. "Hey," she projected to the truck. "So, you might have noticed things moving around. We're about to try and get through a barrier, and it might get a little dicey. Get somewhere you can hold onto things, just in case." She thought about explaining what they were doing to everyone but decided not to. She shut off the communication power.

"You ready?" she called over her shoulder.

Behind her was Jake with the density scanner controls; it was his job to make sure it had the proper settings to show them the way. They'd decided not to have him call out directions from the radar to her. It was too important for Jill to be able to see for herself what turns they had to take. A duplicate of the density display, with all its multicolored hills and valleys, now sat in front of Jill, replacing all the other gauges that were normally before the driver. Right now it was the only thing that mattered.

"I'm a little nervous," he said. "What if I mess this up?"

"You'll be fine," Jill said. "You already did the hard part of finding the path. Just keep me seeing it. Besides, if you screw that up, I'll just hit the brakes." He had found three other candidate ways for getting through the Rift, and they were now headed for the widest. It still didn't offer much clearance.

He breathed out. "I can do that."

"Hell yeah," Jill said and put the truck into motion.

They snaked down the ridge sideways, angling over what seemed to be a flat, descending slope. But it was a strange slope, one that fooled the eye and made the viewer nauseous. The mana field outside wasn't uniform in its intensity—rather, it rose and fell in waves, and every place it rose there was simply more ground to cover. Jill took them down a winding way, following the path of least space as best she could from the detector. Under their tires, the ground crunched by at a steady fifteen miles per hour. To either side, it sped by much faster.

"And . . ." she said to herself, "now!" She pulled the wheel over in a sharp correction and pointed them at the Rift. "I think we're right in the low-density valley." She pushed down the accelerator. She didn't dare take them very fast, not with the truck in this configuration and not with the warping all around them, but she could at least get them up to thirty miles per hour on this straight section. Then, she settled back in her chair.

This part of the drive took hours. The Rift grew brighter and brighter as they got closer, so bright that Jill tinted the windows to filter it out. The path of relatively low mana density they drove on grew narrower and the gradient sharper. By the third hour, the ground just ten feet away blazed past so fast Jill couldn't make any details of it out, just a blur of brown-and-red rock.

"What happens if we drive partway onto that?" Jake asked.

Warning! Spatial warping may interfere with Bertha's dimensional expansion.

"Bad things," Jill said.

On they went for another twenty minutes and then things got harder. The low-mana path that had been a straight line began to twist and curve, and Jill had to follow it. She slowed them down, taking no chances. It wasn't hard driving in the technical sense, but she felt herself sweating, her hands shaking. The air around her vibrated as if she were inside of a drum. The console in front of her was suddenly a hundred feet away, along with her feet. Then it was back.

"What's happening?!" Jake said. "I think—I think—" He cut off and puked.

A horrible rending screech echoed through the truck and pain struck Jill. A diagonal slice of the engine compartment ahead of her and two of the front wheels were just gone, sheared away in an instant by going off course. She twitched the wheel to the side to recenter them on the path, but it was no good. The other side of Bertha's nose sheered off as well, tumbling away at thousands of miles an hour. She hit the brakes before they could go any deeper.

Jill slammed her hands into the wheel in frustration. Their failure had been fast when it had come, and there would be no second try, no crazy maneuvers to pull. It just wouldn't help. She knew that she had been driving perfectly; she had one hundred levels of superhuman reflexes to back up decades of skill, and a connection to the truck like it was her own body, after all. The path was just too narrow for them to get through without being torn apart.

She opened a connection to the conference room where the rest of the bridge crew were waiting. "We've failed," she said. "I'm pulling us out."

They had planned for the possibility, so Jill knew what to do. She used Customization and pulled the cockpit-cab up over the top of Bertha's elongated form, flipping it vertically so that it wouldn't go off the path to either side. She attached it at the back, facing the way they had come, and off they went. Away from the Rift. Away from her home.

It took more hours of painstaking driving to get them back out. A black claw of hopelessness rose from the depths of Jill's mind, but she pushed it down over and over again. So what if they had failed. So what if they had to go back, had to spend days or weeks covering the ground that they had fought their way over once before. She would do it, would get somewhere without this damn space stretching, and she would drive around this blasted Rift. Hell, she'd turn Bertha into a boat and sail around the world if she had to.

They made it back to the edge of the forest of giant trees, and Jill finally stopped driving. Putting Bertha back to her previous form felt like taking off a corset, but Jill felt no relief. She really didn't feel much of anything.

The rest of the cab crew filtered in and took their usual spots in depressed silence.

"Get us on a course back west, Aman," she said. "Maybe we can find a faster way, some sort of shortcut through low-density zones, and get back to normal space a little faster than we got out here."

Aman tried to talk with her, but Jill shook her head. She was done. Her family, Ciara, were farther away than ever, and she just couldn't deal with other people right now.

She went into her room, her every step knocking aside a half dozen potted sunflowers. The progenitor seemed to have gone a bit crazy in the extreme mana. Jill collapsed into bed, and in her exhausted, wrung-out state she didn't notice the thread of mana creeping up on her. She fell asleep without taking off her clothes.

And then she began to dream.

CHAPTER 38

ASK ME IN A DREAM

Jill ran under a brilliant sun, her clawed feet pounding out a rhythm of joy. She was on the hunt! Her crest flared in anticipation, her pace quickened, and then the prey was hers. Her jaws closed around the lesser creature and once, twice, three times she thrashed her head from side to side. Delicious, satisfying power surged into her as she took her share. Then she ate the meat, ripping and tearing and throwing her head back to let the steaming, shredded morsels glide down her throat. That, too, gave itself to her and made her stronger. She roared into the sky.

Day turned to night, night to day, and she stalked the world. Wherever she went she was the strongest. Some came close, some challenged her supremacy and injured her terribly, but in the end, they only fed her. She remembered only tiny snippets of those battles. They weren't important.

She grew in power and others stopped being able to challenge her. She still fed but by the third night, she was bored. When the next prey tried to flee before her, she roared at it and wished it to stop. The chase was no longer fun. Jill felt surprised for the first time when it did stop. It would obey her if only she could get it to understand what she wanted. She ate it eventually anyway.

Time snapped forward, and Jill looked up at the great dark sky studded with glowing fire, drinking in the power all around her. There must be more to hunt over the horizon. So that's where she went. First with her legs as she always had, then in bursts of speed. But all the time creatures kept nipping at her flanks, slowing her down. It was best, fastest, to go unseen. Or was it? Perhaps it would be fastest to simply be where she wanted to be. By the fourth night, she had learned how to slip between here and there, through secret paths that smelled of nothing.

She might have been content to roam forever more, but she found something fascinating, something amazing! Creatures unlike her, creatures that just smelled like the tastiest thing she could imagine! But when she moved in to feast, she again felt surprise.

These tiny burrowing creatures piqued her interest and soothed her boredom. They twisted power about themselves like masters but had the teeth of newborns. Their claws were strange, dead things that spat metal and fire. They should have been harmless, and yet they managed to kill the weak creatures of this area. And when they roared, it wasn't just sound! There was meaning and intention just like when she commanded other creatures, but so much more than that! Hidden in the sounds these weak creatures made were concepts she had no words for, concepts far beyond anything she had ever considered.

She watched them and learned to listen in ways that they couldn't prevent and delighted in what she heard. She danced in the dark, her feathers puffed in sheer joy. They were like her, with minds above the masses that surrounded them and spawned every day. And there were so many of them to learn about!

But there was a problem. She was now on the cusp of something greater, even though she didn't know what she wanted that greatness to be. They were far, far from it. The little things were too weak, too weak by far. They might all become food for something else, and then all that was interesting about them would be lost to her. They would need to be fed, but they would also need to learn how to fight all the different things that could come for them. For that, they needed to fight, but they were hiding too much. Prey either didn't detect them or couldn't get into their burrows.

So she commanded the weak creatures of the area to try harder, to feed themselves to the interesting ones with abandon. She watched, of course, and the carnage was wonderful! The little ones fed so quickly when it was that or die, and most of them lived. She had to step in once or twice when they were too good at hiding, or too bad at feeding, but she would get them there. Get them strong enough to run with her, to see the world and pass meaning back and forth.

They roared that she was wrong, and they tried to leave. Both were hurtful, and she put a stop to the latter. The fire might have been painful to them, but they would learn and heal.

And then, on a flickering patrol of her current territory, rounding up suitable snacks, she felt it. Twisted. Awful. Hungrier than even she had been as a newborn. A walking plague that destroyed magic. It smelled of death, and she would not have it near her precious hatchlings. Jill ambushed it, first throwing all the snacks under her command at the creature to tire it out, then hurling flame at a distance, bouncing from place to place until she knew how dangerous it was. It was fast, far faster than Jill over open ground with its too-many limbs, but it couldn't move in the secret ways, so she stayed always out of reach. She roared fire and it a terrible hungering mist. She tried commanding it to stop moving, but it was too alien, and the commands went unheeded.

Finally, she darted in to attack, accepting that she would be struck in exchange for rending the tiny pest to pieces with her beautiful teeth. She clamped down on it, tearing off a main limb and dozens of smaller ones, but its blood was poison far fouler than she had ever experienced. The venom of a bite sought to kill; this sought to unmake. She staggered away, and the horrible creature's limbs reattached themselves.

She tried to keep fighting, but she was herself weaker, and she couldn't afford to be poisoned again, so her wonderful bite was of no use. In the end, for the first time in her life, she fled from an enemy.

She returned to her hatchlings and brooded, not bothering to feed them for a few days. They didn't seem to appreciate her anyway. Again some left, the strongest among them. Maybe they were strong enough? She would follow and see.

They weren't. Their lifeless creatures of magic and metal were torn from around them and, like the little moles they were, they burrowed underground for safety. She would have to rescue them and shepherd them back to the nest, but for now, she'd let them stew and learn their lesson.

And then, at the very height of her frustration, something new came to Jill. Not quite as big as her on the outside but somehow much bigger on the inside, made of metal and magic, but alive, not like the pale imitations of her hatchlings. It was strong, on the cusp of greatness just like her!

Jill gasped and almost dropped her invisibility. The stranger bore inside of it more of the fascinating hatchlings; she could hear them! So very many more! Hundreds! Thousands! But then the newcomer stopped and scooped up Jill's hatchlings, and she nearly attacked. They were hers. Hers! This potential rival then ran straight for the main nest. Was it going to harm her chicks? If so, they would fight, and she would have so very many more hatchlings to take care of.

But what she saw made her reconsider. Her seven rebellious chicks were being taken care of, healed, and fed, though there had been one dominance tussle in the impossibly large insides of the metal creature. Maybe it was for the best. Maybe this was where the moles had come from in the first place; there were just so many of them, after all!

She still pouted and sent some lesser creatures to harass it. It was only fair to test, to make sure it was really as strong as it smelled. And what fun watching all the little moles inside was! She startled the strongest one enough to make her squawk at her.

That mole confused her a bit; it was maybe the same creature as the metal one that carried them all? She didn't know, and that was confusing, but its roars carried meaning that had Jill dancing in delight. One of its sounds resonated in her mind and she repeated it back, then went back to playing. It even played back, not with the desire to feed but in joyous movement! It was so much fun! If her chicks were going to be taken away by their mother and fed, well, that really wasn't so bad, especially if it was by a fellow enlightened being such as this.

In the end it passed her tests and was a good playmate, maybe even a good friend. She wished her little hatchlings all the prey they could eat, and let her new friend go.

She was extra glad her friend had taken her chicks away because, just a little while later, Jill realized that the nasty thing was coming closer. She attacked that thing again, and again she was repelled. She was speed, she was cunning, she could hide and dance through reality, and could listen and make other creatures obey, but she knew in her bones that all those things had come with a price. She wasn't the killing machine she had started out as, and this thing, this abomination, was nothing but killing and feeding. She wasn't going to be strong enough to defeat it until she crossed her threshold, and she wasn't ready for that. It wasn't time yet. She hadn't figured out what she was going to be.

Jill felt depressed that she might have to abandon this nice territory. Even though the air here was weak and thin compared to where she'd been born, it had become comfortable to her as she watched the hatchlings. Leaving it to the horror felt wrong.

She went to find her friend, to play and have a bit of fun, and was shocked to find that it had fought the horror as well! It was injured, terribly so, but had managed to drive it off, and the hatchlings were safe! Jill realized that her friend might actually be stronger than she was, with all of its mouths spitting fire and death in all directions. It was impressive for sure, and Jill was sure her friend would be fine.

She brought her friend some spicy snacks the next day, making sure it had enough food after recovering from its injuries. The next day they simply ran together. It was nice. Her friend was getting too close to the walls of endless light, though. That was confusing. That wasn't a direction they should go. That wasn't a direction they could go.

But then, Jill's friend proved just how smart it was! It found a hidden path, one that Jill had never thought to look for!

Jill raced ahead, but the path grew too narrow. Too narrow for Jill, too narrow for her friend. She sniffed deeply once, twice, and then she found it. The path grew smaller and smaller, but it never stopped. It was a mere claw wide in the end, but it went through the endless lights. And Jill could make one of her own secret ways, her own glowing hole that smelled of nothing, and she could thread it through that tiny opening. She could take her friend through too!

But Jill hated that she'd been bested by the horrible creature. Hated that it had attacked her friend and her hatchlings. Hated that it poisoned everything around it and was stealing her territory. Maybe, just maybe, her friend would help her to kill it? Lesser creatures hunted as packs sometimes, and Jill wasn't too proud to do the same. Not alongside another protector of the wonderful, strange hatchlings.

There was a problem, though: the abomination would give no power worth consuming, no meat worth eating. What could she offer in exchange to her equal? Her friend was too strong to be ordered. That was why they were friends.

Then Jill realized that her friend wanted to go through the endless lights but couldn't. Her feathers fell limp at the idea of not being able to go where she wanted. It was an awful feeling, one that she could free her friend from as payment. Jill could take her friend through the secret ways with no smell, through the wall of endless lights, and to the other side. It would be a wonderful adventure to go through where they could not, to see past the forbidden horizon.

Jill roared with all her might and pushed her intentions, her longing, and her story at her friend. She hoped that her friend would roar back.

CHAPTER 39

CRUNCH TIME

Jill woke with a gasping start, wondering at the same time where her wonderful claws and teeth had gone and also what the ever-loving fuck had just happened. She sat up, dislodging a particularly adventurously spawned sunflower pot from her chest. The only clear space on the bed was around the cat.

She ran to the cab without coffee and without showering. "Is it here?" she yelled.

Bobby, on the first driving shift, looked at her as if she was crazy. "Is what here, boss?" he asked, tension in his voice.

"The T. rex! Is it following us?"

"Oh," Bobby said and relaxed. "Yeah, Tammy's been doing her portal and run thing for the last hour. I'm starting to get used to her. I tell you ha-whut, I think she just wants to play!"

"No dicks, Watson," Jill said. "Bring us to a stop."

Bobby did. They were driving along a massive dried-out river canyon, walls of layered rock telling an imitation of history around them. A blue-green swirling portal popped into existence three hundred feet in front of them, and out stepped the T. rex, its plumage brilliant in the morning sun. It was so massive that its nose was a third of the way to them by the time its tail cleared the portal. It hopped up and down at them and cocked its head sideways, opening its jaws to reveal blood-stained teeth. It cocked its head to the side, flared its crest, and roared.

"Yes!" Jill yelled and danced as she had in the dream. It involved shaking her ass more than she was comfortable with.

"What the shnikey is going on?" Bobby asked after he'd picked his jaw up off the floor.

"We're going home, Bobby!" Jill said. She reached over and yanked on the horn. Sound exploded outwards, carving a trench in front of them and throwing a billowing cloud of rock and dirt into the air. She held it for a long ten seconds, then released it. The echo of the noise bounced around the canyon followed shortly after by rockslides.

The T. rex danced. It spun around hopping on one leg, then the other, throwing its tail in the air and roaring. It ran at the truck.

"Don't you dare shoot!" Jill projected to the turrets, just in case.

The monster lowered its head down to the cab and turned sideways so that a single eye was pressed up against the glass.

"Hey, buddy," Jill projected outside with Captain Speaking. "I know you can understand me, at least a little bit. You can get through the Rift? Through the, uh, endless lights?"

The T. rex's crest shot straight up. It turned its head to point at Jill, opened its massive maw, and roared. The armored glass shook.

"And you want me to help you kill that rotten sack of a person first?" Jill projected again.

"TWATWAFFLE," it roared back.

"Well, fuck me. You only know one word, but at least it's a good one," Jill said. "You've got a deal!" She made Captain Speaking mimic the sound of Bertha's original horn as loud as she could.

The T. rex leaped back in a cracking explosion of speed, then spun around in place. It opened a swirling portal, revealing on the other side a high arctic cliff, and it charged through, shaking the earth. But the portal didn't close. Instead, the T. rex turned its head to look at her and fluffed its feathers as if saying, "Well? Come on."

"All right, Bobby," Jill said, sitting down and moving the controls over to her. "I'm driving."

The cab door opened. Karen and Aman ran in, looking like they'd just gotten out of bed.

"Jill, what's going on?" Karen asked. "Why are we stopped? Why did you blow the horn?"

"We're—" she started to say but was cut off as Ras appeared, followed just a few seconds later by Babu, who was hopping along on one foot, pulling on his pants.

"Jill!" Ras said. "Is there trouble?"

Jill tapped her fingers on her leg. The T. rex had its head cocked to the side. If Jill were it, and she just had been, she'd be getting impatient. "Okay, listen up—"

"Tammy!" Kevin yelled as he zipped into the room. "Hi, Mr. Bobby," he said in passing, then climbed onto the dashboard and pressed his nose against the glass to get a better look.

"We're finishing this!" Jill said fast before she could be interrupted by the family reunion growing even more. "Our new friend over there is taking us to turbo-murder the abomination, and then it's taking us through the Rift. Ras, get more of the CKs up and gather them in the Cargo Nexus, just in case. Aman, I'll be driving, so you tell Antonio when to shoot. Babu . . ." She hesitated, but Babu smiled.

"I'm going to sit here and watch the action!" he said.

"I was going to say, 'Go somewhere safe,'" Jill said. "Sorry."

"Don't be. My level-nine ass is more fragile than it's been in a while. But I think being in the"—he changed his voice, making it deeper—"Fortress of the Throne"—he laughed—"is safe enough for now. If things get rough, I'll leave. I promise."

The T. rex roared again.

"We gotta go!" Jill said and put her foot down on the accelerator. Bertha shot forward, and the T. rex grinned. It spun, shook its massive tail, and ran ahead.

A flicker of disorientation smacked Jill in the face as they barreled through the portal and onto the icy cliff. Wind whipped around them, strong enough to push even the massive Bertha, but the traction powers of the wheels activated and held them firm. The T. rex led them on, but they were rapidly running out of cliff.

It opened the next portal in the open air just off the edge and leaped through. An idyllic field of flowers and sheep lay on the other side.

"Fucking show off," Jill muttered and held her course.

"Oh no, we are not—" Aman started to say, but by the time he reached "not" they were off the cliff, flying through the portal and onto the field.

"Weeeee!" yelled Kevin. He was sitting on Babu's lap in an observer seat.

"This is amazing!" Babu said.

More people filtered into the cab: a full double crew ready for combat, called by Karen, who'd taken comms back over. There were some screams and demands to know what was going on, but Jill left it to her team to handle them. Aman explained the situation once he'd calmed down from their little fall, and everyone settled into their places. Jill kept driving.

The field proved more difficult to follow the T. rex through than the cliff because the fluffy sheep exploded if Bertha got too close to them. The T. rex delighted in the carnage, bouncing just close enough to a sheep to set it off and then running through the resulting spray of gore with its mouth open. Then, with a sudden spin that left its feathers clean again, it opened another portal. It led to a desert highway: smooth, well repaired, with a clear, yellow-dashed line down the middle.

They blasted through the portal, another tingle washing over Jill as they did, and the tire noise died down. "This isn't so—" Jill started to say, but was interrupted by Jake's scream. The monster-detecting radar console overloaded, showering him with sparks.

"Oh fuck, oh fuck, oh fuck, it's—"

> Warning! It is not recommended to interact with a Regional Mana Concentrator at your Level!

The ground underneath them shifted as the entire section of road they were blasting down began to tilt. What Jill had taken for a hill up ahead rotated around, and six enormous, slitted eyes opened to stare at her. They were driving across the back of a titan, a creature miles long, camouflaged as a desert roadway. The T. rex stood in the road ahead, preening as if it didn't have a care in the world.

The titanic terrain feature opened its mouth, and a spark flared in the depths, brilliantly white hot, with enough magic packed into it that the mana flows inside of Bertha shifted away from it as if blown by a hot wind.

Jill's heart pounded from the surge of fear, but her dominant emotion was exasperation. "Tammy's still showing off," she said, keeping her voice carefully calm. She kept driving.

The T. rex spun around again and summoned a portal right in front of Bertha. It followed the truck through a moment later. They were back in more familiar terrain: the same Montana plains that they'd been crossing for so many days.

"Gah!" Jake said. He flinched back from the radars once again, but this time they didn't explode. "The mana density just dropped by, like, a lot!"

"Aman?" Jill asked. "Where are we?"

He cast his mapping spell. "We're almost back to Maelstrom Base," he said. "Days of travel covered in an instant!" He looked at her with amazement. "Ms. MacLeod, how is this happening? How did you know to go along with it?"

"I'll tell you later," Jill said. The T. rex teleported ahead, spun in place, and roared. Jill stopped Bertha so they wouldn't run into it. The dinosaur threw its head back and forth as if shaking prey between its teeth, then keeled over sideways. It then fell into a portal it opened underneath itself.

"Incredible!" Babu said, the wonder back in his voice. "It's telling us what?"

"Not to try to eat corrupted shit," Jill said. "And—gah!" she yelled in surprise as it portalled in directly on top of Bertha and lowered its jaws right in front of the cab, snapping them shut just a few feet short. "And for us to do an ambush instead," she finished once her heart stopped pounding.

She opened up a Captain Speaking channel to the gunners and the back of the cargo bay. "We're going to be going into combat soon. Gunners, don't shoot until I say. We're going to take Rib Boy by surprise." She gripped the wheel hard and cracked her neck, then pulled on the horn and hit the accelerator.

The T. rex appeared running beside them. As Bertha got faster, it activated its running power to keep up. Then it surged with magic and sped up. Jill pressed down on the accelerator and soon they were going over three hundred miles an hour. The T. rex opened a portal in the distance in front of them.

Through that portal was a brutal fight. Dinosaurs of all kinds threw themselves at the abomination, one after another, and it slaughtered them. Its mist ate at their flesh, its spines pinned them to the ground from range, and any fast enough to keep up with it were unceremoniously rent apart by rib-limbs. The view through the portal kept shifting; while the source portal, which Bertha grew closer to by the second, stayed in place, the destination—the exit—kept moving, following the abomination as it darted to and fro.

Jill activated the eel paint and electric arcs flared over Bertha's surface in snaps of blue and yellow over bright red paint and shining chrome. She hadn't turned it on for the damage but for the speed boost. The mana engine roared, pushed beyond its limits, and Bertha accelerated until the truck was going just shy of four hundred miles per hour.

Jill laughed in delight at the sheer speed.

With just seconds left till Bertha entered the portal, the abomination seemed to finally notice their approach. It turned, opened its mouth, and was too late.

One hundred and fifty metric tons of truck smashed into it at four hundred miles per hour, crushing its relatively fragile body like a house centipede under a boot. Horrible ichor sprayed out, coating the front of Bertha's grille and the window, eating into the armor and making Jill feel like she'd just splashed her face with acid. The abomination was sucked downwards under the brutal wheels, pulverized by Bertha's passage.

Jill slammed on the brakes. "Corrupt that, you unwashed fuck-stick!" she yelled in triumph. She looked in the side mirror and saw it plastered into the ground and in pieces, but she hadn't gotten a kill notification yet. She toggled the mana engine into reverse and began to back them up, projecting the backup beeps of a truck into the cab for everyone to enjoy.

"Jill?" Aman asked, his white knuckles still tightly gripping the sides of his chair. "What do we do about all the monsters around us? Do I tell the hive to attack?"

"Hmm?" Jill asked, her eyes on the side mirror. "Are the monsters going for us?"

"No. They're, well, running."

"Then leave them alone. They belong to Tammy. Oh! And don't shoot Mr. Evil. He's mine."

Behind the truck, the abomination was attempting to pull its shattered body back together. Rib-limbs lay scattered around the ground. The detached rods of flesh and bone twitched and started to crawl back towards their host.

"Oh no, you don't, dillweed," she said. She pressed the accelerator a bit more and, accompanied by beeps, backed the truck over the abomination, crushing it again. She turned off all the truck's traction powers and hit the accelerator one last time, spinning the wheels and tearing the pinned corrupted man to pieces.

> Corrupted Jeremy Song defeated.
> Bonus Experience awarded for: killing a corrupted sapient (x2)
> Your contribution: 48%
> 88,320 Experience Gained! Experience gain deferred until Class Evolution complete.

Jill let out a sigh. "That was satisfying."

"You've gotten a bit more bloodthirsty, don'tcha know," Babu said. He gave her a significant look.

Jill scrunched her nose. "Fair point," she said, "but that fucker really had it coming. Now, let's see if Tammy follows through with our deal."

Moments later, the T. rex appeared in front of them. It grinned at Jill and bobbed its head up and down, crest flaring. "Hell yeah, buddy," Jill protected outside at maximum volume, "but it's time to go, right?"

It spun around in place, then opened another portal.

Their trip back towards the Rift was less exciting than their prior portal adventure. The T. rex kept to safer places and seemed to be drawing the trip out; what had been five hops became ten. But each time, the glow to the east grew brighter, and soon they were back at the top of the endless valley, the walls of the Rift within sight.

The T. rex opened one more portal. The blues and greens were more intense than usual, glowed more brightly, and the normally flat plane of magic was puckered in the center as if being pulled by an irresistible force. The ground on the other side of it just looked like Midwest plains. The dinosaur froze, tilted its head, then ran through.

Jill took a deep breath and gripped the wheel.

"Are you sure about this?" asked Jacob from behind her. He sounded nervous.

"Safe enough for Tammy," Jill said, "is safe enough for us." She opened Captain Speaking to the whole truck. "Hey, everyone. You remember that barrier we couldn't get through? Well, we're trying again. Shit might get weird, so hold on to your butts."

She hit the gas, and Bertha went through the portal. The previous times had been instantaneous and felt like little more than disorientation. This felt like Jill had been stuffed into a washing machine and set on the spin cycle. The windshield stretched away in front of her to infinity, and she felt her heart beating slower and slower. Babu's scream of delight got lower and lower in pitch, along with all other sounds around her, then became too deep to hear.

An eternity passed in an instant, and then they were through. The portal closed behind them.

You have entered the North America Rift Region, Eastern Branch.
Mana flow: Singularities
Status: Wild
Extreme Caution is advised.

"Yes!" Jill yelled and pumped a fist to the ceiling. "We made it!"

A roar shook the glass of the cab. Tammy was celebrating just as Jill was. Then the T. rex froze in place. A blinding light erupted from its body. Its tiny, grasping forelimbs shifted, sliding back until they were on the T. rex's back, then exploded in size, becoming huge feathered wings. Its body grew longer, more sinuous, and its crest stretched until it ran from its head to its mid-back.

The drake roared the same roar as always and leaped into the sky.

"Safe travels, good buddy," Jill said.

A box popped up in her vision.

Legendary Class Evolution unlocked!
Captain of the Infinite Sea: You have taken your vessel where it cannot go, sailed the infinite depths of magic itself, and lived to tell the tale. No other expanses could ever compete, and you will cross them all. Your new Class Powers will enhance you and your chosen vehicle's ability to go where you will.

Jill smiled. "Change the name and you've got a deal."

Congratulations, Jill MacLeod. You are now a Trucker of the Infinite Road.

ABOUT THE AUTHOR

Tom Goldstein is a physicist-turned-writer with a passion for classic fantasy and science fiction. He and his partner live in Vancouver, where he serves his science-cat, Shiva.

Podium

Printed in the USA
CPSIA information can be obtained
at www.ICGtesting.com
JSHW082135260624
65442JS00001B/47

9 781039 44847